David Masson

The three devils

Luther's, Milton's, and Goethe's ; With other essays

David Masson

The three devils
Luther's, Milton's, and Goethe's ; With other essays

ISBN/EAN: 9783337128210

Printed in Europe, USA, Canada, Australia, Japan

Cover: Foto ©Andreas Hilbeck / pixelio.de

More available books at **www.hansebooks.com**

THE THREE DEVILS:

LUTHER'S, MILTON'S, AND GOETHE'S.

WITH OTHER ESSAYS.

THE THREE DEVILS:

LUTHER'S, MILTON'S, AND GOETHE'S.

WITH

OTHER ESSAYS.

BY

DAVID MASSON, M.A., LL.D.,

Professor of Rhetoric and English Literature in the University of Edinburgh.

London:

MACMILLAN AND CO.

1874.

LONDON:
R. CLAY, SONS, AND TAYLOR, PRINTERS,
BREAD STREET HILL.

PREFATORY NOTE.

THE first five of the following Essays are reprinted from the Author's *Essays Biographical and Critical: chiefly on English Poets*, published in 1856. The present Volume and two similar Volumes issued separately (under the titles " *Wordsworth, Shelley, Keats, and other Essays* " and " *Chatterton: A Story of the Year* 1770 ") may be taken together as forming a new and somewhat enlarged edition of the older book. The addition in the present Volume consists of the last Essay.

EDINBURGH :
    November 1874.

CONTENTS.

THE THREE DEVILS:

LUTHER'S, MILTON'S, AND GOETHE'S.[1]

LUTHER, Milton, and Goethe: these are very strange names to bring together. It strikes us, however, that the effect may not be uninteresting if we connect the names of those three great men, as having each represented to us the Principle of Evil, and each represented him in a different way. Each of the three has left on record his conception of a great accursed being, incessantly working in human affairs, and whose function it is to produce evil. There is nothing more striking about Luther than the amazing sincerity of his belief in the existence of such an evil being, the great general enemy of mankind, and whose specific object, in Luther's time, it was to resist Luther's movement, and, if possible, "cut his soul out of God's mercy." What was Luther's exact conception of this being is to

[1] *Fraser's Magazine,* Dec. 1844.

B 2

be gathered from his life and writings. Again, we have
Milton's Satan. Lastly, we have Goethe's Mephistopheles. Nor is it possible to confound the three, or for
a moment to mistake the one for the other. They are as
unlike as it is possible for three grand conceptions of
the same thing to be. May it not, then, be profitable to
make their peculiarities and their differences a subject
of study? Milton's Satan and Goethe's Mephistopheles
have indeed been frequently contrasted in a vague,
antithetic way; for no writer could possibly give a
description of Goethe's Mephistopheles without saying
something or other about Milton's Satan. The exposition, however, of the difference between the two has
never been sufficient; and it may give the whole speculation greater interest if, in addition to Milton's Satan
and Goethe's Mephistopheles, we include Luther's
Devil. It is scarcely necessary to premise that here
there is to be no theological discussion. All that we
propose is to compare, as we find them, three very
striking delineations of the Evil Principle, one of
them experimental, the other two poetical.

These last words indicate one respect in which, it
will be perceived at the outset, Luther's conception of
the Evil Principle on the one hand and Milton's and
Goethe's on the other are fundamentally distinguishable.
All the three, of course, are founded on the Scriptural

proposition of the existence of a being whose express function it is to produce evil. Luther, firmly believing every jot and tittle of Scripture, believed the proposition about the Devil also; and so the whole of his experience of evil in himself and others was cast into the shape of a verification of that proposition. Had he started without such a preliminary conception, his experience would have had to encounter the difficulty of expressing itself in some other way; which, it is likely, would not have been nearly so effective, or so Luther-like. Milton, too, borrows the elements of his conception of Satan from Scripture. The Fallen Angel of the Bible is the hero of *Paradise Lost ;* and one of the most striking things about this poem is that in it we see the grand imagination of the poet blazing in the very track of the propositions of the theologian. And, though there can be no doubt that Goethe's Mephistopheles is conceived less in the spirit of Scripture than either Milton's Satan or Luther's Devil, still even in Mephistopheles we discern the lineaments of the same traditional being. All the three, then, have this in common—that they are founded on the Scriptural proposition of the existence of an accursed being whose function it is to produce evil, and that, more or less, they adopt the Scriptural account of that being. Still, as we have said, Luther's conception of this being belongs to one category; Milton's and Goethe's to another.   Luther's is a biographical phenomenon ; Milton's and Goethe's are literary performances.   Luther illustrated the Evil Being of Scripture to himself by means of his personal experience.   Whatever resistance he met with, whatever obstacle to Divine grace he found in his own heart or in external circumstances, whatever event he saw plainly cast in the way of the progress of the Gospel, whatever outbreak of a bad or unamiable spirit occurred in the Church, whatever strange phenomenon of nature wore a malevolent aspect,—out of that he obtained a clearer notion of the Devil.   In this way it might be said that Luther was all his life gaining a deeper insight into the Devil's character. On the other hand, Milton's Satan and Goethe's Mephistopheles are poetical creations, the one epic, the other dramatic.   Borrowing the elements of his conception from Scripture, Milton set himself to the task of describing the ruined Archangel as he may be supposed to have existed at that epoch of the creation when he had hardly decided his own function, as yet warring with the Almighty, or, in pursuit of a gigantic scheme of revenge, travelling from star to star.   Poetically assuming the device of the same Scriptural proposition, Goethe set himself to the task of representing the Spirit of Evil as he existed six thousand years later, no longer gifted with the same powers of locomotion, or struggling for admission into this part of the universe, but plying his understood function in crowded cities and on the minds of individuals.

So far as the mere fact of Milton's having made Satan the hero of his epic, or of Goethe's having made Mephistopheles a character in his drama, qualifies us to speak of the theological opinions of the one or of the other, we are not entitled to say that either Milton or Goethe believed in a Devil at all as Luther did. Or, again, it is quite conceivable that Milton might have believed in a Devil as sincerely as Luther did, and that Goethe might have believed in a Devil as sincerely as Luther did also, and yet that, in that case, the Devil which Milton believed in might not have been the Satan of the *Paradise Lost*, and the Devil which Goethe believed in might not have been the Mephistopheles of *Faust*. Of course, we have other means of knowing whether Milton did actually believe in the existence of the great accursed being whose fall he sings. It is also plain that Goethe's Mephistopheles resembles Luther's Devil more than Milton's Satan does in this respect— that Mephistopheles is the expression of a great deal of Goethe's actual observation of life and experience in human affairs. Still, neither the fact, on the one hand, that Milton did believe in the existence of the Evil Spirit, nor the fact, on the other, that Mephistopheles is an expression for the aggregate of much profound thinking on the part of Goethe, is of force to obliterate the fundamental distinction between Luther's Devil, as a biographical reality, and Milton's Satan and Goethe's Mephistopheles, as two literary performances. If we might risk summing up under the light of this preliminary distinction, perhaps the following would be near the truth:—Luther had as strong a faith as ever man had in the existence and activity of the Evil Spirit of Scripture: he used to recognise the operation of this Spirit in every individual instance of evil as it occurred; he used, moreover, to conceive that this Spirit and he were personal antagonists; and so, just as one man forms to himself a distinct idea of the character of another man to whom he stands in an important relation, Luther came to form to himself a distinct idea of the Devil, and what this idea was it seems possible to find out by examining his writings. Milton, again, chose the Scripture personage as the hero of an epic poem, and employed his grand imagination in realizing the Scripture narrative: we have reason also to know that he did actually believe in the Devil's existence; and it agrees with what we know of Milton's character to suppose that the Devil thus believed in would be pretty much the same magnificent being he has described in his poem—though, on the whole, we should not say that Milton was a man likely to carry about with him, in daily affairs, any constant recognition of the Devil's presence. Lastly, Goethe, adopting, for a different literary effect, the Scriptural and traditional account of the same being, conceived his Mephistopheles. This Mephistopheles, there is no doubt, had a real allegoric meaning with Goethe; he meant him to typify the Evil Spirit in modern civilization; but whether Goethe did actually believe in the existence of a supernatural intelligence whose function it is to produce evil is a question which no one will feel himself called upon to answer, although, if he did, it may be unhesitatingly asserted that this supernatural intelligence cannot have been Mephistopheles.

From all this it appears that Luther's conception of the Evil Being belongs to one category, Milton's and Goethe's to another. Let us consider, *first*, Milton's Satan, *secondly*, Goethe's Mephistopheles, and, *thirdly*, Luther's Devil.

The difficulties which Milton had to overcome in writing his *Paradise Lost* were immense. The gist of those difficulties may be defined as consisting in this, that the poet had at once to represent a supernatural condition of being and to construct a story. He had to describe the ongoings of Angels, and at the same time to make one event follow another. It is comparatively easy for Milton to sustain his conception of those superhuman beings as mere objects or phenomena —to represent them flying singly through space like huge black shadows, or standing opposite to each other in hostile battalions ; but to construct a story in which these beings should be the agents, to exhibit these beings thinking, scheming, blundering, in such a way as to produce a likely succession of events, was enormously difficult. The difficulty was to make the course of events correspond with the reputation of the objects. To do this perfectly was literally impossible. It is possible for the human mind to conceive twenty-four great supernatural beings existing together at any given moment in space ; but it is utterly impossible to conceive what would occur among those twenty-four beings during twenty-four hours. The value of time, the amount of history that can be transacted in a given period, depends on the nature and prowess of the beings whose volitions make the chain of events ; and so a lower order of beings can have no idea at what rate things happen in a higher. The mode of causation will be different from that with which they are acquainted.

This is the difficulty with which Milton had to struggle ; or, rather, this is the difficulty with which he did not struggle. He had to construct a narrative ; and so, while he represents to us the full stature of his superhuman beings as mere objects or phenomena, he does not attempt to make events follow each other at a higher rate among those beings than they do amongst ourselves, except in the single respect of their being infinitely more powerful physical agents than we are. Whatever feeling of inconsistency is experienced in reading the *Paradise Lost* may be traced, perhaps, to the fact that the necessities of the story obliged the poet not to attempt to make the rate of causation among those beings as extraordinary as his description of them as phenomena. Such a feeling of inconsistency there is ; and yet Milton sustains his flight as nobly as mortal could have done. Throughout the whole poem we see him recollecting his original conception of Satan as an object :—

> " Thus Satan, talking to his nearest mate,
> With head uplift above the waves, and eyes
> That sparkling blazed ; his other parts besides,
> Prone on the flood, extended long and large,
> Lay floating many a rood."

And this is a great thing to have done. If the poet ever flags in his conception of those superhuman beings as objects, it is when he finds it necessary to describe a multitude of them assembled together in some *place ;* and his usual device then is to reduce the bulk of the greatest number. This, too, is for the behoof of the story. If it is necessary, for instance, to assemble the Angels to deliberate, this must be done in an audience-hall, and the human mind refuses to go beyond certain limits in its conception of what an audience-hall is. Again the gate of Hell is described, although the Hell of Milton is a mere vague extent of fiery element, which, in strict keeping, could not be described as having a gate. The narrative, however, requires the conception. And so in other cases. Still, consistency of description is well sustained.

Nor is it merely as objects or phenomena that Milton sustains throughout his whole poem a consistent conception of the Angels. He is likewise consistent in his description of them as physical agents. Lofty stature and appearance carry with them a promise of so much physical power ; and hence, in Milton's case, the necessity of finding words and figures capable of expressing modes and powers of mechanical action, on the part of the Angels, as superhuman as the stature and appearance he has given to them. This complicated his difficulties very much. It is quite conceivable that a man should be able to describe the mere appearance of a gigantic being standing up, as it were, with his back to a wall, and yet utterly break down, and not be able to find words, when he tried to describe this gigantic being stepping forth into colossal activity and doing some characteristic thing. Milton has overcome the difficulty. His conception of the Angels as physical agents does not fall beneath his conception of them as mere objects. In his description, for instance, in the sixth book, of the Angels tearing up mountains by the roots and flinging them upon each other, we have strength suggested corresponding to the reputed stature of the beings. In extension of the same remark, we may observe how skilfully Milton has aggrandized and eked out his conception of the superhuman beings he is describing by endowing them with the power of infinitely swift motion through space. On this point we offer our readers an observation which they may verify for themselves:—Milton, we are persuaded, had it vaguely in his mind, throughout *Paradise Lost*, that the bounding peculiarity between the human condition of being and the angelic one he is describing is the law of gravitation. We, and all that is cognisable by us, are subject to this law; but Creation may be peopled with beings who are not subject to it, and to us these beings are as if they were not. But, whenever one of those beings becomes cognisable by us, he instantly becomes subject to gravitation; and he must resume his own mode of being ere he can be free from its consequences. The Angels were not subject to gravitation; that is to say, they had the means of moving in any direction at will. When they rebelled, and were punished by expulsion from Heaven, they did not *fall* out; for, in fact, so far as the description intimates, there existed no planet, no distinct material element, towards which they could gravitate. They were *driven* out by a pursuing fire. Then, after their fall, they had the power of rising upward, of navigating space, of quitting Hell, directing their flight to one glittering planet, alighting on its rotund surface, and then bounding off again, and away to another. A corollary of this fundamental difference between the human condition of being and the angelic would be that angels are capable of direct vertical action, whereas men are capable mainly of horizontal. An army of men can exist only as a square, or other plane figure, whereas an army of angels can exist as a cube or parallelopiped.

Now, in everything relating to the physical action of the Angels, even in carrying out this notion of their mode of being, Milton is most consistent. But it was impossible to follow out the superiority of these beings to its whole length. The attempt to do so would have made a narrative impossible. Exalting our conception of these beings as mere objects, or as mere physical agents, as much as he could, it would have been suicidal in the poet to attempt to realize history as it must be among such beings. No human mind could do it. He had, therefore, except where the notion of physical superiority assisted him, to make events follow each other just as they would in a human narrative. The motives, the reasonings, the misconceptions of those beings, all that determined the succession of events, he had to make substantially human. The whole narrative, for instance, proceeds on the supposition that those supernatural beings had no higher degree of knowledge than human beings, with equal physical advantages, would have had under similar circumstances. Credit the spirits with a greater degree of insight—credit them even with such a strong conviction of the Divine omnipotence as, in their reputed condition of being, we can hardly conceive them not attaining—and the whole of Milton's story is rendered impossible. The crushing conviction of the Divine omnipotence would have prevented them from rebelling with the alleged motive ; or, after they had rebelled, it would have prevented them from struggling with the alleged hope. In *Paradise Lost* the working notion which the devils have about God is exactly that which human beings have when they hope to succeed in a bad enterprise. Otherwise the poem could not have been written. Suppose the fallen Angels to have had a working notion of the Deity as superhuman as their reputed appearance and physical greatness : then the events of the *Paradise Lost* might have happened nevertheless, but the chain of volitions would not have been the same, and it would have been impossible for any human poet to realize the narrative.

These remarks are necessary to prepare us for conceiving the Satan of Milton. Except, as we have said, for an occasional feeling during a perusal of the poem that the style of thinking and speculating about the issue of their enterprise is too meagre and human for a race of beings physically so superhuman, one's astonishment at the consistency of the poet's conceptions is unmitigated throughout. Such keeping is there between one conception and another, such a distinct material grasp had the poet of his whole subject, so little is there of the mystic or the hazy in his descriptions from beginning to end, that it would be quite possible to prefix to the *Paradise Lost* an illustrative diagram exhibiting the universal space in which Milton conceived his beings moving to and fro, divided, as he conceived it, at first into two or three, and afterwards into four tropics or regions. Then his narrative is so clear that a brief prose version of it would be a history of Satan in the interval between his own fall and the fall of Man.

It is to be noted that Milton as a poet proceeds on the Homeric method, and not on the Shakespearian, devoting the whole strength of his genius to the object, not of being discursive and original, not of making profound remarks on everything as he goes along, but of carrying on a sublime and stately narrative. We should hardly be led to assert, however, that the difference between the epic and the drama lies in this, that the latter may be discursive and reflective while the former cannot. We can conceive an epic written after the Shakespearian method; that is,

one which, while strictly sustaining a narrative, should
be profoundly expository in its spirit. Certain it is, however, that Milton wrote after the Homeric method, and
did not exert himself chiefly in strewing his text with
luminous propositions. One consequence of this is that
the way to obtain an idea of Milton's Satan is not to
lay hold of specific sayings that fall from his mouth,
but to go through his history. Goethe's Mephistopheles, we shall find, on the other hand, reveals himself in the characteristic propositions which he utters.
Satan is to be studied by following his progress ;
Mephistopheles by attending to his remarks.

In the history of Milton's Satan it is important to
begin at the time of his being an Archangel. Before
the creation of our World, there existed, according to
Milton, a grand race of beings altogether different from
what we are. Those beings were Spirits. They did
not lead a planetary existence ; they tenanted space
in some strange, and, to us, inconceivable way. Or,
rather, they did not tenant all space, but only that
upper and illuminated part of infinity called Heaven.
For Heaven, in Milton, is not to be considered as a
locality, but as a region stretching infinitely out on
all sides—an immense extent of continent and kingdom. The infinite darkness, howling and blustering
underneath Heaven, was Chaos or Night. What was
the exact mode of being of the Spirits who lived

D   C in dispersion through Heaven is unknown to us; but it was social. Moreover, there subsisted between the multitudinous far-extending population of Spirits and the Almighty Creator a relation closer, or at least more sensible and immediate, than that which exists between human beings and Him. The best way of expressing this relation in human language is by the idea of physical nearness. They were God's Angels. Pursuing, each individual among them, a life of his own, agreeable to his wishes and his character, yet they all recognised themselves as the Almighty's ministering spirits. At times they were summoned, from following their different occupations in all the ends of Heaven, to assemble near the Divine presence. Among these Angels there were degrees and differences. Some were, in their very essence and constitution, grander and more sublime intelligences than the rest; others, in the course of their long existence, had become noted for their zeal and assiduity. Thus, although really a race of beings living on their own account as men do, they constituted a hierarchy, and were called Angels.

Among all the vast angelic population three or four individuals stood pre-eminent and unapproachable. These were the Archangels. Satan was one of these: if not the highest Archangel in Heaven, he was one of the four highest. After God, he could feel conscious of being the greatest being in the Universe. But, although the relation between the Deity and the angelic population was so close that we can only express it by having recourse to the conception of physical nearness, yet even to the Angels the Deity was so shrouded in clouds and mystery that the highest Archangel might proceed on a wrong notion of his character, and, just as human beings do, might believe the Divine omnipotence as a theological proposition, and yet, in going about his enterprises, might not carry a working consciousness of it along with him. There is something in the exercise of power, in the mere feeling of existence, in the stretching out of a limb, in the resisting of an obstacle, in being active in any way, which generates a conviction that our powers are self-contained, hostile to the recollection of inferiority or accountability. A messenger, employed in his master's business, becomes, in the very act of serving him, forgetful of him. As the feeling of enjoyment in action grows strong, the feeling of a dependent state of being, the feeling of being a messenger, grows weak. Repose and physical weakness are favourable to the recognition of a derived existence : hence the beauty of the feebleness of old age preceding the approach of death. The feebleness of the body weakens the self-sufficient feeling, and disposes to piety. The young man, rejoicing in his strength, cannot believe that his breath is in his nostrils. In some such way the Archangel fell. Rejoicing in his strength, walking colossal through Heaven, gigantic in his conceptions, incessant in his working, ever scheming, ever imagining new enterprises, Satan was in his very nature the most active of God's Archangels. He was ever doing some great thing, and ever thirsting for some greater thing to do. And, alas! his very wisdom became his folly. His notion of the Deity was higher and grander than that of any other Angel: but, then, he was not a contemplative spirit; and his feeling of derived existence grew weak in the glow and excitement of constant occupation. As the feeling of enjoyment in action grew strong, the feeling of being an Angel grew weak. Thus the mere duration of his existence had undermined his strength and prepared him for sin. Although the greatest Angel in Heaven—nay, just because he was such—he was the readiest to fall.

At last an occasion came. When the intimation was made by the Almighty in the Congregation of the Angels that he had anointed his only-begotten Son King on the holy hill of Zion, the Archangel frowned and became a rebel: not because he had weighed the enterprise to which he was committing himself, but because he was hurried on by the impetus of an over-wrought nature. Even had he weighed the enter-sprie, and found it wanting, he would have been a rebel nevertheless; he would have rushed into ruin on the wheels of his old impulses. He could not have said to himself "It is useless to rebel, and I will not;" and, if he could, what a hypocrite to have remained in Heaven! His revolt was the natural issue of the thoughts to which he had accustomed himself; and his crime lay in having acquired a rebellious constitution, in having pursued action too much, and spurned worship and contemplation. Herein lay the difference between him and the other Archangels, Raphael, Gabriel, and Michael.

Satan in his revolt carried a third part of the Angels with him. He had accustomed many of the Angels to his mode of thinking. One of the ways in which he gratified his desire for activity had been that of exerting a moral and intellectual influence over the inferior Angels. A few of these he had liked to associate with, discoursing with them, and observing how they imbibed his ideas. His chief associate, almost his bosom-companion, had been Beelzebub, a princely Angel. Moloch, Belial, and Mammon, had likewise been admitted to his confidence. These five had constituted a kind of clique in Heaven, giving the word to a whole multitude of inferior Angels, all of them resembling their leader in being fonder of action than of contemplation. Thus, in addition to the mere hankering after action, there had grown up in Satan's mind a love of power. This feeling that it was a glorious thing to be a leader seems to have had much to do with his voluntary sacrifice of happiness. We may conceive it to have been voluntary. Foreseeing never so much misery would not have prevented such a spirit from rebelling. Having a third of the Angels away with him in some dark, howling region, where he might rule over them alone, would have seemed, even if he had foreseen it, infinitely preferable to the puny sovereignty of an Archangel in that world of gold and emerald: "better to reign in Hell than serve in Heaven." Thus we conceive him to have faced the anticipation of the future. It required little persuasion to gain over the kindred spirit of Beelzebub. These two appear to have conceived the enterprise from the beginning in a different light from that in which they represented it to their followers. Happiness with the inferior Spirits was a more important consideration than with such Spirits as Satan and Beelzebub; and to have hinted the possibility of losing happiness in the enterprise would have been to terrify them away. Satan and Beelzebub were losing happiness to gain something which they thought better; to the inferior Angels nothing could be mentioned that would appear better. Again, the inferior Angels, judging from narrower premises, might indulge in enthusiastic expectations which the greater knowledge of the leaders would prevent them from entertaining. At all events, the effect of the intercourse with the Angels was that a third of their number joined the standard of Satan. Then began the wars in Heaven, related in the poem.

It may be remarked that the carrying on those wars by Satan with the hope of victory is not inconsistent with what has been said as to the possibility of his not having proceeded on a false calculation. We are apt to imagine those wars as wars between the rebel Angels and the armies of God. Now this is true ; but it is scarcely the proper idea in the circumstances. How could Satan have hoped for victory in that case ? You can only suppose that he did so by lessening his intellect, by making him a mere blundering Fury, and not a keen, far-seeing Intelligence. But in warring with Michael and his followers he was, until the contrary should be proved, warring merely against his fellow-beings of the same Heaven, whose strength he knew and feared not. The idea of physical nearness between the Almighty and the Angels confuses us here. Satan had heard the threat which had accompanied the proclamation of the Messiah's sovereignty; but it may have been problematical in his mind whether the way in which God would fulfil the threat would be to make Michael conquer him. So he made war against Michael and his Angels. At last, when all Heaven was in confusion, the Divine omnipotence interfered. On the third day the Messiah rode forth in his strength, to end the wars and expel the rebel host from Heaven. They fled, driven before his thunder. The crystal wall of Heaven opened wide, and the two lips, rolling inward, disclosed a spacious gap yawning into the wasteful Deep. The reeling Angels saw down, and hung back affrighted; but the terror of the Lord was behind them : headlong they threw themselves from the verge of Heaven into the fathomless abyss, eternal wrath burning after them down through the blackness like a hissing fiery funnel.

And now the Almighty determined to create a new kind of World, and to people it with a race of beings different from that already existing, inferior in the meantime to the Angels, but with the power of working themselves up into the Angelic mode of being. The Messiah, girt with omnipotence, rode out on this creating errand. Heaven opened her everlasting gates, moving on their golden hinges, and the King of Glory, uplifted on the wings of Cherubim, rode on and on into Chaos. At last he stayed his fervid wheels and took the golden compasses in his hand. Centering one point where he stood, he turned the other silently and slowly round through the profound obscurity. Thus were the limits of *our* Universe marked out—that azure region in which the stars were to shine, and the planets were to wheel. On the huge fragment of Chaos thus marked out the Creating Spirit brooded, and the light gushed down. In six days the work of creation was completed. In the centre of the new Universe hung a silvery star. That was the Earth. Thereon, in a paradise of trees and flowers, walked Adam and Eve, the last and the fairest of all God's creatures.

Meanwhile the rebel host lay rolling in the fiery gulf underneath Chaos. The bottom of Chaos was Hell. Above it was Chaos proper, a thick, black, sweltering confusion. Above it again was the new experimental World, cut out of it like a mine, and brilliant with stars and galaxies. And high over all, behind the stars and galaxies, was Heaven itself. Satan and his crew lay rolling in Hell, the fiery element underneath Chaos. Chaos lay between them and the new World. Satan was the first to awake out of stupor and realize the whole state of the case—what had occurred, what was to be their future condition of being, and what remained to be attempted. In the first dialogue between him and Beelzebub we see that, even thus early, he had ascertained what his function was to be for the future, and decided in what precise mode of being he could make his existence most pungent and perceptible.

> " Of this be sure,
> To do aught good never will be our task,
> But ever to do evil our sole delight,
> As being the contrary to His high will
> Whom we resist."

Here the ruined Archangel first strikes out the idea of existing for ever after as the Devil. It is important to observe that his becoming a Devil was not the mere inevitable consequence of his being a ruined Archangel. Beelzebub, for instance, could see in the future nothing but a prospect of continued suffering, until Satan communicated to him his conception of a way of enjoying action in the midst of suffering. Again, some of the Angels appear to have been ruminating the possibility of retrieving their former condition by patient enduring. The gigantic scheme of becoming a Devil was Satan's. At first it existed in his mind only as a vague perception that the way in which he would be most likely to get the full worth of his existence was to employ himself thenceforward in doing evil. The idea afterwards became more definite. After glancing round their new domain, Beelzebub and he aroused their abject followers. In the speech which Satan addresses to them after they had all mustered in order we find him hint an opening into a new career, as if the idea had just occurred to him :—

> " Space may produce new worlds; whereof so rife
> There went a fame in Heaven that He ere long
> Intended to create, and therein plant
> A generation whom His choice regard
> Should favour equal to the sons of Heaven :
> Thither, if but to pry, shall be perhaps
> Our first eruption."

Here is an advance in definiteness upon the first proposal—that, namely, of determining to spend the rest of existence in doing evil. Casting about in his mind for some specific opening, Satan had recollected the talk they used to have in Heaven about the new World that was to be cut out of Chaos, and the new race of beings that was to be created to inhabit it; and it instantly struck his scheming fancy that *this* would be the weak point of the Universe. If he could but insert the wedge here! He did not, however, announce the scheme fully at the moment, but went on thinking. In the council of gods which was summoned some advised one thing, some another. Moloch was for open war; Belial had great faith in the force of circumstances; and Mammon was for organizing their new kingdom so as to make it as comfortable as possible. No one, however, could say the exact thing that was wanted. At last Beelzebub, prompted by Satan, rose and detailed the project of their great leader :—

> " There is a place
> (If ancient and prophetic fame in Heaven
> Err not), another world, the happy seat
> Of some new race called Man, about this time
> To be created, like to us, though less
> In power and excellence, but favoured more
> Of Him who rules above. So was His will
> Pronounced among the gods, and by an oath
> That shook Heaven's whole circumference confirmed.
> Thither let us bend all our thoughts, and learn
> What creatures there inhabit, of what mould

> Or substance, how endued, and what their power
> And where their weakness : how attempted best ;
> By force or subtlety."

This was Satan's scheme. The more he had thought on it the more did it recommend itself to him. It was more feasible than any other. It held out an indefinite prospect of action. Success in it would be the addition of another fragment of the Universe to Satan's kingdom, mingling and confounding the new World with Hell, and dragging down the new race of beings to share the perdition of the old. The scheme was universally applauded by the Angels ; who seem to have differed from their leaders in this, that they were sanguine of being able to better their condition, whereas their leaders sought only the gratification of their desire of action.

The question next was, Who would venture out of Hell to explore the way to the new World ? Satan volunteered the perilous excursion. Immediately, putting on his swiftest wings, he directs his solitary flight towards Hell-gate, where sat Sin and Death. When, at length, the gate was opened to give him exit, it was like a huge furnace-mouth, vomiting forth smoke and flames into the womb of Chaos. Issuing thence, Satan spread his sail-broad wings for flight, and began his toilsome way upward, half on foot, half on wing, swimming, sinking, wading, climbing, flying, through the thick and turbid element. At last he emerged out of Chaos into the glimmer surrounding the new Universe. Winging at leisure now through the balmier ether, and still ascending, he could discern at last the whole empyrean Heaven, his former home, with its opal towers and sapphire battlements, and, depending thence by a golden chain, our little World or Universe, like a star of smallest magnitude on the full moon's edge. At the point of suspension of this World from Heaven was an opening, and by that opening Satan entered.

When Satan thus arrived in the new Creation the whole phenomenon was strange to him, and he had no idea what kind of a being Man was. He asked Uriel, whom he found on the sun fulfilling some Divine errand, in which of all the shining orbs round him Man had fixed his seat, or whether he had a fixed seat at all, and was not at liberty to shift his residence, and dwell now in one star, now in another. Uriel, deceived by the appearance which Satan had assumed, pointed out the way to Paradise.

Alighting on the surface of the Earth, Satan walks about immersed in thought. Heaven's gate was in view. Overhead and round him were the quiet hills and the green fields. Oh, what an errand he had come upon! His thoughts were sad and noble. Fallen as he was, all the Archangel stirred within him. Oh, had he not been made so high, should he ever have fallen so low? Is there no hope even now, no room for repentance? Such were his first thoughts. But he roused himself and shook them off. " The past is gone and away; it is to the future that I must look. Perish the days of my Archangelship! perish the name of Archangel! Such is my name no longer. My future, if less happy, shall be more glorious. Ah, and this is the World I have singled out for my experiment! Formerly, in the days of my Archangelship, I ranged at will through infinity, doing one thing here and another there. Now I must contract the sphere of my activity, and labour nowhere but here. But it is better to apply myself to the task of thoroughly impregnating one point of space with my presence than henceforth to beat my wings vaguely all through infinitude. Ah, but may not my nature suffer by the change? In thus selecting a specific aim, in thus concerning myself exclusively with one point of space, and forswearing all interest in the innumerable glorious things that may be happening out of it, shall I not run the risk of degenerating into a smaller and meaner being? In the course of ages of dealing with the puny offspring of these new beings, may I not dwindle into a mere pungent, pettifogging Spirit? What would Raphael, Gabriel, and Michael say, were they to see their old co-mate changed into such a being? But be it so. If I cannot cope with the Almighty on the grand scale of infinitude, I shall at least make my existence felt by opposing His plans respecting this new race of beings. Besides, by beginning with this, may I not worm my way to a more effective position even in infinitude? At all events, I shall have a scheme on hand, and be incessantly occupied. And, as time makes the occupation more congenial, if I do become less magnanimous, I shall, at the same time, become happier. And, whether my fears on this point are visionary or not, it will, at least, be a noble thing to be able to say that I have caused a whirlpool that shall suck down generation after generation of these new beings, before their Maker's eyes, into the same wretched condition of being to which He has doomed us. It will be something so to vitiate the Universe that, let Him create, create on, as He chooses, it will be like pouring water into a broken vessel."

In the very course of this train of thinking Satan begins to degenerate into a meaner being. He is on the very threshold of that career in which he will cease for ever to be the Archangel and become irrevocably the Devil. The very manner in which he tempts the first pair is devil-like. It is in the shape of a cormorant on a tree that he sits watching his victims. He sat at the ear of Eve "squat like a toad." It was in the shape of a serpent that he tempted her. And, when the evil was done, he slunk away through the brush wood. In the very act of ruining Man he committed himself to a life of ignominious activity: he was to go on his belly and eat dust all his days.

Such is the story of Milton's Satan. It will be easy to express more precisely the idea which we have acquired of him when we come to contrast him with Goethe's Mephistopheles. Meanwhile, we shall be much assisted in our efforts to conceive Goethe's Mephistopheles by keeping in mind what we have been saying about Milton's Satan.

We do not think it possible to sum up in a single expression all that Goethe meant to signify by his Mephistopheles. For one thing, it is questionable whether Goethe kept strictly working out one specific meaning and making it clearer all through Mephistopheles's gambols and devilries, or whether, having once for all allegorized the Spirit of Evil into a living personage, he did not treat him just as he would have treated any other of his characters, making him always consistent, always diabolic, but not intent upon making his actions run parallel to any under-current of exposition. It may be best, therefore, to take Mephistopheles as a character in a drama which we wish to study. On the whole, perhaps, we shall be on the right track if, in the first place, we establish a relation between Satan and Mephistopheles by adopting the notion which we have imagined Satan himself to have entertained when engaged in scheming out his future life, *i.e.* if we suppose Mephistopheles to be what Satan has become after six thousand years. Milton's Satan, then, is the ruined Archangel deciding his future function, and forswearing all interest in other regions of the universe, in order that he may more thoroughly possess and impregnate this. Goethe's Mephistopheles is this same being after the toils and vicissitudes of six thousand years in his new vocation : smaller, meaner, ignobler, but a million times sharper and cleverer. By way of corroboration of this view, we may refer, in passing, to the Satan of the *Paradise Regained;* who, though still a sublime and Miltonic being, dealing in high thoughts and high arguments, yet seems to betray, in his demeanour, the effects of four thousand years spent in a new walk. Is there not something Mephisto-pheles-like, for instance, in the description of the Fiend's appearance when he approached Christ to begin his temptation ? Christ was walking alone and thoughtful one evening in the thick of the forest where he had lived fasting forty days, when he heard the dry twigs behind him snapping beneath approaching footsteps. He turned round, and

> " An aged man in rural weeds,
> Following as seemed the quest of some stray ewe,
> Or withered sticks to gather, which might serve
> Against a winter's day when winds blow keen

> To warm him, wet returned from field at eve,
> He saw approach ; who first with curious eye
> Perused him, then with words thus uttered spake."

Observe how all the particulars of this description are drawn out of the very thick of the civilization of the past four thousand years, and how the whole effect of the picture is to suggest a Mephistophelic-looking man, whom it would be disagreeable to meet alone. Indeed, if one had space, one could make more use of the *Paradise Regained* as exhibiting the transition of Satan into Mephistopheles. But we must pass at once to Goethe.

Viewing Mephistopheles in the proposed light (of course it is not pretended that Goethe himself had any such idea about his Mephistopheles), we obtain a good deal of insight from the " Prologue in Heaven." For here we have Mephistopheles out of his element, and contrasted with his old co-equals. The scene is Miltonic. The Heavenly Hosts are assembled round the throne, and the three Archangels, Raphael, Gabriel, and Michael, come forward to praise the Lord. The theme of their song is Creation—not, as it would have been in Milton, as an event about to take place, and which would vary the monotony of the universe, but as a thing existing and grandly going on. It is to be noted too that, while Milton appeals chiefly to the sight, and is clear and coherent in his imagery, Goethe produces a similar effect in his own manner by appealing to sight and hearing simultaneously, making sounds and metaphors dance and whirl through each other, as in a wild, indistinct, but overpowering dream. Raphael describes the Sun rolling on in thunder through the heavens, singing in chorus with the kindred stars. Gabriel describes the Earth revolving on her axis, one hemisphere glittering in the light, the other dipped in shadow. Michael in continuation sings of the ensphering atmosphere and the storms that rage in it, darting forth tongues of lightning, and howling in gusts over land and sea. And then the three burst forth in symphony, exulting in their nature as beings deriving strength from serene contemplation, and proclaiming all God's works to be as bright and glorious as on the day they were created. Suddenly, while Heaven is still thrilling to the grand undulation, another voice breaks in:

> " Da du, O Herr, dich einmal wieder nahst,
>   Und fragst wie alles sich bei uns befinde,
>   Und du mich sonst gewöhnlich gerne sahst,
>   So siehst du mich auch unter dem Gesinde."

Ugh! what a discord! The tone, the voice, the words, the very metre, so horribly out of tune with what had gone before! Mephistopheles is the speaker. He has been standing behind, looking about him and listening with a sarcastic air to the song of the Archangels; and, when they have done, he thinks it his turn to speak, and immediately begins. (We give the passage in translation.)

> "Since thou, O Lord, approachest us once more,
>   And askest how affairs with us are going,
> And commonly hast seen me here before,
>   To this my presence 'mid the rest is owing.
> Excuse my plainness; I'm no hand at chaffing;
>   I *can't* talk fine, though all around should scorn;
> *My* pathos certainly would set thee laughing,
>   Hadst thou not laughter long ago forborne.
> Of suns and worlds deuce one word can *I* gabble;
> I only know how men grow miserable.
> The little god of Earth is still the same old clay,
> And is as odd this hour as on Creation's day.
> Better somewhat his situation
> Hadst thou not given him that same light of in-
>   spiration:
> Reason he calls 't, and uses 't so that he
> Grows but more beastly than the beasts to be;
> He seems to me, begging your Grace's pardon,
> Like one of those long-legged things in a garden
> That fly about and hop and spring,
> And in the grass the same old chirrup sing.
> Would I could say that here the story closes!
> But in each filthy mess they thrust their noses."

And so shameless, and at the same time so voluble, is he that he would go on longer in the same strain did not the Lord interrupt him.

Now this speech both announces and exhibits Mephistopheles's nature. Without even knowing the language, one could hardly hear the original read as Mephistopheles's without seeing in it shamelessness, impudence, volubility, cleverness, a sneering, sarcastic disposition, want of heart, want of sentiment, want of earnestness, want of purpose, complete, confirmed, irrecoverable devilishness. And, besides, Mephistopheles candidly describes himself in it. When, in sly and sarcastic allusion to the song of the Archangels, he tells that *he* has not the gift of talking fine, he announces in effect that he is not going to be Miltonic. *He* is not going to speak of suns and universes, he says. Raphael, Gabriel, and Michael, are at home in that sort of thing; but *he* is not. Leaving them, therefore, to tell how the universe is flourishing on the grand scale, and how the suns and the planets are going on as beautifully as ever, he will just say a word or two as to how human nature is getting on down yonder; and, to be sure, if comparison be the order of the day, the little godkin, Man, is quite as odd as on the day he was made. And at once, with astounding impudence, he launches into a train of remark the purport of which is that everything down below is at sixes and sevens, and that in his opinion human nature has turned out a failure. And, heedless of the disgust of his audience, he would go on talking for ever, were he not interrupted.

And is this the Satan of the *Paradise Lost?* Is this
the Archangel ruined ? Is this the being who warred
against the Almighty, who lay floating many a rood,
who shot upwards like a pyramid of fire, who navigated
space wherever he chose, speeding on his errands from
star to star, and who finally conceived the gigantic
scheme of assaulting the universe where it was weakest,
and impregnating the new creation with the venom
of his spirit ? Yes, it is he ; but oh, how changed !
For six thousand years he has been pursuing the
walk he struck out at the beginning, plying his self-
selected function, dabbling devilishly in human nature,
and abjuring all interest in the grander physics ; and
the consequence is, as he himself anticipated, that his
nature, once great and magnificent, has become small,
virulent, and shrunken,

> " Subdued
> To what it works in, like the dyer's hand."

As if he had been journeying through a wilderness
of scorching sand, all that was left of the Archangel
has long since evaporated. He is now a dry, shrivelled
up, scoffing spirit. When, at the moment of scheming
out his future existence and determining to become
a Devil, he anticipated the ruin of his nature, he could
not help thinking with what a strange feeling he should
then appear before his old co-equals, Raphael, Gabriel,

and Michael. But now he stands before them disgustingly unabashed, almost ostentatious of not being any longer an Archangel. Even in the days of his glory he was different from them. They luxuriated in contemplation; he in the feeling of innate all-sufficient vigour. And lo, now! They are unchanged, the servants of the Lord, revering the day's gentle going. He, the scheming, enthusiastic Archangel, has been soured and civilized into the clever cold-hearted Mephistopheles.

Mephistopheles is the Spirit of Evil in modern society. Goethe's *Faust* is an illustration of this spirit's working in the history of an individual. The case selected is a noble one. Faust, a man of grand and restless nature, is aspiring after universality of feeling. Utterly dissatisfied and disgusted with all human method and all human acquisition, nay, fretting at the constitution of human nature itself, he longs to spill out his soul, so that, mingling with the winds, it may become a part of the ever-thrilling spirit of the universe and know the essence of everything. He has been contemplating suicide. To this great nature struggling with itself Mephistopheles is linked. It is to be noted that throughout the whole drama there is no evidence that it was an object of very earnest solicitude with Mephistopheles to gain possession of the soul of Faust. Of course, he desired this, and had it in view. Thus, he exacted a bond from Faust; and we find him also now and then chuckling when alone in anticipation of Faust's ultimate ruin. But on the whole he is constant to no earnest plan for effecting it. In fact, he is constant to no single purpose whatever. The desire of doing devilry is his motive all through. Going about with Faust was but being in the way of business and having a companion at the same time. He studies his own gratification, not Faust's, in all that he does. Faust never gets what he had a right to expect from him. He is dragged hither and thither through scenes he has no anxiety to be in, merely that Mephistopheles may enjoy some new and *piquant* piece of devilry. The moment he and Faust enter any place, he quits Faust's side and mixes with the persons present, to do some mischief or other; and, when it is done, he comes back to Faust, who has been standing, with his arms folded, gloomily looking on, and asks him if he could desire any better amusement than this. Now this is not the conduct of a devil intent upon nothing so much as gaining possession of the soul of his victim. A Miltonic devil would have pressed on to the mark more. He would have been more self-denying, and would have kept his victim in better humour. But Mephistopheles is a devil to the very core. He is a devil in his conduct to Faust. What he studies is not to gratify Faust, but to find plenty of congenial occupation for himself, to perpetrate as great a quantity of evil as possible in as short a time as possible. It seems capable of being inferred from this peculiarity in the character of Mephistopheles that Goethe had in his mind all through the poem a certain undercurrent of allegoric meaning. One sees that Mephistopheles, though acting as a dramatic personage, represents an abstract something or other.

The character of Mephistopheles is brought out all through the drama. In the first and second parts we have Faust and him brought into a great variety of situations and into contact with a great variety of individuals; and in watching how Mephistopheles conducts himself in these we obtain more and more insight into his devilish nature. He manifests himself in two ways—by his style of speaking, and by his style of acting. That is to say, Mephistopheles, in the first place, has a habit of making observations upon all subjects, and throwing out all kinds of general propositions in the course of his conversation, and by attending to the spirit of these one can perceive very distinctly his mode of looking at things; and, in the second place, he acts a part in the drama, and this part is, of course, characteristic.

The distinguishing feature in Mephistopheles's conversation is the amazing intimacy which it displays with all the conceivable ways in which crime can be perpetrated. There is positively not a wrong thing that people are in the habit of doing that he does not seem to be aware of. He is profound in his acquaintance with iniquity. If there is a joint loose anywhere in society, he knows of it; if the affairs of the State are going into confusion because of some blockhead's mismanagement, he knows of it. He is versed in all the forms of professional quackery. He knows how pedants hoodwink people, how priests act the hypocrite, how physicians act the rake, how lawyers peculate. In all sorts of police information he is a perfect Fouché. He has gone deep enough into one fell subject to be able to write a book like Duchatelet's. And not only has he accumulated a mass of observations, but he has generalized those observations, and marked evil in its grand educational sources. If the human mind is going out into a hopeless track of speculation, he has observed and knows it. If the universities are frittering away the intellect of the youth of a country in useless and barren studies, he knows it. If atheistic politicians are vehemently defending the religious institutions of a country, he has marked the prognostication. Whatever promises to inflict misery, to lead people astray, to break up beneficial alliances, to make men flounder on in error, to cause them to die blaspheming at the last, he is thoroughly cognisant of it all. He could draw up a catalogue of social vices. He could point out the specific existing grievances to which the disorganization of a people is owing, and lay his finger on the exact parent evils which the philanthropist ought to exert himself in exposing and making away with. But here lies the diabolical peculiarity of his knowledge. It is not in the spirit of a philanthropist that he has accumulated his information; it is in the spirit of a devil. It is not with the benevolent motive of a Duchatelet that he has descended into the lurking-places of iniquity; it is because he delights in knowing the whole extent of human misery. The doing of evil being his function, it is but natural that he should have a taste for even the minutest details of his own profession. Nay more, as the Spirit of all evil, who had been working from the beginning, how could he fail to be acquainted with all the existing varieties of criminal occupation? It is but as if he kept a diary. Now, in this combination of the knowledge of evil with the desire of producing it lies the very essence of his character. The combination is horrible, unnatural, unhuman. Generally the motive to investigate deeply into what is wrong is the desire to rectify it; and it is rarely that profligates possess very valuable information. But in every one of Mephistopheles's speeches there is some profound glimpse into the rottenness of society, some masterly specification of an evil that ought to be rooted out; and yet there is not one of those speeches in which the language is not flippant and sarcastic, not one in which the tone is sorrowful or philanthropic. Everything is going wrong in the world; twaddle and quackery everywhere abounding; nothing to be seen under the sun but hypocritical priests, sharking attorneys, unfaithful wives, children crying for bread to eat, men and women cheating, robbing, murdering each other: hurrah! This is exactly a burst of Mephisto-phelic feeling. In fact it is an intellectual defect in Mephistopheles that his having such an eye for evil and his taking such an interest in it prevent him from allowing anything for good in his calculations. To Mephistopheles the world, seems going to perdition as fast as it can, while in the same universal confusion beings like the Archangels recognise the good struggling with the evil.

Respecting the part which Mephistopheles performs in the drama we have already said something. Going about the world, linked to Faust, is to him only a racy way of acting the devil. Having as his com-panion a man so flighty in his notions did but increase the flavour of whatever he engaged in. All through he is laughing in secret at Faust, and deriving a keen enjoyment from his transcendental style of thinking. Faust's noble qualities are all Greek and Gaelic to his cold and devilish nature. He has a contempt for all strong feeling, all sentiment, all evangelism. He enjoys the Miltonic vastly. Thus in the "Prologue in Heaven" he quizzes the Archangels about the grandiloquence of their song. Not that he does not understand that sort of thing intellectually, but that it is not in his nature to sympathize with anything like sentiment. Hence, when he assumes the sentimental himself and mimicks any lofty strain, although he does it full justice in as far as giving the whole intellectual extent of meaning is concerned, yet he always does so in words so inappropriate emotionally that the effect is a parody. He must have found amusement enough in Faust's company to have reconciled him in some measure to losing him finally.

But to go on. Mephistopheles acts the devil all through. In the first place he acts the devil to Faust himself, for he is continually taking his own way and starting difficulties whenever Faust proposes anything. Then again in his conduct towards the other principal personages of the drama it is the same. In the murder of poor Margaret, her mother, her child, and her brother, we have as fiendish a series of acts as devil could be supposed capable of perpetrating. And, lastly, in the mere filling up and side play, it is the same. He is constantly doing unnecessary mischief. If he enters Auerbach's wine-cellar and introduces himself to the four drinking companions, it is to set the poor brutes fighting and make them cut off each other's noses. If he spends a few minutes in talk with Martha, it is to make the silly old woman expose her foibles. The Second Part of Faust is devilry all through, a tissue of bewilderments and devilries. And while doing all this Mephistopheles is still the same cold, self-possessed, sarcastic being. If he exhibits any emotion at all, it is a kind of devilish anger. Perhaps, too, once or twice we recognise something like terror or flurry. But on the whole he is a spirit bereft of feeling. What could indicate the heart of a devil more than his words to Faust in the harrowing prison scene?

" Komm, komm, ich lasse dich mit ihr im Stich."

And now for a word or two describing Milton's Satan and Goethe's Mephistopheles by each other:—Satan is a colossal figure; Mephistopheles an elaborated portrait. Satan is a fallen Archangel scheming his future existence; Mephistopheles is the modern Spirit of Evil. Mephistopheles has a distinctly marked physiognomy; Satan has not. Satan has a sympathetic knowledge of good; Mephistopheles knows good only as a phenomenon. Much of what Satan says might be spoken by Raphael; a devilish spirit runs through all that

Mephistopheles says. Satan's bad actions are preceded by noble reasonings; Mephistopheles does not reason. Satan's bad actions are followed by compunctious visitings; Mephistopheles never repents. Satan is often "inly racked;" Mephistopheles can feel nothing more noble than disappointment. Satan conducts an enterprise; Mephistopheles enjoys an occupation. Satan has strength of purpose; Mephistopheles is volatile. Satan feels anxiety; Mephistopheles lets things happen. Satan's greatness lies in the vastness of his motives; Mephistopheles's in his intimate acquaintance with everything. Satan has a few sublime conceptions; Mephistopheles has accumulated a mass of observations. Satan declaims; Mephistopheles puts in remarks. Satan is conversant with the moral aspects of things and uses adjectives; Mephistopheles has a preference for nouns, and uses adjectives only to convey significations which he *knows* to exist Satan may end in being a devil; Mephistopheles is a devil irrecoverably.

Milton's Satan and Goethe's Mephistopheles are literary performances; and, for what they prove, neither Milton nor Goethe need have believed in a Devil at all. Luther's Devil, on the other hand, was a being recognised by him as actually existing—as existing, one might say, with a vengeance. The strong conviction which Luther had on this point is a feature in his character. The narrative of his life abounds in anecdotes showing that the Devil with him was no chimera, no mere orthodoxy, no fiction. In every page of his writings we have the word *Teufel*, *Teufel*, repeated again and again. Occasionally there occurs an express dissertation upon the nature and functions of the Evil Spirit; and one of the longest chapters in his *Table Talk* is that entitled "The Devil and his Works"—indicating that his conversation with his friends often turned on the subject of Satanic agency. *Teufel* was actually the strongest signification he had ; and, whenever he was excited to his highest emotional pitch, it came in to assist his utterance at the climax, and give him a correspondingly powerful expression. "This thing I will do," it was common for him to say, " in spite of all who may oppose me, be it duke, emperor, priest, bishop, cardinal, pope, or Devil." Man's heart, he says, is a "Stock, Stein, Eisen, Teufel, hart Herz," (" a stock, stone, iron, Devil, hard heart"). And it was not a mere vague conception he had of this being, such as theology might oblige. On the contrary, he had observed him as a man would his personal enemy, and in so doing had formed a great many conclusions respecting his powers and his character. In general, Luther's Devil may be defined as a personification, in the spirit of Scripture, of the resisting medium which Luther had to toil his way through—

spiritual fears, passionate uprisings, fainting resolutions within himself; error, weakness, envy, in those around him; and, without, a whole world howling for his destruction. It is in effect as if Luther had said, "Scripture reveals to me the existence of a great accursed Being, whose function it is to produce evil. It is for me to ascertain the character of this Being, whom I, of all men, have to deal with. And how am I to do so except by observing him working? God knows I have not far to go in search of his manifestations." And thus Luther went on filling up the Scriptural proposition with his daily experience. He was constantly gaining a clearer conception of his great personal antagonist, constantly stumbling upon some more concealed trait in the Spirit's character. The Being himself was invisible; but men were walking in the midst of his manifestations. It was as if there were some Being whom we could not see, nor directly in the ordinary way have any intercourse with, but who every morning, before it was light, came and left at our doors some exquisite specimen of his workmanship. It would, of course, be difficult under such disadvantages to become acquainted with the character of our invisible correspondent and nightly visitant; still we could arrive at a few conclusions respecting him, and the more of his workmanship we saw the more insight we should come to have. Or again, in striving to realize to himself the Scriptural proposition about the Devil, Luther, to speak in the language of the "Positive Philosophy," was but striving to ascertain the laws according to which evil happens. Only the Positive Philosophy would lay a veto on any such speculation, and pronounce it fundamentally vicious in this respect —that there are not two courses of events, separable from each other, in history, the one good and the other evil, but that evil comes of good and good of evil; so that, if we are to have a science of history at all, the most we can have is a science of the laws according to which, not evil follows evil, but events follow each other. But History to Luther was not a physical course of events. It was God acting, and the Devil opposing.

So far Luther did not differ from his age. Belief in Satanic agency was universal at that period. We have no idea now how powerful this belief was. We realize something of the truth when we read the depositions in an old book of trials for witchcraft. But it is sufficient to glance over any writings of the period to see what a real meaning was then attached to the words "Hell" and "Devil." The spirit of these words has become obsolete, chased away by the spirit of exposition. That was what M. Comte calls the Theological period, when all the phenomena of mind and matter were referred to the agency of Spirits. The going out of the belief in Satanic agency (for even those who retain it

in profession allow it no force in practice) M. Comte
would attribute to the progress of the spirit of that
philosophy of which he is the apostle. We do not
think, however, that the mere progress of the scientific
spirit—that is, the mere disposition of men to pursue
one mode of thinking with respect to all classes of
phenomena—could have been sufficient of itself to work
such an alteration in the general mind. We are fond of
accounting for it, in part at least, by the going out, in
the progress of civilization, of those sensations which
seem naturally fitted to nourish the belief in supernatural beings. The tendency of civilization has been to
diminish our opportunities of feeling terror, of feeling
strongly at all. The horrific plays a much less important part in human experience than it once did. To
mention but a single instance: we are exempted now,
by mechanical contrivances for locomotion, &c., from
the necessity of being much in darkness or wild
physical solitude. This is especially the case with those
who dwell in cities, and therefore exert most conspicuously an intellectual influence. The moaning of
the wind at night in winter is about their highest experience of the kind; and is it not a corroboration of
the view now suggested that the belief in the supernatural is always strongest at the moment of this experience? Scenes and situations our ancestors were in
every day are strange to us. We have not now to

E 2

travel through forests at the dead of night, nor to pass a
lonely spot on a moor where a murderer's body is swing-
ing from a gibbet.   Tam o' Shanter, even before he came
to Allowa' Kirk, saw more than many of us see in a
life-time.

> " By this time he was 'cross the ford
>   Whaur in the snaw the chapman smoored,
>   And past the birks and muckle stane
>   Whaur drunken Charlie brak's neck-bane,
>   And through the whins and by the cairn
>   Whaur hunters fand the murdered bairn,
>   And near the thorn aboon the well
>   Whaur Mungo's mither hanged hersel'."

This effect of civilization in reducing all our sensations to those of comfort is a somewhat alarming circumstance in the point of view we are now taking.   It
is necessary, for many a reason, to resist the universal
application of the " Positive Philosophy," even if we
adopt and adore it as an instrument of explication.
The " Positive Philosophy " commands us to forbear
all speculation into the inexplicable.   For the sake of
many things this order must be disregarded.   Speculation into the metaphysical is the invariable accom-
paniment of strong feeling; and the moral nature of
man would starve upon such chopped straw as the mere
intellectual relations of similitude and succession.   Nor
does it meet the demands of the case to say that the

"Positive Philosophy" would be always far in arrear of the known phenomena, and that here would be mystery enough. No! the "Positive Philosophy" would require to strike a chasm in itself under the title of the Liberty of Hypothesis. We do not mean the liberty of hypothesis merely as a means of anticipating theory, but for spiritual and imaginative purposes. It is in this light that one would welcome Animal Magnetism, or any thing else whatever that would but knock a hole through the paper wall that incloses our mode of being, snub the self-conceit of our present knowledge, and give us other and more difficult phenomena to explain.

But, though Luther and his age were not at variance in the belief in Satanic agency, Luther, of course, did this as he did every thing else, gigantically. The Devil, as Luther conceived him, was not the Satan of Milton; although, had Luther set himself to realize the Miltonic narrative, his conception might not have been dissimilar. But it was as the enemy of mankind, working in human affairs, that Luther conceived the Devil. We should expect his conception therefore to tally with Goethe's in some respects, but only as a conception of Luther's would tally with one of Goethe's. Luther's conception was truer to the strict Scriptural definition than either Milton's or Goethe's. Mephistopheles being a character in a drama, and apparently fully occupied

in his part there, we cannot bring ourselves to recognise in him that virtually omnipotent being to whom
all evil is owing, who is leavening the human mind
everywhere as if the atmosphere round the globe were
charged with the venom of his spirit. In the case of
Milton's Satan we have no such difficulty, because in
his case a whole planet is at stake, and there are only
two individuals on it. But Luther's conception met the
whole exigency of Scripture. His conception was distinctly that of a being to whose operation all the evil of
all times and all places is owing, a veritable $\pi\nu\epsilon\upsilon\mu\alpha$
diffused through the earth's atmosphere. Hence his
mind had to entertain the notion of a plurality of
devils; for he could conceive the Arch-Demon acting
corporeally only through imps or emanations. Goethe's
Mephistopheles might pass for one of these.

It would be possible farther to illustrate Luther's
conception of the Evil Principle by quoting many of
his specific sayings about diabolic agency. It would
be found from these that his conception was that of a
being to whom evil of all kinds was dear. The Devil with
him was a meteorological agent. Devils, he said, are
in woods, and waters, and dark poolly places, ready to
hurt passers-by; there are devils also in the thick
black clouds, who cause hail and thunders and light-
nings, and poison the air and the fields and the pastures.
" When such things happen, philosophers say they are

natural, and ascribe them to the planets, and I know not what all." The Devil he believed also to be the patron of witchcraft. The Devil, he said, had the power of deceiving the senses, so that one should swear he heard or saw something while really the whole was an illusion. The Devil also was at the bottom of dreaming and somnambulism. He was likewise the author of diseases. "I hold," said Luther, "that the Devil sendeth all heavy diseases and sicknesses upon people." Diseases are, as it were, the Devil striking people; only, in striking, he must use some natural instrument, as a murderer uses a sword. When our sins get the upper hand, and all is going wrong, then the Devil must be God's hangman, to clear away obstructions and to blast the earth with famines and pestilences. Whatsoever procures death, that is the Devil's trade. All sadness and melancholy come of the Devil. So does insanity ; but the Devil has no farther power over the soul of a maniac. The Devil works in the affairs of nations. He looks always upward, taking an interest in what is high and pompous ; he does not look downward, taking little interest in what is insignificant and lowly. He likes to work on the great scale, to establish an influence over the central minds which manage public affairs. The Devil is also a spiritual tempter. He is the opponent of the Divine grace in the hearts of individuals. This was the aspect of the doctrine of Satanic agency which was most frequent in preaching; and, accordingly, Luther's propositions on the point are very specific. He had ascertained the laws of Satanic operation upon the human spirit. The Devil, he said, knows Scripture well, and uses it in argument. He shoots fearful thoughts, which are his fiery darts, into the hearts of the godly. The Devil is acquainted even with those mysterious enjoyments, those spiritual excitements, which the Christian would suppose a being like him must be ignorant of. "What gross inexperienced fellows," Luther says, "are those Papist commentators! They are for interpreting Paul's 'thorn in the flesh' to be merely fleshly lust; because they know no other kind of tribulation than that." But, though the Devil has great power over the human mind, he is limited in some respects. He has no means, for instance, of knowing the thoughts of the faithful until they give them utterance. Again, if the Devil be once foiled in argument, he cannot tempt that soul again on the same tack. The Papacy being with Luther the grand existing form of evil, he of course recognised the Devil in *it*. If the Papacy were once overthrown, Satan would lose his stronghold. Never on earth again would he be able to pile up such another edifice. No wonder, then, that at that moment all the energies of the enraged and despairing Spirit were employed to prop up the reeling and tottering fabric. Necessarily, therefore, Luther and Satan were personal antagonists. Satan saw that the grand struggle was with Luther. If he could but crush him by physical violence, or make him forget God, then the world would be his own again. So, often did he wrestle with Luther's spirit; often in nightly heart-agonies did he try to shake Luther's faith in Christ. But he was never victorious. "All the Duke Georges in the universe," said Luther, "are not equal to a single Devil; and I do not fear the Devil." "I should wish," he said, "to die rather by the Devil's hands than by the hands of Pope or Emperor; for then I should die, at all events, by the hands of a great and mighty Prince of the World: but, if I die through him, he shall eat such a bit of me as shall be his suffocation; he shall spew me out again; and, at the last day, I, in requital, shall devour him." When all other means were unavailing, Luther found that the Devil could not stand against humour. In his hours of spiritual agony, he tells us, when the Devil was heaping up his sins before him, so as to make him doubt whether he should be saved, and when he could not drive the Devil away by uttering sentences of Holy Writ, or by prayer, he used to address him thus: "Devil, if, as you say, Christ's blood, which was shed for my sins, be not sufficient to insure my salvation, can't you pray for me yourself, Devil?" At this the Devil invariably fled, "*quia est superbus spiritus et non potest ferre contemptum sui.*"

What Luther called " wrestling with the Devil " we at this day call " low spirits." Life must be a much more insipid thing than it was then. O what a soul that man must have had; under what a weight of feeling, that would have crushed a thousand of us, *he* must have trod the earth !

SHAKESPEARE AND GOETHE.

SHAKESPEARE AND GOETHE.

SHAKESPEARE AND GOETHE.[1]

If there are any two portraits which we all expect to find hung up in the rooms of those whose tastes are regulated by the highest literary culture, they are the portraits of Shakespeare and Goethe.

There are, indeed, many and various gods in our modern Pantheon of genius. It contains rough gods and smooth gods, gods of symmetry and gods of strength, gods great and terrible, gods middling and respectable, and little cupids and toy-gods. Out of this variety each master of a household will select his own Penates, the appropriate gods of his own mantelpiece. The roughest will find some to worship them, and the smallest shall not want domestic adoration. But we suppose a dilettante of the first class, one who, besides excluding from his range of choice the deities of war, and cold

---

[1] *British Quarterly Review*, November, 1852.—1. "Shakspeare and His Times." By M. Guizot. 1852.—2. "Shakspeare's Dramatic Art; and his Relation to Calderon and Goethe." Translated from the German of Dr. Hermann Ulrici. 1846.—3. "Conversations of Goethe with Eckermann and Soret." Translated from the German by John Oxenford. 2 vols. 1850.

thought, and civic action, shall further exclude from it all those even of the gods of modern literature who, whether by reason of their inferior rank, or by reason of their peculiar attributes, fail as models of universal stateliness. What we should expect to see over the mantel-piece of such a rigorous person would be the images of the English Shakespeare and the German Goethe.

On the one side, we will suppose, fixed with due gance against the luxurious crimson of the wall, would be a slab of black marble exhibiting in relief a white plaster-cast of the face of Shakespeare as modelled from the Stratford bust; on the other, in a similar setting, would be a copy, if possible, of the mask of Goethe taken at Weimar after the poet's death. This would suffice; and the considerate beholder could find no fault with such an arrangement. It is true, reasons might be assigned why a third mask should have been added—that of the Italian Dante; in which case Dante and Goethe should have occupied the sides, and Shakespeare should have been placed higher up between. But the master of the house would point out how, in that case, a fine taste would have been pained by the inevitable sense of contrast between the genial mildness of the two Teutonic faces and the severe and scornful melancholy of the poet of the Inferno. The face of the Italian poet, as being so different in kind, must either be reluctantly omitted, he would say, or transferred by itself to the

other side of the room.   Unless, indeed, with a view to
satisfy the claims both of degree and of kind, Shakespeare were to be placed alone over the mantelpiece,
and Dante and Goethe in company on the opposite wall,
where, there being but two, the contrast would be rather
agreeable than otherwise !   On the whole, however, and
without prejudice to new arrangements in the course
of future decorations, he is content that it should be
as it is.

And so, reader, for the present are we.   Let us enter
together, then, if it seems worth while, the room of this
imaginary dilettante during his absence ; let us turn the
key in the lock, so that he may not come in to interrupt
us ; and let us look for a little time at the two masks
he has provided for us over the mantelpiece, receiving
such reflections as they may suggest.   Doubtless we
have often looked at the two masks before ; but that
matters little.

As we gaze at the first of the two masks, what is it
that we see?   A face full in contour, of good oval
shape, the individual features small in proportion to the
entire countenance, the greater part of which is made
up of an ample and rounded forehead and a somewhat
abundant mouth and chin.   The general impression is
that rather of rich, fine, and very mobile tissue, than of
large or decided bone.   This, together with the length

of the upper lip, and the absence of any set expression, imparts to the face an air of lax and luxurious calmness. It is clearly a passive face rather than an active face, a face across which moods may pass and repass rather than a face grooved and charactered into any one permanent show of relation to the outer world. Placed beside the mask of Cromwell, it would fail to impress, not only as being less massive and energetic, but also as being in every way less marked and determinate. It is the face, we repeat, of a literary man, one of those faces which depend for their power to impress less on the sculptor's favourite circumstance of distinct osseous form than on the changing hue and aspect of the living flesh. And yet it is, even in form, quite a peculiar face. Instead of being, as in the ordinary thousand and one portraits of Shakespeare, a mere general face which anybody or nobody might have had, the face in the mask (and the singular portrait in the first folio edition of the poet's works corroborates it) is a face which every call-boy about the Globe Theatre must have carried about with him in his imagination, without any trouble, as specifically Mr. Shakespeare's face. In complexion, as we imagine it, it was rather fair than dark : and yet not very fair either, if we are to believe Shakespeare himself (Sonnet 62)—

> " But when my glass shows me myself indeed,
> Beated and chopped with tanned antiquity—"

a passage, however, in which, from the nature of the
mood in which it was written, we are to suppose ex-
aggeration for the worse. In short, the face of Shakespeare, so far as we can infer what it was from the
homely Stratford bust, was a genuine and even comely,
but still unusual, English face, distinguished by a kind
of ripe intellectual fulness in the general outline, comparative smallness in the individual features, and a look
of gentle and humane repose.

Goethe's face is different. The whole size of the
head is perhaps less, but the proportion of the face to
the head is greater, and there is more of that determinate form which arises from prominence and strength
in the bony structure. The features are individually
larger, and present in their combination more of that
deliberate beauty of outline which can be conveyed with
effect in sculpture. The expression, however, is also
that of calm intellectual repose; and, in the absence of
harshness or undue concentration of the parts, one is at
liberty to discover the proof that this also was the face
of a man whose life was spent rather in a career of
thought and literary effort than in a career of active and
laborious strife. Yet the face, with all its power of fine
susceptibility, is not so passive as that of Shakespeare.
Its passiveness is more the passiveness of self-control,
and less that of natural constitution; the susceptibili-
ties pass and repass over a firmer basis of permanent

D   F

character; the tremors among the nervous tissues do
not reach to such depths of sheer nervous dissolution,
but sooner make impact against the solid bone.   The
calm in the one face is more that of habitual softness
and ease of humour; the calm in the other is more that
of dignified, though tolerant, self-composure.   It would
have been more easy, one thinks, to take liberties with
Shakespeare in his presence than to attempt a similar
thing in the presence of Goethe.   The one carried himself with the air of a man often diffident of himself,
and whom, therefore, a foolish or impudent stranger
might very well mistake till he saw him roused; the
other wore, with all his kindness and blandness, a fixed
stateliness of mien and look that would have checked
undue familiarity from the first.   Add to all this that
the face of Goethe, at least in later life, was browner
and more wrinkled; his hair more dark; his eye also
nearer the black and lustrous in species, if less myste-
riously vague and deep; and his person perhaps the
taller and more symmetrically made.[1]

But a truce to these guesses!   What do we actually
know respecting those two men, whose masks, the preserved similitudes of the living features with which
they once fronted the world, are now before us?   Let
us turn first to the one and then to the other, till, as

---

[1] According to Mr. Lewes, in his Life of Goethe, it is a mistake to
ancy that Goethe was tall.   He seemed taller than he really was.

we gaze at these poor eyeless images, which are all we
now have, some vision of the lives and minds they
typify shall swim into our ken.

Shakespeare, this Englishman who died two hundred
and sixty years ago, what is he now to us his countrymen, who ought to know him best? A great name, in
the first place, of which we are proud! That this little
foggy island of England should have given birth to
such a man is of itself a moiety of our acquittance
among the nations. By Frenchmen Shakespeare is
accepted as at least equal to their own first; Italians
waver between him and Dante; Germans, by race more
our brethren, worship him as their own highest product
too, though born by chance amongst us. All confess
him to have been one of those great spirits, occasionally
created, in whom the human faculties seem to have
reached that extreme of expansion on the slightest
increase beyond which man would burst away into
some other mode of being and leave this behind. And
why all this? What are the special claims of Shakespeare to this high worship? Through what mode of
activity, practised while alive, has he won this immortality after he is dead? The answer is simple. He
was an artist, a poet, a dramatist. Having, during some
five-and-twenty years of a life not very long, written
about forty dramatic pieces, which, after being acted

in several London theatres, were printed either by himself or by his executors, he has, by this means, bequeathed to the memory of the human race an immense number of verses, and to its imagination a great variety of ideal characters and creations—Lears, Othellos, Hamlets, Falstaffs, Shallows, Imogens, Mirandas, Ariels, Calibans. This, understood in its 'fullest extent, is what Shakespeare has done. Whatever blank in human affairs, as they now are, would be produced by the immediate withdrawal of all this intellectual capital, together with all the interest that has been accumulated on it: *that* is the measure of what the world owes to Shakespeare.

This conception, however, while it serves vaguely to indicate to us the greatness of the man, assists us very little in the task of defining his character. In our attempts to do this—to ascend, as it were, to the living spring from which have flowed those rich poetic streams —we unavoidably rely upon two kinds of authority: the records which inform us of the leading events of his life; and the casual allusions to his person and habits left us by his contemporaries.

To enumerate the ascertained events of Shakespeare's life is unnecessary here. How he was born at Stratford-on-Avon, in Warwickshire, in April, 1564, the son of a respectable burgess who afterwards became poor; how, having been educated with some care in his native town, he married there, at the age of eighteen, a farmer's daughter eight years older than himself; how, after employing himself as scrivener or schoolmaster, or something of that kind, in his native county for a few years more, he at length quitted it in his twenty-fourth year, and came up to London, leaving his wife and three children at Stratford; how, connecting himself with the Blackfriars theatre, he commenced the career of a poet and play-writer; how he succeeded so well in this that, after having been a flourishing actor and theatre-proprietor, and a most popular man of genius about town for some seventeen years, he was able to leave the stage while still under forty, and return to Stratford with property sufficient to make him the most considerable man of the place; how he lived here for some twelve years more in the midst of his family, sending up occasionally a new play to town, and otherwise leading the even and tranquil existence of a country gentleman ; and how, after having buried his old mother, married his daughters, and seen himself a grandfather at the age of forty-three, he was cut off rather suddenly near his fifty-third birthday, in the year 1616 :—all this is, or ought to be, as familiar to educated Englishmen of the present day as the letters of the English alphabet. M. Guizot, with a little inaccuracy, has made these leading facts in the life of the English poet tolerably familiar even to our French neighbours.

But, while such facts, if conceived with sufficient distinctness, serve to mark out the life of the poet in general outline, it is rather from the few notices of him that have come down to us from his contemporaries that we derive the more special impressions regarding his character and ways with which we are accustomed to fill up this outline. These notices are various; those of interest may, perhaps, be about a dozen in all; but the only ones that take a very decided hold on the imagination are the three following :—

Fuller's Fancy-picture of Shakespeare and Ben Jonson at the Mermaid Tavern.—" Many were the wit-combats betwixt him and Ben Jonson; which two I behold like a Spanish great galleon and an English man-of-war. Master Jonson, like the former, was built far higher in learning; solid, but slow in his performances.` Shakespeare, with the English man-of-war, lesser in bulk, but lighter in sailing, could turn with all tides, tack about, and take advantage of all winds, by the quickness of his wit and invention."—*Written, about* 1650, *by Thomas Fuller, born in* 1608.

Aubrey's Sketch of Shakespeare at second hand.—" This William, being inclined naturally to poetry and acting, came to London, I guess, about 18; and was an actor at one of the play-houses, and did act exceedingly well. (Now B. Jonson was never a good actor, but an excellent instructor.) He began early to make essays at dramatic poetry, which at that time was very low; and his plays took well. He was a handsome, well-shaped man ; very good company, and of a very ready and pleasant smooth wit. The humour of the constable in '*A Midsummer Night's Dream*,' he happened to take at Grendon, in Bucks, which is the road from London to Stratford; and there was living that constable about 1642, when I first came to Oxon. Mr. Jos. Howe is of that parish; and knew him. Ben Jonson and he did gather humours of men daily wherever they came. . . . . He was wont to go to his native country once a year. I think I have been told that he left 200*l.* or 300*l.* per annum, there and thereabout, to a sister. I have heard Sir William Davenant and Mr. Thomas Shadwell, who is accounted the best comedian we have now, say that he had a most prodigious wit, and did admire his natural parts beyond all other dramatical writers. He was wont to say that he never blotted out a line in his life. Said Ben Jonson, 'I wish he had blotted out a thousand.' "—*Written, about* 1680, *by John Aubrey, born* 1625.

Ben Jonson's own Sketch of Shakespeare.—" I remember the players have often mentioned it as an honour to Shakespeare, that in his writing (whatsoever he penned) he never blotted out a line. My answer hath been ' Would he had blotted a thousand !'; which they thought a malevolent speech. I had not told posterity this but for their ignorance, who chose that circumstance to commend their friend by wherein he most faulted; and to justify mine own candour: for I loved the man, and do honour his memory, on this side idolatry, as much as any. He was, indeed, honest, and of an open and free nature; had an excellent phantasy, brave notions, and gentle expressions; wherein he flowed with that facility that *sometimes it was necessary he should be stopped : ' Suffla-*

minandus erat,' as Augustus said of Haterius. His wit
was in his own power; would the rule of it had been
so too! Many times he fell into those things could
not escape laughter; as when he said, in the person of
Cæsar, one speaking to him, ' Cæsar, thou dost me wrong,'
he replied, ' Cæsar did never wrong but with just cause,'
and such like; which were ridiculous. But he redeemed
his vices with his virtues. There was ever more in him
to be praised than to be pardoned."—*Ben Jonson's "Discoveries."*

It is sheer nonsense, with these and other such passages accessible to anybody, to go on repeating, as people
seem determined to do, the hackneyed saying of the
commentator Steevens, that "all that we know of
Shakespeare is, that he was born at Stratford-on-Avon;
married and had children there; went to London, where
he commenced actor, and wrote plays and poems;
returned to Stratford, made his will, died, and was
buried."[1] It is our own fault, and not the fault of the
materials, if we do not know a great deal more about
Shakespeare than that; if we do not realize, for example,
these distinct and indubitable facts about him—his

[1] This saying of Steevens, though still repeated in books, has lost
its force with the public. The Lives of Shakespeare by Mr. Halliwell
and Mr. Charles Knight, written on such different principles, have
effectually dissipated the old impression. Mr. Knight, by his use of
the principle of synchronism, and his accumulation of picturesque
details, in his Biography of Shakespeare, has left the public without
excuse, if they still believe in Steevens.

special reputation among the critics of his time, as a man not so much of erudition as of prodigious natural genius; his gentleness and openness of disposition; his popular and sociable habits; his extreme ease, and, as some thought, negligence in composition; and, above all, and most characteristic of all, his excessive fluency in speech. "He sometimes required stopping," is Ben Jonson's expression; and whoever does not see a whole volume of revelation respecting Shakespeare in that single trait has no eye for seeing anything. Let no one ever lose sight of that phrase in trying to imagine Shakespeare.

Still, after all, we cannot be content thus. With regard to such a man we cannot rest satisfied with a mere picture of his exterior in its aspect of repose, or in a few of its common attitudes. We seek, as the phrase is, to penetrate into his heart—to detect and to fix in everlasting portraiture that mood of his soul which was ultimate and characteristic; in which, so to speak, he came ready-fashioned from the Creator's hands; towards which he always sank when alone; and on the ground-melody of which all his thoughts and actions were but voluntary variations. As far short of such a result as would be any notion we could form of the poet Burns from a mere chronological outline of his life, together with a few stories such as are current about his moral irregularities, so far short of a true appreciation of Shakespeare would be that idea of him which we could derive from the scanty fund of the external evidence.

And here it is that, in proceeding to make up the deficiency of the external evidence by going to the only other available source of light on the subject, namely the bequeathed writings of the man himself, we find ourselves obstructed at the outset by an obvious difficulty, which does not exist to the same extent in most other cases. We can, with comparative ease, recognise Burns himself in his works; for Burns is a lyrist, pouring out his own feelings in song, often alluding to himself, and generally under personal agitation when he writes. Shakespeare, on the other hand, is a dramatist, whose function it was not to communicate, but to create. Had he been a dramatist of the same school as Ben Jonson, indeed—using the drama as a means of spreading, or, at all events, as a medium through which to insinuate, his opinions, and often indicating his purposes by the very names of his *dramatis personæ* (as Downright, Mercecraft, Eitherside, and the like)—then the task would have been easier. But it is not so with Shakespeare. Less than almost any man that ever wrote does he inculcate or dogmatise. He is the very type of the poet. He paints, represents, creates, holds the mirror up to nature; but from opinion, doctrine, controversy, theory, he holds instinctively aloof. In each of his plays there is a "central idea," to use the favourite term of the German critics—that is, a single thought round which all may be exhibited as consciously or unconsciously crystallized; but there is no pervading maxim, no point set forth to be argued or proved. Of none of all the plays can it be said that it is more than any other a vehicle for fixed articles in the creed of Shakespeare.

One quality or attribute of Shakespeare's genius we do, indeed, contrive to seize out this very difficulty of seizing anything—that quality or attribute of *many-sidedness* of which we have heard so much for the last century and a half. The immense variety of his characters and conceptions, embracing as it does Hamlets and Falstaffs, Kings and Clowns, Prosperos and Dogberrys, and his apparently equal ease in handling them all, are matters that have been noted by one and all of the critics. And thus, while his own character is lost in his incessant shiftings through such a succession of masks, we yet manage, as it were in revenge, to extract from the very impossibility of describing him an adjective which does possess a kind of quasi-descriptive value. It is as if of some one that had baffled all our attempts to investigate him we were to console ourselves by saying that he was a perfect Proteus. We call Shakespeare "many-sided;" not a magazine, nor a young lady at a party, but tells you that; and in adding this to our list of adjectives concerning him we find a certain satisfaction, and even an increase of light.

But it would be cowardice to stop here. The old sea-god Proteus himself, despite his subtlety and versatility, had a real form and character of his own, into which he could be compelled, if one only knew the way. Hear how they served this old gentleman in the Odyssey:

> " We at once,
> Loud shouting, flew on him, and in our arms
> Constrained him fast; nor the sea-prophet old
> Called not incontinent his shifts to mind.
> First he became a long-maned lion grim;
> A dragon then, a panther, a huge boar,
> A limpid stream, and an o'ershadowing tree.
> We, persevering, held him; till, at length,
> The subtle sage, his ineffectual arts
> Resigning weary, questioned me and spoke."

And so with *our* Proteus. The many-sidedness of the dramatist, let it be well believed and pondered, is but the versatility in form of a certain personal and substantial being, which constitutes the specific mind of the dramatist himself. Precisely as we have insisted that Shakespeare's face, as the best portraits represent it to us, is no mere general face or face to let, but a good, decided, and even rather singular face, so, we would insist, he had as specific a character, as

thoroughly a way of his own in thinking about things
and going through his morning and evening hours, as
any of ourselves. "Man is only many-sided," says
Goethe, "when he strives after the highest because he
must, and descends to the lesser because he *will ;*" that
is, as we interpret, when he is borne on in a certain
noble direction in all that he does by the very structure
of his mind, while, at his option, he may keep planting
this fixed path or not with a sportive and flowery
border. By the necessity of his nature, Shakespeare
was compelled in a certain earnest direction in all that
he did; and it is our part to search through the
thickets of imagery and gratuitous fiction amid which
he spent his life, that this path may be discovered.
As the lion, or the limpid stream, or the overshadowing
tree, into which Proteus turned himself, was not a real
lion, or a real stream, or a real tree, but only Proteus as
the one or as the other; so, involved in each of Shakespeare's characters,—in Hamlet, in Falstaff, or in
Romeo,—involved in some deep manner in each of
these diverse characters, is Shakespeare's own nature.
If Shakespeare had not been precisely and wholly
Shakespeare, and not any other man actual or conceivable, could Hamlet or Falstaff, or any other of his
creations, have been what they are ?

But how to evolve Shakespeare from his works, how
to compel this Proteus into his proper and native form,

is still the question. It is a problem of the highest difficulty. Something, indeed, of the poet's personal character and views we cannot help gathering as we read his dramas. Passages again and again occur of which, from their peculiar effect upon ourselves, from their conceivable reference to what we know of the poet's circumstances, or from their evident superfluousness and warmth, we do not hesitate to aver "There speaks the poet's own heart." But to show generally how much of the man has passed into the poet, and how it is that his personal bent and peculiarities are to be surely detected inhering in writings whose essential character it is to be arbitrary and universal, is a task from which a critic might well shrink, were he left merely to the ordinary resources of critical ingenuity without any positive and ascertained clue.

In this case, however, all the world ought to know, there *is* a positive and ascertained clue. Shakespeare has left to us not merely a collection of dramas, the exercises of his creative phantasy in a world of ideal matter, but also certain poems which are assuredly and expressly autobiographic. Criticism seems now pretty conclusively to have determined, what it ought to have determined long ago, that the *Sonnets* of Shakespeare are, and can possibly be, nothing else than a poetical record of his own feelings and experience—a connected series of entries, as it were, in his own diary

—during a certain period of his London life. This, we say, is conclusively determined and agreed upon; and whoever does not, to some extent, hold this view knows nothing about the subject. Ulrici, who is a genuine investigator, as well as a profound critic, is, of course, right on this point. So, also, in the main, is M. Guizot, although he mars the worth of the conclusion by adducing the foolish theory of *Euphuism*—that is, of the adoption of an affected style of expression in vogue in Shakespeare's age—in order to explain away that which is precisely the most important thing about the Sonnets, and the very thing *not* to be explained away: namely, the depth and strangeness of their pervading sentiment, and the curious hyperbolism of their style. In truth, it is the very closeness of the contact into which the right view of the Sonnets brings us with Shakespeare, the very value of the information respecting him to which it opens the way, that operates against it. Where we have so eager a desire to know, there we fear to believe, lest what we have once cherished on so great a subject we should be obliged again to give up, or lest, if our imaginations should dare to figure aught too exact and familiar regarding the traits and motions of so royal a spirit, the question should be put to us, what *we* can know of the halls of a palace, or the mantled tread of a king? Still the fact is as it is. These Sonnets of Shakespeare *are* autobiographic—distinctly.

intensely, painfully autobiographic, although in a style
and after a fashion of autobiography so peculiar that we
can cite only Dante in his *Vita Nuova*, and Tennyson
in his *In Memoriam*, as having furnished similar
examples of it.

We are not going to examine the Sonnets in detail
here, nor to tell the story which they involve as a
whole. We will indicate generally, however, the impression which, we think, a close investigation of them
will infallibly leave on any thoughtful reader, as to the
characteristic personal qualities of that mind the larger
and more factitious emanations from which still cover
and astonish the world.

The general and aggregate effect, then, of these Sonnets, as contributing to our knowledge of Shakespeare
as a man, is to antiquate, or at least to reduce very
much in value, the common idea of him implied in
such phrases as William the Calm, William the Cheerful, and the like. These phrases are true, when understood in a certain very obvious sense; but, if we were
to select that designation which would, as we think,
express Shakespeare in his most intimate and private
relations to man and nature, we should rather say
William the Meditative, William the Metaphysical, or
William the Melancholy. Let not the reader, full of
the just idea of Shakespeare's wonderful concreteness
as a poet, be staggered by the second of these phrases.

The phrase is a good phrase; etymologically, it is perhaps the best phrase we could here use; and whatever of inappropriateness there may seem to be in it proceeds from false associations, and will vanish, we hope, before we have done with it. Nor let it be supposed that, in using, as nearly synonymous, the word Melancholy, we mean anything so absurd as that the author of Falstaff was a Werther. What we mean is that there is evidence in the Sonnets, corroborated by other proof on all hands, that the mind of Shakespeare, when left to itself, was apt to sink into that state in which thoughts of what is sad and mysterious in the universe most easily come and go.

At no time, except during sleep, is the mind of any human being completely idle. All men have some natural and congenial mood into which they fall when they are left to talk with themselves. One man recounts the follies of the past day, renewing the relish of them by the recollection; another uses his leisure to hate his enemy and to scheme his discomfiture; a third rehearses in imagination, in order to be prepared, the part which he is to perform on the morrow. Now, at such moments, as we believe, it was the habit of Shakespeare's mind, obliged thereto by the necessity of its structure, to ponder ceaselessly those questions relating to man, his origin, and his destiny, in familiarity with which consists what is called the spiritual element in human nature. It was Shakespeare's use, as it seems to us, to revert, when he was alone, to that ultimate mood of the soul in which one hovers wistfully on the borders of the finite, vainly pressing against the barriers that separate it from the unknown; that mood in which even what is common and under foot seems part of a vast current mystery, and in which, like Arabian Job of old, one looks by turns at the heaven above, the earth beneath, and one's own moving body between, interrogating whence it all is, why it all is, and whither it all tends. And this, we say, is Melancholy. It is more. It is that mood of man, which, most of all moods, is thoroughly, grandly, specifically human. That which is the essence of all worth, all beauty, all humour, all genius, is open or secret reference to the supernatural; and this is sorrow. The attitude of a finite creature, contemplating the infinite, can only be that of an exile, grief and wonder blending in a wistful longing for an unknown home.

As we consider this frame of mind to have been characteristic of Shakespeare, so we find that as a poet he has not forgotten to represent it. We have always fancied Hamlet to be a closer translation of Shakespeare's own character than any other of his personations. The same meditativeness, the same morbid reference at all times to the supernatural, the same inordinate development of the speculative faculty, the

same intellectual melancholy, that are seen in the
Prince of Denmark, seem to have distinguished Shakespeare. Nor is it possible here to forget that minor
and lower form of the same fancy—the ornament of
As You Like It, the melancholy Jaques.

" *Jaques.* More, more, I prithee, more.
Amiens. It will make you melancholy, Monsieur
Jaques.
Jaques. I thank it. More, I prithee, more! I can
suck melancholy out of a song, as a weasel sucks eggs.
More. I prithee, more!
Amiens. My voice is ragged; I know I cannot
please you.
Jaques. I do not desire you to please me; I desire
you to sing.

* * * * *

Rosalind. They say you are a melancholy fellow.
Jaques. I am so; I do love it better than laughing.
Rosalind. Those that are in extremity of either are
abominable fellows, and betray themselves to every
modern censure worse than drunkards.
Jaques. Why, 'tis good to be sad and say nothing.
Rosalind. Why, then, 'tis good to be a post.
Jaques. I have neither the scholar's melancholy,
which is emulation; nor the musician's, which is fan-
tastical; nor the courtier's, which is proud; nor the
soldier's, which is ambitious; nor the lawyer's, which
is politic; nor the lady's, which is nice; nor the lover's,
which is all these: but it is a melancholy of mine own,
compounded of many simples, extracted from many

objects, and indeed the sundry contemplation of my
travels, in which my often rumination wraps me in a
most humorous sadness."

Jaques is not Shakespeare ; but in writing this
description of Jaques Shakespeare drew from his knowledge of himself. His also was a " melancholy of his
own," a " humorous sadness in which his often rumination wrapt him."   In that declared power of Jaques of
" sucking melancholy out of a song " the reference of
Shakespeare to himself seems almost direct.   Nay
more, as Rosalind, in rating poor Jaques, tells him on
one occasion that he is so abject a fellow that she
verily believes he is " out of love with his nativity,
and almost chides God *for making him of that countenance that he is*," so Shakespeare's melancholy, in one of
his Sonnets (No. 29), takes exactly the same form of
self-dissatisfaction.

> " When, in disgrace with fortune and men's eyes,
>   I all alone beweep my outcast state,
>   And trouble deaf heaven with my bootless cries,
>   And look upon myself and curse my fate,
>   Wishing me like to one more rich in hope,
>   *Featured like him*, like him with friends possessed,
>   Desiring this man's art and that man's scope,
>   With what I most enjoy contented least ;
>   Yet, in these thoughts myself almost despising,
>   Haply I think on thee," &c.

Think of that, reader! That mask of Shakespeare's face, which we have been discussing, Shakespeare himself did not like; and there were moments in which he was so abject as actually to wish that he had received from Nature another man's physical features!

If Shakespeare's melancholy was, like that of Jaques, a complex melancholy, a melancholy "compounded of many simples"—extracted perhaps at first from some root of bitter experience in his own life, and then fed, as his Sonnets clearly state, by a habitual sense of his own "outcast" condition in society, and by the sight of a hundred social wrongs around him, into a kind of abject dissatisfaction with himself and his fate—yet, in the end, and in its highest form, it was rather, as we have already hinted, the melancholy of Hamlet, a meditative, contemplative melancholy, embracing human life as a whole, the melancholy of a mind incessantly tending from the real ($\tau a\ \phi v \sigma i \kappa a$) to the metaphysical ($\tau a\ \mu \epsilon \tau a\ \tau a\ \phi v \sigma i \kappa a$), and only brought back by external occasion from the metaphysical to the real.

Do not let us quarrel about the words, if we can agree about the thing. Let any competent person whatever read the Sonnets, and then, with their impression on him, pass to the plays, and he will inevitably become aware of Shakespeare's personal fondness for certain themes or trains of thought, particularly that of the speed and destructiveness of time.

Death, vicissitude, the march and tramp of generations across life's stage, the rotting of human bodies in the earth—these and all the other forms of the same thought were familiar to Shakespeare to a degree beyond what is to be seen in the case of any other poet. It seems to have been a habit of his mind, when left to its own tendency, ever to indulge by preference in that oldest of human meditations, which is not yet trite: "Man that is born of a woman is of few days, and full of trouble; he cometh forth as a flower, and is cut down: he fleeth as a shadow, and continueth not." Let us cite a few examples from the Sonnets:—

" When I consider everything that grows
Holds in perfection but a little moment,
That this huge stage presenteth nought but shows
Whereon the stars in secret influence comment."—
Sonnet 15.

" If thou survive my well-contented clay,
When that churl Death my bones with dust shall
cover."— *Sonnet* 32.

" No longer mourn for me when I am dead
Than you shall hear the surly sullen bell
Give warning to the world that I am fled
From this vile world, with vilest worms to dwell."—
Sonnet 71

" The wrinkles, which thy glass will truly show,
Of mouthed graves will give thee memory;
Thou by thy dial's shady stealth may'st know
Time's thievish progress to eternity."— *Sonnet* 77.

> " Or I shall live your epitaph to make,
> Or you survive when I in earth am rotten."—
>
> *Sonnet* 81.

These are but one or two out of many such passages occurring in the Sonnets. Indeed, it may be said that, whenever Shakespeare pronounces the words time, age, death, and the like, it is with a deep and cutting personal emphasis, quite different from the usual manner of poets in their stereotyped allusions to mortality. Time, in particular, seems to have tenanted his imagination as a kind of grim and hideous personal existence, cruel out of mere malevolence of nature. Death, too, had become to him a kind of actual being or fury, morally unamiable, and deserving of reproach : " that churl Death."

If we turn to the plays of Shakespeare, we shall find that in them too the same morbid sensitiveness to all associations with mortality is continually breaking out. The vividness, for example, with which Juliet describes the interior of a charnel-house partakes of a spirit of revenge, as if Shakespeare were retaliating, through her, upon an object horrible to himself : —

> " Or hide me nightly in a charnel-house,
> O'ercovered quite with dead men's rattling bones,
> With reeky shanks and yellow chapless skulls."

More distinctly revengeful is Romeo's ejaculation at the tomb :—

> "Thou détestable maw, thou womb of Death,
>   Gorged with the dearest morsel of the earth,
>   Thus I enforce thy rotten jaws to open!"

And who does not remember the famous passage in *Measure for Measure?*—

> "*Claudio.*   Death is a fearful thing.
>   *Isabella.* And shamed life is hateful.
>   *Claudio.* Ay, but to die, and go we know not where;
>   To lie in cold obstruction and to rot;
>   This sensible warm motion to become
>   A kneaded clod; and the delighted spirit
>   To bathe in fiery floods, or to reside
>   In thrilling regions of thick-ribbèd ice;
>   To be imprisoned in the viewless winds,
>   And blown with restless violence round about
>   The pendent world; or to be worse than worst
>   Of those that lawless and incertain thoughts
>   Imagine howling: 'tis too horrible!
>   The weariest and most loathed worldly life
>   That age, ache, penury, and imprisonment,
>   Can lay on nature is a paradise
>   To what we fear of Death."

Again in the grave-digging scene in *Hamlet* we see the same fascinated familiarity of the imagination with all that pertains to churchyards, coffins, and the corruption within them.

> "*Hamlet.* Prithee, Horatio, tell me one thing.
>   *Horatio.* What's that, my lord?

Hamlet. Dost thou think Alexander looked o' this fashion i' the earth?

Horatio. E'en so.

Hamlet. And smelt so? pah!   (*Puts down the skull.*)

Horatio. E'en so, my lord!

Hamlet. To what base uses we may return, Horatio! Why may not imagination trace the noble dust of Alexander till he find it stopping a bung-hole?

Horatio. 'Twere to reason too curiously to consider so.

Hamlet. No, faith, not a jot; but to follow him thither with modesty enough, and likelihood to lead it: as thus:—Alexander died; Alexander was buried; Alexander returneth to dust; the dust is earth; of earth we make loam; and why of that loam whereto he was converted might they not stop a beer-barrel?

> Imperial Cæsar, dead and turned to clay,
> Might stop a hole to keep the wind away:
> O that that earth which kept the world in awe
> Should patch a wall to expel the winter's flaw!"

Observe how Shakespeare here defends, through Hamlet, his own tendency "too curiously" to consider death. To sum up all, however, let us turn to that unparalleled burst of language in the *Tempest*, in which the poet has defeated Time itself by chivalrously proclaiming to all time what Time can do:—

> " And, like the baseless fabric of this vision,
>   The cloud-capped towers, the gorgeous palaces,
>   The solemn temples, the great globe itself,
>   Yea, all which it inherit, shall dissolve,

> And, like this unsubstantial pageant faded,
> Leave not a rack behind.   We are such stuff
> As dreams are made of; and our little life
> Is rounded with a sleep."

This, we contend, is no mere poetic phrenzy, inserted because it was dramatically suitable that Prospero should so express himself at that place; it is the explosion into words of a feeling during which Prospero was forgotten, and Shakespeare swooned into himself.   And what is the continuation of the passage but a kind of postscript, describing, under the guise of Prospero, Shakespeare's own agitation with what he had just written ?—

> " Sir, I am vexed;
> Bear with my weakness; my old brain is troubled:
> Be not disturbed with my infirmity:
> If you be pleased, retire into my cell,
> And there repose : *a turn or two I'll walk,*
> *To still my beating mind.*"

To our imagination the surmise is that Shakespeare here laid down his pen, and began to pace his chamber, too agitated to write more that night.

In this extreme familiarity with the conception of mortality in general, and perhaps also in this extreme sensitiveness to the thought of death as a matter of personal import, all great poets, and possibly all great men whatever, have to some extent resembled Shakespeare.   For these are the feelings of our common nature on which religion and all solemn activity have founded and maintained themselves. Space and Time are the largest and the outermost of all human conceptions ; to stand, therefore, incessantly upon these extreme conceptions, as upon the perimeter of a figure, and to view all inwards from them, is the highest exercise of thought to which a human being can attain. Accordingly, in all great poets there may be discerned this familiarity of the imagination with the world figured as a poor little ball pendent in space and moving forward out of a dark past to a future of light or gloom. But in this respect Shakespeare exceeds them all ; and in this respect, therefore, no poet is more religious, more spiritual, more profoundly metaphysical, than he. Into an inordinate amount of that outward pressure of the soul against the perimeter of sensible things, infuse the peculiar *moral* germ of Christianity, and you have the religion of Shakespeare. Thus :—

> " And our little life
> Is rounded with a sleep."—*Tempest.*

Here the poetic imagination sweeps boldly round the universe, severing it as by a soft cloud-line from the infinite Unknown.

> " Poor soul ! the centre of my sinful earth,
> Fooled by those rebel powers that lead thee 'stray ! "
> *Sonnet* 146.

Here the soul, retracting its thoughts from the far and physical, dwells disgustedly on itself.

> " The dread of something after death,
> The undiscovered country from whose bourn
> No traveller returns."—*Hamlet.*

Here the soul, pierced with the new and awful thought of sin, wings out again towards the Infinite, and finds all dark.

> " How would you be,
> If He, which is the top of judgment, should
> But judge you as you are ?"—*Measure for Measure.*

Here the silver lamp of hope is hung up within the gloomy sphere, to burn softly and faintly for ever !

And so it is throughout Shakespeare's writings. Whatever is special or doctrinal is avoided ; all that intellectual tackling, so to speak, is struck away that would afford the soul any relief whatever from the whole sensation of the supernatural. Although we cannot, therefore, in honest keeping with popular language, call Shakespeare, as Ulrici does, the most Christian of poets, we believe him to have been the man in modern times who, breathing an atmosphere full of Christian conceptions, and walking amid a civilization studded with Christian institutions, had his whole being tied by the closest personal links to those highest generalities of the universe which the greatest minds in all ages have ever

pondered and meditated, and round which Christianity
has thrown its clasp of gold.

Shakespeare, then, we hold to have been essentially
a meditative, speculative, and even, in his solitary hours,
an abject and melancholy man, rather than a man of
active, firm, and worldly disposition. Instead of being
a calm, stony observer of life and nature, as he has been
sometimes represented, we believe him to have been a
man of the gentlest and most troublesome affections, of
sensibility abnormally keen and deep, full of metaphysical longings, liable above most men to self-distrust, de-
spondency, and mental agitation from causes internal
and external, and a prey to many secret and severe
experiences which he did not discuss at the Mermaid
tavern. This, we say, is no guess; it is a thing certified
under his own hand and seal. But, this being allowed,
we are willing to agree with all that is said of him, by
way of indicating the immense variety of faculties, dispositions, and acquirements, of which his character was
built up. Vast intellectual inquisitiveness, the readiest
and most universal humour, the truest sagacity and
knowledge of the world, the richest and deepest capacity
of enjoying all that life presented : all this, as applied
to Shakespeare, is a mere string of undeniable common-
places. The man, as we fancy him, who of all others
trod the oftenest the extreme metaphysic walk which
bounds our universe in, he was also the man of all others

who was related most keenly by every fibre of his being to all the world of the real and the concrete. Better than any man he knew life to be a dream; with as vivid a relish as any man he did his part as one of the dreamers. If at one moment life stood before his mental gaze, an illuminated little speck or disc, softly rounded with mysterious sleep, the next moment this mere span shot out into an illimitable plain, whereon he himself stood—a plain covered with forests, parted by seas, studded with cities and huge concourses of men, mapped out into civilizations, over-canopied by stars. Nay, it was precisely because he came and went with such instant transition between the two extremes that he behaved so genially and sympathetically in the latter. It was precisely because he had done the metaphysic feat so completely once for all, and did not bungle on metaphysicizing bit by bit amid the real, that he stood forth in the character of the most concrete of poets. Life is an illusion, a show, a phantasm : well then, that is settled, and *I* belong to that section of the illusion called London, the seventeenth century, and woody Warwickshire ! So he may have said; and he acted accordingly. He walked amid the woods of Warwickshire, and listened to the birds singing in their leafy retreats; he entered the Mermaid tavern with Ben Jonson after the theatre was over, and found himself quite properly related, as one item in the illusion, to that other item in it, a good supper and a cup of canary. He accepted the world as it was, rejoiced in its joys, was pained by its sorrows, reverenced its dignities, respected its laws, and laughed at its whimsies. It was this very strength and intimacy and universality of his relations to the concrete world of nature and life that caused in him that spirit of acquiescence in things as they were, that evident conservatism of temper, that indifference, or perhaps more, to the specific contemporary forms of social and intellectual movement, with which he has sometimes been charged as a fault. The habit of attaching weight to what are called abstractions, of metaphysicizing bit by bit amid the real, is almost an essential feature in the constitution of men who are remarkable for their faith in social progress. It was precisely, therefore, because Shakespeare was such a votary of the concrete, because he walked so firmly on the green and soli sward of that island of life which he knew to be surrounded by a metaphysic sea, that this or that metaphysical proposal with respect to the island itself occupied him but little.

How, then, *did* Shakespeare relate himself to this concrete world of nature and life in which his lot had been cast? What precise function with regard to it, if not that of an active partisan of progress, did he accept as devolving naturally on *him?* The answer is easy. Marked out by circumstances, and by his own bent and inclination, from the vast majority of men, who, with greater or less faculty, sometimes perhaps with the greatest, pass their lives in silence, appearing in the world at their time, enjoying it for a season, and returning to the earth again,—marked out from among these, and appointed to be one of those whom the whole earth should remember and think of; yet precluded, as we have seen, by his constitution and fortune, from certain modes of attaining to this honour—the special function which, in this high place, he saw himself called upon to discharge, and by the discharge of which he has ensured his place in perpetuity, was simply that of *expressing* what he felt and saw. In other words, Shakespeare was specifically and transcendently a literary man. To say that he was the greatest *man* that ever lived is to provoke a useless controversy, and comparisons that lead to nothing, between Shakespeare and Cæsar, Shakespeare and Charlemagne, Shakespeare and Cromwell; to say that he was the greatest *intellect* that ever lived, is to bring the shades of Aristotle and Plato, and Bacon and Newton, and all the other systematic thinkers, grumbling about us, with demands for a definition of intellect, which we are by no means in a position to give; nay, finally, to say that he is the greatest *poet* that the world has produced (a thing which we would certainly say, were we provoked to it,) would be unnecessarily to hurt the feelings of Homer and

Sophocles, Dante and Milton. What we will say, then, and challenge the world to gainsay, is that he was the greatest *expresser* that ever lived. This is glory enough, and it leaves the other questions open. Other men may have led, on the whole, greater and more impressive lives than he; other men, acting on their fellows through the same medium of speech that he used, may have expended a greater power of thought, and achieved a greater intellectual effect, in one consistent direction; other men, too (though this is very questionable), may have contrived to issue the matter which they did address to the world in more compact and perfect artistic shapes. But no man that ever lived said such splendid things on all subjects universally; no man that ever lived had the faculty of pouring out on all occasions such a flood of the richest and deepest language. He may have had rivals in the art of imagining situations; he had no rival in the power of sending a gush of the appropriate intellectual effusion over the image and body of a situation once conceived. From a jewelled ring on an alderman's finger to the most mountainous thought or deed of man or demon, nothing suggested itself that his speech could not envelope and enfold with ease. That excessive fluency which astonished Ben Jonson when he listened to Shakespeare in person astonishes the world yet. Abundance, ease, redundance, a plenitude of word, sound, and imagery.

D   H

which, were the intellect at work only a little less magnificent, would sometimes end in sheer braggartism and bombast, are the characteristics of Shakespeare's style. Nothing is suppressed, nothing omitted, nothing cancelled. On and on the poet flows; words, thoughts, and fancies crowding on him as fast as he can write, all related to the matter on hand, and all poured forth together, to rise and fall on the waves of an established cadence. Such lightness and ease in the manner, and such prodigious wealth and depth in the matter, are combined in no other writer. How the matter was first accumulated, what proportion of it was the acquired capital of former efforts, and what proportion of it welled up in the poet's mind during and in virtue of the very act of speech, it is impossible to say; but this at least may be affirmed without fear of contradiction, that there never was a mind in the world from which, when it was pricked by any occasion whatever, there poured forth on the instant such a stream of precious substance intellectually related to it. By his powers of expression, in fact, Shakespeare has beggared all his posterity, and left mere practitioners of expression nothing possible to do. There is perhaps not a thought, or feeling, or situation, really common and generic to human life, on which he has not exercised his prerogative; and, wherever he has once been, woe to the man that comes after him! He has overgrown the whole system and face of things like a universal ivy, which has left no wall uncovered, no pinnacle un-climbed, no chink unpenetrated. Since he lived the concrete world has worn a richer surface. He found it great and beautiful, with stripes here and there of the rough old coat seen through the leafy labours of his predecessors ; he left it clothed throughout with the wealth and autumnal luxuriance of his own unparalleled language.

This brings us, by a very natural connexion, to what we have to say of Goethe. For, if, with the foregoing impressions on our mind respecting the character and the function of the great English poet, we turn to the mask of his German successor and admirer, which has been so long waiting our notice, the first question must infallibly be What recognition is it possible that, in such circumstances, we can have left for *him ?* In other words, the first consideration that must be taken into account in any attempt to appreciate Goethe is that he came into a world in which Shakespeare had been before him. For a man who, in the main, was to pursue a course so similar to that which Shakespeare had pursued this was a matter of incalculable importance. Either, on the one hand, the value of all that the second man could do, if he adhered to a course very similar, must suffer from the fact that he was following in the footsteps of a predecessor of such unapproachable excellence; or, on the other hand, the consciousness of this, if it came in time, would be likely to *prevent* too close a resemblance between the lives of the two men, by giving a special direction and character to the efforts of the second. Hear Goethe himself on this very point:—

"We discoursed upon English literature, on the greatness of Shakespeare, and on the unfavourable position held by all English dramatic authors who had appeared after that poetical giant. 'A dramatic talent of any importance,' said Goethe, 'could not forbear to notice Shakespeare's works; nay, could not forbear to study them. Having studied them, he must be aware that Shakespeare has already exhausted the whole of human nature in all its tendencies, in all its heights and depths, and that, in fact, there remains for him, the aftercomer, nothing more to do. And how could one get courage to put pen to paper, if one were conscious, in an earnest appreciating spirit, that such unfathomable and unattainable excellencies were already in existence? It fared better with me fifty years ago in my own dear Germany. I could soon come to an end with all that then existed; it could not long awe me, or occupy my attention. I soon left behind me German literature, and the study of it, and turned my thoughts to life and to production. So on and on I went, in my own natural development, and on and on I fashioned the productions of epoch after epoch. And, at every step of life and development, my standard of excellence was not much higher than what at such a step I was able to attain. But, had I been born an Englishman, and had all those numerous masterpieces been brought before me in all their power at my first dawn of youthful consciousness, they would have overpowered me, and I should not have known what to do. I could not have gone on with such fresh light-heartedness, but should have had to bethink myself, and look about for a long time to find some new outlet.' "—*Eckermann's Conversations of Goethe,* i. pp. 114, 115.

All this is very clear and happily expressed. Most Englishmen that have written since Shakespeare *have* been overawed by the sense of his vast superiority ; and Goethe, if he had been an Englishman, would have partaken of the same feeling, and would have been obliged, as he says, to look about for some path in which competition with such a predecessor would have been avoided. Being, however, a German, and coming at a time when German literature had nothing so great to boast of but that an ardent young man could hope to produce something as good or better, the way was certainly open to him to the attainment, in his own nation, of a position analogous to that which Shakespeare had occupied in his. Goethe might, if he had chosen, have aspired to be the Shakespeare of Germany. Had his tastes and faculties pointed in that direction, there was no reason, special to his own nation, that would have made it very incumbent on him to thwart the tendency of his genius and seek about for a new outlet in order to escape injurious comparisons. But, even in such circumstances, to have pursued a course *very* similar to that of Shakespeare, and to have been animated by a mere ambition to tread in the footsteps of that master, would have been death to all chance of a reputation among the highest. Great writers do not exclusively belong to the country of their birth ; the greatest of all are grouped together on a kind of central platform, in the view of all peoples and tongues; and, as in this select assemblage no duplicates are permitted, the man who does never so well a second time that which the world has already canonized a man for doing once has little chance of being admitted to co-equal honours. More especially in the present case would too close a resemblance to the original, whether in manner or in purpose, have been regarded in the end as a reason for inferiority in place. As the poet of one branch of the great Germanic family of mankind, Shakespeare belonged indirectly to the Germans, even before they recognised him ; in him all the genuine qualities of Teutonic human nature, as well as the more special characteristics of English genius, were embodied once for all in the particular form which had chanced to be his ; and, had Goethe been, in any marked sense, only a repetition of the same form, he might have held his place for some time as the wonder of Germany, but, as soon as the course of events had opened up the communication which was sure to take place at some time between the German and the English literatures, and so made his countrymen acquainted with Shakespeare, he would have lost his extreme brilliance, and become but a star of the second magnitude. In order, then, that Goethe might hold permanently a first rank even among his own countrymen, it was necessary that he should be a man of a genius quite distinct from that of Shakespeare, a man who, having or not having certain Shakespearian qualities, should at all events signalize such qualities as he had by a marked character and function of his own. And, if this was necessary to secure to Goethe a first rank in the literature of Germany, much more was it necessary to ensure him a place as one of the intellectual potentates of the whole modern world. If Goethe was to be admitted into this select company at all, it could not be as a mere younger brother of Shakespeare, but as a man whom Shakespeare himself, when he took him by the hand, would look at with curiosity, as something new in species, produced in the earth since his own time.

Was this, then, the case? Was Goethe, with all his external resemblance in some respects to Shakespeare, a man of such truly individual character, and of so new and marked a function, as to deserve a place among the highest, not in German literature alone, but in the literature of the world as a whole ? We do not think that anyone competent to give an opinion will reply in the negative.

A glance at the external circumstances of Goethe's life alone (and what a contrast there is between the abundance of biographic material respecting Goethe and the scantiness of our information respecting Shakespeare!) will beget the impression that the man who led such a life must have had opportunities for developing a very unusual character. The main facts in the life of Goethe are :—that he was born at Frankfort-on-the-Main in 1749, the only surviving son of parents who ranked among the wealthiest in the town; that, having been educated with extreme care, and having received whatever experience could be acquired by an impetuous student-life, free from all ordinary forms of hardship, first at one German town and then at another, he devoted himself, in accordance with his tastes, to a career of literary activity; that, after unwinding himself from several love-affairs, and travelling for the sake of farther culture in Italy and other parts of Europe, he settled in early manhood at Weimar, as the intimate friend and counsellor of the reigning duke of that state ; that there, during a long and honoured life, in the course of which he married an inferior housekeeper kind of person, of whom we do not hear much, he prosecuted his literary enterprise with unwearied industry, not only producing poems, novels, dramas, essays, treatises, and criticisms in great profusion from his own pen, but also acting, along with Schiller and others, as a director and guide of the whole contemporary intellectual movement of his native land; and that finally, having outlived all his famous associates, become a widower and a grandfather, and attained the position not only of the acknowledged king and patriarch of German literature, but also, as some thought, of the wisest and most serene intellect of Europe, he died so late as 1832, in the eighty-third year of his age. All this, it will be observed, is very different from the life of the prosperous Warwickshire player, whose existence had illustrated the early part of the seventeenth century in England; and it necessarily denoted, at the same time, a very different cast of mind and temper.

Accordingly, such descriptions as we have of Goethe from those who knew him best convey the idea of a character notably different from that of the English poet. Of Shakespeare personally we have but one uniform account—that he was a man of gentle presence and disposition, very good company, and of such boundless fluency and intellectual inventiveness in talk that his hearers could not always stand it, but had sometimes to whistle him down in his flights. In Goethe's case we have two distinct pictures.

In youth, as all accounts agree in stating, he was one of the most impetuous, bounding, ennui-dispelling natures that ever broke in upon a society of ordinary mortals assembled to kill time. " He came upon you," said one who knew him well at this period, "like a wolf in the night." The simile is a splendid one, and it agrees wonderfully with the more subdued representations of his early years given by Goethe himself in his Autobiography. Handsome as an Apollo and welcome everywhere, he bore all before him wherever he went, not only by his talent, but also by an exuberance of animal spirits which swept dulness itself along, took away the breath of those who relied on sarcasm and their cool heads, inspired life and animation into the whole circle, and most especially delighted the ladies. This vivacity became even, at times, a reckless humour, prolific in all kinds of mad freaks and extravagances. Whether this impetuosity kept always within the bounds of mere innocent frolic is a question which we need not here raise. Traditions are certainly afloat of terrible domestic incidents connected with Goethe's youth, both in Frankfort and in Weimar; but to what extent those traditions are founded on fact is a matter which we have never yet seen any attempt to decide upon evidence. More authentic for us, and equally significant, if we could be sure of our ability to appreciate them rightly, are the stories which Goethe himself tells of his various youthful attachments, and the various ways in which they were concluded. In Goethe's own narratives of these affairs there is a confession of error, arising out of his disposition passionately to abandon himself to the feelings of the moment without looking forward to the consequences; but whether this confession is to be converted by his critics into the harsher accusation of heartlessness and want of principle is a thing not to be decided by any general rule as to the matter of inconstancy, but by accurate knowledge in each case of the whole circumstances of that case. One thing these love-romances of Goethe's early life make clear—that, for a being of such extreme sensibility as he was, he had a very strong element of self-control. When he gave up Rica or Lilli, it was with tears, and no end of sleepless nights; and yet he gave them up. Shakespeare, we believe (and there is an instance exactly in point in the story of his Sonnets), had no such power of breaking clear from connexions which his judgment disapproved. Remorse and return, self-reproaches for his weakness at one moment followed the next by weakness more abject than before—such, by his own confession, was the conduct, in one such case, of our more passive and gentle-hearted poet. Where Shakespeare was "past cure," and "frantic-mad with evermore unrest," Goethe but fell into "hypochondria," which reason and resolution enabled him to overcome. Goethe at twenty-five gave up a young, beautiful and innocent girl, from the conviction that it was better to do so. Shakespeare at thirty-five was the abject slave of a dark-complexioned woman, who was faithless to him, and whom he cursed in his heart. The sensibilities in the German poet moved from the first, as we have already said, over a firmer basis of permanent character.

It is chiefly, however, the Goethe of later life that the world remembers and thinks of. The bounding impetuosity is then gone; or rather it is kept back and restrained, so as to form a calm and steady fund of internal energy, capable sometimes of a flash and outbreak, but generally revealing itself only in labour and its fruits. What was formerly the beauty of an Apollo, graceful, light, and full of motion, is now the beauty of a Jupiter, composed, stately, serene. "What a sublime form!" says Eckermann, describing his first interview with him. "I forgot to speak for looking at him: I could not look enough. His face is so powerful and brown, full of wrinkles, and each wrinkle full of expression. And everywhere there is such nobleness and firmness, such repose and greatness. He spoke in a slow, composed manner, such as you would expect from an aged monarch." Such is Goethe, as he lasts now in the imagination of the world. Living among statues, books, and pictures; daily doing something for his own culture and for that of the world ; daily receiving guests and visitors, whom he entertained and instructed with his wise and deep, yet charming and simple, converse ; daily corresponding with friends and strangers, and giving advice or doing a good turn to some young talent or other—never was such a mind consecrated so perseveringly and exclusively to the service of *Kunst* and *Literatur.* One almost begins to wonder if it was altogether right that an old man should go on, morning after morning, and evening after evening, in such a fashion, talking about art and science and literature as if they were the only interests in the world, taking his guests into corners to have quiet discussions with them on these subjects, and always finding something new and nice to be said about them. Possibly, indeed, this is the fault of those who have reported him, and who only took notes when the discourse turned on what they considered the proper Goethean themes. But that Goethe far outdid Shakespeare in this conscious dedication of himself to a life of the intellect is as certain as the testimony of likelihood can make it. Shakespeare did enjoy his art; it was what, in his pensive hours, as he himself hints, he enjoyed most ; and whatever of intellectual ecstasy literary production can bring must surely have been his in those hours when he composed *Hamlet* and the *Tempest.* But Shakespeare's was precisely one of those minds whose strength is a revelation to themselves during the moment of its exercise, rather than a chronic ascertained possession; and from this circumstance, as well as from the attested fact of his carelessness as to the fate of his compositions, we can very well conceive that literature and mental culture formed but a small part of the general system of things in Shakespeare's daily thoughts, and that he would have been absolutely ashamed of himself if, when anything else, from the state of the weather to the quality of the wine, was within the circle of possible allusion, he had said a word about his own plays. If he had not Sir Walter Scott's positive conviction that every man ought to be either a laird or a lawyer, casting in authorship as a mere addition if it were to be practised at all, he at least led so full and keen a life, and was drawn forth on so many sides by nature, society, and the unseen, that Literature, out of the actual moments in which he was engaged in it, must have seemed to him a mere bagatelle, a mere fantastic echo of not a tithe of life. In his home in London, or his retirement at Stratford, he wrote on and on, because he could not help doing so, and because it was his business and his solace; but no play seemed to him worth a day of the contemporary actions of men, no description worth a single glance at the Thames or at the deer feeding in the forest, no sonnet worth the tear it was made to embalm. Literature was

by no means to him, as it was to Goethe, the main
interest of life; nor was he a man so far master of
himself as ever to be able to behave as if it were so,
and to accept, as Goethe did, all that occurred as so
much culture. Yet Shakespeare would have understood Goethe, and would have regarded him, almost
with envy, as one of those men who, as being "lords
and owners of their faces," and not mere "stewards,"
know how to husband Nature's gifts best.

> "They that have power to hurt and will do none,
> That do not do the thing they most do show,
> Who, moving others, are themselves as stone,
> Unmovèd, cold, and to temptation slow,
> They rightly do inherit Heaven's graces,
> And husband nature's riches from expense;
> They are the lords and owners of their faces,
> Others but stewards of their excellence."—*Sonnet* 94.

If Goethe attained this character, however, it was not
because, as it is the fashion to say, he was by nature
cold, heartless, and impassive, but because, uniting will
and wisdom to his wealth of sensibilities, he had dis-
ciplined himself into what he was. A heartless man
does not diffuse geniality and kindliness around him, as
Goethe did; and a statue is not seized, as Goethe
once was, with hæmorrhage in the night, the result
of suppressed grief.

That which made Goethe what he was—namely, his philosophy of life—is to be gathered, in the form of hints, from his various writings and conversations. We present a few important passages here, in what seems their philosophic connexion, as well as the order most suitable for bringing out Goethe's mode of thought in contrast with that of Shakespeare.

Goethe's Thoughts of Death.—" We had gone round the thicket, and had turned by Tiefurt into the Weimar-road, where we had a view of the setting sun. Goethe was for a while lost in thought; he then said to me, in the words of one of the ancients,

> ' Untergehend sogar ist's immer dieselbige Sonne.'
> (Still it continues the self-same sun, even while
>   it is sinking.)

' At the age of seventy-five,' continued he, with much cheerfulness, ' one must, of course, think sometimes of death. But this thought never gives me the least uneasiness, for 1 am fully convinced that our spirit is a being of a nature quite indestructible, and that its activity continues from eternity to eternity. It is like the sun, which seems to set only to our earthly eyes, but which, in reality, never sets, but shines on unceasingly.' "—*Eckermann's Conversations of Goethe*, vol. i. p. 161.

Goethe's Maxim with respect to Metaphysics.—" Man is born not to solve the problem of the universe, but to find out where the problem begins, and then to restrain himself within the limits of the comprehensible."—*Ibid.* vol. i. p. 272.

Goethe's Theory of the intention of the Supernatural with regard to the Visible.—" After all, what does it all come to ?   God did not retire to rest after the well-known six days of creation, but, on the contrary, is constantly active as on the first. It would have been for Him a poor occupation to compose this heavy world out of simple elements, and to keep it rolling in the sunbeams from year to year, if He had not the plan of founding a nursery for a world of spirits upon this material basis. So He is now constantly active in higher natures to attract the lower ones."—*Ibid.* vol. ii. p. 426.

Goethe's Doctrine of Immortality.—" Kant has un-questionably done the best service, by drawing the limits beyond which human intellect is not able to penetrate, and leaving at rest the insoluble problems. What a deal have people philosophised about immortality ! and how far have they got ? I doubt not of our immortality, for nature cannot dispense with the *entelecheia.* But we are not all, in like manner, immortal; and he who would manifest himself in future as a great *entelecheia* must be one now. . . . . To me the eternal existence of my soul is proved from my idea of activity. If I work on incessantly till my death, nature is bound to give me another form of existence when the present one can no longer sustain my spirit."—*Ibid.* vol. ii. pp. 193, 194, and p. 122.

Goethe's Image of Life.—" Child, child, no more ! The coursers of Time, lashed, as it were, by invisible spirits, hurry on the light car of our destiny ; and all that we can do is, in cool self-possession, to hold the reins with a firm hand, and to guide the wheels, now to the left, now

to the right, avoiding a stone here, or a precipice there.
Whither it is hurrying, who can tell ? and who, indeed,
can remember the point from which it started?"—*Egmont.*

Man's proper business.—" It has at all times been said
and repeated that man should strive to know himself.
This is a singular requisition ; with which no one com-
plies, or indeed ever will comply.   Man is by all his
senses and efforts directed to externals—to the world
around him ; and he has to know this so far, and to
make it so far serviceable, as he requires for his own
ends.   It is only when he feels joy or sorrow that he
knows anything about himself, and only by joy or
sorrow is he instructed what to seek and what to shun."
—*Eckermann's Conversations of Goethe*, vol. ii. p. 180.

*The Abstract and the Concrete, and the Subjective and
the Objective.*—" The Germans are certainly strange
people.   By their deep thoughts and ideas, which
they seek in everything, and fix upon everything, they
make life much more burdensome than is necessary.
Only have the courage to give yourself up to your
impressions ; allow yourself to be delighted, moved,
elevated—nay, instructed and inspired by something
great ; but do not imagine all is vanity if it is not
abstract thought and idea.   .   .   .   .   It was not in my
line, as a poet, to strive to embody anything abstract.
I received in my mind impressions, and those of a
sensual, animated, charming, varied, hundred-fold kind,
just as a lively imagination presented them ; and I had,
as a poet, nothing more to do than artistically to round
off and elaborate such views and impressions, and by
means of a lively representation so to bring them forward that others might receive the same impressions in

hearing or reading my representation of them. . . .
A poet deserves not the name while he only speaks out
his few subjective feelings; but as soon as he can appropriate to himself and express the world he is a poet.
Then he is inexhaustible, and can be always new; while
a subjective nature has soon talked out his little internal
material, and is at last ruined by mannerism. People
always talk of the study of the ancients; but what does
that mean, except that it says 'Turn your attention to
the real world, and try to express it, for that is what the
ancients did when they were alive?' Goethe arose and
walked to and fro, while I remained seated at the table,
as he likes to see me. He stood a moment at the stove,
and then, like one who has reflected, came to me, and,
with his finger on his lips, said to me, 'I will now tell
you something which you will often find confirmed in
your own experience. All eras in a state of decline and
dissolution are subjective; on the other hand, all progressive eras have an objective tendency. Our present
time is retrograde, for it is subjective; we see this not
merely in poetry, but also in painting and much besides.
Every healthy effort, on the contrary, is directed from
the inward to the outward world, as you will see in all
great eras, which have been really in a state of pro-
gression, and all of an objective nature.' "—*Ibid.* vol. i.
pp. 415, 416, and pp. 283, 284.

Rule of Individual Activity.—" The most reasonable
way is for every man to follow his own vocation to which
he has been born and which he has learnt, and to avoid
hindering others from following theirs. Let the shoe-
maker abide by his last, the peasant by his plough, and
let the king know how to govern; for this is also a

business which must be learned, and with which no one should meddle who does not understand it."—*Ibid.* vol. i. p. 134.

Right and Wrong: The habit of Controversy.—"The end of all opposition is negation, and negation is nothing. If I call *bad* bad, what do I gain? But, if I call *good* bad, I do a great deal of mischief. He who will work aright must never rail, must not trouble himself at all about what is ill done, but only do well himself. For the great point is not to pull down, but to build up; and in this humanity finds pure joy."—*Ibid.* vol. i. p. 208.

Goethe's own Relation to the Disputes of his Time.—"'You have been reproached,' remarked I, rather inconsiderately, 'for not taking up arms at that great period [the war with Napoleon], or at least co-operating as a poet. 'Let us leave that point alone, my good friend,' returned Goethe. 'It is an absurd world, which knows not what it wants, and which one must allow to have its own way. How could I take up arms without hatred, and how could I hate without youth? If such an emergency had befallen me when twenty years old, I should certainly not have been the last; but it found me as one who had already passed the first sixties. Besides, we cannot all serve our country in the same way; but each does his best, according as God has endowed him. I have toiled hard enough during half a century. I can say that, in those things which nature has appointed for my daily work, I have permitted myself no relaxation night or day, but have always striven, investigated, and done as much, and that as well, as I could. If every-one can say the same of himself, it will prove well with all.   I will not say what I think. There is

more ill-will towards me hidden beneath that remark
than you are aware of. I feel therein a new form of the
old hatred with which people have persecuted me, and en-
deavoured quietly to wound me, for years. I know very
well that I am an eyesore to many; that they would all
willingly get rid of me; and that, since they cannot
touch my talent, they aim at my character. Now, it is
said that I am proud ; now, egotistical ; now, immersed
in sensuality ; now, without Christianity ; and now,
without love for my native country and my own dear
Germans. You have now known me sufficiently for
years, and you feel what all that talk is worth. . . . .
The poet, as a man and citizen, will love his native land ;
but the native land of his *poetic* powers and *poetic* action
is the good, noble, and beautiful : which is confined to
no particular province or country, and which he seizes
upon and forms wherever he finds them. Therein he is
like the eagle, who hovers with free gaze over whole
countries, and to whom it is of no consequence whether
the hare on which he pounces is running in Prussia or
in Saxony.' "—*Ibid.* vol. ii. pp. 257, 258, and p. 427.

Whoever has read these sentences attentively, and
penetrated their meaning in connexion, will see that they
reveal a mode of thought somewhat resembling that
which we have attributed to Shakespeare, and yet essentially different from it. Both poets are distinguished
by this, that they abstained systematically during their
lives from the abstract, the dialectical, and the controversial, and devoted themselves, with true feeling and
enjoyment, to the concrete, the real, and the unques-

tioned; and so far there is an obvious resemblance between them. But the manner in which this characteristic was attained was by no means the same in both cases. In Shakespeare, as we have seen, there was a metaphysical longing, a tendency towards the supersensible and invisible, absolutely morbid, if we take ordinary constitutions as the standard of health in this respect; and, if, with all this, he revelled with delight and moved with ease and firmness in the sensuous and actual, it was because the very same soul which pressed with such energy and wailing against the bounds of this life of man was also related with inordinate keenness and intimacy to all that this life spheres in. In Goethe, on the other hand, the tendency to the real existed under easier constitutional conditions, and in a state of such natural preponderance over any concomitant craving for the metaphysical, that it necessarily took, German though he was, a higher place in his estimate of what is desirable in a human character. That world of the real in which Shakespeare delighted, and which he knew so well, seemed to him, all this knowledge and delight notwithstanding, far more evanescent, far more a mere filmy show, far less considerable a shred of all that is, than it did to Goethe. To Shakespeare, as we have already said, life was but as a little island on the bosom of a boundless sea: men must needs know what the island contains, and act as those who have to till and rule it; still, with that expanse of waters all round in view, and that roar of waters ever in the ear, what can men call themselves or pretend their realm to be? "Poor fools of Nature" is the poet's own phrase—the realm so small that it is pitiful to belong to it! Not so with Goethe. To him also, of course, the thought was familiar of a vast region of the supersensible outlying nature and life; but a higher value on the whole was reserved for nature and life, even on the universal scale, by his peculiar habit of conceiving them, not as distinct from the supersensible and contemporaneously begirt by it, but rather, if we may so speak, as a considerable portion, or even duration, of the *quondam*-supersensible in the new form of the sensible. In other words, Goethe was full of the notion of progress or evolution; the world was to him not a mere spectacle and dominion for the supernatural, but an actual manifestation of the substance of the supernatural itself, on its way through time to new issues. Hence his peculiar notion of immortality; hence his view as to the mere relativeness of the terms right and wrong, good and bad, and the like; and hence also his resolute inculcation of the doctrine, so unpalatable to his countrymen, that men ought to direct their thoughts and efforts to the actual and the outward. Life being the current phase of the universal mystery, the true duty of men could be but to contribute in their various ways to the furtherance of life.

And what then, finally, was Goethe's *own* mode of activity in a life thus defined in his general philosophy ? Like Shakespeare, he was a literary man; his function was literature.   Yes, but in what respect, otherwise than Shakespeare had done before him, did he fulfil this literary function in reference to the world he lived in and enjoyed ?   In the first place, as all know, he differed from Shakespeare in this, that he did not address the world exclusively in the character of a poet.   Besides his poetry, properly so called, Goethe has left behind him numerous prose-writings, ranking under very different heads, abounding with such deep and wise maxims and perceptions, in reference to all things under the sun, as would have entitled him, even had he been no poet, to rank as a sage.   So great, indeed, is Goethe as a thinker and a critic that it may very well be disputed whether his prose-writings, as a whole, are not more precious than his poems.   But even if we set apart this difference, and regard the two men in their special character as poets or artists, a marked difference is still discernible.   Hear Goethe's own definition of his poetical career and aim.

" Thus began that tendency from which I could not deviate my whole life through : namely, the tendency to turn into an image, into a poem, everything that delighted or troubled me, or otherwise occupied me, and to come to some certain understanding with myself upon it, that I might both rectify my conceptions of external things, and set my mind at rest about them. The faculty of doing this was necessary to no one more than to me, for my natural disposition whirled me constantly from one extreme to the other. All, therefore, that has been put forth by me consists of fragments of a great confession."—*Autobiography*, vol. i. p. 240.

Shakespeare's genius we defined to be the genius of universal expression, of clothing objects, circumstances, and feelings with magnificent language, of pouring over the image of any given situation, whether suggested from within or from without, an effusion of the richest intellectual matter that could possibly be related to it. Goethe's genius, as here defined by himself, was something different and narrower. It was the genius of translation from the subjective into the objective, of clothing real feelings with fictitious circumstance, of giving happy intellectual form to states of mind, so as to dismiss and throw them off. Let this distinction be sufficiently conceived and developed, and a full idea will be obtained of the exact difference between the literary many-sidedness attributed to Shakespeare and that also attributed to Goethe.

MILTON'S YOUTH.

MILTON'S YOUTH.[1]

NEVER surely did a youth leave the academic halls of England more full of fair promise than Milton, when, at the age of twenty-three, he quitted Cambridge to reside at his father's house, amid the quiet beauties of a rural neighbourhood some twenty miles distant from London. Fair in person, with a clear fresh complexion, light brown hair which parted in the middle and fell in locks to his shoulders, clear grey eyes, and a well-knit frame of moderate proportions—there could not have been found a finer picture of pure and ingenuous English youth. And that health and beauty which distinguished his outward appearance, and the effect of which was increased by a voice surpassingly sweet and musical, indicated with perfect truth the qualities of the mind within. Seriousness, studiousness, fondness for flowers and music, fondness also for manly exercises in the open air, courage and resolution of character, combined

[1] *North British Review*, February 1852 :—"The Works of John Milton." 8 vols. London : Pickering. 1851.

with the most maiden purity and innocence of life—these were the traits conspicuous in Milton in his early years. Of his accomplishments it is hardly necessary to take particular note. Whatever of learning, of science, or of discipline in logic or philosophy, the University at that time could give, he had duly and in the largest measure acquired. No better Greek or Latin scholar probably had the University in that age sent forth; he was proficient in the Hebrew tongue, and in all the other customary aids to a Biblical Theology; and he could speak and write well in French and Italian. His acquaintance, obtained by independent reading, with the history and with the whole body of the literature of ancient and modern nations, was extensive and various. And, as nature had endowed him in no ordinary degree with that most exquisite of her gifts, the ear and the passion for harmony, he had studied music as an art, and had taught himself not only to sing in the society of others, but also to touch the keys for his solitary pleasure.

The instruments which Milton preferred as a musician were, his biographers tell us, the organ and the bass-viol. This fact seems to us to be not without its significance. Were we to define in one word our impression of the prevailing tone, the characteristic mood and disposition of Milton's mind, even in his early youth, we should say that it consisted in a deep and habitual *seriousness.*

We use the word in none of those special and restricted senses that are sometimes given to it. We do not mean that Milton, at the period of his early youth with which we are now concerned, was, or accounted himself as being, a confessed member of that noble party of English Puritans with which he afterwards became allied, and to which he rendered such vast services. True, he himself tells us, in his account of his education, that "care had ever been had of him, with his earliest capacity, not to be negligently trained in the precepts of the Christian religion;" and in the fact that his first tutor, selected for him by his father, was one Thomas Young, a Scotch-man of subsequent distinction among the English Puri-tans, there is enough to prove that the formation of his character in youth was aided expressly by Puritanical influences. But Milton, if ever in a denominational sense he could be called a Puritan (he wore his hair long, and in other respects did not conform to the usages of the Puritan party), could hardly, with any propriety, be designated as a Puritan in this sense, at the time when he left College. There is evidence that at this time he had not given so much attention, on his own personal account, to matters of religious doctrine as he afterwards bestowed. That seriousness of which we speak was, therefore, rather a constitutional seriousness, ratified and nourished by rational reflection, than the assumed temper of a sect. "A certain reservedness of

natural disposition, and a moral discipline learnt out of
the noblest philosophy "—such, in Milton's own words,
were the causes which, apart from his Christian training,
would have always kept him, as he believed, above the
vices that debase youth. And herein the example of
Milton contradicts much that is commonly advanced by
way of a theory of the poetical character.

Poets and artists generally, it is held, are and ought
to be distinguished by a predominance of sensibility
over principle, an excess of what Coleridge called the
spiritual over what he called the moral part of man. A
nature built on quicksands, an organization of nerve
languid or tempestuous with occasion, a soul falling
and soaring, now subject to ecstasies and now to remorses
—such, it is supposed, and on no small induction of
actual instances, is the appropriate constitution of
the poet. Mobility, absolute and entire destitution
of principle properly so called, capacity for varying
the mood indefinitely rather than for retaining and
keeping up one moral gesture or resolution through all
moods : this, say the theorists, is the essential thing in
the structure of the artist. Against the truth of this,
however, as a maxim of universal application, the
character of Milton, as well as that of Wordsworth after
him, is a remarkable protest. Were it possible to place
before the theorists all the materials which exist for
judging of Milton's personal disposition as a young man,

without exhibiting to them at the same time the actual
and early proofs of his poetical genius, their conclusion,
were they true to their theory, would necessarily be that
the basis of his nature was too solid and immovable, the
platform of personal aims and aspirations over which
his thoughts moved and had footing too fixed and firm,
to permit that he should have been a poet. Nay, who-
soever, even appreciating Milton as a poet, shall come
to the investigation of his writings armed with that
preconception of the poetical character which is sure
to be derived from an intimacy with the character of
Shakespeare will hardly escape some feeling of the same
kind. Seriousness, we repeat, a solemn and even austere
demeanour of mind, was the characteristic of Milton even
in his youth. And the outward manifestation of this
was a life of pure and devout observance. This is a
point that ought not to be avoided, or dismissed in mere
general language; for he who does not lay stress on this
knows not and loves not Milton. Accept, then, by way
of more particular statement, his own remarkable words
in justifying himself against an innuendo of one of his
adversaries in later life, reflecting on the tenor of his
juvenile pursuits and behaviour. "A certain niceness
of nature," he says, "an honest haughtiness and self-
"esteem either of what I was, or what I might be
"(which let envy call pride), and lastly that modesty
"whereof, though not in the title-page, yet here I may

D   K

"be excused to make some beseeming profession, all
"these, uniting the supply of their natural aid together,
"kept me still above those low descents of mind beneath
"which he must deject and plunge himself that can
"agree to saleable and unlawful prostitutions." Fancy,
ye to whom the moral frailty of genius is a consolation,
or to whom the association of virtue with youth and
Cambridge is a jest—fancy Milton, as this passage from
his own pen describes him at the age of twenty-three,
returning to his father's house from the university, full
of its accomplishments and its honours, an auburn-
haired youth, beautiful as the Apollo of a northern
clime, and that beautiful body the temple of a soul pure
and unsoiled. Truly, a son for a mother to take to her
arms with joy and pride !

Connected with this austerity of character, discernible
in Milton even in his youth, may be noted also, as
indeed it is noted in the passage just cited, a haughty
yet modest self-esteem and consciousness of his own
powers. Throughout all Milton's works there may be
discerned a vein of this noble egotism, this unbashful
self-assertion. Frequently, in arguing with an opponent,
or in setting forth his own views on any subject of
discussion, he passes, by a very slight topical connexion,
into an account of himself, his education, his designs,
and his relations to the matter in question; and this
sometimes so elaborately and at such length, that the

impression is as if he said to his readers, " Besides all my other arguments, take this also as the chief and conclusive argument, that it is *I,* a man of such and such antecedents, and with such and such powers to perform far higher work than you see me now engaged in, who affirm and maintain this." In his later years Milton evidently believed himself to be, if not the greatest man in England, at least the greatest writer, and one whose *egomet dixi* was entitled to as much force in the intellectual commonwealth as the decree of a civil magistrate is invested with in the order of civil life. All that he said or wrote was backed in his own consciousness by a sense of the independent importance of the fact that it was he, Milton, who said or wrote it; and often, after arguing a point for some time on a footing of ostensible equality with his readers, he seems suddenly to stop, retire to the vantage-ground of his own thoughts, and bid his readers follow him thither, if they would see the whole of that authority which his words had failed to express.

Such, we say, is Milton's habit in his later writings. In his early life, of course, the feeling which it shows existed rather as an undefined consciousness of superior power, a tendency silently and with satisfaction to compare his own intellectual measure with that of others, a resolute ambition to be and to do something great. Now we cannot help thinking that it will be found that this particular form of self-esteem goes along with that moral austerity of character which we have alleged to be discernible in Milton even in his youth, rather than with that temperament of varying sensibility which is, according to the general theory, regarded as characteristic of the poet. Men of this latter type, as they vary in the entire mood of their mind, vary also in their estimate of themselves. No permanent consciousness of their own destiny, or of their own worth in comparison with others, belongs to them. In their moods of elevation they are powers to move the world; but, while the impulse that has gone forth from them in one of those moods may be still thrilling its way onward in wider and wider circles through the hearts of myriads they have never seen, they, the fountains of the impulse, the spirit being gone from them, may be sitting alone in the very spot and amid the ashes of their triumph, sunken and dead, despondent and self-accusing. It requires the evidence of positive results, the assurance of other men's praises, the visible presentation of effects which they cannot but trace to themselves, to convince such men that they are or can do anything. Whatever manifestations of egotism, whatever strokes of self-assertion come from such men, come in the very burst and phrenzy of their passing resistlessness. The calm, deliberate, and unshaken knowledge of their own superiority is not theirs. True, Shakespeare, the very type, if rightly understood, of this class of minds, is supposed in his Sonnets to have predicted, in the strongest and most deliberate terms, his own immortality as a poet. It could be proved, however, were this the place for such an investigation, that the common interpretation of those passages of the Sonnets which are supposed to supply this trait in the character of Shakespeare is nothing more nor less than a false reading of a very subtle meaning which the critics have missed. Those other passages of the Sonnets which breathe an abject melancholy and discontentment with self, which exhibit the poet as "cursing his fate," as "bewailing his outcast state," as looking about abasedly among his literary contemporaries, envying the "art" of one, and the "scope" of another, and even wishing sometimes that the very features of his face had been different from what they were and like those of some he knew, are, in our opinion, of far greater autobiographic value.

Nothing of this kind is to be found in Milton. As a Christian, indeed, humiliation before God was a duty the meaning of which he knew full well; but, as a man moving among other men, he possessed, in that moral seriousness and stoic scorn of temptation which characterized him, a spring of ever-present pride, dignifying his whole bearing among his fellows, and at times arousing him to a kingly intolerance. In short, instead of that dissatisfaction with self which we trace as a not unfrequent feeling with Shakespeare, we find in Milton, even in his early youth, a recollection firm and habitual that he was one of those servants to whom God had entrusted the stewardship of ten talents. In that very sonnet, for example, written on his twenty-third birthday, in which he laments that he had as yet achieved so little, his consolation is that the power of achievement was still indubitably within him—

> " All is, if I have grace to use it so,
> As ever in my great Task-Master's eye."

And what was that special mode of activity to which Milton, still in the bloom and seed-time of his years, had chosen to dedicate the powers of which he was so conscious ? He had been destined by his parents for the Church ; but this opening into life he had definitively and deliberately abandoned. With equal decision he renounced the profession of the Law ; and it does not seem to have been long after the conclusion of his career at the university when he renounced the prospects of professional life altogether. His reasons for this, which are to be gathered from various passages of his writings, seem to have resolved themselves into a jealous concern for his own absolute intellectual freedom. He had determined, as he says, " to lay up, as the best treasure and solace of a good old age, the honest liberty of free speech from his youth ;" and neither the Church nor the Bar of England, at the time when he formed that resolution, was a place where he could hope to keep it. For a man so situated, the alternative, then as now, was the practice or profession of literature. To this, therefore, as soon as he was able to come to a decision on the subject, Milton had implicitly, if not avowedly, dedicated himself. To become a great writer, and, above all, a great poet; to teach the English language a new strain and modulation ; to elaborate and surrender over to the English nation works that would make it more potent and wise in the age that was passing, and more memorable and lordly in the ages to come : such was the form which Milton's ambition had assumed when, laying aside his student's garb, he went to reside under his father's roof.

Nor was this merely a choice of necessity, the reluctant determination of a young soul " Church-outed by the prelates " and disgusted with the chances of the Law. Milton, in the Church, would certainly have been such an archbishop, mitred or unmitred, as England has never seen; and the very passage of such a man across the sacred floor would have trampled into timely extinction much that has since sprung up amongst us to trouble and perplex, and would have modelled the ecclesiasticism of England into a shape that the world might have gazed

at with no truant glance backward to the splendours of
the Seven Hills. And, doubtless, even amid the traditions of the Law, such a man would have performed the
feats of a Samson, albeit of a Samson in chains. An
inward prompting, therefore, a love secretly plighted to
the Muse, and a sweet comfort and delight in her sole
society, which no other allurement, whether of profit or
pastime, could equal or diminish,—this, less formally perhaps, but as really as care for his intellectual liberty, or
distaste for the established professions of his time, determined Milton's early resolution as to his future way of
life. On this point it will be best to quote his own
words.   "After I had," he says, "from my first years, by
" the ceaseless diligence and care of my father (whom
" God recompense !), been exercised to the tongues and
" some sciences, as my age would suffer, by sundry
" masters and teachers both at home and at the schools,
" it was found that, whether ought was imposed upon
" me by them that had the overlooking or betaken
" to of mine own choice, in English or other tongue,
" prosing or versing, but chiefly this latter, the style,
" by certain vital signs it had, was likely to live."
The meaning of which sentence is that Milton,
before his three-and-twentieth year, knew himself to
be a poet.

He knew this, he says, by "certain vital signs"
discernible in what he had already written. What were

those "vital signs," those proofs indubitable to Milton that he had the art and faculty of a poet? We need but refer the reader for the answer to those smaller poetical compositions of Milton, both in English and in Latin, which survive as specimens of his earliest Muse. Of these, some three or four which happen to be specially dated—such as the *Elegy on the Death of a Fair Infant*, written in 1626, or the author's eighteenth year; the well-known *Hymn on the Morning of Christ's Nativity*, written in 1629, when the author was just twenty-one; and the often-quoted *Lines on Shakespeare*, written not much later—may be cited as convenient materials from which anyone who would convince himself minutely of Milton's youthful vocation to poetry, rather than to anything else, may derive proofs on that head. Here will be found power of the most rare and beautiful conception, choice of words the most exact and exquisite, the most perfect music and charm of verse. Above all, here will be found that ineffable something—call it imagination or what we will—wherein lies the intimate and ineradicable peculiarity of the poet: the art to work on and on for ever in a purely ideal element, to chase and marshal airy nothings according to a law totally unlike that of rational association, never hastening to a logical end like the schoolboy when on errand, but still lingering within the wood like the schoolboy during holiday. This peculiar mental habit, nowhere better

described than by Milton himself when he speaks of
verse

> "Such as the meeting soul may pierce,
> In notes with many a winding bout
> Of linkèd sweetness long drawn out
> With wanton heed and giddy cunning,"

is so characteristic of the poetical disposition that,
though in most of the greatest poets, as, for example, Dante, Goethe, Shakespeare in his dramas,
Chaucer, and almost all the ancient Greek poets,
it is not observable in any extraordinary degree,
chiefly because in them the element of direct reference to human life and its interests had fitting preponderance, yet it may be affirmed that he who,
tolerating or admiring these poets, does not relish also
such poetry as that of Spenser, Keats, and Shakespeare
in his minor pieces, but complains of it as wearisome
and sensuous, is wanting in a portion of the genuine
poetic taste.

There was but one "vital sign" the absence of
which in Milton could, according to any theory of the
poetical character, have begotten doubts in his own
mind, or in the minds of his friends, whether poetry
was his peculiar and appropriate function. The single
source of possible doubt on this head could have been
no other than that native austerity of feeling and

temper, that real though not formal Puritanism of heart and intellect, which we have noticed as distinguishing Milton from his youth upward. The poet, it is said in these days, when, by psychologizing a man, it is supposed we can tell what course of life he is fit for—the poet ought to be universally sympathetic; he ought to hate nothing, despise nothing. And a notion equivalent to this, though by no means so articulately expressed, was undoubtedly prevalent in Milton's own time. As the Puritans, on the one hand, had set their faces against all those practices of profane singing, dancing, masquing, theatre-going, and the like, in which the preservation of the spirit of the arts was supposed to be involved, so the last party in the world from which the reputed devotees of the arts in those days would have expected a poet to arise was that of the Puritans. Even in Shakespeare, and much more in Ben Jonson, Beaumont and Fletcher, and other poets of the Elizabethan age, may be traced evidences of an instinctive enmity to that Puritanical mode of thinking which was then on the increase in English society, and in the triumph of which those great minds foresaw the proscription of their craft and their pleasures. When Sir Toby says to Malvolio, "Dost thou think, because thou art virtuous, there shall be no more cakes and ale?" and when the Clown adds, "Yes, by Saint Anne, and ginger shall be hot i' the mouth too," it is the Knight and the

Clown on the one side against Malvolio the Puritan on the other.   That the defence of the festive in this passage is not borne by more respectable personages than the two who speak is indeed a kind of indication that Shakespeare's personal feelings with regard to the austere movement which he saw gathering around him were by no means so deep or bitter as to discompose him; but, if his profounder soul could behold such things with serenity, and even pronounce them good, they assuredly met with enough of virulence and invective among his lesser contemporaries.   That literary crusade against the Puritans, as canting, sour-visaged, mirth-forbidding, art-abhorring religionists, which came to its height at the time when Butler wrote his *Hudibras*, and Wycherley his plays, was already hot when the wits of King James's days used to assemble after the theatre, in their favourite taverns; and if, sallying out after one of their merry evenings in their most favourite tavern of all, the Mermaid in Bread Street, those assembled poets and dramatists had gone in search of the youth who was likeliest to be the poet of the age then beginning, they certainly would not have gone to that modest residence in the same street where the son of the Puritanic scrivener, then preparing for College, was busy over his books.   Nay, if Ben Jonson, the last twenty-nine years of whose life coincided with the first twenty-nine of Milton's, had followed the young student from the house where he was born in Bread Street to his rooms at Cambridge, and had there become acquainted with him and looked over his early poetical exercises, it is probable enough that, while praising them so far, he would have constituted himself the organ of that very opinion as to the requisites of the poetical character which we are now discussing, and declared, in some strong phrase or other, that the youth would have been all the more hopeful as a poet if he had had a little more of the *bon vivant* in his constitution.

This, then, is a point of no little importance, involving as it does the relations of Milton as a poet to the age in which he lived, that splendid age of Puritan mastery in England which came between the age of Shakespeare and Elizabeth and the age of Dryden and the second Charles. Milton was *the* poet of that intermediate era; that his character was such as we have described it made him only the more truly a representative of all that was then deepest in English society; and, in inquiring, therefore, in what manner Milton's austerity as a man affected his art as a poet, we are, at the same time, investigating the *rationale* of that remarkable fact in the history of English literature, the interpolation of so original and isolated a development as the Miltonic poems between the inventive luxuriousness of the Elizabethan epoch and the witty licentiousness that followed the Restoration.

First, then, it was not *humour* that came to the rescue, in Milton's case, to help him out in those respects wherein, according to the theory in question, the strictness and austerity of his own disposition would have injured his capacity to be a poet. There are and have been men as strict and austere as he, who yet, by means of this quality of humour, have been able to reconcile themselves to much in human life lying far away from, and even far beneath, the sphere of their own practice and conscientious liking. As Pantagruel, the noble and meditative, endured and even loved those immortal companions of his, the boisterous and profane Friar John, and the cowardly and impish Panurge, so these men, remaining themselves with all rigour and punctuality within the limits of sober and exemplary life, are seen extending their regards to the persons and the doings of a whole circle of reprobate Falstaffs, Pistols, Clowns, and Sir Toby Belches. They cannot help it. They may and often do blame themselves for it; they wish that, in their intercourse with the world, they could more habitually turn the austere and judicial side of their character to the scenes and incidents that there present themselves, simply saying of each "That is right and worthy" or "That is wrong and unworthy," and treating it accordingly. But they break down in the trial.

Suddenly some incident presents itself which is not only right but clumsy, or not only wrong but comic, and straightway the austere side of their character wheels round to the back, and judge, jury, and witnesses are convulsed with untimely laughter. It was by no means so with Milton. As his critics have generally remarked, he had little of humour, properly so called, in his composition. His laughter is the laughter of scorn. With one unvarying judicial look he confronted the actions of men, and, if ever his tone altered as he uttered his judgments, it was only because something roused him to a pitch of higher passion. Take, as characteristic, the following passage, in which he replies to the taunt of an opponent who had asked where *he*, the antagonist of profane amusements, had procured that knowledge of theatres and their furniture which certain allusions in one of his books showed him to possess :—

" Since there is such necessity to the hearsay of a tire, a periwig, or a vizard, that plays must have been seen, what difficulty was there in that, when in the colleges so many of the young divines, and those in next aptitude to divinity, have been seen so often upon the stage, writhing and unboning their clergy limbs to all the antic and dishonest gestures of Trinculoes, buffoons, and bawds, prostituting the shame of that ministry which either they had or were nigh having to the eyes of courtiers and court ladies, with their grooms and mademoiselles ? There, whilst they acted and over-acted, among other young scholars, I was a spectator: they thought themselves gallant men, and I thought them fools; they made sport, and I laughed; they mispronounced, and I misliked; and, to make up the atticism, they were out, and I hissed."—*Apology for Smectymnuus.*

Who can doubt that to a man to whom such a scene as this presented itself in a light so different from that in which a Shakespeare would have viewed it Friar John himself, if encountered in the real world, would have been simply the profane and unendurable wearer of the sacred garb, Falstaff only a foul and grey-haired iniquity, Pistol but a braggart and coward, and Sir Toby Belch but a beastly sot?

That office, however, which humour did not perform for Milton, in his intercourse with the world of past and present things, was in part performed by what he did in large measure possess—intellectual *inquisitiveness:* respect for intellect, its accomplishments, and its rights. If any quality in the actions or writings of other men could have won Milton's favourable regards, even where his moral sense condemned, that quality, we believe, was intellectual greatness, and especially greatness of his own stamp, or marked by any of his own features. Hence that tone of almost pitying admiration which pervades his representation of the ruined Archangel; hence his uniformly respectful references to the great intellects of Paganism and of the Catholic world; and hence, we think, his unbounded and, for a time at least, unqualified reverence for Shakespeare. As by the direct exercise of his own intellect, on the one hand, applied to the rational discrimination for himself of what was really wrong from what was only ignorantly reputed to be so, he had kept his mind clear, as Cromwell also did, from many of those sectarian prejudices in the matter of moral observance which were current in his time— justified, for example, his love of music, his liking for natural beauty, his habits of cheerful recreation, his devotion to various literature, and even, most questionable of all, as would then have been thought, his affection for the massy pillars and storied windows of ecclesiastical architecture,—so, reflexly, by a recognition of the intellectual liberty of others, he seems to have distinctly apprehended the fact that there might be legitimate manifestations of intellect of a kind very different from his own. A Falstaff in real life, for example, might have been to Milton the most unendurable of horrors, just as, according to his own confession, a play-acting clergyman was his abomination; and yet, in the pages of his honoured Shakespeare, Sir John as mentor to the Prince, and Parson Hugh Evans as the Welch fairy among the mummers, may have been creations he would con over and very dearly appreciate. And this accounts for the multifarious and unrestricted character of his literary studies. Milton, we believe, was a man whose intellectual inquisitiveness and respect for talent would have led him, in other instances than that of the College theatricals, to see and hear much that his heart derided, to study and know what he would not strictly have wished to imitate. Ovid and Tibullus, for example, contain much that is far from Miltonic; and yet that he read poets of this class with particular pleasure let the following quotation prove:—

"I had my time, readers, as others have who have good learning bestowed upon them, to be sent to those places where, the opinion was, it might be soonest attained; and, as the manner is, was not unstudied in those authors which are most commended: whereof some were grave orators and historians, whose matter methought I loved indeed, but, as my age was, so I understood them; others were the smooth elegiac poets whereof the schools are not scarce, whom, both for the pleasing sound of their numerous writing (which, in imitation, I found most easy, and most agreeable to nature's part in me) and for their matter (which, what it is, there be few who know not), I was so allured to read that no recreation came to me more welcome—for, that it was then those years with me which are excused though they be least severe I may be saved the labour to remember ye."—*Apology for Smectymnuus.*

That Milton, then, notwithstanding his natural austerity and seriousness even in youth, was led by his

keen appreciation of literary beauty and finish, and
especially by his delight in sweet and melodious verse,
to read and enjoy the poetry of those writers who are
usually quoted as examples of the lusciousness and
sensuousness of the poetic nature, and even to prefer
them to all others, is specially stated by himself. But
let the reader, if he should think he sees in this a ground
for suspecting that we have assigned too much importance to Milton's personal seriousness of disposition as
a cause affecting his aims and art as a poet, distinctly
mark the continuation—

" Whence, having observed them [the elegiac and love
poets] to account it the chief glory of their wit, in that
they were ablest to judge, to praise, and by that could
esteem themselves worthiest to love, those high perfec-
tions which, under one or other name, they took to
celebrate, I thought with myself, by every instinct and
presage of nature (which is not wont to be false), that
what emboldened them to this task might, with such
diligence as they used, embolden me, and that what
judgment, wit, or elegance was my share would herein
best appear, and best value itself, by how much more
wisely and with more love of virtue I should choose
(let rude ears be absent!) the object of not unlike
praises. For, albeit these thoughts to some will seem
virtuous and commendable, to others only pardonable,
to a third sort perhaps idle, yet the mentioning of them
now will end in serious. Nor blame it, readers, in those
years to propose to themselves such a reward as the
noblest dispositions above other things in this life have

sometimes preferred; whereof not to be sensible, when good and fair in one person meet, argues both a gross and shallow judgment, and withal an ungentle and swainish breast. For, by the firm settling of these persuasions, I became, to my best memory, so much a proficient that, if I found those authors anywhere speaking unworthy things of themselves, or unchaste those names which before they had extolled, this effect it wrought in me: From that time forward their art I still applauded, but the men I deplored; and above them all preferred the two famous renowners of Beatrice and Laura, who never wrote but honour of them to whom they devote their verse, displaying sublime and pure thoughts without transgression. And long it was not after when I was confirmed in this opinion, that he who would not be frustrate of his hope to write well hereafter in laudable things ought himself to be a true poem—that is, a composition and pattern of the best and honourablest things; not presuming to sing high praises of heroic men or famous cities unless he have in himself the experience and the practice of all that which is praiseworthy."—*Apology for Smectymnuus.*

Here, at last, therefore, we have Milton's own judgment on the matter of our inquiry. He had speculated himself on that subject; he had made it a matter of conscious investigation what kind of moral tone and career would best fit a man to be a poet, on the one hand, or would be most likely to frustrate his hopes of writing well, on the other; and his conclusion, as we see, was dead against the " wild oats " theory.   Had Ben Jonson, according to our previous fancy, proffered him, out of kindly interest, a touch of that theory, while criticising his juvenile poems, and telling him how he might learn to write better, there would have descended on the lecturer, as sure as fate, a rebuke, though from young lips, that would have made his strong face blush.   " *He who would not be frustrate of his hope to write well here-after in laudable things ought himself to be a true poem :*" fancy that sentence, an early and often pronounced formula of Milton's, as we may be sure it was, hurled some evening, could time and chance have permitted it, into the midst of the assembled Elizabethan wits at the Mermaid!   What interruption of the jollity, what mingled uneasiness and resentment, what turning of faces towards the new speaker, what forced laughter to conceal consternation!   Only Shakespeare, one thinks, had he been present, would have fixed on the bold youth a mild and approving eye, would have looked round the room thoroughly to observe the whole scene, and, remembering some passages in his own life, would mayhap have had his own thoughts!   Certainly, at least, the essence of that wonderful and special development of the literary genius of England which came between the Elizabethan epoch and the epoch of the Restoration, and which was represented and consummated in Milton himself, consisted in the fact that then there was a temporary protest, and by a man able to make it good, against the theory of " wild oats," current before and current since. The nearest poet to Milton in this respect, since Milton's time, has undoubtedly been Wordsworth.

DRYDEN, AND THE LITERATURE OF THE RESTORATION.

DRYDEN,

AND THE

LITERATURE OF THE RESTORATION.[1]

IT is a common remark that literature flourishes best in times of social order and leisure, and suffers immediate depression whenever the public mind is agitated by violent civil controversies. The remark is more true than such popular inductions usually are. It is confirmed, on the small scale, by what every one finds in his own experience. When a family is agitated by any matter affecting its interests, there is an immediate cessation from all the lighter luxuries of books and music wherewith it used to beguile its leisure. All the members of the family are intent for the time being on the matter in hand; if books are consulted it is for some purpose of practical reference; and, if pens are active, it is in writing letters of business. Not till the

[1] *British Quarterly Review*, July, 1854. The Annotated Edition of the English Poets : Edited by Robert Bell. " Poetical Works of John Dryden." 3 vols. London. 1854.

matter is fairly concluded are the recreations of music and literature resumed; though then, possibly, with a keener zest and a mind more full and fresh than before. Precisely so it is on the large scale. If everything that is spoken or written be called literature, there is pro-bably always about the same amount of literature going on in a community; or, if there is any increase or decrease, it is but in proportion to the increase of the popu-lation. But, if by literature we mean a certain peculiar kind and quality of spoken or written matter, recog-nisable by its likeness to certain known precedents, then, undoubtedly literature flourishes in times of quiet and security, and wanes in times of convulsion and disorder. When the storm of some great civil contest is blowing, it is impossible for even the serenest man to shut him-self quite in from the noise, and turn over the leaves of his Horace, or practise his violin, as undistractedly as before. Great is the power of *pococurantism;* and it is a noble sight to see, in the midst of some Whig and Tory excitement which is throwing the general com-munity into sixes and sevens, and sending mobs along the streets, the calm devotee of hard science, or the impassioned lover of the ideal, going on his way, aloof from it all, and smiling at it all. But there are times when even these obdurate gentlemen will be touched, in spite of themselves, to the tune of what is going on; when the shouts of the mob will penetrate to the closets of the most studious; and when, as Archimedes of old had to leave his darling diagrams and trudge along the Syracusan streets to superintend the construction of rough cranes and catapults, so philosophers and poets alike will have to quit their favourite occupations, and be whirled along in the common agitation. Those are times when whatever literature there is assumes a character of immediate and practical interest. Just as, in the supposed case, the literary activity of the family is consumed in mere letters of business, so, in this, the literary activity of the community exhausts itself in newspaper articles, public speeches, and pamphlets, more or less elaborate, on the present crisis. There may be a vast amount of mind at work, and as much, on the whole, may be written as before; but the very excess of what may be called the pamphlet literature, which is perishable in its nature, will leave a deficiency in the various departments of literature more strictly so called—philosophical or expository literature, historical literature, and the literature of pure imagination. Not till the turmoil is over, not till the battle has been fairly fought out, and the mental activity involved in it has been let loose for more scattered work, will the calmer muses resume their sway, and the press send forth treatises and histories, poems and romances, as well as pamphlets. Then, however, men may return to literature with a new zest, and the very storm which has interrupted the course of pure literature for a time may infuse into such literature, when it begins again, a fresher and stronger spirit. If the battle has ended in a victory, there will be a tone of joy, of exultation, and of scorn, in what men think and write after it; if it has ended in a defeat, all that is thought and written will be tinged by a deeper and finer sorrow.

The history of English literature affords some curious illustrations of this law.   It has always puzzled historians, for example, to account for such a great unoccupied gap in our literary progress as occurs between the death of Chaucer and the middle of the reign of Elizabeth.   From the year 1250, when the English language first makes its appearance in anything like its present form, to the year 1400, when Chaucer died, forms, as all know, the infant age of our literature.   It was an age of great literary activity; and how much was achieved in it remains apparent in the fact that it culminated in a man like Chaucer—a man whom, without any drawback for the early epoch at which he lived, we still regard as one of our literary princes. Nor was Chaucer the solitary name of his age.   He had some notable contemporaries, both in verse and in prose. When we pass from Chaucer's age, however, we have to overleap nearly a hundred and eighty years before we alight upon a period presenting anything like an adequate show of literary continuation.   A few smaller names, like those of Lydgate, Surrey, and Skelton, are all that can be cited as poetical representatives of this sterile interval in the literary history of England: whatever of Chaucer's genius still lingered in the island seeming to have travelled northward, and taken refuge in a series of Scottish poets, excelling any of their English contemporaries. How is this to be accounted for? Is it that really, during this period, there was less of available mind than before in England, that the quality of the English nerve had degenerated? By no means necessarily so. Englishmen, during this period were engaged in enterprises requiring no small amount of intellectual and moral vigour; and there remain to us, from the same period, specimens of grave and serious prose, which, if we do not place them among the gems of our literature, we at least regard as evidence that our ancestors of those days were men of heart and wit and solid sense. In short, we are driven to suppose that there was something in the social circumstances of England during the long period in question which prevented such talent as there was from assuming the particular form of literature. Fully to make out what this "something" was may baffle us; but, when we remember that this was the period of the Civil Wars of the Roses, and also of the great Anglican Reformation, we have reason enough to conclude that the dearth of pure literature may have been owing, in part, to the engrossing nature of those practical questions which then disturbed English society. When Chaucer wrote, England, under the splendid rule of the third Edward, was potent and triumphant abroad, but large and leisurely at home; but scarcely had that monarch vacated the throne when a series of civil jars began, which tore the nation into factions, and was speedily followed by a religious movement as powerful in its effects. Accordingly, though printing was introduced during this period, and thus Englishmen had greater temptations to write, what they did write was almost exclusively plain grave prose, intended for practical or polemical occasions, and making no figure in a historical retrospect. How different when, passing the controversial reigns of Henry VIII., Edward VI., and Mary, we come upon the golden days of Queen Bess ! Controversy enough remained to give occasion to plenty of polemical prose; but about the middle of her reign, when England, once more great and powerful abroad as in the time of the Edwards, settled down within herself into a new lease of social order and leisure under an ascertained government, there began an outburst of literary genius such as no age or country had ever before witnessed. The literary fecundity of that period of English history which embraces the latter half of the reign of Elizabeth and the whole of the reign of James I. (1580-1625) is a perpetual astonishment to us all. In the entire preceding three centuries and a half we can with difficulty name six men that can, by any charity of judgment, be regarded as stars in our literature, and of these only one that is a star of the first magnitude : whereas in this brief period of forty-five or fifty years we can reckon up a host of poets and prose-writers all noticeable on high literary grounds, and of whom at least thirty were men of extraordinary dimensions. Indeed, in the contemplation of the intellectual abundance and variety of this age—the age of Spenser, Shakespeare, and Bacon, of Raleigh and Hooker, of Ben Jonson, Beaumont and Fletcher, Donne, Herbert, Massinger, and their illustrious contemporaries—we feel ourselves driven from the theory that so rich a literary crop could have resulted from that mere access of social leisure after a long series of national broils to which we do in part attribute it, and are obliged to suppose that there must have been, along with this, an actually finer substance and condition, for the time being, of the national nerve. The very brain of England must have become more " quick, nimble, and forgetive," before the time of leisure came.

We have spoken of this great age of English literature as terminating with the reign of James I., in 1625. In point of fact, however, it extended some way into the reign of his son, Charles I. Spenser had died in 1599, before James had ascended the English throne; Shakespeare and Beaumont had died in 1616, while

James still reigned; Fletcher died in 1625; Bacon died in 1626, when the crown had been but a year on Charles's head. But, while these great men and many of their contemporaries had vanished from the scene before England had any experience of the first Charles, some of their peers survived to tell what kind of men they had been. Ben Jonson lived till 1637, and was poet-laureate to Charles I.; Donne and Drayton lived till 1631; Herbert till 1632; Chapman till 1634; Dekker till 1638; Ford till 1639; and Heywood and Massinger till 1640.

There is one point in the reign of Charles, however, where a clear line may be drawn separating the last of the Elizabethan giants from their literary successors, This is the point at which the Civil War commences. The whole of the earlier part of Charles's reign was a preparation for this war; but it cannot be said to have fairly begun till the meeting of the Long Parliament in 1640, when Charles had been fifteen years on the throne. If we select this year as the commencement of the great Puritan and Republican Revolution in England, and the year 1660, when Charles II. was restored, as the close of the same Revolution, we shall have a period of twenty years to which, if there is any truth in the notion that the Muses shun strife, this notion should be found peculiarly applicable. Is it so? We think it is. In the first place, as we have just said, the last of the Elizabethan giants died off before this period began, as if killed by the mere approach to an atmosphere so lurid and tempestuous. In the second place, in the case of such writers as were old enough to have learnt in the school of those giants and yet young enough to survive them and enter on the period of struggle; —as for example, Herrick (1591–1660), Shirley (1596–1666), Waller (1605–1687), Davenant (1605–1668), Suckling (1608–1643), Milton (1608–1674), Butler (1612–1680), Cleveland (1613–1658), Denham (1615–1668), and Cowley (1618–1667),—it will be found, on examination, either that the time of their literary activity did not coincide with the period of struggle, but came before it, or after it, or lay on both sides of it; or that what they did write of a purely literary character during this period was written in exile; or, lastly, that what they did write at home of a genuine literary character during this period is inconsiderable in quantity, and dashed with a vein of polemical allusion rendering it hardly an exception to the rule. The literary career of Milton illustrates very strikingly this fact of the all but entire cessation of pure literature in England between 1640 and 1660. Milton's life consists of three distinctly marked periods—the first ending with 1640, during which he composed his exquisite minor poems; the second extending precisely

D						M

from 1640 to 1660, during which he wrote no poetry at all, except a few sonnets, but produced his various polemical prose treatises or pamphlets, and served the state as a public functionary; and the third, which may be called the period of his later muse, extending from 1660 to his death in 1674, and famous for the composition of his greater poems. Thus Milton's prose-period, if we may so term it, coincided exactly with the period of civil strife and Cromwellian rule. And, if this was the case with Milton—if he, who was essentially the poet of Puritanism, with his whole heart and soul in the struggle which Cromwell led, was obliged, during the process of that struggle, to lay aside his singing robes, postpone his plans of a great immortal poem, and in the meanwhile drudge laboriously as a prose pamphleteer—how much more must those have been reduced to silence, or brought down into practical prose, who found no such inspiration in the movement as it gave to the soul of Milton, but regarded it all as desolation and disaster! Indeed, one large department of the national literature at this period was proscribed by civil enactment. Stage-plays were prohibited in 1642, and it was not till after the Restoration that the theatres were re-opened. Such a prohibition, though it left the sublime muse of Milton at liberty, had it cared to sing, was a virtual extinction for the time of all the customary literature. In fine, if all the literary produce of England in the interval between 1640 and 1660 is examined, it will be found to consist in the main of a huge mass of controversial prose, by far the greater proportion of which, though effective at the time, is little better now than antiquarian rubbish, astonishing from its bulk, though some small percentage including all that came from the terrible pen of Milton is saved by reason of its strength and grandeur. The intellect of England was as active and as abundant as ever, but it was all required for the current service of the time. Perhaps the only exception of any consequence was in the case of the philosophical and calm-minded Sir Thomas Browne, author of the *Religio Medici.* While all England was in throes and confusion Browne was quietly attending his patients, or pottering along his garden at Norwich, or pursuing his meditations about sepulchral urns and his inquiries respecting the Quincuncial Lozenge. His views of things might have been considerably quickened by billeting upon his household a few of the Ironsides.

Had Cromwell lived longer, or had he established a dynasty capable of maintaining itself, there can be little doubt that there would have come a time of leisure during which, even under a Puritan rule, there would have been a new outburst of English Literature. There were symptoms, towards the close of the Protectorate that Cromwell, having now " reasonable good leisure," was willing and even anxious that the nation should resume its old literary industry and all its innocent liberties and pleasures. He allowed Cowley, Waller, Denham, Davenant, and other Royalists, to come over from France, and was glad to see them employed in writing verses. Waller became one of his courtiers, and composed panegyrics on him. He released Cleveland from prison in a very handsome manner, considering what hard things the witty roysterer had written about "O.P." and his "copper nose." He appears even to have winked at Davenant, when, in violation of the act against stage-plays, that gentlemanly poet began to give private theatrical entertainments under the name of operas. Davenant's heretical friend, Hobbes, too, already obnoxious by his opinions even to his own political party, availed himself of the liberty of the press to issue some fresh metaphysical essays, which the Protector may have read. In fact, had Cromwell survived a few years, there would, in all probability, have arisen, under his auspices, a new literature, of which his admirer and secretary, Milton, would have been the laureate. What might have been the characteristics of this literature of the Commonwealth, had it developed itself to full form and proportions, we can but guess. That, in some respects, it would not have been so broad and various as the literature which took its rise from the

Restoration is very likely; for, so long as the Puritan element remained dominant in English society, it was impossible that, with any amount of liberty of the press, there should have been such an outbreak of the merely comic spirit as did occur when that element succumbed to its antagonist, and genius had official licence to be as profligate as it chose. But, if less gay and riotous, it might have been more earnest, powerful, and impressive. For its masterpiece it would still have had *Paradise Lost*,—a work which, as it is, we must regard as its peculiar offspring, though posthumously born; nor can we doubt that, if influenced by the example and the recognised supremacy of such a laureate as Milton, the younger literary men of the time would have found themselves capable of other things than epigrams and farces.

It was fated, however, that the national leisure requisite for a new development of English literary genius should commence only with the restoration of the Stuarts in 1660; and then it was a leisure secured in very different circumstances from those which would have attended a perpetuation of Cromwell's rule. With Charles II. there came back into the island, after many years of banishment, all the excesses of the cavalier spirit, more reckless than before, and considerably changed by long residence in continental cities, and especially in the French capital. Cavalier noblemen

and gentlemen came back, bringing with them French
tastes, French fashions, and foreign ladies of pleasure.
As Charles II. was a different man from his father,
so the courtiers that gathered round him at Whitehall
were very different from those who had fought with
Charles I. against the Parliamentarians. Their political
principles and prejudices were nominally the same;
but they were for the most part men of a younger
generation, less stiff and English in their demeanour,
and more openly dissolute in their morals. Such was
the court the restoration of which England virtually
confessed to be necessary to prevent a new era of
anarchy. It was inaugurated amid the shouts of the
multitude; and Puritanism, already much weakened
by defections before the event, hastened to disappear
from the public stage, diffusing itself once more as a
mere element of secret efficacy through the veins of
the community, and purchasing even this favour by
the sacrifice of its most notorious leaders.

Miserable in some respects as was this change for
England, it offered, by reason of the very unanimity
with which it was effected, all the conditions necessary
for the forthcoming of a new literature. But where
were the materials for the commencement of this new
literature ?

First, as regards *persons* fit to initiate it. There were

all those who had been left over from the Protectorate, together with such wits as the Restoration itself had brought back, or called into being. There was the old dramatist, Shirley, now in his sixty-fifth year, very glad, no doubt, to come back to town, after his hard fare as a country-schoolmaster during the eclipse of the stage, and to resume his former occupation as a writer of plays in the style that had been in fashion thirty years before. There was Hobbes, older still than Shirley, a tough old soul of seventy-three, but with twenty more years of life in him, and, though not exactly a literary man, yet sturdy enough to be whatever he liked within certain limits. There was mild Izaak Walton, of Chancery-lane, only five years younger than Hobbes, but destined to live as long, and capable of writing very nicely if he could have been kept from sauntering into the fields to fish. There was the gentlemanly Waller, now fifty-six years of age, quite ready to be a poet about the court of Charles, and to write panegyrics on the new side to atone for that on Cromwell. There was the no less gentlemanly Davenant, also fifty-six years of age, steady to his royalist principles, as became a man who had received the honour of knighthood from the royal martyr, and enjoying a wide reputation, partly from his poetical talents, and partly from his want of nose. There was Milton, in his fifty-second year, blind, desolate, and stern, hiding in obscure lodgings till his defences of regicide should be sufficiently forgotten to save him from molestation, and building up in imagination the scheme of his promised epic. There was Butler, four years younger, brimful of hatred to the Puritans, and already engaged on his poem of *Hudibras,* which was to lash them so much to the popular taste. There was Denham, known as a versifier little inferior to Waller, and with such superior claims on the score of loyalty as to be considered worthy of knighthood and the first vacant post. There was Cowley, still only in his forty-third year, and with a ready-made reputation, both as a poet and as a prose-writer, such as none of his contemporaries possessed, and such indeed as no English writer had acquired since the days of Ben Jonson and Donne. Younger still, and with his fame as a satirist not yet made, there was Milton's friend, honest Andrew Marvell, whom the people of Hull had chosen as their representative in Parliament. Had the search been extended to theologians, and such of them selected as were capable of influencing the literature by the form of their writings, as distinct from their matter, Jeremy Taylor would have been noted as still alive, though his work was nearly over, while Richard Baxter, with a longer life before him, was in the prime of his strength, and there was in Bedford an eccentric Baptist preacher, once a tinker, who was to be the author, though no one supposed it, of the greatest prose allegory in the language.   Close about the person of the king, too, there were able men and wits, capable of writing themselves, or of criticising what was written by others, from the famous Clarendon down to such younger and lighter men as Dillon, Earl of Roscommon, Sackville, Earl of Dorset, and Sir Charles Sedley.   Lastly, not to extend the list farther, there was then in London, aged twenty-nine, and going about in a stout plain dress of grey drugget, a Northamptonshire squire's son, named John Dryden, who, after having been educated at Cambridge, had come up to town in the last year of the Protectorate to push his fortune under a Puritan relative then in office, and who had already once or twice tried his hand at poetry.   Like Waller, he had written and published a series of panegyrical stanzas on Cromwell after his death; and, like Waller also, he had attempted to atone for this miscalculation by writing another poem, called *Astræa Redux*, to celebrate the return of Charles.   As a taste of what this poet, in particular, could do, take the last of his stanzas on Cromwell :—

> " His ashes in a peaceful urn shall rest ;
>   His name a great example stands to show
> How strangely high endeavours may be blessed,
>   Where piety and valour jointly go ";

or, in another metre and another strain of politics, the conclusion of the poem addressed to Charles :—

"The discontented now are only they
  Whose crimes before did your just cause betray :
  Of those your edicts some reclaim from sin,
  But most your life and blest example win.
  Oh happy prince! whom Heaven hath taught the way
  By paying vows to have more vows to pay!
  Oh happy age! Oh times like those alone
  By fate reserved for great Augustus' throne,
  When the joint growth of arms and arts foreshow
  The world a monarch, and that monarch you!"

Such were the *personal elements*, if we may so call them, available at the beginning of the reign of Charles II. for the commencement of a new era in English literature. Let us see next what were the more pronounced *tendencies* visible amid these personal elements —in other words, what tone of moral sentiment, and what peculiarities of literary style and method, were then in the ascendant, and likely to determine the character of the budding authorship.

It was pre-eminently clear that the forthcoming literature would be Royalist and anti-Puritan. With the exception of Milton, there was not one man of known literary power whose heart still beat as it did when Cromwell sat on the throne, and whose muse magnanimously disdained the change that had befallen the nation. Puritanism, as a whole, was driven back into the concealed vitals of the community, to sustain itself meanwhile as a sectarian theology lurking in

chapels and conventicles, and only to re-appear after a
lapse of years as an ingredient in the philosophy of
Locke and his contemporaries. The literary men who
stepped forward to lead the literature of the Restoration
were royalists and courtiers: some of them honest
cavaliers, rejoicing at being let loose from the restraints
of the Commonwealth; others timeservers, making up
for delay by the fulsome excess of their zeal for the
new state of things. It was part of this change that
there should be an affectation, even where there was
not the reality, of lax morals. According to the sarcasm
of the time, it was necessary now for those who would
escape the risk of being thought Puritans to contract a
habit of swearing and pretend to be great rakes. And
this increase, both in the practice and in the profession
of profligacy, at once connected itself with that institution of English society which, from the very fact that
it had been suppressed by the Puritans, now became
doubly attractive and popular. The same revolution
which restored royalty in England re-opened the play-
houses; and in them, as the established organs of
popular sentiment, all the anti-Puritanic tendencies of
the time hastened to find vent. The custom of having
female actors on the stage for female parts, instead of
boys as heretofore, was now permanently introduced,
and brought many scandals along with it. Whether,
as some surmise, the very suppression of the theatres

during the reign of Puritanism contributed to their
unusual corruptness when they were again allowed by
law—by damming up, as it were, a quantity of pruriency
which had afterwards to be let loose in a mass—it is not
easy to say; it is certain, however, that never in this
country did impurity run so openly at riot in literary
guise as it did in the Drama of the Restoration. To
use a phrenological figure, it seemed as if the national
cranium of England had suddenly been contracted in
every other direction so as to permit an inordinate
increase of that particular region which is situated
above the nape of the neck. This enormous preponderance of the back of the head in literature was most
conspicuously exhibited in Comedy. Every comedy
that was produced represented life as a meagre action of
persons and interests on a slight proscenium of streets
and bits of green field, behind which lay the real business, transacted in stews. To set against this, it is
true, there was a so-called Tragic Drama. The tragedy
that was now in favour, however, was no longer the old
English tragedy of rich and complex materials, but the
French tragedy of heroic declamation. Familiarized
by their stay in France with the tragic style of Corneille
and other dramatists of the court of Louis XIV., the
Royalists brought back the taste with them into England;
and the poets who catered for them hastened to abandon
the Shakespearian tragedy, with its large range of time

and action and its blank verse, and to put on the stage tragedies of sustained and decorous declamation in the heroic or rhymed couplet, conceived, as much as possible, after the model of Corneille. Natural to the French, this classic or regular style accorded ill with English faculties and habits; and Corneille himself would have been horrified at the slovenly and laborious attempts of the English in imitation of his masterpieces. The effect of French influence at this time, however, on English literary taste, did not consist merely in the introduction of the heroic or rhymed drama. The same influence extended, and in some respects beneficially, to all departments of English literature. It helped, for example, to correct that peculiar style of so-called " wit " which, originating with the dregs of the Elizabethan age, had during a whole generation infected English prose and poetry, but more especially the latter. The characteristic of the " metaphysical school of poetry," as it is called, which took its rise in a literary vice percep- tible even in the great works of the Elizabethan age, and of which Donne and Cowley were the most cele- brated representatives, consisted in the identification of mere intellectual subtlety with poetic genius. To spin out a fantastic conceit, to pursue a thread of quaint thought as long as it could be held between the fingers of the metre without snapping, and, in doing so, to wind it about as many oddities of the real world as possible, and introduce as many verbal quibbles as possible, was the aim of the "metaphysical poets." Some of them, like Donne and Cowley, were men of independent merit; but the style of poetry itself, as all modern readers confess by the alacrity with which they avoid reprinted specimens of it, was as unprofitable an investment of human ingenuity as ever was attempted. At the period of the Restoration, and partly in consequence of French influence, this kind of wit was falling into disrepute. There were still practitioners of it; but, on the whole, a more direct, clear, and light manner of writing was coming into fashion. Discourse became less stiff and pedantic; or, as Dryden himself has expressed it, "the fire of English wit, which was before stifled under a constrained melancholy way of breeding, began to display its force by mixing the solidity of our nation with the air and gaiety of our neighbours." And the change in discourse passed without difficulty into literature, calling into being a nimbler style of wit, a more direct, rapid, and decisive manner of thought and expression, than had beseemed authorship before. In particular, and apart from the tendency to greater directness and concision of thought, there was an increased attention to correctness of expression. The younger literary men began to object to what they called the involved and incorrect syntax of the writers of the previous age, and to pretend to greater neatness and accuracy in the construction of their sentences. It was at this time, for example, that the rule of not ending a sentence with a preposition or other little word began to be attended to. Whether the notion of correctness, implied in this, and other such rules, was a true notion, and whether the writers of the Restoration excelled their Elizabethan predecessors in this quality of correctness, admits of being doubted. Certain it is, however, that a change in the mechanism of writing— this change being on the whole towards increased neatness—did become apparent about this time. The change was visible in prose, but far more in verse. For, to conclude this enumeration of the literary signs or tendencies of the age of the Restoration, it was a firm belief of the writers of the period that then for the first time was the art of correct English versification ex- emplified and appreciated. It was, we say, a firm belief of the time, and indeed it has been a common-place of criticism ever since, that Edmund Waller was the first poet who wrote smooth and accurate verse, that in this he was followed by Sir John Denham, and that these two men were reformers of English metre. " Well- placing of words, for the sweetness of pronunciation, was not known till Mr. Waller introduced it," is a deliberate statement of Dryden himself, meant to apply especially to verse. Here, again, we have to separate a matter of fact from a matter of doctrine. To aver, with such specimens of older English verse before us as the works of Chaucer and Spenser, and the minor poems of Milton, that it was Waller or any other petty writer of the Restoration that first taught us sweetness, or smoothness, or even correctness of verse, is so ridiculous that the currency of such a notion can only be accounted for by the servility with which small critics go on repeating whatever any one big critic has said. That Waller and Denham, however, did set the example of something new in the manner of English versification,—which "something" Dryden, Pope, and other poets who afterwards adopted it, regarded as an improvement,—needs not be doubted. For us it is sufficient in the meantime to recognise the change as an attempt after greater neatness of mechanical structure, leaving open the question whether it was a change for the better.

It was natural that the tendencies of English literature thus enumerated should be represented in the poet-laureate for the time being. Who was the fit man to be appointed laureate at the Restoration? Milton was out of the question, having none of the requisites. Butler, the man of greatest natural power of a different order, and possessing certainly as much of the anti-Puritan sentiment as Charles and his courtiers could have desired in their laureate, was not yet sufficiently known, and was, besides, neither a dramatist nor a fine gentleman. Cowley, whom public opinion would have pointed

out as best entitled to the honour, was somehow not in
much favour at court, and was spending the remainder
of his days on a little property near Chertsey. Waller
and Denham were wealthy men, with whom literature
was but an amusement. On the whole, Sir William
Davenant was felt to be the proper man for the office.
He was an approved royalist; he had, in fact, been laureate to Charles I. after Ben Jonson's death in 1637; and
he had suffered much in the cause of the king. He was,
moreover, a literary man by profession. He had been an
actor and a theatre-manager before the Commonwealth;
he had been the first to start a theatre after the relaxed
rule of Cromwell made it possible; and he was one of
the first to attempt heroic or rhymed tragedies after the
French model. He was also, far more than Cowley, a
wit of the new school; and, as a versifier, he practised,
with no small reputation, the neat, lucid style introduced
by Denham and Waller. He was the author of an epic
called *Gondibert*, written in rhymed stanzas of four
lines each, which Hobbes praised as showing "more
shape of art, health of morality, and vigour and beauty
of expression," than any poem he had ever read. We
defy anyone to read the poem now; but there have
been worse things written; and it has the merit of
being a careful and rather serious composition by a
man who had industry, education, and taste, without
genius. There was but one awkwardness in having

D N

such a man for laureate : he had no nose. This awkwardness, however, had existed at the time of his first appointment in the preceding reign. At least, Suckling adverts to it in the *Session of the Poets*, where he makes the wits of that time contend for the bays—

> " Will Davenant, ashamed of a foolish mischance,
> That he had got lately, travelling in France,
> Modestly hoped the handsomeness of 's muse
> Might any deformity about him excuse.

> " And surely the company would have been content,
> If they could have found any precedent ;
> But in all their records, either in verse or prose,
> There was not one laureate without a nose."

If the more decorous court of Charles I., however, overlooked this deficiency, it was not for that of Charles II. to take objection to it. After all, Davenant, notwithstanding his misfortune, seems to have been not the worst gentleman about Charles's court, either in morals or manners. Milton is said to have known and liked him.

Davenant's laureateship extended over the first eight years of the Restoration, or from 1660 to 1668. Much was done in those eight years both by himself and others. Heroic plays and comedies were produced in sufficient abundance to supply the two chief theatres then open in London—one of them that of the Duke's company, under Davenant's management ; the other, that of the King's company, under the management of an actor named Killigrew. The number of writers for the stage was very great, including not only those whose names have been mentioned, but others new to fame. The literature of the stage formed by far the largest proportion of what was written, or even of what was published. Literary efforts of other kinds, however, were not wanting. Of satires, and small poems in the witty or amatory style, there was no end. The publication by Butler of the first part of his *Hudibras* in 1663, and of the second in 1664, drew public attention, for the first time, to a man, already past his fiftieth year, who had more true wit in him than all the aristocratic poets put together. The poem was received by the king and the courtiers with shouts of laughter; quotations from it were in everybody's mouth; but, notwithstanding large promises, nothing substantial was done for the author. Meanwhile Milton, blind and gouty, and living in his house near Bunhill Fields, where his visitors were hardly of the kind that admired Butler's poem, was calmly proceeding with his *Paradise Lost*. The poem was finished and published in 1667, leaving Milton free for other work. Cowley, who would have welcomed such a poem, and whose praise Milton would have valued more than that of any other contemporary, died in the year of its publication. Davenant may have read it before his death in the following year; but perhaps the only poet of the time who hailed its appearance with enthusiasm adequate to the occasion was Milton's personal friend Marvell. Gradually, however, copies of the poem found their way about town, and drew public attention once more to Cromwell's old secretary.

The laureateship remained vacant two years after Davenant's death; and then it was conferred—on whom? There can be little doubt that, of those eligible to it, Butler had, in some respects, the best title. The author of *Hudibras*, however, seems to have been one of those ill-conditioned men whom patronage never comes near, and who are left, by a kind of necessity, to the bitter enjoyment of their own humours. There does not seem to have been even a question of appointing him; and the office, the income of which would have been a competence to him, was conferred on a man twenty years his junior, and whose circumstances required it less—John Dryden. The appointment, which was made in August, 1670, conferred on Dryden not only the laureateship, but also the office of "historiographer royal," which chanced to be vacant at the same time. The income accruing from the two offices thus conjoined was 200*l.* a-year, which was about as valuable then as 600*l.* a-year would be now; and it was expressly stated in the deed of appointment that these emoluments were conferred on Dryden "in consideration of his many acceptable services done to his majesty, and from an observation of his learning and eminent abilities, and his great skill and elegant style both in verse and prose." At the time of the Restoration, or even for a year or two after it, such language could, by no stretch of courtesy, have been applied to Dryden. At that time, as we have seen, though already past his thirtieth year, he was certainly about the least distinguished person in the little band of wits that were looking forward to the good time coming. He was a stout, fresh-complexioned man, in grey drugget, who had written some robust stanzas on Cromwell's death, and a short poem, also robust, but rather wooden, on Charles's return. That was about all that was then known about him. What had he done, in the interval, to raise him so high, and to make it natural for the Court to prefer him to what was in fact the titular supremacy of English literature, over the heads of others who might be supposed to have claims, and especially over poor battered old Butler? A glance at Dryden's life during Davenant's laureateship, or between 1660 and 1670, will answer this question.

Dryden's connexion with the politics of the Protectorate had not been such as to make his immediate and cordial attachment to the cause of restored Royalty either very strange or very unhandsome. Not committed either by strong personal convictions, or by acts, to the Puritan side, he hastened to show that, whatever the older Northamptonshire Drydens and their relatives might think of the matter, he, for one, was willing to be a loyal subject of Charles, both in church and in state. This main point being settled, he had only farther to consider into what particular walk of industry, now that official employment under government was cut off, he should carry his loyalty and his powers. The choice was not difficult. There was but one career open for him, or suitable to his tastes and qualifications—that of general authorship. We say "general authorship;" for it is important to remark that Dryden was by no means nice in his choice of work. He was ready for anything of a literary kind to which he was, or could make himself, competent. He had probably a preference for verse; but he had no disinclination to prose, if that article was in demand in the market. He had a store of acquirements, academic and other, that fitted him for an intelligent apprehension of whatever was going on in any of the London circles of that day—the circle of the scholars, that of the amateurs of natural science, or that of the mere wits and men of letters. He was, in fact, a man of general intellectual strength, which he was willing to let out in any kind of tolerably honest intellectual service that might be in fashion. This being the case, he set the right way to work to make himself known in quarters where such service was going on. He had about 40*l.* a-year of inherited fortune; which means something more than 120*l.* a-year with us. With this income to supply his immediate wants, he went to live with Herringman, a bookseller and publisher in the New Exchange. What was the precise nature of his agreement with Herringman cannot be ascertained. His literary enemies used afterwards to say that he was Herringman's hack and wrote prefaces for him. However this may be, there were higher conveniences in being connected with Herringman. He was one of the best known of the London publishers of the day, was a personal friend of Davenant, and had almost all the wits of the day as his customers and occasional visitors. Through him, in all probability, Dryden first became acquainted with some of these men, including Davenant himself, Cowley, and a third person of considerable note at that time as an aristocratic dabbler in literature—Sir Robert Howard, son of the Earl of Berkshire. That the impression he made on these men, and on others in or out of the Herringman circle, was no mean one, is proved by the fact that in 1663 we find him a member of the Royal Society, the foundation of which by royal charter had taken place in the previous year. The number of members was then one hundred and fifteen, including such scientific celebrities of the time as Boyle, Wallis, Wilkins, Christopher Wren, Dr.

Isaac Barrow, Evelyn, and Hooke, besides such titled
amateurs of experimental science as the Duke of
Buckingham, the Marquis of Dorchester, the Earls of
Devonshire, Crawford, and Northampton, and Lords
Brouncker, Cavendish, and Berkeley. Among the more
purely literary members were Waller, Denham, Cowley,
and Sprat, afterwards Bishop of Rochester. The
admission of Dryden into such company is a proof
that already he was socially a man of mark. As we
have Dryden's own confession that he was somewhat
dull and sluggish in conversation, and the testimony
of others that he was the very reverse of a bustling
or pushing man, and rather avoided society than sought
it, we must suppose that he had been found out in
spite of himself. We can fancy him at Herringman's,
or elsewhere, sitting as one of a group with Davenant,
Howard, and others, taking snuff and listening, rather
than speaking, and yet, when he did speak, doing so
with such judgment as to make his chair one of the most
important in the room, and impress all with the conviction that he was a solid fellow. He seems also to
have taken an interest in the scientific gossip of
the day about magnetism, the circulation of the blood,
and the prospects of the Baconian system of philosophy;
and this may have helped to bring him into contact
with men like Boyle, Wren, and Wallis. At all events,
if the Society elected him on trust, he soon justified

their choice by taking his place among the best known members of what was then the most important class of literary men—the writers for the stage. His first drama, a lumbering prose-comedy entitled *The Wild Gallant*, was produced at Killigrew's Theatre in February, 1662–3; and, though its success was very indifferent, he was not discouraged from a second venture in a tragi-comedy, entitled *The Rival Ladies*, written partly in blank verse, partly in heroic rhyme, and produced at the same theatre. This attempt was more successful; and in 1664 there was produced, as the joint composition of Dryden and Sir Robert Howard, an attempt in the style of the regular heroic or rhymed tragedy, called *The Indian Queen*. The date of this effort of literary co-partnership between Dryden and his aristocratic friend coincides with the formation of a more intimate connexion between them, by Dryden's marriage with Sir Robert's sister, Lady Elizabeth Howard. The marriage (the result, it would seem, of a visit of the poet, in the company of Sir Robert, to the Earl of Berkshire's seat in Wilts) took place in November, 1663; so that, when *The Indian Queen* was written, the two authors were already brothers-in-law. The marriage of a man in the poet's circumstances with an earl's daughter was neither altogether strange nor altogether such as to preclude remark. The earl was poor, and able to afford his daughter but a small

settlement; and Dryden was a man of sufficiently
good family, his grandfather having been a baronet,
and some of his living relations having landed property
in Northamptonshire. The property remaining for the
support of Dryden's brothers and sisters, however, after
the subduction of his own share, had been too scanty
to keep them all in their original station; and some
of them had fallen a little lower in the world. One
sister, in particular, had married a tobacconist in
London—a connexion not likely to be agreeable to the
Earl of Berkshire and his sons, if they took the trouble
to become cognisant of it. Dryden himself probably
moved conveniently enough between the one relationship and the other. If his aristocratic brother-in-law,
Sir Robert, could write plays with him, his other
brother-in-law, the tobacconist of Newgate-street, may
have administered to his comfort in other ways. It
is known that the poet, in his later life at least, was
peculiarly fastidious in the article of snuff, abhorring
all ordinary snuffs, and satisfied only with a mixture
which he prepared himself; and it is not unlikely that
the foundation of this fastidiousness may have been
laid in the facilities afforded him originally in his
brother-in-law's shop. The tobacconist's wife, of course,
would be pleased now and then to have a visit from
her brother John; but whether Lady Elizabeth ever
went to see her is rather doubtful. According to all

accounts, Dryden's experience of this lady was not such as to improve his ideas of the matrimonial state, or to give encouragement to future poets to marry earls' daughters.

In consequence of the ravages of the Great Plague in 1665 and the subsequent disaster of the Great Fire in 1666 there was for some time a total cessation in London of theatrical performances and all other amusements. Dryden, like most other persons who were not tied to town by business, spent the greater part of this gloomy period in the country. He availed himself of the interruption thus given to his dramatic labours to produce his first writings of any moment out of that field, his *Annus Mirabilis* and his *Essay on Dramatic Poesy*. The first, an attempt to invest with heroic interest, and celebrate in sonorous stanzas, the events of the famous years 1665–6, including not only the Great Fire, but also the incidents of a naval war then going on against the Dutch, must have done more to bring Dryden into the favourable notice of the King, the Duke of York, and other high personages eulogized in it, than anything he had yet written. It was, in fact, a kind of short epic on the topics of the year, such as Dryden might have been expected to write if he had been already doing laureate's duty; and, unless Sir William Davenant was of very easy temper, he must have been rather annoyed at so obvious an invasion of his province, notwithstanding the compliment the poet had paid him by adopting the stanza of his *Gondibert*, and imitating his manner. Scarcely less effective in another way must have been the prose *Essay on Dramatic Poesy*—a vigorous treatise on various matters of poetry and criticism then much discussed. It contained, among other things, a defence of the Heroic or Rhymed Tragedy against those who preferred the older Elizabethan Tragedy of blank verse; and so powerful a contribution was it to this great controversy of the day that it produced an immediate sensation in all literary circles. Sir Robert Howard, who now ranked himself among the partisans of blank verse, took occasion to express his dissent from some of the opinions expounded in it; and, as Dryden replied rather tartly, a temporary quarrel ensued between the two brothers-in-law.

On the re-opening of the theatres in 1667 Dryden, his reputation increased by the two performances just mentioned, stepped forward again as a dramatist. A heroic tragedy called *The Indian Emperor*, which he had prepared before the recess, and which, indeed, had then been acted, was reproduced with great success, and established Dryden's position as a practitioner of heroic and rhymed tragedy. This was followed by a comedy, in mixed blank verse and prose, called *The Maiden Queen;* this by a prose-comedy called *Sir Martin Mar-all;* and this again, by an adaptation, in conjunction with Sir William Davenant, of Shakespeare's *Tempest.* The two last were produced at Davenant's theatre, whereas all Dryden's former pieces had been written for Killigrew's, or the King's company. About this time, however, an arrangement was made which secured Dryden's services exclusively for Killigrew's house. By the terms of the agreement, Dryden engaged to supply the house with three plays every year, in return for which, he was admitted a shareholder in the profits of the theatre to the extent of one share and a-half. The first fruits of the bargain were a prose-comedy called *The Mock Astrologer* and two heroic tragedies entitled *Tyrannic Love* and *The Conquest of Granada*, the latter being in two parts. These were all produced between 1668 and 1670, and the tragedies, in particular, seem to have taken the town by storm, and placed Dryden, beyond dispute, at the head of all the heroic playwrights of the day.

The extent and nature of Dryden's popularity as a dramatist about this time may be judged by the following extract from the diary of the omnipresent Pepys, referring to the first performance of the *Maiden Queen:* —
" After dinner, with my wife to see the *Maiden Queene,*
" a new play by Dryden, mightily commended for the
" regularity of it, and the strain and wit; and the truth
" is, the comical part done by Nell [Nell Gwynn], which

" is Florimell, that I never can hope to see the like done
" again by man or woman. The King and Duke of York
" were at the play. But so great a performance of a
" comical part was never, I believe, in the world before
" as Nell do this, both as a mad girle, then most and
" best of all when she comes in like a young gallant
" and hath the motions and carriage of a spark the most
" that ever I saw any man have. It makes me, I con-
" fess, admire her." But even Nell's performance in
this comedy was nothing compared to one part of her
performance afterwards in the tragedy of *Tyrannic Love*.
Probably there was never such a scene of ecstasy in a
theatre as when Nell, after acting the character of a
tragic princess in this play, and killing herself at the
close in a grand passage of heroism and supernatural
virtue, had to start up as she was being borne off the
stage dead, and resume her natural character, first addressing her bearer in these words :—

> " Hold ! are you mad ? you d——d confounded dog :
>   I am to rise and speak the epilogue.",

and then running to the footlights and beginning her
speech to the audience :—

> " I come, kind gentlemen, strange news to tell ye :
>   I am the ghost of poor departed Nelly.
>   Sweet ladies, be not frighted ; I'll be civil :
>   I'm what I was, a little harmless devil." &c. &c.

It is a tradition that it was this epilogue that effected Nell's conquest of the king, and that he was so fascinated with her manner of delivering it, that he went behind the scenes after the play was over and carried her off. Ah! and it is two hundred years since that fascinating run to the footlights took place, and the swarthy face of the monarch was seen laughing, and the audience shrieked and clapped with delight, and Pepys bustled about the boxes, and Dryden sat looking placidly on, contented with his success, and wondering how much of it was owing to Nelly!

One can see how, even if the choice had been made strictly with a reference to the claims of the candidates, it would have been felt that Dryden, and not Butler, was the proper man to succeed Davenant in the laureate-ship. If Butler had shewn the more original vein of talent in one peculiar walk, Dryden had proved himself the man of greatest general strength, in whom were more broadly represented the various literary tendencies of his time. The author of ten plays, four of which were stately rhymed tragedies, and the rest comedies in prose and blank verse; the author, also, of various occasional poems, one of which, the *Annus Mirabilis,* was noticeable on its own account as the best poem of current history; the author, moreover, of one express prose-treatise, and of various shorter prose dissertations in the shape of prefaces and the like prefixed

to his separate plays and poems, in which the principles
of literature were discussed in a manner at once
masterly and adapted to the prevailing taste : Dryden
was, on the whole, far more likely to perform well that
part of a laureate's duties which consisted in supervis-
ing and leading the general literature of his age than a
man whose reputation, though justly great, had been
acquired by one continuous effort in the single department of burlesque.   Accordingly, Dryden was promoted
to the post, and Butler was left to finish, on his own
scanty resources, the remaining portion of his *Hudibras*,
varying the occupation by jotting down those scraps of
cynical thought which were found among his posthu-
mous papers, and which show that towards the end of
his days there were other things that he hated and
would have lashed besides Puritanism.   Thus :—

> " 'Tis a strange age we've lived in and a lewd
>   As e'er the sun in all his travels viewed."

Again :

> " The greatest saints and sinners have been made
>   Of proselytes of one another's trade."

Again :

> " Authority is a disease and cure
>   Which men can neither want nor well endure."

And again, with an obvious reference to his own case :—

> " Dame Fortune, some men's titular,
> Takes charge of them without their care,
> Does all their drudgery and work,
> Like fairies, for them in the dark ;
> Conducts them blindfold, and advances
> The naturals by blinder chances ;
> While others by desert and wit
> Could never make the matter hit,
> But still, the better they deserve,
> Are but the abler thought to starve."

Dryden, at the time of his appointment to the laureate-ship, was in his fortieth year. This is worth noting, if we would realize his position among his literary con-temporaries. Of those contemporaries there were some who, as being his seniors, would feel themselves free from all obligations to pay him respect. To octogen-arians like Hobbes and Izaak Walton he was but a boy ; and even from Waller, Milton, Butler, and Marvel, all of whom lived to see him in the laureate's chair, he could only look for that approving recognition, totally distinct from reverence, which men of sixty-five, sixty, and fifty-five, bestow on their full-grown juniors. Such an amount of recognition he seems to have re-ceived from all of them. Butler, indeed, does not seem to have taken very kindly to him; and it stands on record, as Milton's opinion of Dryden's powers about

D

this period, that he thought him "a rhymer but no poet." But Butler, who went about snarling at most things, and was irreverent enough to think the Royal Society itself little better than a humbug, was not the man from whom a laudatory estimate of anybody was to be expected; and, though Milton's criticism is too precious to be thrown away, and will even be found on investigation to be not so far amiss, if the moment at which it was given is duly borne in mind, yet it is, after all, not Milton's opinion of Dryden's general literary capacity, but only his opinion of Dryden's claims to be called a poet. Dryden, on his part, to whose charge any want of veneration for his great literary predecessors cannot be imputed, and whose faculty of appreciating the most various kinds of excellence was conspicuously large, would probably have been more grieved than indignant at this indifference of men like Butler and Milton to his rising fame. He had an unfeigned admiration for the author of *Hudibras;* and there was not a man in England who more profoundly revered the poet of *Paradise Lost,* or more dutifully testified this reverence both by acts of personal attention and by written expressions of allegiance to him while he was yet alive. It would have pained Dryden much, we believe, to know that the great Puritan poet, whom he made it a point of duty to go and see now and then in his solitude, and of whom he is reported to have said, on reading the *Paradise Lost*, "This man cuts us all out, and the ancients too," thought no better of him than that he was a rhymer. But, however he may have felt himself related to those seniors who were vanishing from the stage, or whose literary era was in the past, it was in a conscious spirit of superiority that he confronted the generation of his coevals and juniors, the natural subjects of his laureateship. If we set aside such men as Locke and Barrow, belonging more to other departments than to that of literature proper, there were none of these coevals or juniors who were entitled to dispute his authority. There was the Duke of Buckingham, a year or two older than Dryden, at once the greatest wit and the greatest profligate about Charles's court, but whose attempts in the comic drama were little more than occasional eccentricities. There were the Earls of Dorset and Roscommon, both about Dryden's age, and both cultivated men and respectable versifiers. There was Thomas Sprat, afterwards Bishop of Rochester, and now chaplain to his grace of Buckingham, five years younger than Dryden, his fellow-member in the Royal Society, and with considerable pretensions to literary excellence. There was the witty rake, Sir Charles Sedley, a man of frolic, like Buckingham, some seven years Dryden's junior, and the author of at least three comedies and three tragedies. There was the still more witty rake, Sir George Etherege, of about the same age, the author of two comedies, produced between 1660 and 1670, which, for ease and sprightly fluency, surpassed anything that Dryden had done in the comic style. But "gentle George," as he was called, was incorrigibly lazy; and it did not seem as if the public would get anything more from him. In his place had come another gentleman-writer, young William Wycherley, whose first comedy had been written before Dryden's laureateship, though it was not acted till 1672, and who was already famous as a wit. Of precisely the same age as Wycherley, and with a far greater *quantity* of comic writing in him, whatever might be thought of the quality, was Thomas Shadwell, whose bulky body was a perpetual source of jest against him, though he himself vaunted it as one of his many resemblances to Ben Jonson. The contemporary opinion of these two last-named comic poets, Wycherley and Shadwell, after they came to be better known, is expressed in these lines from a poem of Rochester's :—

> "Of all our modern wits none seem to me
>   Once to have touched upon true comedy
>   But hasty Shadwell and slow Wycherley.
>   Shadwell's unfinished works do yet impart
>   Great proofs of force of Nature, none of Art.
>   With just bold strokes he dashes here and there,
>   Showing great mastery with little care;
>   Scorning to varnish his good touches o'er,
>   To make the fools and women praise the more.

> But Wycherley earns hard whate'er he gains ;
> He wants no judgment, and he spares no pains ;
> He frequently excels, and, at the least,
> Makes fewer faults than any of the rest."

The author of these lines, the notorious Wilmot, Earl of Rochester, was also one of Dryden's literary subjects. He was but twenty-two years of age when Dryden became laureate ; but before ten years of that laureateship were over he had blazed out, in rapid debauchery, his wretchedly-spent life. Younger by three years than Rochester, and also destined to a short life, though more of misery than of crime, was Thomas Otway, of whose six tragedies and four comedies, all produced during the laureateship of Dryden, one at least has taken a place in our dramatic literature, and is read still for its power and pathos. Associated with Otway's name is that of Nat. Lee, more than Otway's match in fury, and who, after a brief career as a tragic dramatist and drunkard, became an inmate of Bedlam. Another writer of tragedy, whose career began with Dryden's laureateship, was John Crowne, "little starched Johnny Crowne," as Rochester calls him, but whom so good a judge as Charles Lamb has thought worthy of commemoration as having written some really fine things. Finally, the list includes a few Nahum Tates, Elkanah Settles, Tom D'Urfeys, and other small celebrities, in whose company we may place Aphra Behn, the poetess.

Doing our best to fancy this cluster of wits and play-writers, in the midst of which, from his appointment to the laureateship in 1670, at the age of thirty-nine, to his deposition from that office in 1688, at the age of fifty-eight, Dryden is historically the principal figure, we can very well see that not one of them all could wrest the dictatorship from him. With an income from various sources, including his salary as laureate and historiographer and his receipts from his engagement with Killigrew's company, amounting in all to about 600*l.* a-year—which, according to Sir Walter Scott's computation, means about 1,800*l.* in our value—he had, during a portion of this time at least, all the means of external respectability in sufficient abundance. His reputation as the first dramatic author of the day was already made; and if, as yet, there were others who had done as well or better as poets out of the dramatic walk, he more than made up for this by the excellence of his prologues and epilogues, and by his readiness and power as a prose-critic of general literature. No one could deny that, though a rather heavy man in private society, and so slow and silent among the wits of the coffee-house that, but for the pleasure of seeing his placid face, the deeply indented leather chair on which he sat would have done as well to represent literature there as his own presence in it, John Dryden was, all in all, the first wit of the age. There was not a Buckingham, nor

an Etherege, nor a Shadwell, nor a starched Johnny
Crowne, of them all, that singly would have dared to
dispute his supremacy. And yet, as will happen, what
his subjects could not dare to do singly, or ostensibly,
some of them tried to compass by cabal and systematic
depreciation on particular points. In fact, Dryden had
to fight pretty hard to maintain his place, and had
to make an example or two of a rebel subject before the
rest were terrified into submission.

He was first attacked in the very field of his greatest
triumphs, the drama. The attack was partly directed
against himself personally, partly against that style of
heroic or rhymed tragedy of which he was the advocate
and representative. There had always been dissenters
from this new fashion ; and among these was the Duke
of Buckingham, who had a natural genius for making fun
of anything. Assisted, it is said, by his chaplain Sprat,
and by Butler, who had already satirized this style of
tragedy by writing a dialogue in which two cats are
made to caterwaul to each other in heroics, the duke had
amused his leisure by preparing a farce in which heroic
plays were held up to ridicule. In the original draft of
the farce Davenant was made the butt under the name
of Bilboa; but, after Davenant's death, the farce was
recast, and Dryden substituted under the name of Bayes.
The plot of this famous farce, *The Rehearsal*, is much
the same as that of Sheridan's *Critic*. The poet Bayes

invites two friends, Smith and Johnson, to be present at
the rehearsal of a heroic play which he is on the point
of bringing out, and the humour consists in the supposed
representation of this heroic play, while Bayes alternately
directs the actors, and expounds the drift of the play
and its beauties to Smith and Johnson, who all the
while are laughing at him, and thinking it monstrous
rubbish.   Conceive a farce like this, written with
amazing cleverness, and full of absurdities, produced in
the very theatre where the echoes of Dryden's last
sonorous heroics were still lingering, and acted by the
same actors; conceive it interspersed with parodies of
well-known passages from Dryden's plays, and with
allusions to characters in those plays; conceive the actor
who played the part of Bayes dressed to look as like
Dryden as possible, instructed by the duke to mimic
Dryden's voice, and using phrases like " i'gad" and
" i'fackins," which Dryden was in the habit of using
in familiar conversation; and an idea may be formed
of the sensation made by *The Rehearsal* in all theatrical circles on its first performance in the winter of
1671.   Its effect, though not immediate, was decisive.
From that time the heroic or rhymed tragedy was
felt to be doomed.   Dryden, indeed, did not at once
recant his opinion in favour of rhymed tragedies; but he
yielded so far to the sentence pronounced against them
as to write only one more of the kind.

Though thus driven out of his favourite style of the rhymed tragedy, he was not driven from the stage. Bound by his agreement with the King's Company to furnish three plays a-year, he continued to make dramatic writing his chief occupation; and almost his sole productions during the first ten years of his laureateship were ten plays. Three of these were prose-comedies; one, a tragi-comedy, in blank verse and prose; one, an opera in rhyme; five, tragedies in blank verse; and one, the rhymed tragedy above referred to. It will be observed that this was at the rate of only one play a-year, whereas, by his engagement, he was to furnish three. The fact was that the company were very indulgent to him, and let him have his full share of the receipts, averaging 300*l.* a-year, in return for but a third of the stipulated work. Notwithstanding this, we find them complaining, in 1679, that Dryden had behaved unhandsomely to them in carrying one of his plays to the other theatre, and so injuring their interests. As, from that year, none of Dryden's plays were produced at the King's Theatre, but all at the Duke's, till 1682, when the two companies were united, it is probable that in that year the bargain made with Killigrew terminated. It deserves notice, by the way, that the so-called "opera" was one entitled *The State of Innocence; or, The Fall of Man*, founded on Milton's *Paradise Lost*, and brought out in 1674-5, immediately

after Milton's death. That this was an equivocal
compliment to Milton's memory Dryden himself lived
to acknowledge. He confessed to Dennis, twenty years
afterwards, that at the time when he wrote that opera
"he knew not half the extent of Milton's excellence."
A striking proof of Dryden's veneration for Milton,
when we consider how high his admiration of Milton
had been even while Milton was alive!

Of these dramatic productions of Dryden during the
first ten years of his laureateship some were very carefully written. Thus *Marriage à-la-mode*, performed in
1672, is esteemed one of his best comedies; and of
the rhymed tragedy, *Aurung-Zebe*, performed in 1675,
he himself says in the Prologue—

> "What verse can do he has performed in this,
> Which he presumes the most correct of his."

The tragedy of *All for Love*, which followed *Aurung-Zebe*,
in 1678, and in which he falls back on blank verse,
is pronounced by many critics to be the very best of all
his dramas; and perhaps none of his plays has been
more read than the *Spanish Friar*, written in 1680. Yet
it may be doubted if in any of these plays Dryden
achieved a degree of immediate success equal to that
which had attended his *Tyrannic Love* and his *Conquest
of Granada*, written before his laureateship. This was
not owing so much to the single blow struck at his
fame by Buckingham's *Rehearsal* as to the growth of

that general spirit of criticism and disaffection which pursues every author after the public have become sufficiently acquainted with his style to expect the good, and look rather for the bad, in what he writes. Thus, we find one critic of the day, Martin Clifford, who was a man of some note, addressing Dryden, a year or two after his laureateship, in this polite fashion : "You do live in as much ignorance and darkness as you did in the womb; your writings are like a Jack-of-all-trades' shop; they have a variety, but nothing of value; and, if thou art not the dullest plant-animal that ever the earth produced, all that I have conversed with are strangely mistaken in thee." This onslaught of Mr. Clifford's is clearly to be regarded as only that gentleman's; but what young Rochester said and thought about Dryden at this time is more likely to have been what was said and thought generally by the critical part of the town.

> " Well sir, 'tis granted : I said Dryden's rhymes
> Were stolen, unequal—nay, dull, many times.
> What foolish patron is there found of his
> So blindly partial to deny me this ?
> But that his plays, embroidered up and down
> With wit and learning, justly pleased the town,
> In the same paper I as freely own.
> Yet, having this allowed, the heavy mass
> That stuffs up his loose volumes must not pass.
> *   *   *   *   *   *

> But, to be just, 'twill to his praise be found
> His excellencies more than faults abound;
> Nor dare I from his sacred temples tear
> The laurel which he best deserves to wear.
>
>   *   *   *   *   *
>
> And may I not have leave impartially
> To search and censure Dryden's works, and try
> If these gross faults his choice pen doth commit
> Proceed from want of judgment or of wit,
> Or if his lumpish fancy doth refuse
> Spirit and grace to his loose slattern muse?"

We have no doubt the opinion thus expressed by the scapegrace young earl was very general. Dryden's own prose disquisitions on the principles of poetry may have helped to diffuse many of those notions of genuine poetical merit by which he was now tried. But, undoubtedly, what most of all tended to expose Dryden's reputation to the perils of criticism was the increasing number of his dramatic competitors and the evident ability of some of them. True, most of those competitors were Dryden's personal friends, and some of the younger of them, as Lee, Shadwell, Crowne, and Tate, were in the habit of coming to him for prologues and epilogues, with which to increase the attractions of their plays. On more than one occasion, too, Dryden clubbed with Lee or Shadwell in the composition of a dramatic piece. But, though thus on a friendly footing with most of his contemporary dramatists, and almost in a fatherly relation to some of them, Dryden found his popularity not the less affected by their competition. In the department of prose comedy, Etherege, whose last and best comedy, *Sir Fopling Flutter*, was produced in 1676, and Wycherley, whose four celebrated comedies were all produced between 1672 and 1677, had introduced a style compared with which Dryden's best comic attempts were but heavy horse-play. Even the hulking Shadwell, who dashed off his comedies as fast as he could write, had a vein of coarse natural humour which Dryden lacked. It was in vain that Dryden tried to keep his pre-eminence against these rivals by increased strength of language, increased intricacy of plot, and an increased use of those indecencies upon which they all relied so much in their efforts to please. One comedy in which Dryden, trusting too confidently to this last element of success, pushed grossness to the utmost conceivable limit, was hissed off the stage. In tragedy, it is true, his position was more firm. But even in this department some niches were cut in the body of his fame. His friend Nat. Lee had produced one or two tragedies displaying a tenderness and a wild force of passion to which Dryden's more masculine genius could not pretend; Crowne had also done one or two things of a superior character; and, though it was not till 1682 that Otway produced his *Venice Preserved*, he had already given evidence of his mastery of dramatic pathos. All this Dryden might have seen without allowing himself to be much disturbed, conscious as he must have been that in general strength he was still superior to all about him, however they might rival him in particulars. The deliberate resolution, however, of Rochester and some other aristocratic leaders of the fashion to make good their criticisms on his writings, by setting up first one and then another of the dramatists of the day as patterns of a higher style of art than his, provoked him out of his composure. To show what he could do, if called upon to defend his rights against pretenders, he made a terrible example of one poor wretch, who had been puffed for the moment into undue popularity. This unfortunate was Elkanah Settle, and the occasion of the attack was a heroic tragedy written by Settle, acted with great success both on the stage and at Whitehall, and published with illustrative woodcuts. On this performance Dryden made a most merciless onslaught in a prose-criticism prefixed to his next published play, tearing Settle's metaphors and grammar to pieces. Settle replied with some spirit, but little effect, and was, in fact, "settled" for ever. Rochester next patronized Crowne and Otway for a time, but soon gave them up, and contented himself with assailing Dryden more directly in such lampoons as we have quoted. In the year 1679, however, suspecting Dryden to have had a share in the authorship of a poem, then circulating in manuscript, in which certain liberties were taken with his name, he caused him to be way-laid and beaten as he was going home one evening through Rose-alley to his house in Gerard-street. The poem, entitled *An Essay on Satire*, is usually printed among Dryden's works; but it remains uncertain whether Dryden was really the author.

` It was fortunate for Dryden and for English literature that, just about this time, when he was beginning to be regarded as a veteran among the dramatists, whose farther services in that department the town could afford to spare, circumstances led him, almost without any wish of his own, into a new path of literature. He was now arrived at the ripe age of fifty years, and, if an inventory had been made of his writings, they would have been found to consist of twenty-one dramas, with a series of critical prose-essays for the most part bound up with these dramas, but nothing in the nature of non-dramatic poetry, except a few occasional pieces, of which the *Annus Mirabilis* was still the chief. Had a discerning critic examined those works with a view to discover in what peculiar vein of verse Dryden, if he abandoned the drama, might still do justice to his powers, he would certainly have selected the vein of reflective satire. Of the most nervous and emphatic lines that could have been quoted from his plays a large proportion would have been found to consist of what may be called *maxim* metrically expressed; while in his dramatic prologues and epilogues, which were always thought among the happiest efforts of his pen, the excellence would have been found to consist in very much the same power of direct didactic declamation applied satirically to the humours, manners, and opinions of the day. Whether any critic, observing all this, would have been bold enough to advise Dryden to take the hint, and quit the drama for satirical, controversial, and didactic poetry, we need not inquire. Circumstances compelled what advice might have failed to bring about. After some twenty years of political stagnation, or rather of political confusion, relieved only by the occasional cabals of leading statesmen, and by rumours of Catholic and Protestant plots, the old Puritan feeling and the general spirit of civil liberty which the Restoration had but pent up within the vitals of England broke forth in a regular and organized form as modern English Whiggism. The controversy had many ramifications; but its immediate phase at that moment was an antagonism of two parties on the question of the succession to the crown after Charles should die—the Tories and Catholics maintaining the rights of the Duke of York as the legal heir, and the Whigs and Protestants rallying, for want of a better man, round Charles's illegitimate son, the handsome and popular Duke of Monmouth, then a puppet in the hands of Shaftesbury, the

recognised leader of the Opposition. Charles himself
was forced by reasons of state to take part with his
brother, and to frown on Monmouth; but this did not
prevent the lords and wits of the time from distributing
themselves pretty equally between the two parties, and
fighting out the dispute with all the weapons of intrigue
and ridicule. Shadwell, Settle, and some other minor
poets, lent their pens to the Whigs, and wrote squibs
and satires in the Whig service. Lee, Otway, Tate, and
others, worked for the Court party. Dryden, as laureate
and Tory, had but one course to take. He plunged into
the controversy with the whole force of his genius; and
in November, 1681, when the nation was waiting for the
trial of Shaftesbury, then a prisoner in the Tower, he
published his satire of *Absalom and Achitophel*, in which,
under the thin veil of a story of Absalom's rebellion
against his father David, the existing political state of
England was represented from the Tory point of view.
Among the characters portrayed in it Dryden had the
satisfaction of introducing his old critic, the Duke of
Buckingham, upon whom he now took ample revenge.

The satire of *Absalom and Achitophel*, than which
nothing finer of the kind had ever appeared in England,
and which indeed surpassed all that could have been
expected even from Dryden at that time, was the first of
a series of polemical or satirical poems the composition
of which occupied the last eight years of his laureateship.

D   P

The Medal, a Satire against Sedition, appeared in March, 1682, as the poet's comment on the popular enthusiasm occasioned by the acquittal of Shaftesbury; *Mac Flecknoe*, in which Shadwell, as poet-in-chief of the Whigs, received a thrashing all to himself, was published in October in the same year; and, a month later, there appeared the so-called *Second Part of Absalom and Achitophel*, written by Nahum Tate, under Dryden's superintendence, and with interpolations from Dryden's pen. In the same avowed character, as literary champion of the government and the party of the Duke of York, Dryden continued to labour during the remainder of the reign of Charles. His *Religio Laici*, indeed, produced early in 1683, and forming a metrical statement of the grounds and extent of his own attachment to the Church of England, can hardly have been destined for immediate political service. But the solitary play which he wrote about this period—a tragedy called *The Duke of Guise* —was certainly intended for political effect, as was also a translation from the French of a work on the history of French Calvinism.

How ill-requited Dryden was for these services appears but too clearly from evidence proving that, at this time, he was in great pecuniary difficulties. At the time when the king's cast-off mistresses were receiving pensions of 10,000*l.* a-year, and when 130,000*l.* or more was squandered every year on secret court-

purposes, Dryden's salary as laureate remained unpaid
for four years ; and when, in consequence of his repeated
solicitations, an order for part-payment of the arrears
was at last issued in May 1684, it was for the miserable
pittance of one quarter's salary, due at midsummer
1680, leaving fifteen quarters, or 750*l.* still in arrears.
It appears, however, from a document published for the
first time by Mr. Bell, that an additional pension of
100*l.* a-year was at this time conferred on Dryden—
that pension to date retrospectively from 1680, and the
arrears to be paid, as convenient, along with the larger
arrears of salary.   How far Dryden benefited by this
nominal increase of his emoluments from government,
or whether any further portion of the arrears was paid
up while Charles continued on the throne, can hardly be
ascertained.   Charles died in February, 1684-5, and
Dryden, as in duty bound, wrote his funeral panegyric.
In this Pindaric, which is entitled *Threnodia Augustalis*,
the poet seems to hint, as delicately as the occasion
would permit, at the limited extent of his pecuniary
obligations to the deceased monarch.

> " As, when the new-born phœnix takes his way
>   His rich paternal regions to survey,
>   Of airy choristers a numerous train
>   Attends his wondrous progress o'er the plain,
>   So, rising from his father's urn,
>   So glorious did our Charles return.

The officious muses came along—
A gay harmonious choir, like angels ever young;
The muse that mourns him now his happy triumph
     sung.
   Even they could thrive in his auspicious reign;
And such a plenteous crop they bore
   Of purest and well-winnowed grain
As Britain never knew before:
   Though little was their hire, and light their gain,
Yet somewhat to their share he threw.
Fed from his hand, they sung and flew,
Like birds of Paradise, that lived on morning dew.
Oh, never let their lays his name forget:
The pension of a prince's praise is great."

If there was any literary man in whose favour James
II., on his accession, might have been expected to relax
his parsimonious habits, it was Dryden. The poet had
praised him and made a hero of him for twenty years,
and had during the last four years been working for
him incessantly. In acknowledgment of these services,
James could not do otherwise than continue him in the
laureateship; but this was all that he seemed inclined to
do. In the new patent issued for the purpose, not only
was there no renewal of the deceased king's private
grant of 100*l.* a-year, but even the annual butt of sherry,
hitherto forming part of the laureate's allowance, was
discontinued, and the salary limited to the precise money
payment of 200*l.* a-year. If, as is probable, the salary

was now more punctually paid than it had been under
Charles, the reduction may have been of less consequence.   In March 1685-6, however, James opened his
purse, and, by fresh letters patent, conferred on Dryden
a permanent additional salary of 100*l.* a-year, thus raising
the annual income of the laureateship to 300*l.*   The explanation of this unusual piece of liberality on the part
of James has been generally supposed to lie in the fact
that, in the course of the preceding year, Dryden had
proved the thorough and unstinted character of his
loyalty by declaring himself a convert to the king's
religion.   That Dryden's passing over to the Catholic
church was contemporaneous with the increase of his
pension is a fact; but what may have been the exact
relation between the two events is a question which one
ought to be cautious in answering.   Lord Macaulay's
view of the case is harsh enough.   " Finding," he says,
" that, if he continued to call himself a Protestant, his
" services would be overlooked, he declared himself a
" Papist.   The king's parsimony instantly relaxed
" Dryden was gratified with a pension of one hundred
" pounds a-year, and was employed to defend his new
" religion both in prose and verse."   Sir Walter Scott's
view is more charitable, and, we believe, more just.   He
regards Dryden's conversion as having been, in the main,
honest to the extent professed by himself, though his
situation and expectations may have co-operated to effect

it.　In support of this view Mr. Bell points out the fact that the pension granted by James was, after all, only a renewal of a pension granted by Charles, and which, not being secured by letters patent, had lapsed on that king's decease.　Dryden, it is also to be remarked, remained sufficiently staunch to his new faith during the rest of his life, and seems even to have felt a kind of comfort in it.　Probably, therefore, the true state of the case is that conformity to the Catholic religion, at the time when Dryden embraced it, was the least troublesome mode of systematizing for his own mind a number of diverse speculations, personal and political, that were then perplexing him, and that, afterwards, in consequence of the very obloquy which his change of religion drew upon him from all quarters, he hugged his new creed more closely, so as to coil round him, for the first time in his life, a few threads of private theological conviction.　This is not very different from the notion entertained by Sir Walter Scott, who argues that Dryden's conversion was not, except in outward profession, a change from Protestant to Catholic belief, but rather, like that of Gibbon, a choice of Catholicism as the most convenient resting-place for a mind tired of Pyrrhonism, and disposed to cut short the process of emancipation from it by taking a decisive step at once.

At all events, Dryden showed sufficient polemical energy in the service of the religion which he had adopted. He became James's literary factotum, the defender in prose and in verse of the worst measures of his rule ; and he was ready to do battle with Stilling-fleet, Burnet, or anyone else that dared to use a pen on the other side. As if to make the highest display of his powers as a versifier at a time when his character as a man was lowest, he published in 1687 his controversial allegory of *The Hind and the Panther*, by far the largest and most elaborate of his original poems. In this poem, in which the various churches and sects of the day figure as beasts—the Church of Rome as a " milk-white hind," innocent and unchanged ; the Church of England as a " panther," spotted, but still beautiful ; Presbyterianism as a haggard ugly " wolf ; " Independency as the " bloody bear ; " the Baptists as the "bristled boar ; " the Unitarians as the " false fox ; " the Freethinkers as the " buffoon ape ; " and the Quakers as the timid " hare "—Dryden showed that, whatever his new faith had done for him, it had not changed his genius for satire. In fact, precisely as during James's reign Dryden appears personally as a solitary giant, warring on the wrong side, so this poem remains as the sole literary work of any excellence in which the wretched spirit of that reign is fully represented. Dryden himself, as if he had thrown all his force into it, wrote little else in verse till the year 1688, when, on the occasion of the birth of James's son, afterwards the

Pretender, he made himself the spokesman of the exulting Catholics, and published his *Britannia Rediviva.*

> "See how the venerable infant lies
>   In early pomp; how through the mother's eyes
>   The father's soul, with an undaunted view,
>   Looks out, and takes our homage as his due.
>   See on his future subjects how he smiles,
>   Nor meanly flatters, nor with craft beguiles;
>   But with an open face, as on his throne,
>   Assures our birthrights, and secures his own."

Within a few months after these lines were written,
the father, the mother, and the baby, were out of
England, Dutch William was king, and the Whigs had
it all to themselves.   Dryden, of course, had to give up
the laureateship; and, as William had but a small
choice of poets, Shadwell was put in his place.

The concluding period of Dryden's career, extending
from the Revolution to his death in 1701, exhibits him
as a Tory patriarch lingering in the midst of a Whig
generation, and still, despite the change of dynasty, retaining his literary pre-eminence.   For a while, of course,
he was under a cloud; but after it had passed away he
was at liberty to make his own terms with the public.
The country could have no literature except what he
and such as he chose to furnish.   Locke, Sir William
Temple, and others, indeed, were now in a position to
bring forward speculations smothered during the previous

reigns, and to scatter seeds that might spring up in new literary forms. Burnet, Tillotson, and others might represent Whiggism in the Church. But all the especially literary men whose services were available at the beginning of the new reign were men who, whatever might be their voluntary relations to the new order of things, had been more or less trained in the school of the Restoration, and accustomed to the supremacy of Dryden. The Earl of Rochester, the Earl of Roscommon, the Duke of Buckingham, Etherege, and poor Otway, were dead; but Shadwell, Settle, Lee, Crowne, Tate, Wycherley, the Earl of Dorset, Tom D'Urfey, and Sir Charles Sedley, were still alive. Shadwell, coarse and fat as ever, enjoyed the laureateship till his death in 1692, when Nahum Tate was appointed to succeed him. Settle had degenerated in the City showman. Lee, liberated from Bedlam, continued to write tragedies till April 1692, when he tumbled over a bulk going home drunk at night through Clare Market, and was killed or stifled among the snow. "Little starched Johnny Crowne" kept up the respectability of his character. Wycherley lived as a man of fashion about town, and wrote no more. Sedley and the Earl of Dorset were also idle; and Tom D'Urfey made small witticisms, and called them "pills to purge melancholy." Among such men Dryden, so long as he cared to be seen among them, held necessarily his old place. Nor were there any of

the younger men, as yet known, in whom the critics
recognised, or who recognised in themselves, any title
to renounce allegiance to the ex-laureate.   Thomas
Southerne had begun his prolific career as a dramatist in
1682, when Dryden furnished him with a prologue to
his first play; but, though after the Revolution he made
more money by his dramas than ever Dryden had made
by his, he was ashamed to admit the fact to Dryden
himself.   Matthew Prior, twenty-four years of age at the
Revolution, had made his first literary appearance before
it, in no less important a character than that of one of
Dryden's political antagonists; but, though *The Town
and Country Mouse* had been a decided hit, and Dryden
himself was said to have winced under it, no one pretended that the author was anything more than a
clever young man who had sat in Dryden's company and
turned his opportunities to account.   Five years after
the Revolution, Congreve produced his first comedy at
the age of twenty-four; but it was Congreve's greatest
boast in after life that that comedy had won him the
warm praises of Dryden, and laid the foundation of the
extraordinary friendship which subsisted between them
during Dryden's last years, when they used to walk
together and dine together as father and son.   During
these last years Dryden, had he been willing to see
merit in any other comedies than those of his young
friend Congreve, might have hailed his equal in Van-

brugh, and his superior in Farquhar, then beginning to write for the stage. Among their coevals, destined to some distinction, he might have marked Colley Cibber, Nicholas Rowe, and John Philips, the pleasing parodist of Milton. Of the epics of Blackmore he had quite enough, at least three of those performances having been given to the world before Dryden died. At the time of Dryden's death his kinsman, Jonathan Swift, was thirty-three years of age; Richard Steele was thirty; Daniel Defoe was thirty; Addison was twenty-nine; Shaftes-bury, the essayist, was twenty-nine; Bolingbroke was twenty-two; and Parnell, the poet, twenty-one. With these men a new literary movement was to take its origin; but they had hardly yet begun their work; and there was not one of them, Swift excepted, that would not, in the height of his subsequent fame, have been proud to acknowledge his obligations to Dryden. Alexander Pope, the next Englishman that was to take a place in general literature as high as that occupied by Dryden, had been born only in the year of the Revolution, and was consequently but a precocious boy of thirteen when Dryden left the scene. *Virgilium tantum vidit*, as he used himself to say.

Living, a hale patriarch, among these newer men, Dryden partly influenced them, and was partly influenced by them. On the one hand, it was from his chair in Will's Coffee-house that those literary decrees were issued which still ruled the judgment of the town; and for a young author, on visiting Will's, to receive a pinch from Dryden's snuff-box was equivalent to his formal admission into that society of wits. On the other hand, the times were so changed and the men were so changed that Dryden, dictator though he was, had to yield in some points, and defend himself in others. His cousin Swift, whom he had offended by an unfavourable judgment given in private on some of his poems, was the only man who would have made a general attack upon his literary reputation; but the moral character of his writings was a subject on which adverse criticism was likely to be more general. At first, indeed, there was little perceptible improvement in the moral tone of the literature of the Revolution, as compared with that of the Restoration—the elder dramatists, such as Shadwell, still writing in the fashion to which they had been accustomed, and the younger ones, such as Congreve and Vanbrugh, deeming it a point of honour to be as immoral as their predecessors. In the course of a few years, however, what with the influence of a Whig court, what with other causes, a more delicate taste crept in, and people became ashamed of what their fathers had delighted in. Dryden lived to see the beginnings of this important change, and, with many expressions of regret for his own past delinquencies in this respect, to welcome the appearance of a purer literature.

Those of Dryden's writings which were produced during the twelve years of his life subsequent to the Revolution constitute an important part of his literary remains, not merely in point of bulk, but also in respect of a certain general peculiarity of their character. They may be described as for the most part belonging to the department of pure, as distinct from that of controversial, literature. Dryden did not indeed wholly abandon satire and controversy after the Revolution; but his aim after that period seemed rather to be to produce such literature as would at once be acceptable to the public and earn for himself most money with the least trouble. Deprived of his laureateship, and so rendered almost entirely dependent on his pen at a time when age was creeping upon him and the expenses of his family were greater than ever, he was obliged to make considerations of economy paramount in his choice of work. As was natural, he fell back at first on the drama; and his five last plays, two of which are tragedies, one an opera, and two comedies, were all produced between 1689 and 1694. The profits of these dramas, however, were insufficient; and he was obliged to eke them out by all those devices of dedication to private noblemen, execution of literary commissions for elegiac poems, and the like, which then formed part of the professional author's means of livelihood. Sums of 50*l.*, 100*l.*, and even, in one or two cases, 500*l.*, were earned by Dryden in this disagreeable

way from earls, squires, and clubs of gentlemen. His
poem of *Eleonora* was a 500*l.* commission, executed for
the Earl of Abingdon, who wanted a poem in memory
of his deceased wife, and, without knowing anything of
Dryden personally, applied to him to write it, just as
now, in a similar case, a commission might be given to
a popular sculptor for a *post mortem* statue. In spite of
the utmost allowance for the custom of the time, no one
knowing the circumstances, can read the poem now,
without disgust ; and it does show a certain lowness of
mind in Dryden to have been able, under any pressure
of necessity, to write for hire such extravagan s as that
poem contains respecting a person he had never seen.
Far more honourable were Dryden's earnings by work
done for Jacob Tonson, the publisher. His dealings
with Tonson had begun before the Revolution ; but
after the Revolution Tonson was his mainstay. First
came several volumes of miscellanies, consisting of
select poems, published and unpublished, with scraps of
prose and translation. Then, catching at the hint
furnished by the success of some of the scraps of translation from the Latin and Greek poets, Dryden and
Tonson found it mutually advantageous to prosecute
that vein. Juvenal and Persius were translated under
Dryden's care ; and in 1697, after three years of labour,
he gave to the world his completed translation of *Virgil*.
Looking about for a task to succeed this, he undertook

to furnish Tonson with so many thousands of lines of narrative verse, to be published under the title of *Fables.* Where the fables came from Tonson did not care, provided they would sell; and Dryden, with his rapid powers of versification, soon produced versions of some tales of Chaucer and Boccaccio which answered the purpose exceedingly well.   They were printed in 1699.   Of the other poems written by Dryden in his last years his *Alexander's Feast* is the most celebrated.   He continued his literary labours till within a few days of his death, which happened on the 1st of May, 1701.

When we inquire what it is that makes Dryden's name so important as to entitle it to rank, as it seems to do, the fifth in the series of great English poets after Chaucer, Spenser, Shakespeare, and Milton, we find that it is nothing else than the fact, brought out in the preceding sketch, that, steadily and industriously, for a period of forty-two years, he kept in the front of the national literature, such as it then was.   It is because he represents the entire literary development of the Restoration—it is because he fills up the whole interval between 1658 and 1701, thus connecting the age of Puritanism and Milton with the age of the Queen Anne wits—that we give him such a place in such a list.   The reason is a chronological one, rather than one of strict comparison of personal merits.   Though we place Dryden fifth in the list, after Chaucer, Spenser, Shakespeare, and

Milton, it is not necessarily because we regard him as the co-equal of those men in genius; it is only because, passing onward in time, we find his the next name of very distinguished magnitude after theirs. Personally there is no one that would compare Dryden with Shakespeare or Milton; and there are not many now that would compare him with Chaucer or Spenser. On the whole, if the estimate is one of general intellectual strength, he takes rank only with the first of the second class, as with the Jonsons, the Fletchers, and others of the Elizabethan age; while, if the estimate have regard to genuine poetic or imaginative power, he sinks below even these. Yet, if historical reasons only are regarded, Dryden has perhaps a better right to his place in the list than any of the others. At least as strictly as Chaucer is the representative of the English literature of the latter half of the fourteenth century, far more strictly than Spenser and Shakespeare are the representatives of the literature of their times, and in a more broad and obvious manner than Milton is the literary representative of the Commonwealth, Dryden represents the literary activity of the reigns of Charles II. and James II., and of the greater part of that of William III. Davenant, Butler, Waller, Etherege, Otway, Wycherley, Southerne, Prior, and Congreve, are names leading us over the same period, and illustrating perhaps more exquisitely than Dryden some of its individual characteristics; but for a solid representative of the period as a whole, resuming in himself all its more prominent characteristics in one substantial aggregate, we are obliged to take Dryden. Twelve years of his literary life he laboured as a strong junior among the Davenants, the Butlers, and the Wallers, qualifying himself to set them aside; eighteen years more were spent in acknowledged lordship over the Ethereges, Otways, and Wycherleys, who occupied the middle of the period; and during the twelve concluding years he was a patriarch among the Southernes, and Priors, and Congreves, in whose lives the period wove itself into the next.

And yet, personally as well as historically, Dryden is a man of no mean importance. Not only is he the largest figure in one era of our literature; he is a very considerable figure also in our literature as a whole. To begin with the most obvious, but at the same time not the least noteworthy, of his claims, the *quantity* of his contributions to our literature was large. He was a various and voluminous writer. In Scott's collected edition of his works they fill seventeen octavo volumes. About seven of these volumes consist of dramas, with accompanying prefaces and dedications, the number of dramas being in all twenty-eight. Two volumes more embrace the polemical poems, the satires, and the poems of contemporary historical allusion, written chiefly between 1681 and 1683. One volume is filled with

D   Q

odes, songs, and lyrical pieces, written at various times.
The Fables, or Metrical Tales, redacted in his old age
from Chaucer and Boccaccio, occupy a volume and a
half. Three volumes and a half are devoted to the
translations from the classic poets, including the Translation of Virgil. The remaining two volumes consist of
miscellaneous prologues, epilogues, and witty pieces of
verse, and of miscellaneous prose-writings, original and
translated, including the critical Essay on Dramatic
Poetry. Considered as a whole, the matter of the
seventeen volumes is a goodly contribution from one
man as respects both extent and variety. Spread over
forty-two years, it does not argue that excessive industry
which Scott, of all men in the world, has found in it;
but it fairly entitles Dryden to take his place among
those writers who deserve regard for the quantity of
their writings, in addition to whatever regard they may
be entitled to on the score of quality. And it is a fact
worth noting, and remarked by Scott more than once,
that most writers who have taken a high place in literature have been voluminous—have not only written well,
but also written much. Moreover there are two ways
of writing much. One may write much and variously,
or one may write much all of one kind. Dryden was
various as well as voluminous.

Of all that Dryden wrote, however, there is but
a comparatively small portion that has won for itself

a permanent place in our literature; and in this he differs from other writers that have been equally voluminous. It is indeed a significant fact about Dryden that the proportion of that part of his matter which survives, or deserves to survive, to that part which was squandered away on the age it was first written for, and there ended, is unusually small. In Shakespeare there is very little that is felt to be of such inferior quality as not to be worth reading in due time and place. In Milton there is, if we consider only his poetry, still less. All Chaucer, almost, is felt to be worth preservation by those who like Chaucer; all Wordsworth, almost, by those who like Wordsworth. But, except for library purposes, there is no admirer of Dryden that would care to save more than a small select portion of what he wrote. His satires and polemical poems; one or two of his odes; his Translation of Virgil; his fables; one of his comedies, and one of his tragedies, by way of specimen of his dramatic powers; a complete set of his prologues, for the sake of their allusions to contemporary manners and humours; and a few pieces of his prose, to show his style of criticism :—these would together form a collection not much more than a fourth part of the whole, and which would require to be yet farther winnowed, were the purpose to leave only what is sterling and in Dryden's best manner. Mr. Bell's edition, which comprise in three volumes all Dryden's original non-dramatic poetry, and the best collection of his prologues and epilogues yet made, is itself a surfeit of matter. It is such an edition of Dryden as ought to be included in a series of the English poets intended to be complete; but even in it there is more of dross than of ore.

What is the reason of this? How is it that in Dryden the proportion of what is now rubbish to what is still precious as a literary possession is so much greater than in most other writers of great celebrity? There are two reasons for it. The first is, that originally, and in its own nature, much of the matter that Dryden put forth was not of a kind for which his genius was fitted. Whatever his own imagination constructed on the large scale was mean and conventional. Wherever, as in his translations of Virgil and his imitations of Chaucer and Boccaccio, he employed his powers of language and verse in refurbishing matter invented by others, the poetical substance of his writings is valuable; but the sheer produce of his own imagination, as in his dramas, is in general such stuff as nature disowns and no creature can take pleasure in. There is no fine power of dramatic story, no exquisite invention of character or circumstance, no truth to nature in ideal landscape: at the utmost, there is conventional dramatic situation, with an occasional flash of splendid imagery such as may be struck out in the heat of heroic declamation. Thus—

> "I am as free as Nature first made man,
> Ere the base laws of servitude began,
> When wild in woods the noble savage ran."

Dryden's natural powers, as all his critics have remarked, lay not so much in the imaginative as in the didactic, the declamatory, and the ratiocinative. What Johnson claims for him, and what seems to have been claimed for him in his own lifetime, was the credit of being one of the best reasoners in verse that ever wrote. Lord Macaulay means very much the same thing when he calls Dryden a great "critical poet," and the founder of the "critical school of English poetry." Probably Milton meant something of the kind when he said that Dryden was a rhymer, but no poet. It was in declamatory and didactic rhyme, with all that could consist with it, that Dryden excelled. It was in the metrical utterance of weighty sentences, in the metrical conduct of an argument, in vehement satirical invective, and in such passages of lyric passion as depended for their effect on rolling grandeur of sound, that he was pre-eminently great. Even his imagination worked more powerfully, and his perceptions of physical circumstance became keener and truer, under the influence of polemical rage, the pursuit of terse maxim, or the passion for sonorous declamation. Thus—

> "And every shekel which he can receive
> Shall cost a limb of his prerogative."

Or, in his character of Shaftesbury,—

> " Of these the false Achitophel was first :
> A name to all succeeding ages curst ;
> For close designs and crooked counsels fit ;
> Sagacious, bold, and turbulent of wit ;
> Restless, unfixed in principles and place ;
> In power unpleased, impatient of disgrace ;
> A fiery soul, which, working out its way,
> Fretted the pigmy body to decay,
> And o'er-informed the tenement of clay.
> A daring pilot in extremity,
> Pleased with the danger when the waves went high,
> He sought the storms ; but, for a calm unfit,
> Would steer too nigh the sands, to boast his wit.
> Great wits are sure to madness near allied,
> And thin partitions do their bounds divide."

Or, in the lines which he sent to Tonson the publisher
as a specimen of what he could do in the way of portrait-
painting if Tonson did not send him supplies—

> " With leering looks, bull-faced, and freckled fair,
> With two left legs, and Judas-coloured hair,
> And frowzy pores that taint the ambient air."

And, again, in almost every passage in the noble ode on
Alexander's Feast, *e.g.*—

> " With ravished ears
> The monarch hears ;
> Assumes the god,
> Affects to nod,
> And seems to shake the spheres."

In satire, in critical disquisition, in aphoristic verse, or in lyrical grandiloquence, Dryden was in his natural element; and one reason why, of all the matter of his voluminous works, so small a portion is of permanent literary value, is that, in his attempts after literary variety, he could not or would not restrict himself within these proper limits of his genius.

But, besides this, Dryden was a slovenly worker within his own field. Even of what he could do best he did little continuously in a thoroughly careful manner. In his best poem there are not twenty consecutive lines without some logical incoherence, some confusion of metaphor, some inaccuracy of language, or some evident strain of the meaning for the sake of the metre. His strength lies in passages and weighty interspersed lines, not in whole poems. Even in Dryden's lifetime this complaint was made. It was hinted at in *The Rehearsal;* Rochester speaks of Dryden's " slattern muse ;" and Blackmore, who criticised Dryden in his old age, expresses the common opinion distinctly and deliberately—

> " Into the melting-pot when Dryden comes,
> What horrid stench will rise, what noisome fumes !
> How will he shrink, when all his lewd allay
> And wicked mixture shall be purged away !
> When once his boasted heaps are melted down,
> A chest-full scarce will yield one sterling crown ;
> But what remains will be so pure, 'twill bear
> The examination of the most severe."

This is true, though it was Blackmore who said it.

Dryden's slovenliness, however, consisted not so much in a disposition to spare pains as in a constitutional robustness which rendered artistic perfection all but impossible to him even when he laboured hardest to attain it. One's notion of Dryden is that he was originally a *robust* man, who, when he first engaged in poetry, could produce nothing better than strong stanzas of rather wóoden sound and mechanism, but who, by perseverance and continual work, drilled his genius into higher susceptibility and a conscious aptitude and mastery in certain directions, so that, the older he grew, he became mellower, more musical, and more imaginative, what had been robustness at first having by long practice been subdued into flexibility and nerve. It is stated of Dryden that, in his earlier life at least, he used, as a preparation for writing, to induce on himself an artificial state of languor by taking medicine or letting blood. The trait is characteristic. Dryden's whole literary career was a metaphor of it. Had he died before 1670, or even before 1681, when his *Annus Mirabilis* was still his most ambitious production, he would have been remembered as little more than a robust versifier; but, living as he did till 1701, he performed work which has entitled him to rank among English poets. As a contributor to the actual body of our literature, and as a man who produced by his influence a lasting effect on its literary methods, Dryden's place is certainly high.

DEAN SWIFT.

DEAN SWIFT.[1]

IN dividing the history of English literature into periods it is customary to take the interval between the year 1688 and the year 1727 as constituting one of those periods. This interval includes the reigns of William III., Anne, and George I. If we do not bind ourselves too precisely to the year 1727 as closing the period, the division is proper enough. There *are* characteristics about the time thus marked out which distinguish it from previous and from subsequent portions of our literary history. Dryden, Locke, and some other notabilities of the Restoration, lived into this period, and may be regarded as partly belonging to it; but the names more peculiarly representing it are those of Swift, Burnet, Addison, Steele, Pope, Shaftesbury, Gay, Arbuthnot, Atterbury, Prior, Parnell, Bolingbroke, Congreve, Vanbrugh, Farquhar, Rowe, Defoe, and Cibber. The names in this cluster disperse

[1] *British Quarterly Review*, October 1854.—1. "The English Humourists of the Eighteenth Century." A Series of Lectures. By W. M. Thackeray. London: 1853. 2. "The Life of Swift." By Sir Walter Scott. Edinburgh: 1848.

themselves over the three reigns which the period
includes, some of them having already been known as
early as the accession of William, while others survived
the first George and continued to add to their celebrity
during the reign of his successor ; but the most brilliant
portion of the period was from 1702 to 1714, when
Queen Anne was on the throne.   Hence the name of
" Wits of Queen Anne's reign," commonly applied to the
writers of the whole period.

A while ago this used to be spoken of as the Golden
or Augustan age of English literature.   We do not talk
in that manner now.   We feel that when we get among
the authors of the times of Queen Anne and the first
George we are among very pleasant and very clever
men, but by no means among giants.   In coming down
to this period from those going before it, we have an
immediate sensation of having left the region of "greatness" behind us.   We still find plenty of good writing,
characterized by certain qualities of trimness, artificial
grace, and the like, to a degree not before attained ; here
and there also, we discern something like real power
and strength, breaking through the prevailing element ;
but, on the whole, there is an absence of what, except
by a compromise of language, could be called "great."
It is the same whether we regard largeness of imaginative
faculty, loftiness of moral spirit, or vigour of speculative
capacity, as principally concerned in imparting the

character of "greatness" to literature. What of genius in the ideal survived the seventeenth century in England contented itself with nice little imaginations of scenes and circumstances connected with the artificial life of the time; the moral quality most in repute was kindliness or courtesy; and speculation did not go beyond that point where thought retains the form either of ordinary good sense, or of keen momentary wit. No sooner, in fact, do we pass the time of Milton than we feel that we have done with the sublimities. A kind of lumbering largeness does remain in the intellectual gait of Dryden and his contemporaries, as if the age still wore the armour of the old literary forms, though not at home in it; but in Pope's days even the affectation of the "great" had ceased. Not slowly to build up a grand poem of continuous ideal action, not quietly and at leisure to weave forth tissues of fantastic imagery, not perseveringly and laboriously to prosecute one track of speculation and bring it to a close, not earnestly and courageously to throw one's whole soul into a work of moral agitation and reform, was now what was regarded as natural in literature. On the contrary, he was a wit, or a literary man, who, living in the midst of the social bustle, or on the skirts of it, could throw forth in the easiest manner little essays, squibs, and *jeux d'esprit*, pertinent to the rapid occasions of the hour, and never tasking the mind too long or too much. This was the time when that great distinction between Whiggism and Toryism which for a century-and-a-half has existed in Great Britain as a kind of permanent social condition, affecting the intellectual activity of all natives from the moment of their birth, first began to be practically operative. It has, on the whole, been a wretched thing for the mind of England to have had this necessity of being either a Whig or a Tory put so prominently before it. Perhaps, in all times, some similar necessity of taking one side or the other in some current form of controversy has afflicted the leading minds, and tormented the more genial among them; but we question if ever in this country in previous times there was a form of controversy, so little to be identified, in real reason, with the one only true controversy between good and evil, and so capable, therefore, of breeding confusion and mischief, when so identified in practice, as this poor controversy of Whig and Tory which came in with the Revolution. To be called upon to be either a Puritan or a Cavalier— there was some possibility of complying with *that* call and still leading a tolerably free and large intellectual life; though possibly it was one cause of the rich mental development of the Elizabethan era that the men of that time were exempt from any personal obligation of attending even to this distinction. But to be called upon to be either a Whig or a Tory—why, how on earth can one retain any of the larger humanities about him if society is to hold him by the neck between two chairs such as these, pointing alternately to the one and to the other, and incessantly asking him on which of the two he means to sit? Into a mind trained to regard adhesiveness to one or other of these chairs as the first rule of duty or of prudence what thoughts of any high interest can find their way? Or, if any such do find their way, how are they to be adjusted to so mean a rule? Now-a-days, our higher spirits solve the difficulty by kicking both chairs down, and plainly telling society that they will not bind themselves to sit on either, or even on both put together. Hence partly it is that, in recent times, we have had renewed specimens of the "great" or "sublime" in literature—the poetry, for example, of a Byron, a Wordsworth, or a Tennyson. But in the interval between 1688 and 1727 there was not one wit alive whom society let off from the necessity of being, and declaring himself to be, either a Whig or a Tory. Constitutionally, and by circumstances, Pope was the man who could have most easily obtained the exemption; but even Pope professed himself a Tory. Addison and Steele were Whigs. In short, every literary man was bound, by the strongest of all motives, to keep in view, as a permanent fact qualifying his literary undertakings, the distinction between Whiggism and Toryism, and to give to at least a considerable part of his writings the character of pamphlets or essays in the service of his party. To minister by the pen to the occasions of Whiggism and Toryism was, therefore, the main business of the wits both in prose and verse. Out of those occasions of ministration there of course arose personal quarrels, and these furnished fresh opportunities to the men of letters. Critics of previous writings could be satirized and lampooned, and thus the circle of subjects was widened. Moreover, there was abundant matter, capable of being treated consistently with either Whiggism or Toryism, in the social foibles and peculiarities of the day, as we see in the *Tatler* and the *Spectator*. Nor could a genial mind like that of Steele, a man of taste and fine thought like Addison, and an intellect so keen, exquisite, and sensitive as that of Pope, fail to variegate and surround all the duller and harder literature thus called into being with more lasting touches of the humorous, the fanciful, the sweet, the impassioned, the meditative, and the ideal. Thus from one was obtained the character of a *Sir Roger de Coverley*, from another a *Vision of Mirza*, and from the third a *Windsor Forest*, an *Epistle of Héloïse*, and much else that delights us still. After all, however, it remains true that the period of English literature now in question, whatever admirable characteristics it may possess, exhibits a remarkable deficiency of what, with recollections of former periods to guide us in our use of epithets, we should call great or sublime.

With the single exception of Pope, and that exception made from deference to the peculiar position of Pope as the poet or metrical artist of his day, the greatest name in the history of English literature during the early part of last century is that of Swift. In certain fine and deep qualities, Addison and Steele, and perhaps Farquhar, excelled him, just as in the succeeding generation Goldsmith had a finer vein of genius than was to be found in Johnson with all his massiveness; but in natural brawn and strength, in original energy, force, and imperiousness of brain, he excelled them all. It was about the year 1702, when he was already thirty-five years of age, that this strangest specimen of an Irishman, or of an Englishman born in Ireland, first attracted attention in London literary circles. The scene of his first appearance was Button's coffee-house : the witnesses were Addison, Ambrose Philips, and other wits belonging to Addison's little senate, who used to assemble there.

"They had for several successive days observed a strange clergyman come into the coffee-house, who seemed utterly unacquainted with any of those who frequented it, and whose custom it was to lay his hat down on a table, and walk backward and forward at a good pace for half an hour or an hour, without speaking to any mortal, or seeming in the least to attend to anything that was going forward there. He then used to take up his hat, pay his money at the bar, and walk away without opening his lips. After having observed

this singular behaviour for some time, they concluded
him to be out of his senses; and the name that he went
by among them was that of 'the mad parson.' This
made them more than usually attentive to his motions;
and one evening, as Mr. Addison and the rest were
observing him, they saw him cast his eyes several times
on a gentleman in boots, who seemed to be just come
out of the country, and at last advance towards him as
intending to address him. They were all eager to hear
what this dumb mad parson had to say, and immediately
quitted their seats to get near him. Swift went up to
the country gentleman, and in a very abrupt manner,
without any previous salute, asked him, 'Pray, sir,
do you remember any good weather in the world?' The
country gentleman, after staring a little at the singularity
of his manner, and the oddity of the question, answered
'Yes, sir. I thank God I remember a great deal of good
weather in my time.' 'That is more,' said Swift, 'than
I can say; I never remember any weather that was not
too hot or too cold, too wet or too dry; but, however
God Almighty contrives it, at the end of the year 'tis all
very well.' Upon saying this, he took up his hat, and
without uttering a syllable more, or taking the least
notice of anyone, walked out of the coffee-house; leaving
all those who had been spectators of this odd scene
staring after him, and still more confirmed in the opinion
of his being mad."—*Dr. Sheridan's Life of Swift, quoted
in Scott's Life.*

If the company present had had sufficient means of
information, they would have found that the mad
parson with the harsh, swarthy features, and eyes

"azure as the heavens," whose oddities thus amused them, was Jonathan Swift, then clergyman of Laracor, a rural parish in the diocese of Meath in Ireland. They would have found that he was an Irishman by birth, though of pure English descent; that he could trace a relationship to Dryden; that, having been born after his father's death, he had been educated, at the expense of his relatives, at Trinity College, Dublin; that, leaving Ireland in his twenty-second year, with but a sorry character from the College authorities, he had been received as a humble dependent into the family of Sir William Temple, at Sheen and Moorpark, near London, that courtly Whig and ex-ambassador being distantly connected with his mother's family; that here, while acting as Sir William's secretary, amanuensis, librarian, and what not, he had begun to write verses and other trifles, some of which he had shown to Dryden, who had told him in reply that they were sad stuff, and that he would never be a poet; that still, being of a restless, ambitious temper, he had not given up hopes of obtaining introduction into public employment in England through Sir William Temple's influence; that, at length, at the age of twenty-eight, despairing of anything better, he had quarrelled with Sir William, returned to Ireland, taken priest's orders, and settled in a living; and that again, disgusted with Ireland and his prospects in that country, he had come back to Moorpark, and resided there till

.1699, when Sir William's death had obliged him finally to return to Ireland, and accept first a chaplaincy to Lord Justice Berkeley, and then his present living in the diocese of Meath.   If curious about the personal habits of this restless Irish parson, they might have found that he had already won the reputation of an eccentric in his own parish and district: performing his parochial duties when at home with scrupulous care, yet by his language and manners often shocking all ideas of clerical decorum and begetting a doubt as to his sincerity in the religion he professed; boisterous, fierce, overbearing, and insulting to all about him, yet often doing acts of real kindness; exact and economical in his management of his income to the verge of actual parsimony, yet sometimes spending money freely, and never without pensioners living on his bounty.   They would have found that he was habitually irritable, and that he was subject to a recurring giddiness of the head, or vertigo, which he had brought on, as he thought himself, by a surfeit of fruit while he was staying with Sir William Temple at Sheen.   And, what might have been the best bit of gossip of all, they would have found that, though unmarried, and entertaining a most unaccountable and violent aversion to the very idea of marriage, he had taken over to reside with him, or close to his neighbourhood, in Ireland, a certain young and beautiful girl, named Hester Johnson, with whom he had formed

an acquaintance in Sir William Temple's house, where
she had been brought up, and where, though she passed
as a daughter of Sir William's steward, she was believed
to be, in reality, a natural daughter of Sir William himself. They would have found that his relations to this
girl, whom he had himself educated from her childhood
at Sheen and Moorpark, were of a very singular and
puzzling kind; that on the one hand she was devotedly
attached to him, and on the other he cherished a passionate affection for her, wrote and spoke of her as his
" Stella," and liked always to have her near him ; yet
that a marriage between them seemed not to be thought
of by either; and that, in order to have her near him
without giving rise to scandal, he had taken the precau-
tion to bring over an elderly maiden lady, called Mrs.
Dingley, to reside with her as a companion, and was
most careful to be in her society only when this Mrs.
Dingley was present.

There was mystery and romance enough, therefore,
about the wild, black-browed Irish parson, who attracted
the regards of the wits in Button's coffee-house. What
had brought him there ? That was partly a mystery
too ; but the mystery would have been pretty well
solved if it had been known that, uncouth-looking
clerical lout as he was, he was an author like the rest of
them, having just written a political pamphlet which
was making or was to make a good deal of noise in the

world, and having at that moment in his pocket at least one other piece which he was about to publish. The political pamphlet was an *Essay on the Civil Discords in Athens and Rome,* having an obvious bearing on certain dissensions then threatening to break up the Whig party in Great Britain. It was received as a vigorous piece of writing on the ministerial side, and was ascribed by some to Lord Somers, and by others to Burnet. Swift had come over to claim it, and to see what it and his former connexion with Temple could do for him among the leading Whigs. For the truth was, an ambition equal to his consciousness of power gnawed at the heart of this furious and gifted man, whom a perverse fate had flung away into an obscure vicarage on the wrong side of the channel. His books, his garden, his canal with its willows at Laracor; his dearly-beloved Roger Coxe, and the other perplexed and admiring parishioners of Laracor over whom he domineered; his clerical colleagues in the neighbourhood; and even the society of Stella, the wittiest and best of her sex, whom he loved better than any other creature on earth: all these were insufficient to occupy the craving void in his mind. He hated Ireland, and regarded his lot there as one of banishment; he longed to be in London, and struggling in the centre of whatever was going on. About the date of his appointment to the living of Laracor he had lost the rich deanery of Derry, which Lord Berkeley had meant to give him, in consequence of a notion on the part of the bishop of the diocese that he was a restless, ingenious young man, who, instead of residing, would be "eternally flying backwards and forwards to London." The bishop's perception of his character was just. At or about the very time when the wits at Button's saw him stalking up and down in the coffee-house, the priest of Laracor was introducing himself to Somers, Halifax, Sunderland, and others, and stating the terms on which he would support the Whigs with his pen. Even then, it seems, he took high ground, and let it be known that he was no mere hireling. The following, written at a much later period, is his own explanation of the nature and limits of his Whiggism at the time when he first offered the Whigs his services :—

" It was then (1701-2) I began to trouble myself with the differences between the principles of Whig and Tory ; having formerly employed myself in other, and, I think, much better speculations. I talked often upon this subject with Lord Somers; told him that, having been long conversant with the Greek and Latin authors, and therefore a lover of liberty, I found myself much inclined to be what they call a Whig in politics ; and that, besides, I thought it impossible, upon any other principles, to defend or submit to the Revolution ; but, as to religion, I confessed myself to be a High-Churchman, and that I could not conceive how anyone who wore the habit of a clergyman could be otherwise; that I had observed very well with what insolence and haughtiness some lords of the High-Church party treated not only their own chaplains, but all other clergymen whatsoever, and thought this was sufficiently recompensed by their professions of zeal to the Church: that I had likewise observed how the Whig lords took a direct contrary measure, treated the persons of particular clergymen with particular courtesy, but showed much contempt and ill-will for the order in general: that I knew it was necessary for their party to make their bottom as wide as they could, by taking all denominations of Protestants to be members of their body: that I would not enter into the mutual reproaches made by the violent men on either side; but that the connivance or encouragement given by the Whigs to those writers of pamphlets who reflected upon the whole body of the clergy, without any exception, would unite the Church to one man to oppose them; and that I doubted his lordship's friends did not consider the consequences of this."

Even with these limitations the assistance of so energetic a man as the parson of Laracor was doubtless welcome to the Whigs. His former connexion with the stately old Revolution Whig, Sir William Temple, may have prepared the way for him, as it had already been the means of making him known in some aristocratic families. But there was evidence in his personal bearing and his writings that he was not a man to be neglected. And, if there had been any doubt on the subject on his first presentation of himself to ministers, the publication of his *Battle of the Books* and his *Tale of a*

Tub in 1703 and 1704 would have set it overwhelmingly at rest. The author of these works (and, though they were anonymous, they were at once referred to Swift) could not but be acknowledged as the first prose satirist, and one of the most formidable writers, of the age. On his subsequent visits to Button's, therefore (and they were frequent enough; for, as the Bishop of Derry had foreseen, he was often an absentee from his parish), the mad Irish parson was no longer a stranger to the company. Addison, Steele, Tickell, Philips, and the other Whig wits came to know him well, and to feel his weight among them in their daily convivial meetings. "To Dr. Jonathan Swift, the most agreeable companion, the truest friend, and the greatest genius of the age" was the inscription written by Addison on a copy of his *Travels* presented to Swift; and it shows what opinion Addison and those about him had formed of the author of the *Tale of a Tub.*

Thus, passing and repassing between Laracor and London, now lording it over his Irish parishioners, and now filling the literary and Whig haunts of the great metropolis with the terror of his merciless wit and with talk behind his back of his eccentricities and rude manners, Swift spent the interval between 1702 and 1710, or between his thirty-sixth and his forty-fourth year. His position as a High-Church Whig, however, was an anomalous one. In the first place, it was difficult to see how such a man could honestly be in the Church at all. People were by no means strict in those days in their notions of the clerical character; but the *Tale of a Tub* was a strong dose even then to have come from a clergyman. If Voltaire afterwards recommended the book as a masterly satire against religion in general, it cannot be wondered at that an outcry arose among Swift's contemporaries respecting the profanity of the book. It is true, Peter and Jack, as the representatives of Popery and Presbyterianism, came in for the greatest share of the author's scurrility; and Martin, as the representative of the Church of England, was left with the honours of the story; but the whole structure and spirit of the story, to say nothing of the oaths and other irreverences mingled with its language, were well calculated to shock the more serious even of Martin's followers, who could not but see that rank infidelity alone would be a gainer by the book. Accordingly, despite all that Swift could afterwards do, the fact that he had written this book left a public doubt as to his Christianity. It is quite possible, however, that, with a very questionable kind of belief in Christianity, he may have been a conscientious High-Churchman, zealous for the social defence and aggrandisement of the ecclesiastical institution with which he was connected. Whatever that institution was originally based upon, it existed as part and parcel of the commonwealth of

England, rooted in men's habits and interests, and intertwined with the whole system of social order; and, just as a Brahmin, lax enough in his own speculative allegiance to the Brahminical faith, might still desire to maintain Brahminism as a vast pervading establishment in Hindostan, so might Swift, with a heart and a head dubious enough respecting men's eternal interest in the facts of the Judæan record, see a use notwithstanding in that fabric of bishoprics, deaneries, prebends, parochial livings, and curacies, which ancient belief in those facts had first created and put together. This kind of respect for the Church Establishment is still very prevalent. It is a most excellent thing, it is thought by many, to have a cleanly, cultured, gentlemanly man invested with authority in every parish throughout the land, who can look after what is going on, fill up schedules, give advice, and take the lead in all parish business. That Swift's faith in the Church included no more than this perception of its uses as a vast administrative and educational establishment we will not say. Mr. Thackeray, indeed, openly avows his opinion that Swift had no belief in the Christian religion. "Swift's," he says, " was a reverent, was a pious spirit—he could love and could pray;" but such religion as he had, Mr. Thackeray hints, was a kind of mad, despairing Deism, and had nothing of Christianity in it. Hence, "having put that cassock on, it poisoned him; he was strangled in his bands." The question thus broached as to the nature of Swift's religion is too deep to be discussed here. Though we would not exactly say, with Mr. Thackeray, that Swift's was a " reverent " and " pious " spirit, there are, as he phrases it, breakings out of " the stars of religion and love" shining in the serene blue through " the driving clouds and the maddened hurricane of Swift's life ; " and this, though vague, is about all that we have warrant for saying. As to the zeal of his Churchmanship, however, there is no doubt at all. There was not a man in the British realms more pugnacious in the interests of his order, more resolute in defending the prerogatives of the Church of England against Dissenters and others desirous of limiting them, or more anxious to elevate the social position and intellectual character of the clergy, than the author of the *Tale of a Tub.* No veteran commander of a regiment could have had more of the military than the parson of Laracor had of the ecclesiastical *esprit de corps;* and, indeed, Swift's known dislike to the military may be best explained as the natural jealousy of the surplice at the larger consideration accorded by society to the scarlet coat. Almost all Swift's writings between 1702 and 1710 are assertions of his High-Church sentiments and vindications of the Establishment against its assailants. Thus in 1708 came forth his *Letter on the Sacramental Test,* a hot High-Church and anti-Dissenter pamphlet;

and this was followed in the same year by his *Sentiments of a Church of England man with respect to Religion and Government,* and by his ironical argument, aimed at free-thinkers and latitudinarians, entitled *Reasons against Abolishing Christianity.* In 1709 he published a graver pamphlet, under the name of *A Project for the Advancement of Religion,* in which he urged certain measures for the reform of public morals and the strengthening of the Establishment, recommending in particular a scheme of Church-extension. Thus, with all his readiness to help the Whigs politically, Swift was certainly faithful to his High-Church principles. But, as we have said, a High-Church Whig was an anomaly which the Whigs refused to comprehend. Latitudinarians, Low Churchmen, and Dissenters, did not know what to make of a Whiggism in state-politics which was conjoined with the strongest form of ecclesiastical Toryism. Hence, in spite of his ability, Swift was not a man that the Whigs could patronise and prefer. They were willing to have the benefit of his assistance, but their favours were reserved for men more wholly their own. Various things were, indeed, talked of for Swift—the secretaryship to the proposed embassy of Lord Berkeley in Vienna, a prebend of Westminster, the office of historiographer-royal ; nay, even a bishopric in the American colonies : but all came to nothing. Swift, at the age of forty-three, and certified by Addison as "the greatest genius of the age," was still only an Irish parson, with some 350*l.* or 400*l.* a year. How strange if the plan of the Transatlantic bishopric had been carried out, and Swift had settled in Virginia !

Meanwhile, though neglected by the English Whigs, Swift had risen to be a leader among the Irish clergy, a great man in their convocations and other ecclesiastical assemblies. The object which the Irish clergy then had at heart was to procure from the Government an extension to Ireland of a boon granted several years before to the clergy of England : namely, the remission of the tax levied by the Crown on the revenues of the Church since the days of Henry VIII. in the shape of tenths and first-fruits. This remission, which would have amounted to about 16,000*l.* a year, the Whigs were not disposed to grant, the corresponding remission in the case of England not having been followed by the expected benefits. Archbishop King and the other prelates were glad to have Swift as their agent in this business ; and, accordingly, he was absent from Ireland for upwards of twelve months continuously in the years 1708 and 1709. It was during this period that he set London in a roar by his famous Bickerstaff hoax, in which he first predicted the death of Partridge, the astrologer, at a particular day and hour, and then nearly drove the wretched tradesman mad by declaring, when the time was come, that the prophecy had been fulfilled, and publishing a detailed account of the circumstances. Out of this Bickerstaff hoax, and Swift's talk over it with Addison and Steele, arose the *Tatler*, prolific parent of so many other periodicals.

The year 1710 was an important one in the life of Swift. In that year he came over to London, resolved in his own mind to have a settlement of accounts with the Whigs, or to break with them for ever. The Irish ecclesiastical business of the tenths and first-fruits was still his pretext, but he had many other arrears to introduce into the account. Accordingly, after some civil skirmishing with Somers, Halifax, and his other old friends, then just turned out of office, he openly transferred his allegiance to the new Tory administration of Harley and Bolingbroke. The 4th of October, not quite a month after his arrival in London, was the date of his first interview with Harley; and from that day forward till the dissolution of Harley's administration by the death of Queen Anne, in 1714, Swift's relations with Harley, St. John, and the other ministers, were more those of an intimate friend and adviser than a literary dependent. How he dined almost daily with Harley or St. John ; how he bullied them, and made them beg his pardon when by chance they offended him—either, as Harley once did, by offering him a fifty-pound note, or, as St. John once did, by appearing cold and abstracted when Swift was his guest at dinner; how he obtained from them not only the settlement of the Irish business, but almost everything else he asked ; how he used his influence to prevent Steele, Addison, Congreve, Rowe, and his other Whig literary friends, from suffering loss of office by the change in the state of politics, at the same time growing cooler in his private intercourse with Addison and poor Dick, and tending more to young Tory writers, such as Pope and Parnell ; how, with Pope, Gay, Arbuthnot, Harley, and St. John, he formed the famous club of the *Scriblerus* brotherhood, for the satire of literary absurdities ; how he wrote squibs, pamphlets, and lampoons innumerable for the Tories and against the Whigs, and at one time actually edited a Tory paper called the *Examiner:* all this is to be gathered, in most interesting detail, from his epistolary journal to Stella, in which he punctually kept her informed of all his doings during his long three years of absence. The following is a description of him at the height of his Court influence during this season of triumph, from the Whiggish, and therefore somewhat adverse, pen of Bishop Kennet :—

" When I came to the antechamber [at Court] to wait before prayers, Dr. Swift was the principal man of talk and business, and acted as master of requests. He was soliciting the Earl of Arran to speak to his brother, the Duke of Ormond, to get a chaplain's place established in the garrison of Hull for Mr. Fiddes, a clergyman in that neighbourhood, who had lately been in jail, and published sermons to pay the fees. He was promising Mr. Thorold to undertake with my lord-treasurer that, according to his petition, he should obtain a salary of 200*l.* per annum as minister of the English church at Rotterdam. He stopped F. Gwynne, Esq., going in with the red bag to the Queen, and told him aloud he had something to say to him from my lord-treasurer. He talked with the son of Dr. Davenant, to be sent abroad, and took out his pocket-book, and wrote down several things as *memoranda* to do for him. He turned to the fire, and took out his gold watch, and, telling him the time of day, complained it was very late. A gentleman said he was too fast. ' How can I help it,' says the Doctor, ' if the courtiers give me a watch that won't go right ? ' Then he instructed a young nobleman that the best poet in England was Mr. Pope (a Papist), who had begun a translation of Homer into English verse, for which he must have them all subscribe ; ' for,' says he, ' the author shall not begin to print till I have a thousand guineas for him.' Lord-treasurer, after leaving the Queen, came through the room, beckoning Dr. Swift to follow him : both went off just before prayers."

Let us see, by a few pickings from the journal to Stella, in what manner the black-browed Irish vicar, who was thus figuring in the mornings at Court as the friend and confidant of Ministers, and almost as their domineering colleague, was writing home from his lodging in the evenings to the " dear girls " at Laracor.

Dec. 3, 1710. " Pshaw, I must be writing to those dear

D   S

saucy brats every night whether I will or no, let me
have what business I will, or come home ever so late, or
be ever so sleepy ; but it is an old saying and a true one,
'Be you lords or be you earls, you must write to naughty
girls.'   I was to-day at Court, and saw Raymond [an
Irish friend] among the beefeaters, staying to see the
Queen ; so I put him in a better station, made two or
three dozen bows, and went to church, and then to
Court again to pick up a dinner, as I did with Sir John
Stanley : and then we went to visit Lord Mountjoy, and
just left him ; and 'tis near eleven at night, young
women, and methinks this letter comes very near to the
bottom," &c. &c.

Jan. 1, 1711. Morning. " I wish my dearest pretty
Dingley and Stella a happy new year, and health, and
mirth, and good stomachs, and *Fr's* company. Faith, I
did not know how to write *Fr.* I wondered what
was the matter ; but now I remember I always write
Pdfr [by this combination of letters, or by the word
Presto, Swift designates himself in the Journal] * *
Get the *Examiners*, and read them ; the last nine or
ten are full of reasons for the late change and of the
abuses of the last ministry ; and the great men assure
me that all are true. They were written by their
encouragement and direction. I must rise, and go see
Sir Andrew Fountain ; but perhaps to-morrow I may
answer *M.D.'s* [Stella's designation in the Journal]
letter: so good morrow, my mistresses all, good morrow.
I wish you both a merry new year; roast beef, minced
pies, and good strong beer ; and me a share of your good
cheer; that I was there or you were here ; and you're a
little saucy dear," &c. &c.

Jan. 13, 1711. "O faith, I had an ugly giddy fit

last night in my chamber, and I have got a new box of
pills to take, and I hope shall have no more this good
while. I would not tell you before, because it would
vex you, little rogues ; but now it is better. I dined
to-day with Lord Shelburn," &c. &c.

Jan. 16, 1711. " My service to Mrs. Stode and
Walls. Has she a boy or a girl ? A girl, hmm !, and
died in a week, hmmm !, and was poor Stella forced
to stand for godmother ?—Let me know how accounts
stand, that you may have your money betimes. There's
four months for my lodging ; that must be thought on
too. And zoo go dine with Manley, and lose your
money, doo extravagant sluttikin ? But don't fret. It
will just be three weeks when I have the next letter:
that is, to-morrow. Farewell, dearest beloved *M.D.*,
and love poor, poor Presto, who has not had one happy
day since he left you, as hope to be saved."

March 7, 1711. " I am weary of business and
ministers. I don't go to a coffee-house twice a month.
I am very regular in going to sleep before eleven. And
so you say that Stella's a pretty girl ; and so she be ;
and methinks I see her just now, as handsome as the
day's long. Do you know what ? When I am writing
in our language [a kind of baby-language of endearment
used between him and Stella, and called ' the little
language '] I make up my mouth just as if I was
speaking it. I caught myself at it just now. * * Poor
Stella, won't Dingley leave her a little daylight to write
to Presto ? Well, well, we'll have daylight shortly,
spite of her teeth ; and zoo must cly Zele, and Hele, and
Hele aden. Must loo minitate *Pdfr*, pay ? Iss, and
so la shall. And so leles fol ee rettle. Dood Mollow.

[You must cry There and Here and Here again. Must
you imitate *Pdfr*, pray ? Yes, and so you shall. And
so there's for the letter. Good morrow.]"

And so on, through a series of daily letters, forming
now a goodly octavo volume or more, Swift chats and
rattles away to the "dear absent girls," giving them all
the political gossip of the time, and informing them about
his own goings-out and comings-in, his dinings with
Harley, St. John, and occasionally with Addison and
other old Whig friends, the state of his health, his
troubles with his drunken servant Patrick, his lodging-
expenses, and a host of other things. Such another
journal has, perhaps, never been given to the world;
and but for it we should never have known what depths
of tenderness and power of affectionate prattle there
were in the heart of this harsh and savage man.

Only on one topic, affecting himself during his long
stay in London, is he in any degree reserved. Among
the acquaintanceships he had formed was one with a Mrs.
Vanhomrigh, a widowed lady of property, who had a
family of several daughters. The eldest of these, Hester
Vanhomrigh, was a girl of more than ordinary talent
and accomplishments, and of enthusiastic and impetuous
character ; and, as Swift acquired the habit of dropping
in upon the "Vans," as he called them, when he had no
other dinner engagement, it was not long before he and
Miss Vanhomrigh fell into the relationship of teacher

and pupil. He taught her to think and to write verses ; and, as among Swift's peculiarities of opinion, one was that he entertained what would even now be called very advanced notions as to the intellectual capabilities and rights of women, he found no more pleasant amusement, in the midst of his politics and other business, than that of superintending the growth of so hopeful a mind.

> " His conduct might have made him styled
> A father, and the nymph his child :
> The innocent delight he took
> To see the virgin mind her book
> Was but the master's secret joy
> In school to hear the finest boy."

But, alas ! Cupid got among the books.

> " Vanessa, not in years a score,
> Dreams of a gown of forty-four ;
> Imaginary charms can find
> In eyes with reading almost blind ;
> She fancies music in his tongue,
> Nor farther looks, but thinks him young."

Nay, more : one of Swift's lessons to her had been that frankness, whether in man or women, was the chief of the virtues, and

> " That common forms were not design'd
> Directors to a noble mind."

"Then," said the nymph,

> " I'll let you see
> My actions with your rules agree;
> That I can vulgar forms despise,
> And have no secrets to disguise."

She told her love, and fairly argued it out with the startled tutor, discussing every element in the question, whether for or against—the disparity of their ages, her own five thousand guineas, their similarity of tastes, his views of ambition, the judgment the world would form of the match, and so on; and the end of it was that she reasoned so well that Swift could not but admit that there would be nothing after all so very incongruous in a marriage between him and Esther Vanhomrigh. So the matter rested, Swift gently resisting the impetuosity of the young woman, when it threatened to take him by storm, but not having the courage to adduce the real and conclusive argument—the existence on the other side of the channel of another and a dearer Esther. Stella, on her side, knew that Swift visited a family called the "Vans"; she divined that something was wrong; but that was all.

That Swift, the Mentor of ministers, their daily companion, at whose bidding they dispensed their patronage and their favour, should himself be suffered to remain a mere vicar of an Irish parish, was, of course, impossible. Vehement and even boisterous and overdone as was his

zeal for his own independence—"If we let these great
ministers pretend too much, there will be no governing
them," was his maxim; and, in order to act up to it,
he used to treat Dukes and Earls as if they were dogs—
there were yet means of honourably acknowledging his
services in a way to which he would have taken no
exception.   Nor can we doubt that Oxford and St. John,
who were really and heartily his admirers, were anxious
to promote him in some suitable manner.   An English
bishopric was certainly what he coveted, and what
they would at once have given him.   But, though the
bishopric of Hereford fell vacant in 1712, there was, as
Sir Walter Scott says, "a lion in the path."   Queen Anne,
honest dowdy woman,—her instinctive dislike of Swift
strengthened by the private influence of the Archbishop
of York, and that of the Duchess of Somerset, whose
red hair Swift had lampooned—obstinately refused to
make the author of the *Tale of a Tub* a bishop.   Even an
English deanery could not be found for so questionable
a Christian; and in 1713 Swift was obliged to accept,
as the best thing he could get, the Deanery of St.
Patrick's in his native city of Dublin.   He hurried
over to Ireland to be installed, and came back just in
time to partake in the last struggles and dissensions of
the Tory administration before Queen Anne's death.   By
his personal exertions with ministers, and his pamphlet
entitled *Public Spirit of the Whigs,* he tried to buoy up the

sinking Tory cause.　But the Queen's death destroyed all; with George I. the Whigs came in again; the late Tory ministers were dispersed and disgraced, and Swift shared their fall.　"Dean Swift," says Arbuthnot, "keeps up his noble spirit; and, though like a man knocked down, you may behold him still with a stern countenance, and aiming a blow at his adversaries." He returned, with rage and grief in his heart, to Ireland, a disgraced man, and in danger of arrest on account of his connexion with the late ministers.　Even in Dublin he was insulted as he walked in the streets.

For twelve years—that is, from 1714 to 1726—Swift did not quit Ireland.　At his first coming, as he tells us in one of his letters, he was "horribly melancholy;" but the melancholy began to wear off; and, having made up his mind to his exile in the country of his detestation, he fell gradually into the routine of his duties as Dean.　How he boarded in a private family in the town, stipulating for leave to invite his friends to dinner at so much a head, and only having two evenings a week at the deanery for larger receptions; how he brought Stella and Mrs. Dingley from Laracor, and settled them in lodgings on the other side of the Liffey, keeping up the same precautions in his intercourse with them as before, but devolving the management of his receptions at the deanery upon Stella, who did all the honours of the house; how he had his own way in all cathedral business, and had always a few clergymen and others in his train, who toadied him, and took part in the facetious horse-play of which he was fond; how gradually his physiognomy became known to the citizens, and his eccentricities familiar to them, till the "Dean" became the lion of Dublin, and everybody turned to look at him as he walked in the streets; how, among the Dean's other oddities, he was popularly charged with stinginess in his entertainments and a sharp look-out after the wine; how sometimes he would fly off from town, and take refuge in some country-seat of a friendly Irish nobleman; how all this while he was reading books of all kinds, writing notes and jottings, and corresponding with Pope, Gay, Prior, Arbuthnot, Oxford, Bolingbroke, and other literary and political friends in London or abroad: these are matters in the recollection of all who have read any of the biographies of Swift. It is also known that it was during this period that the Stella-and-Vanessa imbroglio reached its highest degree of entanglement. Scarcely had the Dean located Stella and Mrs. Dingley in their lodging in Dublin when, as he had feared, the impetuous Vanessa crossed the Channel to be near him too. Her mother's death, and the fact that she and her younger sister had a small property in Ireland, were pretext enough. A scrap or two from surviving letters will tell the sequel, and will suggest the state of the relations at this time between

Swift and this unhappy and certainly very extraordinary, woman :—

Swift to Miss Vanhomrigh: London, Aug. 12, 1714. "1 had your letter last post, and before you can send me another I shall set out for Ireland. * * * If you are in Ireland when I am there, I shall see you very seldom. It is not a place for any freedom, but where everything is known in a week, and magnified a hundred degrees. These are rigorous laws that must be passed through; but it is probable we may meet in London in winter; or, if not, leave all to fate."

Miss Vanhomrigh to Swift: Dublin, 1714 (*some time after August*). "You once had a maxim, which was to act what was right, and not mind what the world would say. I wish you would keep to it now. Pray, what can be wrong in seeing and advising an unhappy young woman? I cannot imagine. You cannot but know that your frowns make my life unsupportable. You have taught me to distinguish, and then you leave me miserable."

Miss Vanhomrigh to Swift: Dublin, 1714. "You bid me be easy, and you would see me as often as you could. You had better have said as often as you could get the better of your inclinations so much, or as often as you remembered there was such a one in the world. If you continue to treat me as you do, you will not be made uneasy by me long. It is impossible to describe what I have suffered since I saw you last. I am sure I could have bore the rack much better than those killing, killing words of

yours. Sometimes I have resolved to die without seeing you more ; but those resolves, to your misfortune,
did not last long ; for there is something in human
nature that prompts one to find relief in this world. I
must give way to it, and beg you'd see me, and speak
kindly to me ; for I am sure you'd not condemn any
one to suffer what I have done, could you but know it.
The reason I write to you is because I cannot tell it to
you should I see you. For, when I begin to complain,
then you are angry ; and there is something in your
looks so awful that it strikes me dumb."

Here a gap intervenes, which record fills up with but
an indication here and there. Swift saw Vanessa,
sometimes with that " something awful in his looks which
struck her dumb," sometimes with words of perplexed
kindness ; he persuaded her to go out, to read, to amuse
herself ; he introduced clergymen to her—one of them
afterwards Archbishop of Cashel—as suitors for her
hand ; he induced her to leave Dublin, and go to her
property at Selbridge, about twelve miles from Dublin,
where now and then he went to visit her, where she
used to plant laurels against every time of his coming,
and where "Vanessa's bower," in which she and the
Dean used to sit, with books and writing materials
before them, during those happy visits, was long an
object of interest to tourists ; he wrote kindly letters
to her, some in French, praising her talents, her conversation, and her writing, and saying that he found in her

"*tout ce que la nature a donnée à un mortel, l'honneur, la vertu, le bon sens, l'esprit, la douceur, l'agrément et la fermeté d'âme.*" All did not suffice; and one has to fancy, during those long years, the restless beatings, on the one hand, of that impassioned woman's heart, now lying as cold undistinguishable ashes in some Irish grave, and, on the other hand, the distraction, and anger, and daily terror, of the man she clung to. For, somehow or other, there *was* an element of terror mingled with the affair. What it was is beyond easy scrutiny, though possibly the data exist if they were well sifted. The ordinary story is that some time in the midst of those entanglements with Vanessa, and in consequence of their effects on the rival-relationship—Stella having been brought almost to death's door by the anxieties caused her by Vanessa's proximity, and by her own equivocal position in society—the form of marriage was gone through by Swift and Stella, and they became legally husband and wife, although with an engagement that the matter should remain secret, and that there should be no change in their manner of living. The year 1716, when Swift was forty-nine years of age, and Stella thirty-two, is assigned as the date of this event; and the ceremony is said to have been performed in the garden of the deanery by the Bishop of Clogher. But more mystery remains. "Immediately subsequent to the ceremony," says Sir Walter Scott, "Swift's state of mind appears to have been dreadful. Delany (as I have learned from a friend of his widow) said that about the time it was supposed to have taken place he observed Swift to be extremely gloomy and agitated—so much so that he went to Archbishop King to mention his apprehensions. On entering the library, Swift rushed out with a countenance of distraction, and passed him without speaking. He found the archbishop in tears, and, upon asking the reason, he said, 'You have just met the most unhappy man on earth; but on the subject of his wretchedness you must never ask a question.'" What are we to make of this? Nay more, what are we to make of it when we find that the alleged marriage of Swift with Stella, with which Scott connects the story, is after all denied by some as resting on no sufficient evidence: even Dr. Delany, though he believed in the marriage, and supposed it to have taken place about the time of this remarkable interview with the archbishop, having no certain information on the subject? If we assume a secret marriage with Stella, indeed, the subsequent portion of the Vanessa story becomes more explicable. On this assumption we are to imagine Swift continuing his letters to Vanessa, and his occasional visits to her at Selbridge on the old footing, for some years after the marriage, with the undivulged secret ever in his mind, increasing tenfold his former awkwardness in encountering her presence. And so we come to the year 1720, when, as the following scraps will show, a new paroxysm on the part of Vanessa brought on a new crisis in their relations.

Miss Vanhomrigh to Swift: Selbridge, 1720.   " Believe me, it is with the utmost regret that I now write to you, because I know your good-nature such that you cannot see any human creature miserable without being sensibly touched.   Yet what can I do?   I must either unload my heart, and tell you all its griefs, or sink under the inexpressible distress I now suffer by your prodigious neglect of me.   It is now ten long weeks since I saw you, and in all that time I have never received but one letter from you, and a little note with an excuse.   Oh, have you forgot me?   You endeavour by severities to force me from you.   Nor can I blame you ; for, with the utmost distress and confusion, I behold myself the cause of uneasy reflections to you.   Yet I cannot comfort you, but here declare that it is not in the power of art, time, or accident, to lessen the inexpressible passion I have for ——.   Put my passion under the utmost restraint, send me as distant from you as the earth will allow ; yet you cannot banish those charming ideas which will ever stick by me whilst I have the use of memory.   Nor is the love I bear you only seated in my soul ; for there is not a single atom of my frame that is not blended with it.   Therefore do not flatter yourself that separation will ever change my sentiments ; for I find myself unquiet in the midst of silence, and my heart is at once pierced with sorrow and love.   For Heaven's sake, tell me what has caused this prodigious change in you which I have found of late."

Miss Vanhomrigh to Swift: Dublin, 1720. * * " I
believe you thought I only rallied when I told you the
other night that I would pester you with letters. Once
more I advise you, if you have any regard for your quiet,
to alter your behaviour quickly ; for I do assure you I
have too much spirit to sit down contented with this
treatment. Because I love frankness extremely, I here
tell you now that I have determined to try all manner
of human arts to reclaim you; and, if all these fail, I
am resolved to have recourse to the black one, which, it
is said, never does. Now see what inconveniency you
will bring both yourself and me unto * *. When I
undertake a thing, I don't love to do it by halves."

Swift to Miss Vanhomrigh: Dublin, 1720. " If you
write as you do, I shall come the seldomer on purpose
to be pleased with your letters, which I never look into
without wondering how a brat that cannot read can
possibly write so well. * * Raillery apart, I think it
inconvenient, for a hundred reasons, that I should make
your house a sort of constant dwelling-place. I will
certainly come as often as I conveniently can; but my
health and the perpetual run of ill weather hinder me
from going out in the morning, and my afternoons are
taken up I know not how; so that I am in rebellion
with a hundred people besides yourself for not seeing
them. For the rest, you need make use of no other
black art besides your ink. It is a pity your eyes are
not black, or I would have said the same; but you are
a white witch, and can do no mischief."

Swift to Miss Vanhomrigh: Dublin, 1720. " I received
your letter when some company was with me on Satur-

day night, and it put me in such confusion that I could not tell what to do. This morning a woman who does business for me told me she heard I was in love with one, naming you, and twenty particulars; that little master —— and I visited you, and that the Archbishop did so; and that you had abundance of wit, &c. I ever feared the tattle of this nasty town, and told you so; and that was the reason why I said to you long ago that I would see you seldom when you were in Ireland; and I must beg you to be easy, if, for some time, I visit you seldomer, and not in so particular a manner."

Miss Vanhomrigh to Swift: Selbridge, 1720. * * "Solitude is unsupportable to a mind which is not easy. I have worn out my days in sighing and my nights in watching and thinking of ——, who thinks not of me. How many letters shall I send you before I receive an answer? * * Oh that I could hope to see you here, or that I could go to you! I was born with violent passions, which terminate all in one—that inexpressible passion I have for you. * * Surely you cannot possibly be so taken up but you might command a moment to write to me and force your inclinations to so great a charity. I firmly believe, if I could know your thoughts (which no human creature is capable of guessing at, because never anyone living thought like you), I should find you had often in a rage wished me religious, hoping then I should have paid my devotions to Heaven. But that would not spare you; for, were I an enthusiast, still you'd be the deity I should worship. What marks are there of a deity but what you are to be known by? You are present everywhere; your dear image is always before my eyes. Sometimes you strike me with that prodigious awe I tremble with fear; at other times a charming compassion shines through your countenance, which revives my soul. Is it not more reasonable to adore a radiant form one has seen than one only described?"

Swift to Miss Vanhomrigh: Dublin, October 15, 1720. "All the morning I am plagued with impertinent visits, below any man of sense or honour to endure, if it were any way avoidable. Afternoons and evenings are spent abroad in walking to keep off and avoid spleen as far as I can; so that, when I am not so good a correspondent as I could wish, you are not to quarrel and be governor, but to impute it to my situation, and to conclude infallibly that I have the same respect and kindness for you I ever professed to have."

Swift to Miss Vanhomrigh: Gaullstoun, July 5, 1721. * * " Settle your affairs, and quit this scoundrel-island, and things will be as you desire. I can say no more, being called away. *Mais soyez assurée que jamais personne au monde n'a été aimée, honorée, estimée, adorée par votre ami que vous.*"

Vanessa did not quit the " scoundrel-island ; " but, on the contrary, remained in it, unmanageable as ever. In 1722, about a year after the date of the last scrap, the catastrophe came. In a wild fit Vanessa, as the story is, took the bold step of writing to Stella, insisting on an explanation of the nature of Swift's engagements to her; Stella placed the letter in Swift's hands; and Swift, in a paroxysm of fury, rode instantly to Selbridge, saw Vanessa without speaking, laid a letter on her table, and rode off again. The letter was Vanessa's death-warrant. Within a few weeks she was dead, having previously revoked a will in which she had bequeathed all her fortune to Swift.

Whatever may have been the purport of Vanessa's communication to Stella, it produced no change in Swift's relations to the latter. The pale pensive face of Hester Johnson, with her " fine dark eyes " and hair " black as a raven," was still to be seen on reception-evenings at the deanery, where also she and Mrs. Dingley would sometimes take up their abode when Swift was suffering from one of his attacks of vertigo and required to be nursed. Nay, during those very years in which, as we have just seen, Swift was attending to the movements to and fro of the more imperious Vanessa in the background, and assuaging her passion by visits and letters, and praises of her powers, and professions of his admiration of her beyond all her sex, he was all the while keeping up the same affectionate style of intercourse as ever with the more gentle Stella, whose happier lot it was to be stationed in the centre of his domestic circle, and addressing to her, in a less forced manner, praises singularly like those he addressed to her rival. Thus, every year, on Stella's birth-day, he wrote a little poem in honour of the occasion.   Take the one for 1718, beginning thus :—

> " Stella this day is thirty-four
>   (We sha'n't dispute a year or more) :
>   However, Stella, be not troubled ;
>   Although thy size and years be doubled
>   Since first I saw thee at sixteen,
>   The brightest virgin on the green,
>   So little is thy form declined,
>   Made up so largely in thy mind."

Stella would reciprocate these compliments by verses on the Dean's birth-day ; and one is struck with the similarity of her acknowledgments of what the Dean had taught her and done for her to those of Vanessa. Thus, in 1721,—

> " When men began to call me fair,
>   You interposed your timely care ;
>   You early taught me to despise
>   The ogling of a coxcomb's eyes ;
>   Show'd where my judgment was misplaced,
>   Refined my fancy and my taste.
>   You taught how I might youth prolong
>   By knowing what was right and wrong ;
>   How from my heart to bring supplies
>   Of lustre to my fading eyes ;
>   How soon a beauteous mind repairs
>   The loss of changed or falling hairs ;

> How wit and virtue from within
> Send out a smoothness o'er the skin :
> Your lectures could my fancy fix,
> And I can please at thirty-six."

The death of Vanessa in 1722 left Swift from that time entirely Stella's. How she got over the Vanessa affair in her own mind, when the full extent of the facts became known to her, can only be guessed. When some one alluded to the fact that Swift had written beautifully about Vanessa, she is reported to have said " That doesn't signify, for we all know the Dean could write beautifully about a broomstick." " A woman, a true woman ! " is Mr. Thackeray's characteristic comment.

To the world's end those who take interest in Swift's life will range themselves either on the side of Stella or on that of Vanessa. Mr. Thackeray prefers Stella, but admits that, in doing so, though the majority of men may be on his side, he will have most women against him. Which way Swift's *heart* inclined him it is not difficult to see. Stella was the main influence of his life ; the intimacy with Vanessa was but an episode. And yet, when he speaks of the two women as a critic, there is a curious equality in his appreciation of them. Of Stella he used to say that her wit and judgment were such that " she never failed to say the best thing that was said wherever she was in company ; " and one of his epistolary compliments to Vanessa is that he had "always remarked that, neither in general nor in particular conversation, had any word ever escaped her lips that could by possibility have been better." Some little differences in his preceptorial treatment of them may be discerned—as when he finds it necessary to admonish poor Stella for her incorrigibly bad spelling, no such admonition, apparently, being required for Vanessa; or when, in praising Stella, he dwells chiefly on her honour and gentle kindliness, whereas in praising Vanessa he dwells chiefly on her genius and force of mind. But it is distinctly on record that his regard for both was founded on his belief that in respect of intellect and culture both were above the majority of their sex. And here it may be repeated that, not only from the evidence afforded by the whole story of Swift's relations to these two women, but also from the evidence of distinct doctrinal passages scattered through his works, it appears that those who in the present day maintain the co-equality of the two sexes, and the right of women to as full and varied an education, and as free a social use of their powers, as is allowed to men, may claim Swift as a pioneer in their cause. Both Stella and Vanessa have left their testimony that from the very first Swift took care to indoctrinate them with peculiar views on this subject; and both thank him for having done so. Stella even goes further, and almost urges Swift to do

on the great scale what he had done for her individually :—

> "O turn your precepts into laws;
> Redeem the woman's ruin'd cause;
> Retrieve lost empire to our sex,
> That men may bow their rebel necks."

This fact that Swift had a *theory* on the subject of the
proper mode of treating and educating women, which
theory was in antagonism to the ideas of his time,
explains much both in his conduct as a man and in his
habits as a writer.

For the first six years of his exile in Ireland after the
death of Queen Anne, Swift had published nothing of
any consequence, and had kept aloof from politics,
except when they were brought to his door by local
quarrels. In 1720, however, he again flashed forth as
a political luminary, in a character that could hardly
have been anticipated—that of an Irish patriot. Taking
up the cause of the "scoundrel-island," to which he
belonged by birth, if not by affection, and to which fate
had consigned him in spite of all his efforts, he made
that cause his own. Virtually saying to his old Whig
enemies, then in power on the other side of the water,
"Yes, I am an Irishman, and I will show you what an
Irishman is," he constituted himself the representative

of the island, and hurled it, with all its pent-up mass of rage and wrongs, against Walpole and his administration. First, in revenge for the commercial wrongs of Ireland came his *Proposal for the Universal Use of Irish Manufactures, utterly Rejecting and Renouncing Everything Wearable that comes from England;* then, amidst the uproar and danger excited by this proposal, other and other defiances in the same tone; and lastly, in 1723, on the occasion of the royal patent to poor William Wood to supply Ireland, without her own consent, with a hundred and eight thousand pounds' worth of copper half-pence of English manufacture, the unparalleled *Drapier's Letters,* which blasted the character of the coppers and asserted the nationality of Ireland. All Ireland, Catholic as well as Protestant, blessed the Dean of St. Patrick's; associations were formed for the defence of his person; and, had Walpole and his Whigs succeeded in bringing him to trial, it would have been at the expense of an Irish rebellion. From that time till his death Swift was the true King of Ireland; only when O'Connell arose did the heart of the nation yield equal veneration to any single chief; and even at this day the grateful Irish, forgetting his gibes against them, and forgetting his continual habit of distinguishing between the Irish population as a whole and the English and Protestant part of it to which he belonged himself, cherish his memory with loving enthusiasm, and speak of him as the "great Irishman." Among the phases of Swift's life this of his having been an Irish patriot and agitator deserves to be particularly remembered.

In the year 1726 Swift, then in his sixtieth year, and in the full flush of his new popularity as the champion of Irish nationality, visited England for the first time since Queen Anne's death. Once there, he was loth to return; and a considerable portion of the years 1726 and 1727 was spent by him in or near London. This was the time of the publication of *Gulliver's Travels*, which had been written some years before, and also of some *Miscellanies*, which were edited for him by Pope. It was at Pope's villa at Twickenham that most of his time was spent; and it was there and at this time that the long friendship between Swift and Pope ripened into that extreme and affectionate intimacy which they both lived to acknowledge. Gay, Arbuthnot, and Bolingbroke, now returned from exile, joined Pope in welcoming their friend. Addison had been dead several years. Prior was dead, and also Vanbrugh and Parnell. Steele was yet alive; but between him and Swift there was no longer any tie. Political and aristocratic acquaintances, old and new, there were in abundance, all anxious once again to have Swift among them to fight their battles. Old George I. had not long to live, and the Tories were trying again to come into power in the train of the Prince of Wales. There were even chances of an arrangement with Walpole, with possibilities, in that or in some other way, that Swift should not die a mere Irish dean. These prospects were but temporary. The old King died; and, contrary to expectation, George II. retained Walpole and his Whig colleagues. In October, 1727, Swift left England for the last time. He returned to Dublin just in time to watch over the death-bed of Stella, who expired, after a lingering illness, in January, 1728. Swift was then in his sixty-second year.

The story of the remaining seventeen years of Swift's life—for, with all his maladies, bodily and mental, his strong frame withstood, for all that time of solitude and gloom, the wear of mortality—is perhaps better known than any other part of his biography. How his irritability and eccentricities and avarice grew upon him, so that his friends and servants had a hard task in humouring him, we learn from the traditions of others; how his memory began to fail, and other signs of breaking-up began to appear, we learn from himself;—

> "See how the Dean begins to break!
> Poor gentleman he droops apace;
> You plainly find it in his face.

> That old vertigo in his head
> Will never leave him till he's dead.
> Besides, his memory decays;
> He recollects not what he says;
> He cannot call his friends to mind,
> Forgets the place where last he dined,
> Plies you with stories o'er and o'er;
> He told them fifty times before."

The fire of his genius, however, was not yet burnt out. Between 1729 and 1736 he continued to throw out satires and lampoons in profusion, referring to the men and topics of the day, and particularly to the political affairs of Ireland; and it was during this time that his *Directions to Servants*, his *Polite Conversation*, and other well-known facetiæ, first saw the light. From the year 1736, however, it was well known in Dublin that the Dean was no more what he had been, and that his recovery was not to be looked for. The rest will be best told in the words of Sir Walter Scott :—

"The last scene was now rapidly approaching, and the stage darkened ere the curtain fell. From 1736 onward the Dean's fits of periodical giddiness and deafness had returned with violence; he could neither enjoy conversation nor amuse himself with writing, and an obstinate resolution which he had formed not to wear glasses prevented him from reading. The following dismal letter to Mrs. Whiteway [his cousin, and chief attendant in his last days] in 1740 is almost the last document which we possess of the celebrated Swift as a rational and reflecting being. It awfully foretells the catastrophe which shortly after took place.

'I have been very miserable all night, and to-day extremely deaf and full of pain. I am so stupid and confounded that I cannot express the mortification I am under both in body and mind. All I can say is that I am not in torture, but I daily and hourly expect it. Pray let me know how your health is and your family. I hardly understand one word I write. I am sure my days will be very few; few and miserable they must be.

'I am, for these few days,

'Yours entirely,

'J. SWIFT.'

'If I do not blunder, it is Saturday, July 26th, 1740.'

"His understanding having totally failed soon after these melancholy expressions of grief and affection, his first state was that of violent and furious lunacy. His estate was put under the management of trustees, and his person confided to the care of Dr. Lyons, a respectable clergyman, curate to the Rev. Robert King, prebendary of Dunlavin, one of Swift's executors. This gentleman discharged his melancholy task with great fidelity, being much and gratefully attached to the object of his care. From a state of outrageous frenzy, aggravated by severe bodily suffering, the illustrious Dean of St. Patrick's sank into the situation of a helpless changeling. In the course of about three years he is only known to have spoken once or twice. At length,

when this awful moral lesson had subsisted from 1743
until the 19th of October, 1745, it pleased God to release
him from this calamitous situation.　He died upon that
day without a single pang, so gently that his attendants
were scarce aware of the moment of his dissolution."

Swift was seventy-eight years of age at the time
of his death, having outlived all his contemporaries
of the Queen Anne cluster of wits, with the exception of Bolingbroke, Ambrose Philips, and Cibber.
Congreve had died in 1729; Steele in the same year;
Defoe in 1731; Gay in 1732; Arbuthnot in 1735;
Tickell in 1740; and Pope, who was Swift's junior by
twenty-one years, in 1744.　Swift, therefore, is entitled
in our literary histories to the place of patriarch as well
as to that of chief among the Wits of Queen Anne's
reign; and he stands nearest to our own day of any of
them whose writings we still read.　As late as the year
1820 a person was alive who had seen Swift as he lay
dead in the deanery before his burial, great crowds going
to take their last look of him.　"The coffin was open;
he had on his head neither cap nor wig; there was not
much hair on the front or very top, but it was long and
thick behind, very white, and was like flax upon the
pillow."　Such is the last glimpse we have of Swift on
earth.　Exactly ninety years afterwards the coffin was
taken up from its resting-place in the aisle of the
cathedral; and the skull of Swift, the white locks now

all mouldered away from it, became an object of scientific curiosity. Phrenologically, it was a disappointment, the extreme lowness of the forehead striking everyone, and the so-called organs of wit, causality, and comparison being scarcely developed at all. There were peculiarities, however, in the shape of the interior, indicating larger capacity of brain than would have been inferred from the external aspect. Stella's coffin was exhumed, and her skull examined at the same time. The examiners found the skull "a perfect model of symmetry and beauty."

Have we said too much in declaring that of all the men who illustrated that period of our literary history which lies between the Revolution of 1688 and the beginning or middle of the reign of George II. Swift alone (Pope excepted, and he only on certain definite and peculiar grounds) fulfils to any tolerable extent those conditions which would entitle him to the epithet of " great," already refused to his age as a whole ? We do not think so. Swift *was* a great genius ; nay, if by *greatness* we understand general mass and energy rather than any preconceived peculiarity of quality, he was the greatest genius of his age. Neither Addison, nor Steele, nor Pope, nor Defoe, possessed, in anything like the same degree, that which Goethe and Niebuhr, seeking a name for a certain attribute found often present, as they thought, in the higher and more forcible order of historic characters, agreed to call the *demonic* element. Indeed very few men in our literature, from first to last, have had so much of this element in them—perhaps the sign and source of all real greatness—as Swift. In him it was so obvious as to attract notice at once. "There is something in your looks," wrote Vanessa to him, "so awful that it strikes me dumb;" and again, "Sometimes you strike me with that prodigious awe I tremble with fear;" and again, "What marks are there of a deity that you are not known by?" True, these are the words of a woman infatuated with love; but there is evidence that, wherever Swift went, and in whatever society he was, there was this magnetic power in his presence. Pope felt it; Addison felt it; they all felt it. We question if, among all our literary celebrities, from first to last, there has been one more distinguished for being personally formidable to all who came near him.

And yet, in calling Swift a great genius, we clearly do not mean to rank him in the same order of greatness with such men among his predecessors as Spenser, or Shakespeare, or Milton, or such men among his successors as Scott, Coleridge, and Wordsworth. We even retain instinctively the right of not according to him a certain kind of admiration which we bestow on such men of his own generation as Pope, Steele, and Addison. How is this? What is the drawback about Swift's genius which prevents us from referring him to that highest order of literary greatness to which we do refer others who in respect of hard general capacity were apparently not superior to him, and on the borders of which we also place some who in that respect were certainly his inferiors? To make the question more special, why do we call Milton great in quite a different sense from that in which we consent to confer the same epithet on Swift?

Altogether, it will be said, Milton was a greater man than Swift; his intellect was higher, richer, deeper, grander, his views of things were more profound, grave, stately, and exalted. This is a true enough statement of the case; and one likes that comprehensive use of the word intellect which it implies, wrapping up, as it were, all that is in and about a man in this one word, so as to dispense with the distinctions between imaginative and non-imaginative, spiritual and unspiritual natures, and make every possible question about a man a mere question in the end as to the size or degree of his intellect. But such a mode of speaking is too violent and recondite for common purposes. According to the common use of the word intellect, it might be maintained (we do not say it would) that Swift's intellect, his strength of mental grasp, was equal to Milton's, and yet that, by reason of the fact that his intellectual style was different, or that he did not grasp things precisely in the

Miltonic way, a distinction might be drawn unfavourable to his genius as compared with that of Milton. According to such a view, we must seek for that in Swift's genius upon which it depends that, while we accord to it all the admiration we bestow on strength, our sympathies with height or sublimity are left unmoved. Nor have we far to seek. When Goethe and Niebuhr generalized in the phrase "the demonic element" that mystic something which they seemed to detect in men of unusual potency among their fellows, they used the word "demonic," not in its English sense, as signifying what appertains specially to the demons or powers of darkness, but in its Greek sense, as equally implying the unseen agencies of light and good. The demonic element in a man, therefore, may in one case be the demonic of the etherial and celestial, in another the demonic of the Tartarean and infernal. There is a demonic of the *super*natural—angels, and seraphs, and white-winged airy messengers, swaying men's phantasies from above; and there is a demonic of the *infra*-natural —fiends and shapes of horror tugging at men's thoughts from beneath. The demonic in Swift was of the latter kind. It is false, it would be an entire mistake as to his genius, to say that he regarded, or was inspired by, only the worldly and the secular—that men, women, and their relations in the little world of visible life, were all that his intellect cared to recognise. He also, like our Miltons and our Shakespeares, and all our men who have been anything more than prudential and pleasant writers, had his being anchored in things and imaginations beyond the visible verge. But, while it was given to them to hold rather by things and imaginations belonging to the region of the celestial, to hear angelic music and the rustling of seraphic wings, it was his unhappier lot to be related rather to the darker and subterranean mysteries. One might say of Swift that he had far less of belief in a God than of belief in a Devil. He is like a man walking on the earth and among the busy haunts of his fellow-mortals, observing them and their ways, and taking his part in the bustle, all the while, however, conscious of the tuggings downward of secret chains reaching into the world of the demons. Hence his ferocity, his misanthropy, his *sæva indignatio*, all of them true forms of energy, imparting unusual potency to a life, but forms of energy bred of communion with what outlies nature on the lower or infernal side.

Swift, doubtless, had this melancholic tendency in him constitutionally from the beginning. From the first we see him an unruly, rebellious, gloomy, revengeful, unforgiving spirit, loyal to no authority, and gnashing under every restraint. With nothing small or weak in his nature, too proud to be dishonest, bold and fearless in his opinions, capable of strong attachments and of

D U

hatred as strong, it was to be predicted that, if the swarthy Irish youth, whom Sir William Temple received into his house when his college had all but expelled him for contumacy, should ever be eminent in the world, it would be for fierce and controversial, and not for beautiful or harmonious, activity. It is clear, however, on a survey of Swift's career, that the gloom and melancholy which characterized it were not altogether congenital, but, in part at least, grew out of some special circumstance, or set of circumstances, having a precise date and locality among the facts of his life. In other words, there was some secret in Swift's life, some root of bitterness or remorse, diffusing a black poison throughout his whole existence. That communion with the invisible almost exclusively on the infernal side—that consciousness of chains wound round his own moving frame at the one end, and at the other held by demons in the depths of their populous pit, while no cords of love were felt sustaining him from the countervailing heaven—had its origin, in part at least, in some one recollection or cause of dread. It was some one demon down in that pit that held the chains; the others but assisted him. Thackeray's perception seems to us exact when he says of Swift that "he goes through life, tearing, like a man possessed with a devil;" or again, changing the form of the figure, that "like Abudah, in the Arabian story, he is always looking out for the Fury, and knows that the

night will come, and the inevitable hag with it."
What was this Fury, this hag that duly came in the
night, making the mornings horrible by the terrors of
recollection, the evenings horrible by those of anticipation, and leaving but a calm hour at full mid-day?
There was a secret in Swift's life: what was it? His
biographers as yet have failed to agree on this dark
topic. Thackeray's hypothesis, that the cause of
Swift's despair was chiefly his consciousness of disbelief
in the creed to which he had sworn his professional
faith, does not seem to us sufficient. In Swift's days,
and even with his frank nature, we think that difficulty
could have been got over. There was nothing, at least,
so unique in the case as to justify the supposition that
this was what Archbishop King referred to in that
memorable saying to Dr. Delany, " You have just met
the most miserable man on earth ; but on the subject
of his wretchedness you must never ask a question."
Had Swift made a confession of scepticism to the Archbishop, we do not think the prelate would have been
taken so very much by surprise. Nor can we think,
with some, that Swift's vertigo (now pronounced to have
been increasing congestion of the brain), and his life-
long certainty that it would end in idiocy or madness,
are the true explanation of this interview and of the
mystery which it shrouds. There was cause enough for
melancholy here, but not exactly the cause that meets

the case. Another hypothesis there is of a physical
kind, which Scott and others hint at, and which finds
great acceptance with the medical philosophers. Swift, it
is said, was of "a cold temperament," &c.,&c. But why
a confession on the part of Swift that he was not a mar-
riageable man, even had he added that he desired, above
all things in the world, to be a person of that sort, should
have so moved the heart of an Archbishop as to make
him shed tears, one cannot conceive. Besides, although
this hypothesis might explain much of the Stella and
Vanessa imbroglio, it would not explain all ; nor do we
see on what foundation it could rest. Scott's assertion
that all through Swift's writings there is no evidence of
his having felt the tender passion is simply untrue. On
the whole, the hypothesis which has been started of a
too near consanguinity between Swift and Stella, either
known from the first to one or both, or discovered too
late, would most nearly suit the conditions of the case.
And yet, as far as we have seen, this hypothesis also
rests on air, with no one fact to support it. Could we
suppose that Swift, like another Eugene Aram, went
through the world with a murder on his mind, it might
be taken as a solution of the mystery ; but, as we cannot
do this, we must be content with supposing that either
some one of the foregoing hpyotheses, or some combination of them, is to be accepted, or that the
matter is altogether inscrutable.

Such by constitution as we have described him—with
an intellect strong as iron, much acquired knowledge,
an ambition all but insatiable, and a decided desire to
be wealthy—Swift, almost as a matter of course, flung
himself impetuously into that Whig and Tory controversy which was the question paramount in his time.
In that he laboured as only a man of his powers could,
bringing to the side of the controversy on which he
chanced to be (and we believe when he was on a side it
was honestly because he found a certain preponderance
of right in it) a hard and ruthless vigour which served
it immensely. But from the first, or at all events after
the disappointments of a political career had been
experienced by him, his nature would not work merely
in the narrow warfare of Whiggism and Toryism, but
overflowed in general bitterness of reflection on all the
customs and ways of humanity. The following passage
in *Gulliver's Voyage to Brobdingnay*, describing how the
politics of Europe appeared to the King of Brobdingnag,
shows us Swift himself in his larger mood of thought.

"This prince took a pleasure in conversing with me,
inquiring into the manners, religion, laws, government,
and learning of Europe; wherein I gave him the best
account I was able. His apprehension was so clear, and
his judgment so exact, that he made very wise reflections
and observations upon all I said. But I confess that,
after I had been a little too copious in talking of my
own beloved country, of our trade, and wars by sea and

land, of our schisms in religion and parties in the state, the prejudices of his education prevailed so far that he could not forbear taking me up in his right hand, and, stroking me gently with the other, after a hearty fit of laughing asking me whether *I* was a •Whig or Tory. Then, turning to his first minister, who waited behind him with a white staff nearly as tall as the mainmast of the 'Royal Sovereign,' he observed how contemptible a thing was human grandeur, which could be mimicked by such diminutive insects as I; 'And yet,' says he, ' I dare engage these creatures have their titles and distinctions of honour; they contrive little nests and burrows, that they call houses and cities; they make a figure in dress and equipage ; they love, they fight, they dispute, they cheat, they betray.' And thus he continued on, while my colour came and went several times with indignation to hear our noble country, the mistress of arts and arms, the scourge of France, the arbitress of Europe, the seat of virtue, piety, honour, truth, the pride and envy of the world, so contemptuously treated."

Swift's writings, accordingly, divide themselves, in the main, into two classes,—pamphlets, tracts, lampoons, and the like, bearing directly on persons and topics of the day, and written with the ordinary purpose of a partisan ; and satires of a more general aim, directed, in the spirit of a cynic philosopher, against humanity on the whole, or against particular human classes, arrangements, and modes of thinking. In some of his writings the politician and the general satirist are seen together. The *Drapier's Letters* and most of the poetical lampoons exhibit Swift in his direct character as a party-writer; in the *Tale of a Tub* we have the ostensible purpose of a partisan masking a reserve of general scepticism; in the *Battle of the Books* we have a satire partly personal to individuals, partly with a reference to a prevailing tone of opinion; in the *Voyage to Laputa* we have a satire on a great class of men; and in the *Voyages to Lilliput and Brobdingnag,* and still more in the story of the *Houyhnhnms* and *Yahoos,* we have human nature itself analysed and laid bare.

Swift took no care of his writings, never acknowledged some of them, never collected them, and suffered them to find their way about the world as chance, demand, and the piracy of publishers, directed. As all know, it is in his character as a humourist, an inventor of the preposterous as a medium for the reflective, and above all as a master of irony, that he takes his place as one of the chiefs of English literature. There can be no doubt that, as regards the literary form which he affected most, he took hints from Rabelais as the greatest original in the realm of the absurd. Sometimes, as in his description of the Strulbrugs in the *Voyage to Laputa,* he approaches the ghastly power of that writer; but on the whole there is more of stern English realism in him, and less of sheer riot and wildness. Sometimes, however, Swift throws off the disguise of the humourist, and speaks seriously and in his own name. On such occasions we find ourselves in the presence of a man of strong, sagacious, and thoroughly English mind, content, as is the habit of most Englishmen, with vigorous proximate sense, expressed in plain and rather coarse idiom. For the speculative he shows in these cases neither liking nor aptitude: he takes obvious reasons and arguments as they come to hand, and uses them in a robust, down-right, Saxon manner. In one respect he stands out conspicuously even among plain Saxon writers—his total freedom from cant. Johnson's advice to Boswell, "above all things to clear his mind of cant," was perhaps never better illustrated than in the case of Dean Swift. Indeed, it might be given as a summary definition of Swift's character that he had cleared his mind of cant without having succeeded in filling the void with song. It was Swift's intense hatred of cant—cant in religion, cant in morality, cant in literature—that occasioned many of those peculiarities which shock people in his writings. His principle being to view things as they are, with no regard to the accumulated cant of orators and poets, he naturally prosecuted his investigations into those classes of facts which orators and poets have omitted as unsuitable for their purposes. If they had viewed men as Angels, he would view them as

Yahoos. If they had placed the springs of action among the fine phrases and the sublimities, he would trace them down into their secret connections with the bestial and the obscene. Hence, as much as for any of those physiological reasons which some of his biographers assign for it, his undisguised delight in filth. And hence, also, probably—since among the forms of cant he included the traditional manner of speaking of women in their relations to men—his studious contempt, whether in writing for men or for women, of all the accustomed decencies. It was not only the more obvious forms of cant, however, that Swift had in aversion. Even to that minor form of cant which consists in the "trite" he gave no quarter. Whatever was habitually said by the majority of people seemed to him, for that very reason, not worthy of being said at all, much less put into print. A considerable portion of his writings, as, for example, his *Tritical Essay on the Faculties of the Mind*, and his *Art of Polite Conversation*—in the one of which he strings together a series of the most threadbare maxims and quotations to be found in books, offering the compilation as a gravely original disquisition, while in the other he imitates the insipidity of ordinary table-talk in society—may be regarded as showing a systematic determination on his part to turn the trite into ridicule. Hence, in his own writings, though he refrains from the profound, he never falls into the commonplace.

Apart from Swift's other views, there are to be found scattered through his writings not a few distinct propositions of an innovative character respecting our social arrangements. We have seen his doctrine as to the education of women; and we may mention, as another instance of the same kind, his denunciation of the system of standing armies as incompatible with freedom. Curiously enough, also, it was Swift's belief that, Yahoos though we are, the world is always in the right.

HOW LITERATURE MAY ILLUSTRATE

HISTORY.

HOW LITERATURE MAY ILLUSTRATE

HISTORY.[1]

SOME of the ways in which Literature may illustrate
History are obvious enough. In the poems, the songs,
the dramas, the novels, the satires, the speeches, even
the speculative treatises, of any time or nation, there
is imbedded a wealth of direct particulars respecting
persons and events, additional to the information that
has been transmitted in the formal records of that time
or nation, or in its express histories of itself. "It has
often come to my ears that it is a saying too frequently
in your mouth that you have lived long enough for
yourself:" so did Cicero, if the speech in which the
passage occurs is really his, address Cæsar face to face,
in the height of his power, and not long before his
assassination, remonstrating with him on his melancholy, and his carelessness of a life so precious to Rome
and to the world. If the words are any way authentic,
what a flash they are into the mind of the great Roman

[1] *Macmillan's Magazine*, July 1871.

in his last years, when, *blasé* with wars and victories, and all the sensations that the largest life on earth could afford, he walked about the streets of Rome, consenting to live on so long as there might be need, but, so far as he himself was concerned, heedless when the end might come, the conspirators in a ring round him, the short scuffle, the first sharp stab of the murderous knife!

Let this pass as one instance of a valuable illustration of Biography and History derived from casual reading. Literature teems with such : no one can tell what particles of direct historical and biographical information lie yet undiscovered and unappropriated in miscellaneous books. But there is an extension of the use for the historian of the general literature of the time with which he may be concerned. Not only does Literature teem with yet unappropriated anecdotes respecting the persons and events of most prominent interest in the consecutive history of the world ; but quite apart from this, the books, and especially the popular books, of any time, are the richest possible storehouses of the kind of information the historian wants. Whatever may be the main thread of his narrative, he has to re-imagine more or less vividly what is called the general life of the time, its manners, customs, humours, ways of thinking, the working of its institutions, all the peculiarities of that patch of the never-ending, ever-changing rush and bustle of human affairs, to-day above the ground, and to-morrow under. Well, here in the books of the time he has his materials and aids. They were formed in the conditions of the time; the time played itself into them; they are saturated with its spirit; and costumes, customs, modes of eating and drinking, town-life, country life, the traveller on horseback to his inn, the shoutings of mobs in riot, what grieved them, what they hated, what they laughed at, all are there. No matter of what kind the book is, or what was its author's aim; it is, in spite of itself, a bequest out of the very body and being of that time, reminding us thereof by its structure through and through, and by a crust of innumerable allusions. It has been remarked by Hallam, and by others, how particularly useful in this way for the historian, as furnishing him with social details of past times, are popular books more especially of the humorous order— comic dramas and farces, poems of occasion, and novels and works of prose-fiction generally. How the plays of Aristophanes admit us to the public life of Athens! How, as we read the Satires and Epistles of Horace, we see old Rome, like another huge London, only with taller houses, and the masons mending the houses, and the poet himself, like a modern official in Somerset House, trudging along to his office, jostled by the crowds, and having to get out of the way of the ladders and the falling rubbish, thinking all the while of his appointment with Mæcenas! Or, if it is the reign of George II. in Britain that we are studying, where shall we find better illustration of much of the life, and especially the London life, of that coarse, wig-wearing age, than in the novels of Fielding and Smollett?

These, and perhaps other ways in which Literature may illustrate History, are tolerably obvious, and need no farther exposition. There is, however, a higher and somewhat more subtle service which Literature may perform towards illustrating History and modifying our ideas of the Past.

What the historian chiefly and finally wants to get at, through all his researches, and by all his methods of research, is the *mind* of the time that interests him, its mode of thinking and feeling. Through all the trappings, all the colours, all the costumes, all those circumstances of the picturesque which delight us in our recollections of the past, this is what we seek, or ought to seek. The trappings and picturesque circumstances are but our optical helps in our quest of this; they are the thickets of metaphor through which we push the quest, interpreting as we go. The metaphors resolve themselves; and at last it is as if we had reached that vital and essential something—a clear transparency, we seem to fancy it, and yet a kind of throbbing transparency, a transparency with pulses and powers—which we call the mind or spirit of the time. As in the case of the individual, so in that of a time or a people, we seem to have got at the end of our language when we use this word, mind or spirit. We know what we mean, and it is the last thing that we can mean; but, just on that account, it eludes description or definition. At best we can go to and fro among a few convenient synonyms and images. Soul, mind, spirit, these old and simple words are the strongest, the profoundest, the surest; age cannot antiquate them, nor science undo them; they last with the rocks, and still go beyond. But, having in view rather the operation than the cause, we find a use also in such alternative phrases as "mode of thinking," "mode of feeling and thinking," "habit of thought," "moral and intellectual character or constitution," and the like. Or, again, if we will have an image of that which from its nature is unimaginable, then, in our efforts to be as pure and abstract as possible, we find ourselves driven, as I have said, into a fancy of mind as a kind of clear aërial transparency, unbounded or of indefinite bounds, and yet not a dead transparency, but a transparency full of pulses, powers, motions, and whirls, capable in a moment of clouding itself, ceasing to be a transparency, and becoming some strange solid phantasmagory, as of a landscape smiling in sunshine or a sky dark with a storm. Yet again there is another and more mechanical conception of mind which may be of occasional use. The thinking power, the thinking principle, the substance which feels and thinks, are phrases for mind from of old: what if we were to agree, for a momentary advantage, to call mind rudely the thinking apparatus? What the advantage may be will presently appear.

Mind, mode of thinking, mode of thinking and feeling, moral and intellectual constitution, that mystic transparency full of pulses and motions, this thinking apparatus,—whichever phrase or image we adopt, there are certain appertaining considerations which we have to take along with us.

(1.) There is the consideration of differences of degree, quality, and worth. Mind may be great or small, noble or mean, strong or weak; the mode of thinking of one person or one time may be higher, finer, grander than that of another; the moral and intellectual constitutions of diverse individuals or peoples may present all varieties of the admirable and lovely or the despicable and unlovely; the pulses and motions in that mystic transparency which we fancy as one man's mind may be more vehement, more awful, more rhythmical and musical, than are known in that which we fancy as the mind of some other; the thinking apparatus which A possesses, and by which he performs the business of his life, may be more massive, more complex, more exquisite, capable of longer reaches and more superb combinations, than that which has fallen to the lot of B. All this is taken for granted everywhere; all our speech and conduct proceed on the assumption.

(2.) Somewhat less familiar, but not unimportant, is a consideration which I may express by calling it the necessary instability of mind, its variability from moment to moment. Your mind, my mind, every mind, is continually sustaining modifications, disintegrations, reconstructions, by all that acts upon it, by all it comes to know. We are much in the habit, indeed, of speaking of experience, of different kinds of knowledge, as so much material for the mind—material delivered into it, outspread as it were on its floor, and which it, the lord and master, may survey, let lie there for occasion, and now and then select from and employ. True! but not the whole truth! The mind does not stand amid what it knows, as something distinct and untouched; the mind is actually composed at any one moment of all that it has learnt or felt up to that moment. Every new information received, every piece of knowledge gained, every joy enjoyed, every sorrow suffered, is then and there transmuted into mind, and becomes incorporate with the prior central substance. To resort now to that mechanical figure which I said might be found useful: every new piece of information, every fact that one comes to apprehend, every probability brought before one in the course of life, is not only so much new matter for the thinking apparatus to lay hold of and work into the warp and woof of thought; it is actually also a modification of the thinking apparatus itself. The mind thinks *with* what it knows; and, if you alter the knowledge in any one whit, you alter the thinking instrumentality in proportion. Our whole practice of education is based on this idea, and yet somehow the idea is allowed to lurk. It may be brought out best perhaps by thinking what may happen to a mind that has passed the period of education in the ordinary sense. A person of mature age, let us say, betakes himself, for the first time, to the study of geology. He gains thereby so much new and important knowledge of a particular kind. Yes! but he does more. He modifies his previous mind; he introduces a difference into his mode of thinking by a positive addition to that instrumentality of notions *with* which he thinks. The geological conceptions which he has acquired become an organic part of that reason, that intellect, which he applies to all things whatsoever; he will think and imagine thenceforward with the help of an added potency, and, consequently, never again precisely as he did before. Generalize this hint, and let it run through history. The mind of Man cannot remain the same through two consecutive generations, if only because the knowledge which feeds and makes mind, the notions that constitute the thinking power, are continually varying. In this age of a hundred sciences, all tramping on Nature's outside with their flags up, and marching her round and round, and searching her through and through for her secrets, and flinging into the public forum their heaps of results, how is it possible to call mind the same as it was a generation or two ago, when the sciences were fewer, their industry more leisurely, and their discoveries less frequent? Nay, but we may go back not a generation or two only, but to generation beyond generation through a long series, still, as we ascend, finding the sciences fewer, earth's load of knowledge lighter, and man's very imagination of the physical universe which he tenants cruder and more diminutive. Till two hundred years ago the Mundus, or physical system of things, to even the most learned of men, with scarcely an exception, was a finite spectacular sphere, or succession of spheres, that of the fixed stars nearly outermost, wheeling round the central earth for her pleasure; as we penetrate through still prior centuries, even this finite spherical Mundus is seen to shrink and shrink in men's fancies of it till a radius of some hundreds of miles would sweep from the earth to the starry roof; back beyond that again the very notion of sphericity disappears, and men were walking, as it seemed, on the upper side of a flat disc, close under a concave of blue, travelled by fiery caprices. How is it possible to regard man's mode of thinking and feeling, man's mind, as in any way constant through such vicissitude in man's notions respecting his very housing in space, and the whole encircling touch of his physical belongings?

(3.) A third consideration, however, administers a kind of corrective to the last. It is that, though the last consideration is not unimportant, its importance practically, and as far as the range of historic time is concerned, may be easily exaggerated. We have supposed a person betaking himself to the study of geology, and have truly said that his very mode of thinking would be thereby affected, that his geological knowledge would pass into his reason, and determine so far the very cast of his mind, the form of his ability. Well, but he might have betaken himself to something else; and who can tell, without definite investigation, but that out of that something else he might have derived as much increase of his mental power, or even greater? There are thousands of employments for all minds, and, though all may select, and select differently, there are thousands for all in common. Life itself, all the inevitable activity of life, is one vast and most complex schooling. Books or no books, sciences or no sciences, we live, we look, we love, we laugh, we fear, we hate, we wonder; we are sons, we are brothers, we have friends; the seasons return, the sun shines, the moon walks in beauty, the sea roars and beats the land, the winds blow, the leaves fall; we are young, we grow old; we commit others to their graves, we see somewhere the little grassy mound which shall conceal ourselves: —is not this a large enough primary school for all and sundry; are not these sufficient and everlasting rudiments? That so it is we all recognise. Given some original force or goodness of nature, and out of even this primary school, and from the teaching of these common rudiments, may there not come, do there not come, minds worthy of mark—the shrewd, keen wit, the upright and robust judgment, the disposition tender and true, the bold and honest man? And though, for perfection, the books and the sciences must be superadded, yet do not the rudiments persist in constant over-proportion and incessant compulsory repetition through all the process of culture, and is not the great result of culture itself a reaction on the rudiments? And so, without prejudice to our foregone conclusion that mind is variable with knowledge, that every new science or body of notions conquered for the world modifies the world's mode of thinking and feeling, alters the cast and the working trick of its reason and imagination, we can yet fall back, for historic time at least, on the notion of a human mind so essentially permanent and traditional that we cannot decide by mere chronology where we may justly be fondest of it, and certainly cannot assume that its latest individual specimens, with all their advantages, are necessarily the ablest, the noblest, or the cleverest. In fact, however we may reconcile it with our theories of vital evolution and progressive civilization, we all instinctively agree in this style of sentiment. Shakespeare lived and died, we may say, in the pre-scientific period; he lived and died in the belief of the fixedness of our earth in space and the diurnal wheeling round her of the ten spectacular spheres. Not the less was he Shakespeare; and none of us dares to say that there is now in the world, or has recently been, a more superb thinking apparatus of its order than his mind was, a spiritual transparency of larger diameter, or vivid with grander gleamings and pulses. Two hundred and fifty years, therefore, chock-full though they are of new knowledges and discoveries, have not been a single knife-edge of visible advance in the world's power of producing splendid individuals; and, if we add two hundred and fifty to that, and again two hundred and fifty, and four times two hundred and fifty more without stopping, still we cannot discern that there has been a knife-edge of advance in that particular. For at this last remove we are among the Romans, and beyond them there lie the Greeks; and side by side with both, and beyond both, are other Mediterranean Indo-Europeans, and, away in Asia, clumps and masses of various Orientals. For ease of reference, let us go no farther than the Greeks. Thinking apparatuses of first-rate grip! mental transparencies of large diameter and tremulous with great powers and pulses! What do we say to Homer, Plato, Æschylus, Sophocles, Euripides, Aristophanes, Thucydides, Aristotle, Demosthenes, and the rest of the great Hellenic cluster which these represent! True, their cosmology was in a muddle (perhaps *ours* is in a muddle too, for as little as we think so); but somehow they contrived to be such that the world doubts to this day whether, on the whole, at any time since, it has exhibited, in such close grouping, such a constellation of spirits of the highest magnitude. And the lesson enforced by this Greek instance may be enforced, less blazingly perhaps, but still clearly, as by the light of scattered stars, by instances from the whole course of historic time. Within that range, despite the vicissitudes of the mode of human thought caused by continued inquisitiveness and its results in new knowledges, despite the change from age to age in mankind's very image of its own whereabouts in space, and the extent of that whereabouts, and the complexity of the entanglement in which it rolls, it is still true that you may probe at any point with the sure expectation of finding at least *some* minds as good intrinsically, as strong, as noble, as valiant, as inventive, as any in our own age of latest appearances and all the newest lights.

I am aware, of course, where the compensation may be sought. The philosophical historian may contend that, though some minds of early ages have been as able intrinsically as any minds of later ages, these later minds being themselves the critics and judges, yet an enormous general progress may be made out in the increased *number* in the later ages of minds tolerably able, in the heightening of the general level, in the more equable diffusion of intelligence, in the gradual extension of freedom, and the humanizing of manners and institutions. On that question I am not called upon to enter now, nor is my opinion on it to be inferred from anything I am now saying. I limit myself to the assertion that within historic time we find what we are obliged to call an intrinsic' co-equality of *some* minds at various successive points and at long-separated intervals, and that consequently, if the human race *is* gradually acquiring a power of producing individuals more able than their ablest predecessors, the rate of its law in this respect is so slow that 2,500 years have not made the advance appreciable. The assertion is limited; it is reconcilable, I believe, with the most absolute and extreme doctrine of evolution; but it seems to be both important and curious, inasmuch as it has not yet been sufficiently attended to in any of the phrasings of that doctrine that have been speculatively put forward. No doctrine is rightly phrased, I would submit, when, if it were true according to that phrasing, it would be man's highest duty to proceed as if it weren't.

History itself, the mere tradition and records of the human race, would have authorized our assertion. Pericles, Epaminondas, Alexander the Great, Hannibal, Julius Cæsar, Charlemagne: would not the authenticated tradition of the lives and actions of those men, and others of their order, or of other orders, prove that possible capacity of the individual mind has not, for the last 2,500 years of our earth's history, been a mere affair of chronological date? But it is Literature that reads us the lesson most fully and convincingly. Some of those great men of action have left little or no direct speech of themselves. They mingled their minds with the rage of things around them; they worked, and strove, and died. But the books we have from all periods, the poems, the songs, the treatises, the pleadings—some of them from men great also in the world of action, but most from men who only looked on, and thought, and tried to rule the spirit, or to find how it might be ruled—these remain with us and can be studied yet microscopically. If what the Historian wants to get at is the mind of the time that interests him, or of the past generally, here it is for him in no disguised form, but in actual specimens. Poems, treatises, and the like, are actual transmitted *bits* of the mind of the past; every fragment of verse or prose from a former period preserves something of the thought and sentiment of that period expressed by some one belonging to it; the masterpieces of the world's literature are the thought and feeling of successive generations expressed, in and for each generation, by those who could express them best. What a purblind perversity then it is for History, professing that its aim is to know the mind or real life of the past, to be fumbling for that mind or life amid old daggers, rusty iron caps and jingling jackets, and other such material relics as the past has transmitted, or even groping for it, as ought to be done most strictly, in statutes and charters and records, if all the while those literary remains of the past are neglected from which the very thing searched for stares us face to face!

There is a small corollary to our main proposition. It is that ages which we are accustomed to regard as crude, barbarous, and uncivilized, may turn out perhaps, on due investigation and a better construction of the records, to have been not so crude and barbarous after all, but to have contained a great deal of intrinsic humanity, interesting to us yet, and capable, through all intervening time and difference, of folding itself round our hearts. And here I will quit those great, but perhaps too continually obtrusive, Greeks and

Romans, and will take my examples, all the homelier though they must be, from our own land and kindred.

The Fourteenth Century in our island was not what we should now hold up as a model age, a soft age, an orderly age, an instructed age, a pleasant age for a lady or gentleman that has been accustomed to modern ideas and modern comforts to be transferred back into. It was the age of the three first Edwards, Richard II., and Henry IV. in England, and of the Wallace Interregnum, Bruce, David II., and the two first Stuarts in Scotland. Much was done in it, as these names will suggest, that has come down as picturesque story and stirring popular legend. It is an age, on that account, in which schoolboys and other plain uncritical readers of both nations revel with peculiar relish. Critical inquirers, too, and real students of history, especially of late, have found it an age worth their while, and have declared it full of important facts and powerful characters. Not the less the inveterate impression among a large number of persons of a rapid modern way of thinking is that all this interesting vision of the England and Scotland of the fourteenth century is mere poetical glamour or antiquarian make-believe, and that the real state of affairs was one of mud, mindlessness, fighting and scramble generally, no tea and no newspapers, but plenty of hanging, and murder almost *ad libitum*. Now these are most wrong-headed persons,

and they might be beaten black and blue by sheer force
of records. But out of kindliness one may take a
gentler method with them, and try to bring them right
by æsthetic suasion. It so chances, for example, that
there are literary remains of the fourteenth century,
both English and Scottish, and that the authors of the
chief of these were Geoffrey Chaucer, the father of
English literature proper, and John Barbour, the father
of the English literature of North Britain. Let us take
a few bits from Chaucer and Barbour. Purposely, we
shall take bits that may be already familiar.

Here is Chaucer's often-quoted description of the
scholar, or typical student of Oxford University, from
the Prologue to his *Canterbury Tales :—*

> A Clerk there was of Oxenford also,
> That unto logic haddè long ygo,
> As leanè was his horse as is a rake,
> And *he* was not right fat, I undertake;
> But lookèd hollow, and thereto soberly.
> Full threadbare was his overest courtepy;
> For he had getten him yet no benefice,
> Ne was so worldly for to have oflice;
> For him was liefer have at his bed's head
> A twenty books, clothèd in black and red,
> Of Aristotle and his philosophie
> Than robès rich, or fiddle, or sautrie.
> But, albe that he was a philosópher,
> Yet had he but a little gold in coffer;

But all that he might of his friendès hent
On bookès and on learning he it spent,
And busily gan for the soulès pray
Of hem that gave him wherewith to scholay.
Of study took he most cure and most heed ;
Not oe word spak he morè than was need ;
And that was said in form and reverence,
And short and quick, and full of high sentence ;
Souning in moral virtue was his speech,
And gladly would he learn, and gladly teach.

Or take an out-of-doors' scene from one of Chaucer's reputed minor poems. It is a description of a grove or wood in spring, or early summer : —

In which were oakès great, straight as a line,
Under the which the grass, so fresh of hue,
Was newly sprung, and an eight foot or nine
Every tree well fro his fellow grew,
With branches broad, laden with leavès new,
That sprungen out agen the sunnè-sheen,
Some very red, and some a glad light green.

Or, for a tidy scene indoors, take this from another poem :—

And, sooth to sayen, my chamber was
Full well depainted, and with glass
Were all the windows well yglazed
Full clear, and not an hole ycrased,
That to behold it was great joy ;
For wholly all the story of Troy

Was in the glazing ywrought thus,
Of Hector and of King Priamus,
Of Achilles and of King Laomedon,
And eke of Medea and Jason,
Of Paris, Helen, and Lavine;
And all the walls with colours fine
Weren paint, both text and glose,
And all the Rómaunt of the Rose:
My windows weren shut each one,
And through the glass the sunnè shone
Upon my bed with brighte beams.

Or take these stanzas of weighty ethical sententious-
ness (usually printed as Chaucer's, but whether his or
not does not matter):—

Fly from the press, and dwell with soothfastness;
Suffice unto thy good, though it be small;
For hoard hath hate, and climbing tickleness,
Press hath envy, and weal is blent in all;
Savour no more than thee behovè shall;
Rede well thyself that other folk canst rede;
And truth shall thee deliver, it is no drede.

Painè thee not each crooked to redress
In trust of her that turneth as a ball.
Great rest standeth in little business;
Beware also to spurn against an awl;
Strive not as doth a crockè with a wall;
Deemè thyself that deemest others dead;
And truth shall thee deliver, it is no drede.

> That thee is sent receive in buxomness;
> The wrestling of this world asketh a fall;
> Here is no home, here is but wilderness:
> Forth, pilgrim! forth, beast, out of thy stall!
> Look up on high, and thankè God of all:
> Waivè thy lusts, and let thy ghost thee lead;
> And truth shall thee deliver, it is no drede.

Or, finally, take a little bit of Chaucer's deep, keen slyness, when he is speaking smilingly about himself and his own poetry. He has represented himself as standing in the House or Temple of Fame, observing company after company going up to the goddess, and petitioning for renown in the world for what they have done. Some she grants what they ask, others she dismisses crestfallen, and Chaucer thinks the *levée* over:—

> With that I gan about to wend,
> For one that stood right at my back
> Methought full goodly to me spak,
> And said, " Friend, what is thy name?
> Art *thou* come hither to have fame?"
> " Nay, forsoothè, friend," quoth I;
> " I came not hither, grammercy,
> For no such causè, by my head.
> Sufficeth me, as I were dead,
> That no wight have *my* name in hand:
> I wot myself best how I stand;
> For what I dree or what I think
> I will myselfè all it drink,
> Certain for the morè part,
> As farforth as I ken mine art!"

Chaucer ranks to this day as one of the very greatest
and finest minds in the entire literature of the English
speech, and stands therefore on a level far higher than
can be assumed for his contemporary Barbour.   But
Barbour was a most creditable old worthy too.   Let us
have a scrap or two from his *Bruce.*   Who does not
know the famous passage which is the very key-note of
that poem ?   One is never tired of quoting it :—

> Ah ! freedom is a noble thing ;
> Freedom makes man to have liking :
> Freedom all solace to man gives ;
> He lives at ease that freely lives.
> A noble heart may have nane ease,
> Ne ellys nought that may him please
> Gif freedom faileth ; for free liking
> Is yearnit ower all other thing ;
> Nor he that aye has livit free
> May not know weel the propertie,
> The anger, ne the wretched doom,
> That is couplit to foul thirldom ;
> But, gif he had essayit it,
> Then all perquére he suld it wit,
> And suld think freedom mair to prize
> Than all the gold in the warld that is.

Or take the portrait of the good Sir James, called
" The Black Douglas," the chief companion and ad-
herent of Bruce, introduced near the beginning of the
poem, where he is described as a young man living
moodily at St. Andrews before the Bruce revolt :—

Ane weel great while there dwellit he :
All men loved him for his bountie ;
For he was of full fair effere,
Wise, courteous, and debonair ;
Large and lovand also was he,
And ower all thing loved loyauty.
Loyautie to love is gretumly ;
Through loyautie men lives richtwisely ;
With a virtue of loyautie
Ane man may yet sufficiand be ;
And, but loyautie, may nane have prize,
Whether he be wicht or be he wise ;
For, where *it* failis, nae virtue
May be of prize, ne of value
To mak ane man sae good that he
May simply callit good man be.
He was in all his deedès leal ;
For him dedeignit not to deal
With treachery ne with falsét.
His heart on high honóur was set,
And him contened in sic manére
That all him loved that war him near.
But he was not sae fair that we
Suld speak greatly of his beautie.
In visage was he somedeal grey,
And had black hair, as I heard say ;
But of his limbs he was well made,
With banès great and shoulders braid ;
His body was well made leanlie,
As they that saw him said to me.
When he was blythe, he was lovely
And meek and sweet in company ;

> But wha in battle micht him see
> All other countenance had he.
> And in speech lispit he somedeal;
> But that set him richt wonder weel.
> To Good Hector of Troy micht he
> In mony thingès likenit be.
> Hector had black hair as he had,
> And stark limbès and richt weel made,
> And lispit also as did he,
> And was fulfillit of loyantie,
> And was courteous, and wise, and wicht.

My purpose in quoting these passages from Chaucer and Barbour will have been anticipated. Let me, however, state it in brief. We hear sometimes in these days of a certain science, or rather portion of a more general science, which takes to itself the name of *Social Statics*, and professes, under that name, to have for its business—I give the very phrase of those who define it — the investigation of "possible social simultaneities." That is to say, there may be a science of what can possibly go along with what in any social state or stage; or, to put it otherwise, any one fact or condition of a state of society being given, there may be inferred from that fact or condition some of the other facts and conditions that must necessarily have co-existed with it. Thus at length perhaps, by continued inference, the whole state of an old society might be imaged out, just as Cuvier, from the sight of one bone, could infer with tolerable accuracy the general structure of the animal. Well, will *Social Statics* be so good as to take the foregoing passages, and whirr out of them their " possible social simultaneities " ? Were this done, I should be surprised if the England and Scotland of the fourteenth century were to turn out so very unlovely, so atrociously barbarian, after all. These passages are actual transmitted bits of the English and Scottish mind of that age, and surely the substance from which they are extracts cannot have been so very coarse or bad. Where such sentiments existed and were expressed, where the men that could express them lived and were appreciated, the surrounding medium of thought, of institutions, and of customs, must have been to correspond. There must have been truth, and honour, and courtesy, and culture, round those men ; there must have been high heart, shrewd sense, delicate art, gentle behaviour, and, in one part of the island at least, a luxuriant complexity of most subtle and exquisite circumstance.

The conclusion which we have thus reached vindicates that mood of mind towards the whole historical past which we find to have been actually the mood of all the great masters of literature whenever they have ranged back in the past for their themes. When

Shakespeare writes of Richard II., who lived two hundred years before his own time, does he not overleap those two hundred years as a mere nothing, plunge in among Richard's Englishmen as intrinsically not different from so many great Elizabethans, make them talk and act as co-equals in whom Elizabethans could take an interest, and even fill the mouth of the weak monarch himself with soliloquies of philosophic melancholy and the kingliest verbal splendours? And so when the same poet goes back into a still remoter antique, as in the council of the Greek chiefs in his *Troilus and Cressida*. We speak of Shakespeare's anachronisms in such cases. There they are certainly for the critic to note; but they only serve to bring out more clearly his main principle in his art—his sense or instinct, for all historic time, of a grand over-matching synchronism. And, indeed, without something of this instinct — this sense of an intrinsic traditional humanity persisting through particular progressive variations, this belief in a co-equality of at least some minds through all the succession of human ages in what we call the historic period—what were the past of mankind to us much more than a history of dogs or ruminants? Nay, and with that measure with which we mete out to others, with the same measure shall it not be meted out to ourselves? If to be dead is to be inferior, and if to be long dead is to be despicable, to the generation in possession, shall not we who are in possession now have passed into the state of inferiority to-morrow, with all the other defunct beyond us, and will not a time come when some far future generation will lord it on the earth, and *we* shall lie deep, deep down, among the strata of the despicable?

THE END.

LONDON ; R. CLAY, SONS, AND TAYLOR, PRINTERS.

BEDFORD STREET, COVENT GARDEN, LONDON,
October 1879.

MACMILLAN & CO.'S CATALOGUE of Works in BELLES LETTRES, including Poetry, Fiction, etc.

Allingham.—LAURENCE BLOOMFIELD IN IRELAND; OR, THE NEW LANDLORD. By WILLIAM ALLINGHAM. New and Cheaper Issue, with a Preface. Fcap. 8vo. cloth. 4*s.* 6*d.*

An Ancient City, and other Poems.—By A NATIVE OF SURREY. Extra fcap. 8vo. 6*s.*

Anderson.—BALLADS AND SONNETS. By ALEXANDER ANDERSON (Surfaceman). Extra fcap. 8vo. 5*s.*

"*As an instance of culture under difficulties this work is of the highest interest.*"—ACADEMY.

Archer.—CHRISTINA NORTH. By E. M. ARCHER. New and Cheaper Edition. Crown 8vo. 6*s.*

Arnold. — THE POETICAL WORKS OF MATTHEW ARNOLD. Vol. I. EARLY POEMS, NARRATIVE POEMS, AND SONNETS. Vol. II. LYRIC, DRAMATIC, AND ELEGIAC POEMS. New and Complete Edition. Two Vols. Crown 8vo. Price 7*s.* 6*d.* each.

SELECTED POEMS OF MATTHEW ARNOLD. With Vignette engraved by C. H. JEENS (GOLDEN TREASURY SERIES). 18mo. 4*s.* 6*d.*

Large Paper Edition. Crown 8vo. 12*s.* 6*d.*

Art at Home Series.—Edited by W. J. LOFTIE, F.S.A.

"*If the whole series but continue as it has been begun—if the volumes yet to be rival these two initial—it will be beyond price as a library of household art.*"—EXAMINER.

A PLEA FOR ART IN THE HOUSE. With especial reference to the Economy of Collecting Works of Art, and the importance of Taste in Education and Morals. By W. J. LOFTIE, B.A., F.S.A. With Illustrations. Fifth Thousand. Crown 8vo. 2*s.* 6*d.*

SUGGESTIONS FOR HOUSE DECORATION IN PAINTING, WOODWORK, AND FURNITURE. By RHODA and AGNES GARRETT. With Illustrations. Sixth Thousand. Crown 8vo. 2*s.* 6*d.*

Art at Home Series—*continued.*

MUSIC IN THE HOUSE. By JOHN HULLAH. With Illustrations. Fourth Thousand. Crown 8vo. 2s. 6d.

THE DRAWING ROOM; ITS DECORATIONS AND FURNITURE. By Mrs. ORRINSMITH. Illustrated. Fifth Thousand. Crown 8vo. 2s. 6d.

THE DINING ROOM. By Mrs. LOFTIE. Illustrated. Fourth Thousand. Crown 8vo. 2s. 6d.

THE BED ROOM AND BOUDOIR. By LADY BARKER. Illustrated. Fourth Thousand. Crown 8vo. 2s. 6d.

DRESS. By Mrs. OLIPHANT. Illustrated. Crown 8vo. 2s. 6d.

PRIVATE THEATRICALS. By Lady POLLOCK. Illustrated.
[*Shortly.*

[Other vols. in preparation.]

Atkinson. — AN ART TOUR TO THE NORTHERN CAPITALS OF EUROPE. By J. BEAVINGTON ATKINSON. 8vo. 12s.

"*We can highly recommend it; not only for the valuable information it gives on the special subjects to which it is dedicated, but also for the interesting episodes of travel which are interwoven with, ana lighten, the weightier matters of judicious and varied criticism on art and artists in northern capitals.*"—ART JOURNAL.

Atkinson (J. P.)—A WEEK AT THE LAKES, AND WHAT CAME OF IT; OR, THE ADVENTURES OF MR. DOBBS AND HIS FRIEND MR. POTTS. A Series of Sketches by J. P. ATKINSON. Oblong 4to. 7s. 6d.

Baker.—CAST UP BY THE SEA; OR, THE ADVENTURES OF NED GREY. By Sir SAMUEL BAKER, Pasha, F.R.G.S. With Illustrations by HUARD. Sixth Edition. Crown 8vo. cloth gilt. 6s.

"*An admirable tale of adventure, of marvellous incidents, wild exploits, and terrible dénouements.*"—DAILY NEWS. "*A story of adventure by sea and land in the good old style.*"—PALL MALL GAZETTE.

Barker(Lady).—A YEAR'S HOUSEKEEPING IN SOUTH AFRICA. With Illustrations. Cheaper Edition. Crown 8vo. 6s.

"*We doubt whether in any of her previous books she has written more pleasantly than in this. . . . The great charm of these letters is that she is always natural, and tells of what she sees and hears in a strange country, just as if she were quietly chatting to her friends by their own fireside.*"—STANDARD.

Beesly.—STORIES FROM THE HISTORY OF ROME. By Mrs. BEESLY. Fcap. 8vo. 2s. 6d.

"*A little book for which every cultivated and intelligent mother will be grateful.*"—EXAMINER.

Betsy Lee; A FO'C'S'LE YARN. Extra fcap. 8vo. 3s. 6d.

"*We can at least say that it is the work of a true poet.*"—ATHE-NÆUM.

Black (W.)—Works by W. BLACK, Author of "A Daughter of Heth."

THE STRANGE ADVENTURES OF A PHAETON. Thirteenth Thousand. Illustrated. Crown 8vo. 6s.

"*The book is a really charming description of a thousand English landscapes and of the emergencies and the fun and the delight of a picnic journey through them by a party determined to enjoy themselves, and as well matched as the pair of horses which drew the phaeton they sat in.*"—TIMES.

A PRINCESS OF THULE. Fourteenth Thousand. Crown 8vo. 6s.

The SATURDAY REVIEW says :—"*A novel which is both romantic and natural, which has much feeling, without any touch of mawkishness, which goes deep into character without any suggestion of painful analysis—this is a rare gem to find amongst the débris of current literature, and this, or nearly this, Mr. Black has given us in the 'Princess of Thule.'*" "*A beautiful and nearly perfect story.*"—SPECTATOR.

THE MAID OF KILLEENA, and other Stories. Fifth Thousand. Crown 8vo. 6s.

"*A collection of pretty stories told in the easiest and pleasantest manner imaginable.*"—TIMES. "*We shall not be satisfied till 'The Maid of Killeena' rests on our shelves.*"—SPECTATOR.

MADCAP VIOLET. Eighth Thousand. Crown 8vo. 6s.

"*In the very first rank of Mr. Black's heroines ; proud as Sheila, and sweet as Coquette, stands Madcap Violet. The true, proud, tender nature of her, her beauty, her mischief, her self-sacrifice, endear her to the reader.*"—DAILY NEWS.

GREEN PASTURES AND PICCADILLY. Cheaper Edition. Seventh Thousand. Crown 8vo. 6s.

MACLEOD OF DARE. With Illustrations. Cheaper Edition. Crown 8vo. 6s.

"*The best book that Mr. Black has written ; the best novel that has been published in England for some years.*"—ACADEMY.

Blackie.—THE WISE MEN OF GREECE. In a Series of Dramatic Dialogues. By J. E. BLACKIE, Professor of Greek in the University of Edinburgh. Crown 8vo. 9*s.*

Blakiston.—MODERN SOCIETY IN ITS RELIGIOUS AND SOCIAL ASPECTS. By PEYTON BLAKISTON, M.D., F.R.S. Crown 8vo. 5*s.*

Borland Hall.—By the Author of "Olrig Grange." Cr. 8vo. 7*s.*

Bramston.—RALPH AND BRUNO. A Novel. By M. BRAMSTON. 2 vols. crown 8vo. 21*s.*

Bright.—A YEAR IN A LANCASHIRE GARDEN. By HENRY A. BRIGHT. Crown 8vo. 3*s.* 6*d.*
[*Second Edition now ready.*

" *It is full of admirable suggestions for the practical gardener as to the choice and arrangement of his plants, but it will also be read with interest in the arm-chair in town. It is the true story of a year's gardening written by an accomplished man, whose flowers tell him many stories and pleasant things not to be found in the nurseryman's catalogue. . . . A faithful and fascinating garden story.*"—TIMES.

Brooke.—THE FOOL OF QUALITY; OR, THE HISTORY OF HENRY, EARL OF MORELAND. By HENRY BROOKE. Newly revised, with a Biographical Preface by the Rev. CHARLES KINGSLEY, M.A., Rector of Eversley. Crown 8vo. 6*s.*

Bunce.—FAIRY TALES, THEIR ORIGIN AND MEANING. With some Account of the Dwellers in Fairy Land. By J. THACKRAY BUNCE. Extra fcap. 8vo. 3*s.* 6*d.*

Burnand.—MY TIME, AND WHAT I'VE DONE WITH IT. By F. C. BURNAND. Crown 8vo. 6*s.*

Burnett.—HAWORTH'S. A Novel. By FRANCES HODGSON BURNETT, Author of "That Lass o' Lowrie's." Two Vols. Crown 8vo. 21*s.*

Burns.—THE POETICAL WORKS OF. Edited from the best printed and manuscript Authorities, with Glossarial Index and a Biographical Memoir, by ALEXANDER SMITH. Two Vols., fcap. 8vo, hand-made paper, with Portrait of Burns, and Vignette of the Twa Dogs, engraved by SHAW, and printed on India Paper.
[*Shortly*

Carroll.—Works by " LEWIS CARROLL : "—

ALICE'S ADVENTURES IN WONDERLAND. With Forty-two Illustrations by TENNIEL. 57th Thousand. Crown 8vo. cloth. 6*s*.

> "*An excellent piece of nonsense.*"—TIMES. "*Elegant and delicious nonsense.*"—GUARDIAN. "*That most delightful of children's stories.*"—SATURDAY REVIEW.

A GERMAN TRANSLATION OF THE SAME. With TENNIEL'S Illustrations. Crown 8vo. gilt. 6*s*.

A FRENCH TRANSLATION OF THE SAME. With TENNIEL'S Illustrations. Crown 8vo. gilt. 6*s*.

AN ITALIAN TRANSLATION OF THE SAME. By T. P. ROSSETTE. With TENNIEL'S Illustrations. Crown 8vo. 6*s*.

THROUGH THE LOOKING-GLASS, AND WHAT ALICE FOUND THERE. With Fifty Illustrations by TENNIEL. Crown 8vo. gilt. 6*s*. 45th Thousand.

> "*Will fairly rank with the tale of her previous experiences.*"—DAILY TELEGRAPH. "*Many of Mr. Tenniel's designs are masterpieces of wise absurdity.*"—ATHENÆUM.

THE HUNTING OF THE SNARK. An Agony in Eight Fits. With Nine Illustrations by H. Holiday. Crown 8vo. cloth extra, Gilt edges. 4*s*. 6*d*. 18th Thousand.

> "*This glorious piece of nonsense. . . . . Everybody ought to read it—nearly everybody will—and all who deserve the treat will scream with laughter.*"—GRAPHIC.

DOUBLETS. A Word Puzzle. 18mo. 2*s*.

Cautley.—A CENTURY OF EMBLEMS. By G. S. CAUTLEY, Vicar of Nettleden, author of "The After Glow," etc. With numerous Illustrations by LADY MARION ALFORD, REAR-ADMIRAL LORD W. COMPTON, the VEN. LORD A. COMPTON, R. BARNES, J. D. COOPER, and the author. Pott 4to. cloth elegant, gilt edges. 10*s*. 6*d*.

Christmas Carol (A). Printed in Colours from Original Designs by Mr. and Mrs. TREVOR CRISPIN, with Illuminated Borders from MSS. of the 14th and 15th Centuries. Imp. 4to. cloth elegant. Cheaper Edition, 21*s*.

> "*A most exquisitely got-up volume.*"—TIMES.

Church (A. J.)—HORÆ TENNYSONIANÆ, Sive Eclogæ e Tennysono Latine redditæ. Cura A. J. CHURCH, A.M. Extra fcap. 8vo. 6*s*.

Clough (Arthur Hugh).—THE POEMS AND PROSE REMAINS OF ARTHUR HUGH CLOUGH. With a Selection from his Letters and a Memoir. Edited by his Wife. With Portrait. Two Vols. Crown 8vo. 21*s.*

> "*Taken as a whole,*" the SPECTATOR *says,* "*these volumes cannot fail to be a lasting monument of one of the most original men of our age.*"

THE POEMS OF ARTHUR HUGH CLOUGH, sometime Fellow of Oriel College, Oxford. Fifth Edition. Fcap. 8vo. 6*s.*

> "*From the higher mind of cultivated, all-questioning, but still conservative England, in this our puzzled generation, we do not know of any utterance in literature so characteristic as the poems of Arthur Hugh Clough.*"—FRASER'S MAGAZINE.

Clunes.—THE STORY OF PAULINE: an Autobiography. By G. C. CLUNES. Crown 8vo. 6*s.*

Coleridge.—HUGH CRICHTON'S ROMANCE. A Novel. By CHRISTABEL R. COLERIDGE. Second Edition. Crown 8vo. 6*s.*

Collects of the Church of England. With a beautifully Coloured Floral Design to each Collect, and Illuminated Cover. Crown 8vo. 12*s.* Also kept in various styles of morocco.

> "*This is beyond question,*" the ART JOURNAL *says,* "*the most beautiful book of the season.*" The GUARDIAN *thinks it* "*a successful attempt to associate in a natural and unforced manner the flowers of our fields and gardens with the course of the Christian year.*"

Colquhoun.—RHYMES AND CHIMES. By F. S. COLQUHOUN (née F. S. FULLER MAITLAND). Extra fcap. 8vo. 2*s.* 6*d.*

Cooper.—SEBASTIAN. A Novel. By KATHERINE COOPER. Crown 8vo. 6*s.*

Dante; AN ESSAY. With a Translation of the "De Monarchia." By the Very Rev. W. R. CHURCH, D.C.L., Dean of St. Paul's. Crown 8vo. 6*s.*

THE "DE MONARCHIA." Separately. 8vo. 4*s.* 6*d.*

THE PURGATORIO. A Prose Translation, with Notes by A. J. BUTLER. Post 8vo. [*Shortly.*

Day.—BENGAL PEASANT LIFE. By the Rev. LAL BEHARI DAY. New Edition. Crown 8vo. 6*s.*

> "*The book presents a careful, minute, and well-drawn picture of Hindoo peasant life.*"—DAILY NEWS.

Days of Old ; STORIES FROM OLD ENGLISH HISTORY. By the Author of "Ruth and her Friends." New Edition. 18mo. cloth, extra. *2s. 6d.*

Duff (Grant).—MISCELLANIES, POLITICAL and LITE-RARY. By M. E. GRANT DUFF, M.P. 8vo. *10s. 6d.*

Elsie.—A LOWLAND SKETCH. By A. C. M. Crown 8vo. *6s.*

Estelle Russell.—By the Author of "The Private Life o Galileo." New Edition. Crown 8vo. *6s.*

Evans.—Works by SEBASTIAN EVANS.

BROTHER FABIAN'S MANUSCRIPT, AND OTHER POEMS. Fcap. 8vo. cloth. *6s.*
"In this volume we have full assurance that he has 'the vision and the faculty divine.' . . . Clever and full of kindly humour."—GLOBE.

IN THE STUDIO : A DECADE OF POEMS. Extra fcap. 8vo. *5s.*
" The finest thing in the book is 'Dudman in Paradise,' a wonderfully vigorous and beautiful story. The poem is a most remarkable one, full of beauty, humour, and pointed satire."—ACADEMY.

Farrell.—THE LECTURES OF A CERTAIN PROFESSOR. By the Rev. JOSEPH FARRELL. Crown 8vo. *7s. 6d.*

Fawcett.—TALES IN POLITICAL ECONOMY. By MIL-LICENT FAWCETT, Author of "Political Economy for Beginners." Globe 8vo. *3s.*
" The idea is a good one, and it is quite wonderful what a mass of economic teaching the author manages to compress into a small space. . . The true doctrines of international trade, currency, and the ratio between production and population, are set before us and illustrated in a masterly manner."—ATHENÆUM.

Fleming.—Works by GEORGE FLEMING.

A NILE NOVEL. Third and Cheaper Edition. Crown 8vo.

MIRAGE. A Novel. Cheaper Edition. Crown 8vo. *6s.*

Fletcher.—THOUGHTS FROM A GIRL'S LIFE. By LUCY FLETCHER. Second Edition. Fcap. 8vo. *4s. 6d.*

Freeman. — HISTORICAL AND ARCHITECTURAL SKETCHES; CHIEFLY ITALIAN. By E. A. FREEMAN, D.C.L., LL.D. With Illustrations by the Author. Crown 8vo. 10s. 6d.

> "*Those who know Italy well will retrace their steps with delight in Mr. Freeman's company, and find him a most interesting guide and instructor.*" —EXAMINER.

Garnett.—IDYLLS AND EPIGRAMS. Chiefly from the Greek Anthology. By RICHARD GARNETT. Fcap. 8vo. 2s. 6d.

> "*A charming little book. For English readers, Mr. Garnett's translations will open a new world of thought.*"—WESTMINSTER REVIEW.

Gilmore.—STORM WARRIORS; or, LIFE-BOAT WORK ON THE GOODWIN SANDS. By the Rev. JOHN GILMORE, M.A., Rector of Holy Trinity, Ramsgate, Author of "The Ramsgate Life-Boat," in *Macmillan's Magazine*. Second Edition. Crown 8vo. 6s.

> "*The stories, which are said to be literally exact, are more thrilling than anything in fiction. Mr. Gilmore has done a good work as well as written a good book.*"—DAILY NEWS.

Guesses at Truth.—By TWO BROTHERS. 18mo. 4s. 6d. Golden Treasury Series.

Hamerton.—A PAINTER'S CAMP. Second Edition, revised. Extra fcap. 8vo. 6s.

> "*These pages, written with infinite spirit and humour, bring into close rooms, back upon tired heads, the breezy airs of Lancashire moors and Highland lochs, with a freshness which no recent novelist has succeeded in preserving.*"—NONCONFORMIST.

Harry.—A POEM. By the Author of "Mrs. Jerningham's Journal." Extra fcap. 8vo. 3s. 6d.

Hawthorne.—THE LAUGHING MILL; and Other Stories. By JULIAN HAWTHORNE. Cheaper Edition. Crown 8vo. 6s.

> "*A volume of permanent value, and among recent books quite alone for subtle blending of individual and general human interest, poetic and psychological suggestion, and rare humour . . . . We cordially commend the stories to readers of all classes, hoping they will not pay the slightest attention to any one who tells them beforehand they are wanting in human interest.*"—CONTEMPORARY REVIEW.

Heine.—SELECTIONS FROM THE POETICAL WORKS OF HEINRICH HEINE. Translated into English. Crown 8vo. 4s. 6d.

Higginson.—MALBONE: An Oldport Romance. By T. W. HIGGINSON. Fcap. 8vo. 2s. 6d.

Hilda among the Broken Gods.—By the Author of "Olrig Grange." Extra fcap. 8vo. 7s. 6d.

Hobday. — COTTAGE GARDENING; OR, FLOWERS, FRUITS AND VEGETABLES FOR SMALL GARDENS. By E. HOBDAY. Crown 8vo. 1s. 6d.
"*A sensible and useful little book.*"—ATHENÆUM.

Hooper and Phillips.—A MANUAL OF MARKS ON POTTERY AND PORCELAIN. A Dictionary of Easy Reference. By W. H. HOOPER and W. C. PHILLIPS. With numerous Illustrations. Second Edition, revised. 16mo. 4s. 6d.
"*It is one of the most complete, and beyond all comparison, the handiest volume of the kind.*"—ATHENÆUM.

Hopkins.—ROSE TURQUAND. A Novel. By ELLICE HOPKINS. Cheaper Edition. Crown 8vo. 6s.
"*Rose Turquand is a noble heroine, and the story of her sufferings and of her sacrifice is most touching. A tale of rare excellence.*"— STANDARD.

Horace.—WORD FOR WORD FROM HORACE. The Odes literally versified. By W. T. THORNTON, C.B. Crown 8vo. 7s. 6d.

Hunt.—TALKS ABOUT ART. By WILLIAM HUNT. With a Letter by J. E. MILLAIS. Crown 8vo. 3s. 6d.
"*They are singularly racy and suggestive.*"—— PALL MALL GAZETTE.

Irving.—Works by WASHINGTON IRVING.

OLD CHRISTMAS. From the Sketch Book. With upwards of 100 Illustrations by Randolph Caldecott, engraved by J. D. Cooper. Second Edition. Crown 8vo. cloth elegant. 6s.
"*This little volume is indeed a gem.*"—DAILY NEWS. "*One of the best and prettiest volumes we have seen this year. . . . . All the illustrations are equally charming and equally worthy of the immortal words to which they are wedded.*"—SATURDAY REVIEW.

BRACEBRIDGE HALL. With 120 illustrations by R. Caldecott. Crown 8vo. cloth gilt. 6s.
"*No one who has seen 'Old Christmas,' issued last year with charming illustrations by Mr. Caldecott, is likely to forget the pleasure he derived from turning over its pages. Text and illustrations, both having a flavour of quaint, old-fashioned humour, fit into each other to perfection, and leave an impression absolutely unique. . . . This work is in no respect behind its predecessor.*"—GLOBE.

James.—Works by HENRY JAMES, jun.

FRENCH POETS AND NOVELISTS. Crown 8vo. 8*s.* 6*d.*

CONTENTS :—Alfred de Musset—Théophile Gautier—Baudelaire—Honoré de Balzac—George Sand—Turgénieff, etc.
"There has of late years appeared nothing upon French literature so intelligent as this book—so acute, so full of good sense, so free from affectation and pretence."—ATHENÆUM.

THE EUROPEANS. A Novel. Cheaper Edition. Crown 8vo. 6*s.*

THE AMERICAN. Crown 8vo. 6*s.*

DAISY MILLER ; and Other Stories. 2 vols. Crown 8vo. 21*s.*

RODERICK HUDSON. Three Vols. Crown 8vo. 31*s.* 6*d.*

THE MADONNA OF THE FUTURE ; and other Tales. Two Vols. Crown 8vo. [*Shortly.*

Joubert.—PENSÉES OF JOUBERT. Selected and Translated with the Original French appended, by HENRY ATTWELL, Knight of the Order of the Oak Crown. Crown 8vo. 5*s.*

Keary (A.)—Works by ANNIE KEARY :—

CASTLE DALY : THE STORY OF AN IRISH HOME THIRTY YEARS AGO. New Edition. Crown 8vo. 6*s.*
"Extremely touching, and at the same time thoroughly amusing."—MORNING POST.

JANET'S HOME. New Edition. Globe 8vo. 2*s.* 6*d.*

CLEMENCY FRANKLYN. New Edition. Globe 8vo. 2*s.* 6*d.*

OLDBURY. New and Cheaper Edition. Crown 8vo. 6*s.*

A YORK AND A LANCASTER ROSE. Crown 8vo. 6*s.*
"A very pleasant and thoroughly interesting book."—JOHN BULL.

A DOUBTING HEART. Three Vols. Crown 8vo. 31*s.* 6*d.*
[*Shortly.*

Keary (E.) — THE MAGIC VALLEY ; or, PATIENT ANTOINE. With Illustrations by E. V. B. Globe 8vo. gilt. 4*s.* 6*d.*
"A very pretty, tender, quaint little tale."—TIMES.

Kingsley.—Works by the Rev. CHARLES KINGSLEY, M.A., Rector of Eversley, and Canon of Westminster :—

WESTWARD HO ! or, The Voyages and Adventures of Sir Amyas Leigh. Forty-third Thousand. Crown 8vo. 6*s.*

TWO YEARS AGO. 24th Thousand. Crown 8vo. 6*s.*

Kingsley (C.)—*continued.*

HYPATIA ; or, New Foes with an Old Face. Tenth Edition. Crown 8vo. 6s.

HEREWARD THE WAKE—LAST OF THE ENGLISH. Fifth Edition. Crown 8vo. 6s.

YEAST : A Problem. Tenth Edition. Crown 8vo. 6s.

ALTON LOCKE. New Edition. With a Prefatory Memoir by THOMAS HUGHES, Q.C., and Portrait of the Author. Crown 8vo. 6s.

THE WATER BABIES. A Fairy Tale for a Land Baby. With Illustrations by Sir NOEL PATON, R.S.A., and P. SKELTON. New Edition. Crown 8vo. 6s.

> "*In fun, in humour, and in innocent imagination, as a child's book we do not know its equal.*"—LONDON REVIEW. "*Mr. Kingsley must have the credit of revealing to us a new order of life. . . . There is in the 'Water Babies' an abundance of wit, fun, good humour, geniality, élan, go.*"—TIMES.

THE HEROES ; or, Greek Fairy Tales for my Children. With Illustrations. New Edition. Crown 8vo. 6s.

> "*We do not think these heroic stories have ever been more attractively told. . . There is a deep under-current of religious feeling traceable throughout its pages which is sure to influence young readers power-fully.*"—LONDON REVIEW. "*One of the children's books that will surely become a classic.*"—NONCONFORMIST.

PHAETHON ; or, Loose Thoughts for Loose Thinkers. Third Edition. Crown 8vo. 2s.

POEMS ; including The Saint's Tragedy, Andromeda, Songs, Ballads, etc. Complete Collected Edition. Extra fcap. 8vo. 6s.

> *The* SPECTATOR *calls "Andromeda" "the finest piece of English hexameter verse that has ever been written. It is a volume which many readers will be glad to possess."*

PROSE IDYLLS. NEW AND OLD. Fourth Edition. Crown 8vo. 6s.

> CONTENTS :—*A Charm of Birds ; Chalk-Stream Studies ; The Fens ; My Winter-Garden ; From Ocean to Sea ; North Devon.*
> "*Altogether a delightful book. . . . . It exhibits the author's best traits, and cannot fail to infect the reader with a love of nature and of out-door life and its enjoyments. It is well calculated to bring a gleam of summer with its pleasant associations, into the bleak winter-time ; while a better companion for a summer ramble could hardly be found.*"—BRITISH QUARTERLY REVIEW.

GLAUCUS ; OR, THE WONDERS OF THE SEA-SHORE. With Coloured Illustrations. Sixth Edition. Crown 8vo. 6s.

Kingsley (C.)—*continued.*

MADAM HOW AND LADY WHY; or, First Lessons in Earth-Lore for Children. New Edition. Crown 8vo. 6s.

HEALTH EDUCATION. New Edition. Crown 8vo. 6s.

Kingsley (H.)—Works by HENRY KINGSLEY :—

THE LOST CHILD. With Eight Illustrations by FRÖLICH. Crown 4to. cloth gilt. 3s. 6d.

"A pathetic story, and told so as to give children an interest in Australian ways and scenery."—GLOBE. *"Very charmingly and very touchingly told."*—SATURDAY REVIEW.

TALES OF OLD TRAVEL. Re-narrated. With Eight full-page Illustrations by HUARD. Fifth Edition. Crown 8vo. cloth, extra gilt. 5s.

"We know no better book for those who want knowledge or seek to refresh it. As for the 'sensational,' most novels are tame compared with these narratives."—ATHENÆUM. *"Exactly the book to interest and to do good to intelligent and high-spirited boys."*—LITERARY CHURCHMAN.

Knatchbull-Hugessen.—Works by E. H. KNATCHBULL-HUGESSEN, M.P. :—

CRACKERS FOR CHRISTMAS. More Stories. With Illustrations by JELLICOE and ELWES. Fifth Edition. Crown 8vo. 5s.

" A fascinating little volume, which will make him friends in every household in which there are children."—DAILY NEWS.

QUEER FOLK. FAIRY STORIES. Illustrated by S. E. WALLER. Fourth Edition. Crown 8vo. Cloth gilt. 5s.

"Decidedly the author's happiest effort. . . . One of the best story books of the year."—HOUR.

Knox.—SONGS OF CONSOLATION. By ISA CRAIG KNOX. Extra fcap. 8vo. Cloth extra, gilt edges. 4s. 6d.

" The verses are truly sweet; there is in them not only much genuine poetic quality, but an ardent, flowing devotedness, and a peculiar skill in propounding theological tenets in the most graceful way, which any divine might envy."—SCOTSMAN.

Leading Cases done into English. By an Apprentice of Lincoln's Inn. Third Edition. Crown 8vo. 2s. 6d.

" The versifier of these 'Leading Cases' has been most successful. He has surrounded his legal distinctions with a halo of mock passion which is in itself in the highest degree entertaining, especially when the style of the different modern poets is so admirably hit off that the cloud of associations which hangs round one of Mr. Swinburne's, or Mr. Rossetti's, or Mr. Browning's, or Mr. Clough's, or Mr. Tennyson's poems, is summoned up to set off the mock tenderness or mock patriotism of the strain itself."—SPECTATOR.

Leland.—JOHNNYKIN AND THE GOBLINS. By C. G. LELAND, Author of "Hans Breitmann's Ballads." With numerous Illustrations by the Author. Crown 8vo. 6s.

"*Mr. Leland is rich in fantastic conception and full of rollicking fun, and youngsters will amazingly enjoy his book.*"—BRITISH QUARTERLY REVIEW.

Life and Times of Conrad the Squirrel. A Story for Children. By the Author of "Wandering Willie," "Effie's Friends," &c. With a Frontispiece by R. FARREN. Second Edition. Crown 8vo. 3s. 6d.

"*Having commenced on the first page, we were compelled to go on to the conclusion, and this we predict will be the case with every one who opens the book.*"—PALL MALL GAZETTE.

Little Estella, and other FAIRY TALES FOR THE YOUNG. 18mo. cloth extra. 2s. 6d.

Loftie.—FORTY-SIX SOCIAL TWITTERS. By MRS. LOFTIE. Second Edition. 16mo. 2s. 6d.

"*Many of these essays are bright and pleasant, and extremely sensible remarks are scattered about the book.*"—ATHENÆUM.

Lorne.—Works by the MARQUIS OF LORNE :—
GUIDO AND LITA : A TALE OF THE RIVIERA. A Poem. Third Edition. Small 4to. cloth elegant, with Illustrations. 7s. 6d.

"*Lord Lorne has the gifts of expression as well as the feelings of a poet.*"—TIMES. "*A volume of graceful and harmonious verse.*"— STANDARD. "*We may congratulate the Marquis on something more than a mere succès a'estime.*"—GRAPHIC. "*Lucidity of thought and gracefulness of expression abound in this attractive poem.*"—MORNING POST.

THE BOOK OF THE PSALMS, LITERALLY RENDERED IN VERSE. With Three Illustrations. Third Edition. Crown 8vo. 7s. 6d.

"*His version is such a great improvement upon Rous that it will be surprising should it not supplant the old version in the Scottish churches. . . . on the whole, it would not be rash, to call Lord Lorne's the best rhymed Psalter we have.*"—ATHENÆUM.

Lowell.—COMPLETE POETICAL WORKS of JAMES RUSSELL LOWELL. With Portrait, engraved by Jeens. 18mo. cloth extra. 4s. 6d.

"*All readers who are able to recognise and appreciate genuine verse will give a glad welcome to this beautiful little volume.*"—PALL MALL GAZETTE.

Lyttelton.—Works by LORD LYTTELTON :—

THE "COMUS" OF MILTON, rendered into Greek Verse. Extra fcap. 8vo. 5*s.*

THE "SAMSON AGONISTES" OF MILTON, rendered into Greek Verse. Extra fcap. 8vo. 6*s.* 6*d.*

Maclaren.—THE FAIRY FAMILY. A series of Ballads and Metrical Tales illustrating the Fairy Mythology of Europe. By ARCHIBALD MACLAREN. With Frontispiece, Illustrated Title, and Vignette. Crown 8vo. gilt. 5*s.*

Macmillan's Magazine.—Published Monthly. Price 1*s.* Volumes I. to XXXIX. are now ready. 7*s.* 6*d.* each.

Macquoid.—Works by KATHARINE S. MACQUOID.

PATTY. Third and Cheaper Edition. Crown 8vo. 6*s.*
    "*A book to be read.*"—STANDARD. "*A powerful and fascinating story.*"—DAILY TELEGRAPH.

THE BERKSHIRE LADY. Crown 8vo. 10*s.* 6*d.*

Maguire.—YOUNG PRINCE MARIGOLD, AND OTHER FAIRY STORIES. By the late JOHN FRANCIS MAGUIRE, M.P. Illustrated by S. E. WALLER. Globe 8vo. gilt. 4*s.* 6*d.*

Mahaffy.—Works by J. P. MAHAFFY, M.A., Fellow of Trinity College, Dublin.

SOCIAL LIFE IN GREECE FROM HOMER TO MENANDER. Third Edition, enlarged, with New Chapter on Greek Art. Crown 8vo. 9*s.*
    "*Should be in the hands of all who desire thoroughly to understand and to enjoy Greek literature, and to get an intelligent idea of the old Greek life.*"—GUARDIAN.

RAMBLES AND STUDIES IN GREECE. Illustrated. Second Edition, revised and enlarged, with Map. Crown 8vo. 10*s.* 6*d.*
    "*A singularly instructive and agreeable volume.*"—ATHENÆUM.
    "*This charmingly picturesque and lively volume.*"—EXAMINER.

Massey.—SONGS OF THE NOONTIDE REST. By LUCY MASSEY, Author of "Thoughts from a Girl's Life." Fcap. 8vo. cloth extra. 4*s.* 6*d.*

Masson (Mrs.)—THREE CENTURIES OF ENGLISH POETRY : being selections from Chaucer to Herrick, with Introductions and Notes by Mrs. MASSON and a general introduction by PROFESSOR MASSON. Extra fcap. 8vo. 3*s.* 6*d.*
    "*Most excellently done. The selections are made with good taste and discrimination. The notes, too, are to the point. We can most strongly recommend the book.*"—WESTMINSTER REVIEW.

Masson (Professor).—Works by DAVID MASSON, M.A., Professor of Rhetoric and English Literature in the University of Edinburgh.

WORDSWORTH, SHELLEY, KEATS, AND OTHER ESSAYS. Crown 8vo. 5*s.*

CHATTERTON : A Story of the Year 1770. Crown 8vo. 5*s.*

THE THREE DEVILS : LUTHER'S, MILTON'S, and GOETHE'S ; and other Essays. Crown 8vo. 5*s.*

Mazini.—IN THE GOLDEN SHELL ; A Story of Palermo. By LINDA MAZINI. With Illustrations. Globe 8vo. cloth gilt. 4*s.* 6*d.*

Merivale.—KEATS' HYPERION, rendered into Latin Verse. By C. MERIVALE, B.D. Second Edition. Extra fcap. 8vo. 3*s.* 6*d.*

Milner.—THE LILY OF LUMLEY. By EDITH MILNER. Crown 8vo. 7*s.* 6*d.*

Milton's Poetical Works.—Edited with Text collated from the best Authorities, with Introduction and Notes by DAVID MASSON. Three vols. 8vo. 42*s.* With Three Portraits engraved by C. H. JEENS. (Uniform with the Cambridge Shakespeare.)

"An edition of Milton which is certain to be the standard edition for many years to come, and which is as complete and satisfactory as can be conceived."—EXAMINER.

Golden Treasury Edition. By the same Editor. With Two Portraits. 2 vols. 18mo. 9*s.*

Mistral (F.)—MIRELLE, a Pastoral Epic of Provence. Translated by H. CRICHTON. Extra fcap. 8vo. 6*s.*

Mitford (A. B.)—TALES OF OLD JAPAN. By A. B. MITFORD, Second Secretary to the British Legation in Japan. With Illustrations drawn and cut on Wood by Japanese Artists. New and Cheaper Edition. Crown 8vo. 6*s.*

"They will always be interesting as memorials of a most exceptional society ; while, regarded simply as tales, they are sparkling, sensational, and dramatic."—PALL MALL GAZETTE.

Molesworth. — Works by Mrs. MOLESWORTH (ENNIS GRAHAM) :—

GRANDMOTHER DEAR. Illustrated by WALTER CRANE. Eighth Thousand. Extra fcap. 8vo. cloth gilt. 4*s.* 6*d.*

"Charmingly written pages, full of delightful but simple adventures, healthy in tone."—EXAMINER.

TELL ME A STORY. Illustrated by WALTER CRANE. Globe 8vo. gilt. 4*s.* 6*d.* Fifth Thousand.

"So delightful that we are inclined to join in the petition, and we hope she may soon tell us more stories."—ATHENÆUM.

Molesworth (Mrs.)—*continued.*

"CARROTS": JUST A LITTLE BOY. Illustrated by WALTER CRANE. Ninth Thousand. Globe 8vo. gilt. 4*s.* 6*d.*

> " *One of the cleverest and most pleasing stories it has been our good fortune to meet with for some time. ' Carrots' and his sister are delightful little beings, whom to read about is at once to be become very fond of.*—EXAMINER.

THE CUCKOO CLOCK. Illustrated by WALTER CRANE. Eighth Thousand. Globe 8vo. gilt. 4*s.* 6*d.*

> "*A beautiful little story. . . . It will be read with delight by every child into whose hands it is placed. . . . Ennis Graham deserves all the praise that has been, is, and will be, bestowed on ' The Cuckoo Clock. Children's stories are plentiful, but one like this is not to be met with every day.*"—PALL MALL GAZETTE.

THE TAPESTRY ROOM. Illustrated by WALTER CRANE Globe 8vo, gilt. 4*s.* 6*d.*   [*Immediately*

Moulton.—SWALLOW FLIGHTS. Poems by LOUISA CHANDLER MOULTON. Extra fcap. 8vo. 4*s.* 6*d.*

> The ATHENÆUM says :—" *Mrs. Moulton has a real claim to attention. It is not too much to say of these poems that they exhibit delicate and rare beauty, marked originality, and perfection of style. What is still better, they impress us with a sense of vivid and subtle imagination, and that spontaneous feeling which is the essence of lyrical poetry.*"

Moultrie.—POEMS by JOHN MOULTRIE. Complete Edition. 2 vols. Crown 8vo. 7*s.* each.

Vol. I. MY BROTHER'S GRAVE, DREAM OF LIFE, &c. With Memoir by the Rev. Prebendary COLERIDGE.

Vol. II. LAYS OF THE ENGLISH CHURCH, and other Poems. With notices of the Rectors of Rugby, by M. H. BLOXHAM. F.R.A.S.

Mrs. Jerningham's Journal. A Poem purporting to be the Journal of a newly-married Lady. Third Edition. Fcap. 8vo. 3*s.* 6*d.*

> "*It is nearly a perfect gem. We have had nothing so good for a long time, and those who neglect to read it are neglecting one of the jewels of contemporary history.*"—EDINBURGH DAILY REVIEW. " *One quality in the piece, sufficient of itself to claim a moment's attention, is that it is unique—original, indeed, is not too strong a word—in the manner of its conception and execution.*" —PALL MALL GAZETTE.

Mudie.—STRAY LEAVES. By C. E. MUDIE. New Edition. Extra fcap. 8vo. 3*s.* 6*d.* Contents:—"His and Mine"—"Night and Day"—"One of Many," &c.

This little volume consists of a number of poems, mostly of a genuinely devotional character. " They are for the most part so exquisitely sweet and delicate as to be quite a marvel of composition. They are worthy of being laid up in the recesses of the heart, and recalled to memory from time to time."—ILLUSTRATED LONDON NEWS.

Murray.—ROUND ABOUT FRANCE. By E. C. GRENVILLE MURRAY. Crown 8vo. 7*s.* 6*d.*
"A most amusing series of articles.'—ATHENÆUM.

Myers (Ernest).—Works by ERNEST MYERS :—

THE PURITANS. Extra fcap. 8vo. cloth. 2*s.* 6*d.*

POEMS. Extra fcap. 8vo. 4*s.* 6*d.*
" The diction is excellent, the rhythm falls pleasantly on the ear, there is a classical flavour in the verse which is eminently grateful, the thought and imagery are poetical in character."—PALL MALL GAZETTE.

Myers (F. W. H.)—POEMS. By F. W. H. MYERS. Containing "St. Paul," "St. John," and others. Extra fcap. 8vo 4*s.* 6*d.*
" It is rare to find a writer who combines to such an extent the faculty of communicating feelings with the faculty of euphonious expression."—SPECTATOR.

ST. PAUL. A Poem. New Edition. Extra fcap. 8vo. 2*s.* 6*d.*

Nichol.—HANNIBAL, A HISTORICAL DRAMA. By JOHN NICHOL, B.A. Oxon., Regius Professor of English Language and Literature in the University of Glasgow. Extra fcap. 8vo. 7*s.* 6*d.*

Nine Years Old.—By the Author of "St. Olave's," "When I was a Little Girl," &c. Illustrated by FRÖLICH. Fourth Edition. Extra fcap. 8vo. cloth gilt. 4*s.* 6*d.*

Noel.—BEATRICE AND OTHER POEMS. By the HON. RODEN NOEL. Fcap. 8vo. 6*s.*

Noel (Lady Augusta).—Works by LADY AUGUSTA NOEL :—

OWEN GWYNNE'S GREAT WORK. Cheaper Edition. Crown 8vo. 6*s.*

FROM GENERATION TO GENERATION. Two Vols. Crown 8vo. [*Shortly.*

Norton.—Works by the Hon. Mrs. NORTON :—

THE LADY OF LA GARAYE. With Vignette and Frontispiece. Eighth Edition. Fcap. 8vo. 4*s.* 6*d.*
"Full of thought well expressed, ana may be classed among her best efforts."—TIMES.

OLD SIR DOUGLAS. New Edition. Crown 8vo. 6*s.*

Oliphant.—Works by Mrs. OLIPHANT :—

AGNES HOPETOUN'S SCHOOLS AND HOLIDAYS. New Edition with Illustrations. Royal 16mo. gilt leaves. 4*s.* 6*d.*

A SON OF THE SOIL. New Edition. Crown 8vo. 6*s.*

THE CURATE IN CHARGE. Crown 8vo. 6*s.* Sixth Edition
" We can pronounce it one of the happiest of her recent efforts."— TIMES.

THE MAKERS OF FLORENCE : Dante, Giotto, Savonarola, and their City. With Illustrations from Drawings by Professor Delamotte, and a Steel Portrait of Savonarola, engraved by C. H. JEENS. Second Edition with Preface. Medium 8vo. Cloth extra. 21*s.*
The EDINBURGH REVIEW *says " We cannot leave this subject without expressing our admiration for the beautiful volume which Mrs. Oliphant has devoted to the ' Makers of Florence'—one of the most elegant and interesting books which has been inspired in our time by the arts and annals of that celebrated Republic."*

YOUNG MUSGRAVE. Cheaper Edition. Crown 8vo. 6*s.*

THE BELEAGUERED CITY. Crown 8vo.   [*Shortly*.

Our Year. A Child's Book, in Prose and Verse. By the Author of " John Halifax, Gentleman." Illustrated by CLARENCE DOBELL. Royal 16mo. 3*s.* 6*d.*

Palgrave.—Works by FRANCIS TURNER PALGRAVE, M.A., late Fellow of Exeter College, Oxford :—

THE FIVE DAYS' ENTERTAINMENTS AT WENTWORTH GRANGE. A Book for Children. With Illustrations by ARTHUR HUGHES, and Engraved Title-page by JEENS. Small 4to. cloth extra. 6*s.*

LYRICAL POEMS. Extra fcap. 8vo. 6*s.*
" A volume of pure quiet verse, sparkling with tender melodies, and alive with thoughts of genuine poetry. . . . Turn where we will throughout the volume, we find traces of beauty, tenderness, and truth ; true poet's work, touched and refined by the master-hand of a real artist, who shows his genius even in trifles."—STANDARD.

Palgrave—*continued.*

ORIGINAL HYMNS. Third Edition, enlarged, 18mo. 1s. 6d.

> "*So choice, so perfect, and so refined, so tender in feeling, and so scholarly in expression, that we look with special interest to everything that he gives us.*"—LITERARY CHURCHMAN.

GOLDEN TREASURY OF THE BEST SONGS AND LYRICS Edited by F. T. PALGRAVE. 18mo. 4s. 6d.

SHAKESPEARE'S SONNETS AND SONGS. Edited by F. T. PALGRAVE. With Vignette Title by JEENS. (Golden Treasury Series.) 18mo. 4s. 6d.

THE CHILDREN'S TREASURY OF LYRICAL POETRY. Selected and arranged with Notes by F. T. PALGRAVE. 18mo. 2s. 6d., and in Two Parts, 1s. each.

HERRICK: SELECTIONS FROM THE LYRICAL POEMS. With Notes. (Golden Treasury Series.) 18mo. 4s. 6d.

PRINCESS SNOWDROP. A Child's Story. Extra fcap. 8vo.
[*Shortly*.

Pater.—THE RENAISSANCE. Studies in Art and Poetry. By WALTER PATER, Fellow of Brasenose College, Oxford. Second Edition, Revised, with Vignette, engraved by C. H. Jeens. Crown 8vo. 10s. 6d.

> "*Mr. Pater's Studies in the history of the Renaissance, constitute the most remarkable example of this younger movement towards a fresh and inner criticism, and they are in themselves a singular and interesting addition to literature. The subjects are of the very kind in which we need instruction and guidance, and there is a moral in the very choice of them. From the point of view of form and literary composition they are striking in the highest way. They introduce to English readers a new and distinguished master in the great and difficult art of writing prose. Their style is marked by a flavour at once full and exquisite, by a quality that mixes richness with delicacy and a firm coherency with infinite subtlety.*"—FORTNIGHTLY REVIEW.

Patmore.—THE CHILDREN'S GARLAND, from the Best Poets. Selected and arranged by COVENTRY PATMORE. New Edition. With Illustrations by J. LAWSON. Crown 8vo. gilt. 6s. Golden Treasury Edition. 18mo. 4s. 6d.

Peel.—ECHOES FROM HOREB, AND OTHER POEMS. By EDMUND PEEL, Author of "An Ancient City," etc. Crown 8vo. 3s. 6d.

Pember.—THE TRAGEDY OF LESBOS. A Dramatic Poem. By E. H. PEMBER. Fcap. 8vo. 4*s.* 6*d.*

Phillips.—BENEDICTA. A Novel. By Mrs. ALFRED PHILLIPS. 3 Vols. Crown 8vo. 31*s.* 6*d.*

Phillips (S. K.)—ON THE SEABOARD; and Other Poems. By SUSAN K. PHILLIPS. Second Edition. Crown 8vo. 5*s.*
"There is much that is charming in these poems, and well worth preserving."—EXAMINER.

Philpot. — A POCKET OF PEBBLES, WITH A FEW SHELLS; Being Fragments of Reflection, now and then with Cadence, made up mostly by the Sea-shore. By the Rev. W. B. PHILPOT. Second Edition, picked, sorted, and polished anew; with Two Illustrations by GEORGE SMITH. Fcap. 8vo. 5*s.*

Poets (English).—A SELECTION OF ENGLISH POETRY, with Introductions. Edited by T. H. WARD, M.A. Four Vols. Crown 8vo. (Vols. I. and II. will be published in November.)

Poole.—PICTURES OF COTTAGE LIFE IN THE WEST OF ENGLAND. By MARGARET E. POOLE. New and Cheaper Edition. With Frontispiece by R. Farren. Crown 8vo. 3*s.* 6*d.*

Population of an Old Pear Tree. From the French of E. VAN BRUYSSEL. Edited by the Author of "The Heir of Redclyffe." With Illustrations by BECKER. Cheaper Edition. Crown 8vo. gilt. 4*s.* 6*d.*
" A whimsical and charming little book."—ATHENÆUM.

Potter.—LANCASHIRE MEMORIES. By LOUISA POTTER. Crown 8vo. 6*s.*
" A short and simple story of family life in 'One Sweet Village,' told with an unpretending grace and gentle humour which we should often be glad to meet with in more ambitious pages."—DAILY NEWS.

Prince Florestan of Monaco, The Fall of. By HIMSELF. New Edition, with Illustration and Map. 8vo. cloth. Extra gilt edges, 5*s.* A French Translation, 5*s.* Also an Edition for the People. Crown 8vo. 1*s.*

Quin.—GARDEN RECEIPTS. Edited by CHARLES QUIN. Crown 8vo. 2*s.* 6*d.*
The most useful book for the garden that has been published for some time."—FLORIST AND POMOLOGIST.

Rachel Olliver—a Novel. 3 vols. Crown 8vo. 31s. 6d.

Realmah.—By the Author of "Friends in Council." Crown 8vo. 6s.

Rhoades.—POEMS. By JAMES RHOADES. Fcap. 8vo. 4s. 6d.

Richardson.—THE ILIAD OF THE EAST. A Selection of Legends drawn from Valmiki's Sanskrit Poem, "The Ramayana." By FREDERIKA RICHARDSON. Crown 8vo. 7s. 6d.

Rimmer.—ANCIENT STREETS AND HOMESTEADS OF ENGLAND. By ALFRED RIMMER. With Introduction by the Very Rev. J. S. HOWSON, D.D., Dean of Chester. With 150 Illustrations by the Author. Royal 8vo, cloth elegant. Cheaper issue. 10s. 6d.

*"All the illustrations are clear and good, and they are eminently truthful. . . . A book which gladdens the eye while it instructs and improves the mind."—*STANDARD. *"One of the most interesting and beautiful books we have seen this season. . . . It is full of knowledge, the result of exact and faithful study, most readable and interesting; the illustrations are simply exquisite."* —NONCONFORMIST.

Robinson.—GEORGE LINTON; OR, THE FIRST YEARS OF AN ENGLISH COLONY. By JOHN ROBINSON, F.R.G.S. Crown 8vo. 7s. 6d.

Rossetti.—Works by CHRISTINA ROSSETTI :—

POEMS. Complete Edition, containing "Goblin Market," "The Prince's Progress," &c. With Four Illustrations. Extra fcap. 8vo. 6s.

SPEAKING LIKENESSES. Illustrated by ARTHUR HUGHES. Crown 8vo. gilt edges. 4s. 6d.
*"Certain to be a delight to many a juvenile fireside circle."—*MORNING POST.

Ruth and her Friends. A Story for Girls. With a Frontispiece. Seventh Edition. Extra fcap. 8vo. 4s. 6d.

Scouring of The White Horse; or, the Long VACATION RAMBLE OF A LONDON CLERK. Illustrated by DOYLE. Imp. 16mo. Cheaper Issue. 3s. 6d.

Shakespeare.—The Works of WILLIAM SHAKESPEARE. Cambridge Edition. Edited by W. GEORGE CLARK, M.A. and W. ALDIS WRIGHT, M.A. Nine vols. 8vo. cloth.

Shakespeare's Plays.—An attempt to determine the Chronological Order. By the Rev. H. PAINE STOKES, B.A. Extra fcap. 8vo. 4s. 6d.

Shakespeare Scenes and Characters.—A Series of Illustrations designed by ADAMO, HOFMANN, MAKART, PECHT, SCHWOERER, and SPEISS, engraved on Steel by BANKEL, BAUER, GOLDBERG, RAAB, and SCHMIDT; with Explanatory Text, selected and arranged by Professor DOWDEN. Royal 8vo. Cloth elegant. 2l. 12s. 6d.

Also a LARGE PAPER EDITION, India Proofs. Folio, half-morocco elegant. 4l. 14s. 6d.

Shakespeare's Tempest. Edited with Glossarial and Explanatory Notes, by the Rev. J. M. JEPHSON. New Edition. 18mo. 1s.

Slip (A) in the Fens.—Illustrated by the Author. Crown 8vo. 6s.

Smedley.—TWO DRAMATIC POEMS. By MENELLA BUTE SMEDLEY, Author of " Lady Grace," &c. Extra fcap. 8vo. 6s.
" *May be read with enjoyment and profit.*"—SATURDAY REVIEW.

Smith.—POEMS. By CATHERINE BARNARD SMITH. Fcap. 8vo. 5s.

Smith (Rev. Walter).—HYMNS OF CHRIST AND THE CHRISTIAN LIFE. By the Rev. WALTER C. SMITH, M.A. Fcap. 8vo. 6s.

Southesk.—THE MEDA MAIDEN : AND OTHER POEMS By the Earl of Southesk, K.T. Extra fcap. 8vo. 7s.
" *It is pleasant in these days, when there is so much artificial and sensuous verse published, to come across a book so thoroughly fresh and healthy as Lord Southesk's. . . . There is an infinite charm about them in their spontaneity and their healthful philosophy, in the fervent love for nature which is their distinguishing characteristic, and the manly and wholesome tone which pervades every page.*"—SCOTSMAN.

Stephen (C. E.)—THE SERVICE OF THE POOR ; being an Inquiry into the Reasons for and against the Establishment of Religious Sisterhoods for Charitable Purposes. By CAROLINE EMILIA STEPHEN. Crown 8vo. 6s. 6d.
" *It touches incidentally and with much wisdom and tenderness on so many of the relations of women, particularly of single women, with society, that it may be read with advantage by many who have never thought of entering a Sisterhood.*"—SPECTATOR.

Stephens (J. B.)—CONVICT ONCE. A Poem. By J. BRUNTON STEPHENS. Extra fcap. 8vo. 3*s*. 6*d*.
"It is as far more interesting than ninety-nine novels out of a hundred, as it is superior to them in power, worth, and beauty. We should most strongly advise everybody to read 'Convict Once.'"—WESTMINSTER REVIEW.

Streets and Lanes of a City: Being the Reminiscences of AMY DUTTON. With a Preface by the BISHOP OF SALISBURY. Second and Cheaper Edition. Globe 8vo. 2*s*. 6*d*.
"One of the most really striking books that has ever come before us."—LITERARY CHURCHMAN.

Thompson.—A HANDBOOK TO THE PUBLIC PICTURE GALLERIES OF EUROPE. With a brief sketch of the History of the various schools of Painting from the thirteenth century to the eighteenth, inclusive. By KATE THOMPSON. Second Edition, Revised and Enlarged. Extra fcap. 8vo. 6*s*.
" A very remarkable memoir of the several great schools of painting, and a singularly lucid exhibition of the principal treasures of all the chief and some of the smaller picture galleries of Europe. This unpretending book which does so much for the history of art is also a traveller's guide-book; a guide-book, moreover, so convenient in arrangement and comprehensive in design that it will not fail to become the companion of the majority of English tourists. . . . The large crowd of ordinary connoisseurs who only care to know a little about pictures, and the choicer body of intelligent students of all artistic objects that fall in their way, will extol the compact little volume as the model of what an art explorer's vade mecum *should be. It will also be found in the highest degree serviceable to the more learned connoisseurs and erudite authorities on the matter of art."*—MORNING POST.

Thring.—SCHOOL SONGS. A Collection of Songs for Schools. With the Music arranged for four Voices. Edited by the Rev. E. THRING and H. RICCIUS. Folio. 7*s*. 6*d*.

Tom Brown's School Days.—By AN OLD BOY.
Golden Treasury Edition, 4*s*. 6*d*. People's Edition, 2*s*.
With Seven Illustrations by A. HUGHES and SYDNEY HALL. Crown 8vo. 6*s*.
" The most famous boy's book in the language."—DAILY NEWS.

Tom Brown at Oxford.—New Edition. With Illustrations. Crown 8vo. 6*s*.
" In no other work that we can call to mind are the finer qualities of the English gentleman more happily portrayed."—DAILY NEWS.
"A book of great power and truth."—NATIONAL REVIEW.

Tourgenief.—VIRGIN SOIL. By I. TOURGENIEF. Translated by ASHTON W. DILKE. Cheaper Edition. Crown 8vo. 6s.

> *"If we want to know Russian life and society in all its phases . . . we cannot do better than take up the works of the greatest of Russian novelists, and one of the greatest in all European literature, Ivan Tourgenief."*—DAILY NEWS.

Trench.—Works by R. CHENEVIX TRENCH, D.D., Archbishop of Dublin. (For other Works by this Author, see THEOLOGICAL, HISTORICAL, and PHILOSOPHICAL CATALOGUES.)

POEMS. Collected and arranged anew. Fcap. 8vo. 7s. 6d.

HOUSEHOLD BOOK OF ENGLISH POETRY. Selected and arranged, with Notes, by Archbishop TRENCH. Third Edition, revised, extra fcap. 8vo. 5s. 6d.

> *"The Archbishop has conferred in this delightful volume an important gift on the whole English-speaking population of the world."*—PALL MALL GAZETTE.

SACRED LATIN POETRY, Chiefly Lyrical. Selected and arranged for Use. By Archbishop TRENCH. Third Edition, Corrected and Improved. Fcap. 8vo. 7s.

Turner.—Works by the Rev. CHARLES TENNYSON TURNER :—
SONNETS. Dedicated to his Brother, the Poet Laureate. Fcap. 8vo. 4s. 6d.

SMALL TABLEAUX. Fcap. 8vo. 4s. 6d.

Tyrwhitt.—OUR SKETCHING CLUB. Letters and Studies on Landscape Art. By Rev. R. ST. JOHN TYRWHITT, M.A. With an Authorized Reproduction of the Lessons and Woodcuts in Professor Ruskin's "Elements of Drawing." Second Edition. Crown 8vo. 7s. 6d.

Under the Limes.—By the Author of "Christina North." Second Edition. Crown 8vo. 6s.

Webster.—Works by AUGUSTA WEBSTER :—

> *"If Mrs. Webster only remains true to herself, she will assuredly take a higher rank as a poet than any woman has yet done."*—WESTMINSTER REVIEW.

DRAMATIC STUDIES. Extra fcap. 8vo. 5s.

> *"A volume as strongly marked by perfect taste as by poetic power."*—NONCONFORMIST.

Webster (Augusta)—*continued.*

A WOMAN SOLD, AND OTHER POEMS. Crown 8vo. 7*s.* 6*d.*
"*Mrs. Webster has shown us that she is able to draw admirably from the life; that she can observe with subtlety, and render her observations with delicacy; that she can impersonate complex conceptions and venture into recesses of the ideal world into which few living writers can follow her.*"—GUARDIAN.

PORTRAITS. Second Edition. Extra fcap. 8vo. 3*s.* 6*d.*
"*Mrs. Webster's poems exhibit simplicity and tenderness . . . her taste is perfect . . . This simplicity is combined with a subtlety of thought, feeling, and observation which demand that attention which only real lovers of poetry are apt to bestow.*"—WESTMINSTER REVIEW.
"*Closeness and simplicity combined with literary skill.*"—ATHENÆUM. "*Mrs. Webster's 'Dramatic Studies' and 'Translation of Prometheus' have won for her an honourable place among our female poets. She writes with remarkable vigour and dramatic realization, and bids fair to be the most successful claimant of Mrs. Browning's mantle.*"—BRITISH QUARTERLY REVIEW.

MEDEA OF EURIPIDES. Literally translated into English Verse. Extra fcap. 8vo. 3*s.* 6*d.*
"*Mrs. Webster's translation surpasses our utmost expectations. It is a photograph of the original without any of that harshness which so often accompanies a photograph.*"—WESTMINSTER REVIEW.

THE AUSPICIOUS DAY. A Dramatic Poem. Extra fcap. 8vo. 5*s.*
"*The 'Auspicious Day' shows a marked advance, not only in art, but, in what is of far more importance, in breadth of thought and intellectual grasp.*"—WESTMINSTER REVIEW. "*This drama is a manifestation of high dramatic power on the part of the gifted writer, and entitled to our warmest admiration, as a worthy piece of work.*"—STANDARD.

YU-PE-YA'S LUTE. A Chinese Tale in English Verse. Extra fcap. 8vo. 3*s.* 6*d.*
"*A very charming tale, charmingly told in dainty verse, with occasional lyrics of tender beauty.*"—STANDARD. "*We close the book with the renewed conviction that in Mrs. Webster we have a profound and original poet. The book is marked not by mere sweetness of melody—rare as that gift is—but by the infinitely rarer gifts of dramatic power, of passion, and sympathetic insight.*"—WESTMINSTER REVIEW.

A HOUSEWIFE'S OPINIONS. Crown 8vo. 7*s.* 6*d.*
"*Mrs. Webster has studied social subjects profoundly, and her opinions are worthy of every consideration. . . . No one can read Mrs. Webster's books without immediately perceiving she is a woman of genius, possessed of remarkable commonsense and a rare faculty of expression.*"—MORNING POST.

White.—RHYMES BY WALTER WHITE. 8vo. 7s. 6d.

Whittier.—JOHN GREENLEAF WHITTIER'S POETICAL
WORKS. Complete Edition, with Portrait engraved by C. H.
JEENS. 18mo. 4s. 6d.
*"Mr. Whittier has all the smooth melody and the pathos of the author
of 'Hiawatha,' with a greater nicety of description and a
quainter fancy."*—GRAPHIC.

Willoughby.—FAIRY GUARDIANS. A Book for the Young.
By F. WILLOUGHBY. Illustrated. Crown 8vo. gilt. 5s.
"A dainty and delicious tale of the good old-fashioned type."—
SATURDAY REVIEW.

Wolf.—THE LIFE AND HABITS OF WILD ANIMALS.
Twenty Illustrations by JOSEPH WOLF, engraved by J. W. and E.
WHYMPER. With descriptive Letter-press, by D. G. ELLIOT,
F.L.S. Super royal 4to, cloth extra, gilt edges. 21s.
*This is the last series of drawings which will be made by Mr. Wolf,
either upon wood or stone. The* PALL MALL GAZETTE *says:
" The fierce, untamable side of brute nature has never received a
more robust and vigorous interpretation, and the various incidents
in which particular character is shown are set forth with rare dramatic power. For excellence that will endure, we incline to place
this very near the top of the list of Christmas books." And the*
ART JOURNAL *observes, " Rarely, if ever, have we seen animal
life more forcibly and beautifully depicted than in this really
splendid volume."*

Also, an Edition in royal folio, Proofs before Letters, each Proo
signed by the Engravers.

Woolner.—MY BEAUTIFUL LADY. By THOMAS WOOLNER.
With a Vignette by A. HUGHES. Third Edition. Fcap. 8vo. 5s.
*" No man can read this poem without being struck by the fitness and
finish of the workmanship, so to speak, as well as by the chastened
and unpretending loftiness of thought which pervades the whole."*
—GLOBE.

Words from the Poets. Selected by the Editor of " Rays
of Sunlight." With a Vignette and Frontispiece. 18mo. limp. 1s.
" The selection aims at popularity, and deserves it."—GUARDIAN.

Wordsworth, SELECT POEMS OF. Chosen and Edited,
with Preface by MATTHEW ARNOLD. Fine Edition of the
Golden Treasury Volume. Crown 8vo, hand-made paper, with
Portrait of Wordsworth, engraved by C. H. JEENS, and Printed
on India Paper. [Shortly.

Yonge (C. M.)—New Illustrated Edition of Novels and Tales by CHARLOTTE M. YONGE.

In Sixteen Monthly Volumes :—

VOL. I. THE HEIR OF REDCLYFFE. With Illustrations by KATE GREENAWAY. Crown 8vo. 6s.

II. HEARTSEASE. With Illustrations by KATE GREENAWAY. Crown 8vo. 6s.

III. HOPES AND FEARS. With Illustrations by HERBERT GANDY. Crown 8vo. 6s.

IV. DYNEVOR TERRACE. With Illustrations by ADRIAN STOKES.

Yonge (C. M.)—Works by CHARLOTTE M. YONGE.

THE DAISY CHAIN. New Edition. With Illustrations. Crown 8vo. 6s.

THE TRIAL: MORE LINKS OF THE DAISY CHAIN. New Edition. With Illustrations. Crown 8vo. 6s.

THE YOUNG STEPMOTHER. New Edition. Crown 8vo. 6s.

CLEVER WOMAN OF THE FAMILY. New Edition. Crown 8vo. 6s.

THE DOVE IN THE EAGLE'S NEST. New Edition. Crown 8vo. 6s.

THE CAGED LION. Illustrated. New Edition. Crown 8vo. 6s.

THE CHAPLET OF PEARLS; OR, THE WHITE AND BLACK RIBAUMONT. New Edition. Crown 8vo. 6s.

THE PRINCE AND THE PAGE. A Tale of the Last Crusade. Illustrated. New Edition. 18mo. 2s. 6d.

THE LANCES OF LYNWOOD. New Edition, with Coloured Illustrations. 18mo. 4s. 6d.

THE LITTLE DUKE: RICHARD THE FEARLESS. New Edition. Illustrated. 18mo. 2s. 6d.

A BOOK OF GOLDEN DEEDS OF ALL TIMES AND ALL COUNTRIES. Gathered and Narrated Anew. GOLDEN TREASURY SERIES). 4s. 6d. Cheap Edition. 1s.

CAMEOS FROM ENGLISH HISTORY. From ROLLO to EDWARD II. Extra fcap. 8vo. 5s. Third Edition, enlarged. 5s.

SECOND SERIES. THE WARS IN FRANCE. Third Edition. Extra fcap. 8vo. 5s.
"Instead of dry details," says the NONCONFORMIST, *"we have living pictures, faithful, vivid, and striking."*

Yonge (C. M.)—*continued.*

THIRD SERIES. THE WARS OF THE ROSES. Extra fcap. 8vo. 5s.

FOURTH SERIES. [*Nearly ready.*

P's AND Q's; OR, THE QUESTION OF PUTTING UPON. With Illustrations by C. O. MURRAY. New Edition. Globe 8vo, cloth gilt. 4s. 6d.

"*One of her most successful little pieces . . . . just what a narrative should be, each incident simply and naturally related, no preaching or moralizing, and yet the moral coming out most powerfully, and the whole story not too long, or with the least appearance of being spun out.*"—LITERARY CHURCHMAN.

THE PILLARS OF THE HOUSE; OR, UNDER WODE, UNDER RODE. New Edition. Two vols. crown 8vo. 12s.

LADY HESTER; OR, URSULA'S NARRATIVE. New Edition. Crown 8vo. 6s.

MY YOUNG ALCIDES; OR, A FADED PHOTOGRAPH. New Edition. Crown 8vo. 6s.

THE THREE BRIDES. New Edition. 2 vols. Crown 8vo. 12s.

MAGNUM BONUM; or, Mother Carey's Brood. Three Vols. Crown 8vo. 31s. 6d. [*Shortly.*

A VOLUME OF TALES. Crown 8vo. [*Shortly.*

MACMILLAN'S GOLDEN TREASURY SERIES.

UNIFORMLY printed in 18mo., with Vignette Titles by J. E. MILLAIS, T. WOOLNER, W. HOLMAN HUNT, Sir NOEL PATON, ARTHUR HUGHES, &c. Engraved on Steel by JEENS. Bound in extra cloth, 4s. 6d. each volume. Also kept in morocco and calf bindings.

> *" Messrs. Macmillan have, in their Golden Treasury Series, especially provided editions of standard works, volumes of selected poetry, and original compositions, which entitle this series to be called classical. Nothing can be better than the literary execution, nothing more elegant than the material workmanship."*—BRITISH QUARTERLY REVIEW.

The Golden Treasury of the Best Songs and LYRICAL POEMS IN THE ENGLISH LANGUAGE. Selected and arranged, with Notes, by FRANCIS TURNER PALGRAVE.

> *" This delightful little volume, the Golden Treasury, which contains many of the best original lyrical pieces and songs in our language, grouped with care and skill, so as to illustrate each other like the pictures in a well-arranged gallery."*—QUARTERLY REVIEW.

The Children's Garland from the best Poets. Selected and arranged by COVENTRY PATMORE.

> *" It includes specimens of all the great masters in the art of poetry, selected with the matured judgment of a man concentrated on obtaining insight into the feelings and tastes of childhood, and desirous to awaken its finest impulses, to cultivate its keenest sensibilities."*—MORNING POST.

The Book of Praise. From the Best English Hymn Writers. Selected and arranged by LORD SELBORNE. *A New and Enlarged Edition.*

> *" All previous compilations of this kind must undeniably for the present give place to the Book of Praise. . . . The selection has been made throughout with sound judgment and critical taste. The pains involved in this compilation must have been immense, embracing, as it does, every writer of note in this special province of English literature, and ranging over the most widely divergent tracks of religious thought."*—SATURDAY REVIEW.

The Fairy Book; the Best Popular Fairy Stories. Selected and rendered anew by the Author of "John Halifax, Gentleman."

*"A delightful selection, in a delightful external form; full of the physical splendour and vast opulence of proper fairy tales."—*SPECTATOR.

The Ballad Book. A Selection of the Choicest British Ballads. Edited by WILLIAM ALLINGHAM.

*"His taste as a judge of old poetry will be found, by all acquainted with the various readings of old English ballads, true enough to justify his undertaking so critical a task."—*SATURDAY REVIEW.

The Jest Book. The Choicest Anecdotes and Sayings. Selected and arranged by MARK LEMON.

*"The fullest and best jest book that has yet appeared."—*SATURDAY REVIEW.

Bacon's Essays and Colours of Good and Evil. With Notes and Glossarial Index. By W. ALDIS WRIGHT, M.A.

*"The beautiful little edition of Bacon's Essays, now before us, does credit to the taste and scholarship of Mr. Aldis Wright. . . . It puts the reader in possession of all the essential literary facts and chronology necessary for reading the Essays in connection with Bacon's life and times."—*SPECTATOR.

The Pilgrim's Progress from this World to that which is to come. By JOHN BUNYAN.

*"A beautiful and scholarly reprint."—*SPECTATOR.

The Sunday Book of Poetry for the Young. Selected and arranged by C. F. ALEXANDER.

*"A well-selected volume of Sacred Poetry."—*SPECTATOR.

A Book of Golden Deeds of All Times and All Countries Gathered and narrated anew. By the Author of "THE HEIR OF REDCLYFFE."

*"... To the young, for whom it is especially intended, as a most interesting collection of thrilling tales well told; and to their elders, as a useful handbook of reference, and a pleasant one to take up when their wish is to while away a weary half-hour. We have seen no prettier gift-book for a long time."—*ATHENÆUM.

The Adventures of Robinson Crusoe. Edited from the Original Edition by J. W. CLARK, M.A. Fellow of Trinity College, Cambridge.

*"Mutilated and modified editions of this English classic are so much the rule, that a cheap and pretty copy of it, rigidly exact to the original, will be a prize to many book-buyers."—*EXAMINER.

The Republic of Plato. TRANSLATED into ENGLISH, with Notes by J. Ll. DAVIES, M.A. and D. J. VAUGHAN, M.A.

*"A dainty and cheap little edition."—*EXAMINER.

The Song Book. Words and Tunes from the best Poets and Musicians. Selected and arranged by JOHN HULLAH, Professor of Vocal Music in King's College, London.

> "*A choice collection of the sterling songs of England, Scotland, and Ireland, with the music of each prefixed to the Words. How much true wholesome pleasure such a book can diffuse, and will diffuse, we trust through many thousand families.*"—EXAMINER.

La Lyre Française. Selected and arranged, with Notes, by GUSTAVE MASSON, French Master in Harrow School.

> *A selection of the best French songs and lyrical pieces.*

Tom Brown's School Days. By AN OLD BOY.

> "*A perfect gem of a book. The best and most healthy book about boys for boys that ever was written.*"—ILLUSTRATED TIMES.

A Book of Worthies. Gathered from the Old Histories and written anew by the Author of "THE HEIR OF REDCLYFFE.' With Vignette.

> "*An admirable addition to an admirable series.*"—WESTMINSTER REVIEW.

A Book of Golden Thoughts. By HENRY ATTWELL, Knight of the Order of the Oak Crown.

> "*Mr. Attwell has produced a book of rare value . . . . Happily it is small enough to be carried about in the pocket, and of such a companion it would be difficult to weary.*"—PALL MALL GAZETTE.

Guesses at Truth. By TWO BROTHERS. New Edition.

The Cavalier and his Lady. Selections from the Works of the First Duke and Duchess of Newcastle. With an Introductory Essay by EDWARD JENKINS, Author of "Ginx's Baby," &c.

> "*A charming little volume.*"—STANDARD.

Theologia Germanica.—Which setteth forth many fair Lineaments of Divine Truth, and saith very lofty and lovely things touching a Perfect Life. Edited by DR. PFEIFFER, from the only complete manuscript yet known. Translated from the German, by SUSANNA WINKWORTH. With a Preface by the REV. CHARLES KINGSLEY, and a Letter to the Translator by the Chevalier Bunsen, D.D.

Milton's Poetical Works.—Edited, with Notes, &c. by PROFESSOR MASSON. Two vols. 18mo. 9*s.*

Scottish Song. A Selection of the Choicest Lyrics of Scotland. Compiled and arranged, with brief Notes, by MARY CARLYLE AITKIN.

> "*Miss Aitkin's exquisite collection of Scottish Song is so alluring, and suggests so many topics, that we find it difficult to lay it down. The book is one that should find a place in every library, we had almost said in every pocket, and the summer tourist who wishes to carry with him into the country a volume of genuine poetry, will find it difficult to select one containing within so small a compass so much of rarest value.*"—SPECTATOR.

Deutsche Lyrik.—The Golden Treasury of the best German Lyrical Poems, selected and arranged with Notes and Literary Introduction. By Dr. BUCHHEIM.

" This collection of German poetry is compiled with care and conscientiousness. . . . . The result of his labours is satisfactory. Almost all the lyrics dear to English readers of German will be found in this little volume."—PALL MALL GAZETTE.

Robert Herrick.—SELECTIONS FROM THE LYRICAL POEMS OF. Arranged with Notes by F. T. PALGRAVE.

" A delightful little book. Herrick, the English Catullus, is simply one of the most exquisite of poets, and his fame and memory are fortunate in having found one so capable of doing honour to them as the present editor ; who contributes a charming dedication and a preface full of delicate and sensitive criticism to a volume than which one would hardly desire a choicer companion for a journey or for hours of ease in the country."—DAILY NEWS.

Poems of Places.—Edited by H. W. LONGFELLOW. England and Wales. Two Vols.

" After a careful perusal we must pronounce his work an excellent collection. . . . In this compilation we find not only a guide-book for future travels, but a fund of reminiscences of the past. To many of us it will seem like a biography of our best and happiest emotions. . . . For those who know not all these places the book will be an excellent travelling companion or guide, or may even stand some in good stead in place of travel."—TIMES.

Matthew Arnold's Selected Poems.
Also a Large Paper Edition. Crown 8vo. 12*s.* 6*d.*

The Story of the Christians and Moors in Spain.
—By CHARLOTTE M. YONGE. With a Vignette by HOLMAN HUNT.

Lamb's Tales from Shakespeare.—Edited with Preface by the Rev. ALFRED AINGER, Reader at the Temple.

Wordsworth's Select Poems.—Chosen and Edited, with Preface by MATTHEW ARNOLD.

Shakespeare's Songs and Sonnets.—Edited by FRANCIS TURNER PALGRAVE.   [*Shortly.*

Selections from Addison.—Edited by JOHN RICHARD GREEN.   [*Shortly.*

Selections from Shelley.—Edited by STOPFORD A. BROOKE.   [*Shortly*

MACMILLAN'S GLOBE LIBRARY.

Beautifully printed on toned paper price 3s. 6d. each.   Also kept in a variety of calf and morocco bindings at moderate prices.

BOOKS, Wordsworth says, are
> "the spirit breathed
> By dead men to their kind;"

and the aim of the publishers of the Globe Library has been to make it possible for the universal kin of English-speaking men to hold communion with the loftiest "spirits of the mighty dead;" to put within the reach of all classes *complete* and *accurate* editions, carefully and clearly printed upon the best paper, in a convenient form, at a moderate price, of the works of the MASTER-MINDS OF ENGLISH LITERATURE, and occasionally of foreign literature in an attractive English dress.

The Editors, by their scholarship and special study of their authors, are competent to afford every assistance to readers of all kinds: this assistance is rendered by original biographies, glossaries of unusual or obsolete words, and critical and explanatory notes.

The publishers hope, therefore, that these Globe Editions may prove worthy of acceptance by all classes wherever the English Language is spoken, and by their universal circulation justify their distinctive epithet; while at the same time they spread and nourish a common sympathy with nature's most "finely touched" spirits, and thus help a little to "make the whole world kin."

The SATURDAY REVIEW *says: "The Globe Editions are admirable for their scholarly editing, their typographical excellence, their compendious form, and their cheapness." The* BRITISH QUARTERLY REVIEW *says: "In compendiousness, elegance, and scholarliness, the Globe Editions of Messrs. Macmillan surpass any popular series of our classics hitherto given to the public. As near an approach to miniature perfection as has ever been made."*

Shakespeare's Complete Works. Edited by W. G. CLARK, M.A., and W. ALDIS WRIGHT, M.A., of Trinity College,

Cambridge, Editors of the "Cambridge Shakespeare." With Glossary. Pp. 1,075.

The ATHENÆUM *says this edition is " a marvel of beauty, cheapness, and compactness. . . . For the busy man, above all for the working student, this is the best of all existing Shakespeares." And the* PALL MALL GAZETTE *observes: " To have produced the complete works of the world's greatest poet in such a form, and at a price within the reach of every one, is of itself almost sufficient to give the publishers a claim to be considered public bene-factors."*

Spenser's Complete Works. Edited from the Original Editions and Manuscripts, by R. MORRIS, with a Memoir by J. W. HALES, M.A. With Glossary. pp. lv., 736.

"Worthy—and higher praise it needs not—of the beautiful 'Globe Series.' The work is edited with all the care so noble a poet deserves."—DAILY NEWS.

Sir Walter Scott's Poetical Works. Edited with a Biographical and Critical Memoir by FRANCIS TURNER PALGRAVE, and copious Notes. pp. xliii., 559.

"We can almost sympathise with a middle-aged grumbler, who, after reading Mr. Palgrave's memoir and introduction, should exclaim —'Why was there not such an edition of Scott when I was a school boy?'"—GUARDIAN.

Complete Works of Robert Burns.—THE POEMS, SONGS, AND LETTERS, edited from the best Printed and Manuscript Authorities, with Glossarial Index, Notes, and a Biographical Memoir by ALEXANDER SMITH. pp. lxii., 636.

"Admirable in all respects."—SPECTATOR. *"The cheapest, the most perfect, and the most interesting edition which has ever been published."*—BELL'S MESSENGER.

Robinson Crusoe. Edited after the Original Editions, with a Biographical Introduction by HENRY KINGSLEY. pp. xxxi., 607.

"A most excellent and in every way desirable edition."—COURT CIRCULAR. *"Macmillan's ' Globe' Robinson Crusoe is a book to have and to keep."*—MORNING STAR.

Goldsmith's Miscellaneous Works. Edited, with Biographical Introduction, by Professor MASSON. pp. lx., 695.

"Such an admirable compendium of the facts of Goldsmith's life, and so careful and minute a delineation of the mixed traits of his peculiar character as to be a very model of a literary biography in little."—SCOTSMAN.

Pope's Poetical Works. Edited, with Notes and Intro-ductory Memoir, by ADOLPHUS WILLIAM WARD, M.A., Fellow of St. Peter's College, Cambridge, and Professor of History in Owens College, Manchester. pp. lii., 508.

The LITERARY CHURCHMAN *remarks : " The editor's own notes and introductory memoir are excellent, the memoir alone would be cheap and well worth buying at the price of the whole volume."*

Dryden's Poetical Works. Edited, with a Memoir, Revised Text, and Notes, by W. D. CHRISTIE, M.A., of Trinity College, Cambridge. pp. lxxxvii., 662.

"An admirable edition, the result of great research and of a careful revision of the text. The memoir prefixed contains, within less than ninety pages, as much sound criticism and as comprehensive a biography as the student of Dryden need desire."—PALL MALL GAZETTE.

Cowper's Poetical Works. Edited, with Notes and Biographical Introduction, by WILLIAM BENHAM, Vicar of Addington and Professor of Modern History in Queen's College, London. pp. lxxiii., 536.

"Mr. Benham's edition of Cowper is one of permanent value. The biographical introduction is excellent, full of information, singularly neat and readable and modest—indeed too modest in its comments. The notes are concise and accurate, and the editor has been able to discover and introduce some hitherto unprinted matter. Altogether the book is a very excellent one."—SATURDAY REVIEW.

Morte d'Arthur.—SIR THOMAS MALORY'S BOOK OF KING ARTHUR AND OF HIS NOBLE KNIGHTS OF THE ROUND TABLE. The original Edition of CAXTON, revised for Modern Use. With an Introduction by Sir EDWARD STRACHEY, Bart. pp. xxxvii., 509.

"It is with perfect confidence that we recommend this edition of the old romance to every class of readers."—PALL MALL GAZETTE.

The Works of Virgil. Rendered into English Prose, with Introductions, Notes, Running Analysis, and an Index. By JAMES LONSDALE, M.A., late Fellow and Tutor of Balliol College, Oxford, and Classical Professor in King's College, London ; and SAMUEL LEE, M.A., Latin Lecturer at University College, London. pp. 288.

"A more complete edition of Virgil in English it is scarcely possible to conceive than the scholarly work before us."—GLOBE.

The Works of Horace. Rendered into English Prose, with Introductions, Running Analysis, Notes, and Index. By JOHN LONSDALE, M.A., and SAMUEL LEE, M.A.

The STANDARD *says,* " *To classical and non-classical readers it will be invaluable as a faithful interpretation of the mind and meaning of the poet, enriched as it is with notes and dissertations of the highest value in the way of criticism, illustration, and explanation.*"

Milton's Poetical Works.—Edited with Introductions by Professor MASSON.

" *A worthy addition to a valuable series."*—ATHENÆUM.

" *In every way an admirable book."*—PALL MALL GAZETTE.

MACMILLAN'S POPULAR NOVELS.

In Crown 8vo. cloth, price 6s. each Volume.

BY WILLIAM BLACK.

A PRINCESS OF THULE.

MADCAP VIOLET.

THE MAID OF KILLEENA; and other Tales.

THE STRANGE ADVENTURES OF A PHAETON. Illustrated.

GREEN PASTURES AND PICCADILLY.

MACLEOD OF DARE. Illustrated.

BY CHARLES KINGSLEY.

TWO YEARS AGO.

"WESTWARD HO!"

ALTON LOCKE. With Portrait.

HYPATIA.

YEAST.

HEREWARD THE WAKE.

BY THE AUTHOR OF "JOHN HALIFAX, GENTLEMAN."

THE HEAD OF THE FAMILY. Illustrated.

THE OGILVIES. Illustrated.

AGATHA'S HUSBAND. Illustrated.

OLIVE. Illustrated.

BY CHARLOTTE M. YONGE.

THE HEIR OF REDCLYFFE. With Illustrations.

HEARTSEASE. With Illustrations.

THE DAISY CHAIN. With Illustrations.

THE TRIAL: More Links in the Daisy Chain. With Illustrations.

HOPES AND FEARS.

DYNEVOR TERRACE. With Illustrations.

MY YOUNG ALCIDES.

THE PILLARS OF THE HOUSE. 2 Vols.

CLEVER WOMAN OF THE FAMILY.

THE YOUNG STEPMOTHER.

THE DOVE IN THE EAGLE'S NEST.

THE CAGED LION. Illustrated.